FAR FROM HOME

When Georgiana and her maid, Kitty, make the long sea journey from their native East Yorkshire to America, they are seeking a new life of freedom and emancipation, but in New York, Georgiana encounters an imposter posing as Edward Newmarch, her cousin's husband. Meanwhile the real Edward, having escaped his disastrous marriage in England, is now running from a bigamous union with the daughter of a plantation owner. As he flees, and as Georgiana and Kitty journey to the land of the Iroquois, the dangers and passions of this new country and its people threaten to overwhelm them all.

FAR FROM HOME

FAR FROM HOME

by

Valerie Wood

Magna Large Print Books
Long Preston, North Yorkshire,
BD23 4ND, England.

British Library Cataloguing in Publication Data

Wood, Valerie
    Far from home.

A catalogue record of this book is
available from the British Library

    ISBN   0-7505-2261-5

First published in Great Britain in 2003 by Bantam Press
a division of Transworld Publishers

Copyright © Valerie Wood 2003

Cover illustration © Gordon Crabb by arrangement with
Alison Eldred

The right of Valerie Wood to be identified as the author of this work
has been asserted in accordance with sections 77 and 78 of the
Copyright, Designs and Patents Act, 1988

Published in Large Print 2004 by arrangement with
Transworld Publishers

Magna Large Print is an imprint of Library Magna Books Ltd.

Printed and bound in Great Britain by
T.J. (International) Ltd., Cornwall, PL28 8RW

For my family, with love

ACKNOWLEDGEMENTS

Thanks to Nick Evans, B.A., Maritime Historical Centre, Blaydes House, Hull, for information on nineteenth-century shipping and emigration to New York and New Orleans. Any fabrications or improvisations on fact are mine.

Thanks to Peter and Ruth for their constant support and to Catherine for reading the manuscript and checking my geography.

Books for general reading:

The Lure of the Frontier by Ralph Henry Gabriel. Yale University Press, New Haven, 1929.
Frontier America by Thomas D. Clark. Charles Scribner's Sons, New York.
History of the American People by Paul Johnson. Phoenix Giant.
The American West by John A. Hawgood. Frontier Library, Eyre & Spottiswoode, London, 1967.

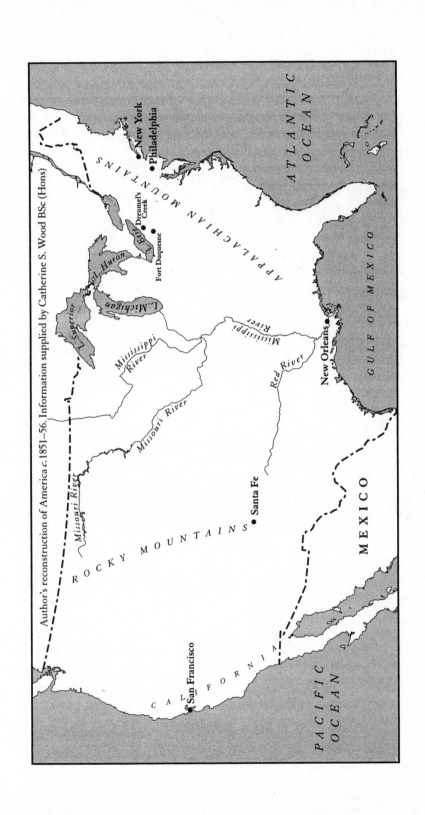

Author's reconstruction of America c.1851–56. Information supplied by Catherine S. Wood BSc (Hons)

ATLANTIC OCEAN

GULF OF MEXICO

PACIFIC OCEAN

MEXICO

New York
Philadelphia

APPALACHIAN MOUNTAINS

Dreumel's Creek

Fort Duquesne

L. Huron

L. Superior

L. Michigan

Mississippi River

Mississippi River

Missouri River

Red River

New Orleans

Missouri River

ROCKY MOUNTAINS

Santa Fe

CALIFORNIA

San Francisco

CHAPTER ONE

Georgiana leaned her arms on the rails of the packet ship *Wilberforce* and watched the shores of Hull receding. The vessel drew away from the Humber dock basin, down the estuary, heading towards Spurn Point and the open sea. She turned for a moment to watch the opposite shore, that of Lincolnshire, a county she had seldom visited. On its flat plain, smoke was issuing from factory chimneys. It seems so near, she thought, now that I am travelling so far.

Turning again she looked back for the last time at the buildings of Hull, the towers and turrets of the Holy Trinity, St John's and the Mariner's churches, and the towering Wilberforce Monument. She saw the thick smoke issuing from the tall chimneys of mills and factories which lined the banks of the river Hull, and the ships' masts in the Humber dock which gradually receded, their silhouettes framed in the bright morning sky.

Am I doing right? she questioned herself. Cousin May and her parents are convinced that I am not and expect me to come back on the next ship! And they are right that I had a comfortable existence living with Aunt Clarissa, though it couldn't be described as eventful. Oh, but I must be right! I couldn't have lived in limbo any longer, waiting for someone to come along and rescue me and give me a different life.

She nodded her head vigorously as she confirmed her own decision. Surely, better by far to take this opportunity and shape something for myself, she thought.

'Is everything all right, Miss Gregory?' Her maid, Kitty, plump in numerous woollen shawls, cloak and bonnet, appeared at her side. 'Wouldn't you like to come inside? It's so cold here on deck.'

'No,' Georgiana refused. 'I might be seeing this for the last time. I must watch it disappear into the past so that I can remember it.'

'That's what I'm scared of, Miss Gregory. I've never known anything else but this place. Hull and Hessle, I mean. Born in Hull I was, though my ma and da were Irish.'

'And you hadn't travelled anywhere else until you came to work for my aunt?'

'No, miss.' The girl smiled, dimples showing in her cheeks. 'And I thought I was travelling to 'ends of the earth when coachie drove me to Hessle.' Her smile faded. 'I wish Ma and Da could have seen 'fine house I was working in. They both died 'following year,' she added with a catch in her voice. 'Cholera.'

'They would have been glad for you, I'm sure,' Georgiana said softly, 'and perhaps pleased that you are making this journey now?'

'I don't know about that, Miss Gregory.' Kitty's eyes started to water as the breeze freshened. She tucked a wisp of red hair beneath her bonnet. 'They'd have been worried that I was travelling to America with just my mistress and no-one to look after us.'

'Mmm,' Georgiana said thoughtfully. 'Everyone is worried about that, including me,' she added. 'I once said that I couldn't imagine a time when a woman would travel alone, and,' she remembered, 'someone replied that there would always be some women who would be independent enough to do that. I took it as a kind of challenge!'

'But you've never been afraid to speak out, have you, miss?' Kitty said boldly. 'With your Women's Rights and suchlike. Not like me who daren't say boo to a goose!'

'You heard about that, did you, Kitty?' Georgiana smiled. 'Well, I suppose that was one of the reasons for my making this journey. I'll be long dead before women get equality in England.'

But that is only partly the reason for leaving England to sail to the New World, she reflected. I do long for some excitement in my life, but it was Cousin May who made me take this drastic decision. She sighed. I was so heartily sick of her moaning and carping on about her husband who had gone off and left her after such a short marriage. May never thought that I might become weary of her constant demands that we discuss the rights and wrongs of Edward and her marital situation. Nor did she consider that I might have interests of my own! And of course I felt obliged to indulge her, as her father supports me.

But not any more, she thought gleefully. I have my freedom! Though my uncle has been generous towards me in funding this voyage. But I'll pay him back one day. I swear I will. I'll show him, and everyone else who has said that I'm out of my senses, that I can stand on my own feet, even though I'm a mere woman who has never lifted a finger in her life.

'I want freedom and independence, Kitty,' she said aloud. 'To change my life if it is possible.'

'Yes, ma'am,' Kitty agreed, then, glancing at her employer, said bashfully, 'we'll be all right, don't you worry. I'll look after you in that new country of America.'

Georgiana nodded. 'We'll look after each other, Kitty.'

Kitty went off to check their luggage, first putting one of her own shawls around the shoulders of Georgiana's travelling gown and jacket, to save her catching a chill. Georgiana wanted to catch a last glimpse of the villages on the edge of the Humber banks. Places such as Paull with its dilapidated medieval fort and shrimp boats, the strange-sounding Sunk Island, reclaimed from the river bed, and the tongue of Spurn at the mouth of the Humber which two years before had been breached by a great storm, changing its shape and making it almost an island.

What will I do when I get to this new country? she wondered. I've heard such wild rumours that some of it is untamed with ferocious natives, but also that the cities of Philadelphia and Boston are well established. New York is a fine city, so it is said, a melting pot of nationalities. I should like that, to meet people from other cultures.

Perhaps I could teach, she considered. English or French. Or open a shop! How appalled Cousin May would be. At any rate I must think of earning a living for the first time in my life.

It was a sharp cold morning and she started to

18

feel chilled in spite of the extra shawl, and returned to the cabin, where she found Kitty boiling a kettle on a small oil stove to make a drink.

'There'll be food in the saloon at two o'clock, Miss Gregory,' Kitty said. 'I've been talking to some of 'other passengers, them as have travelled this way before. There's about fifteen of us all told. Some are businessmen, and they said that going to London by ship is better than by train. There's some bullocks on board,' she added, 'and a pack of dogs, they're all howling!

'We'll have got our sea legs by 'time we arrive in London, I expect,' she continued, pouring boiling water onto tea leaves in a pot as she chatted. 'Proper sailors we'll be by then. Put that blanket round you, miss, you'll soon get warm.'

Georgiana laughed. 'I'm glad you came with me, Kitty. You'll cheer me up when I'm worrying whether I've made the right decision.'

'Well, look at it this way, miss.' Kitty poured tea into a cup, added milk and handed it to Georgiana. 'What would you have gained by staying? You might have got married, but there's no guarantee you'd have been satisfied with that, and me neither,' she added. 'There's been nobody that I've fancied enough to tie myself to for life. And look at your cousin, Mrs Edward Newmarch. She picked a wrong 'un there – if you'll pardon my impertinence.' She blushed and stopped, conscious that in her chattering she had overstepped the mark.

'I suppose everyone has heard of that?' Georgiana asked. 'Everyone downstairs?'

'Oh yes, miss. It's been gossip for weeks in

19

'kitchen. How Mr Newmarch had a mistress and wanted her to travel with him to America. Onny she wouldn't go, so he went on his own anyway and left his wife behind to fend for herself. But they don't talk about them now, they talk about his brother Martin and how he's marrying a woman who's pulled herself up from poverty and made a name for herself.'

'Yes.' Georgiana drew in a breath, then took a sip of tea. 'So he is.' And Martin would have married me, she thought, if I had held him to his offer. Only I couldn't. He is too nice a man to be married to someone like me, a restless soul looking for who knows what.

They went back on deck as they approached Spurn Point, holding fast to the rails as the ship dipped and rolled and made headway into the open sea. Other passengers came on deck as they passed the Spurn lighthouse, and waved goodbye to the returning pilot boat and the eastern shores of England.

'That's it, then, Kitty,' Georgiana murmured as she clung onto her bonnet and huddled into her cloak. 'We're on our way.'

Kitty's face was turning a shade of pale green. 'Yes, miss,' she whispered. 'Excuse me. I think I'm going to be sick!'

They disembarked at London Bridge, their legs decidedly unsteady for the passage had been unseasonably rough. A porter called to them as he stood by their luggage. 'Come on lady, you and your gel! You going to the Brunswick? Yes? Take this growler.' He whistled to the driver of a four-wheeled hire vehicle, who drew up on the wharf in front of them. 'Brunswick Hotel, me lad,' he shouted, 'and look snappy.'

'There's no real hurry,' Georgiana began, for they were not sailing for two more days, but they were no sooner seated and their luggage on board than the driver was cracking his whip and they were buffeted around as the carriage wove in and out of other vehicles, gigs, hansoms, waggonettes, victorias, waggons and handcarts.

'What bedlam, miss!' Kitty exclaimed. 'What a row.' A barrage of sound had hit their ears: the raucous tones of porters and dock workers, the clatter of iron hooves and racket of wheels on cobbles, the lash of whips, the shrieking and crying of children and the strident voices of harassed adults as they tried in vain to quieten them.

Georgiana put her hand over her nose. 'And the stench!' she said. 'It's dreadful.'

'No worse than 'river Hull, miss,' Kitty declared. 'If you lived along 'Groves like I once did, you got used to 'stink from 'river. Just like this it was,' she added cheerfully. 'I could feel quite at home. Except,' she sniffed, 'I can smell oranges.'

Georgiana took a tentative sniff. 'You're right.' She breathed in again and found, mingling with the odours of the river, the sweet nectareous scent of oranges which were packed in crates at the dockside.

The driver took them to the Brunswick Hotel where they had rooms booked until their day of departure. From their window they looked across the Thames at the Greenwich Peninsula, and below onto the wharf from where they would sail.

21

'*Millions* of people, miss!' Kitty cried excitedly. 'Just look at them, I've never seen so many folk! Some have come by train, I expect. Railway station's just down there.'

'We'll walk out tomorrow,' Georgiana said. 'We'll get our bearings, buy extra provisions and see where our ship sails from.' She was beginning to become animated too, now that they were here in London. The nagging doubts that she had had were starting to fade away, and her dream of a new life began to take on a reality.

The next day they stepped out to look at the ships being made ready for voyages across the Atlantic. It seemed like pandemonium as porters rushed around rolling barrels, carrying casks, heaving crates and baskets, and all the while shouting to one another. 'Come on, Jack. Get a move on!' 'Here, Harry. Give us a hand with this!' 'Now then, me lad, look sharp, the ship sails today not tomorrer.'

Tipsy seamen, who were not on duty and had spent the previous night in alehouses, rollicked around the wharf with merry girls on their arms. Some had parrots on their shoulders which shrieked obscenities and whistled at passers-by. Other seamen, their shirtsleeves rolled up to reveal brown tattooed muscles, coiled ropes, scrutinized rigging and climbed over passengers who had settled themselves on the decks of their ships to check tickets, trunks, food, count their money and their children.

Georgiana and Kitty pinpointed their vessel, the *Paragon*, a three-masted iron ship with three decks which they were due to board the following day. Then they walked away from the dockside to find shops where they could buy provisions. A butcher sold them salt beef, and a grocer's shop supplied eggs, rice and a fruit cake to supplement the food which they would get on board. Itinerant salesmen carrying wooden trays and boxes attempted to persuade them to buy Union flags, crude paintings of London, watches which were *genuine* gold and all manner of items which they were assured would be very necessary for their journey to the New World.

When they returned to the wharf the sound of singing greeted them. An assembly of passengers had gathered on the top deck of one of the ships and were gustily singing hymns. A queue of people waiting to board joined in the hymn-singing as they patiently stood with their tickets in their hands and a bright expectant expression on their faces.

'Mormons,' Georgiana murmured, and one of the waiting male passengers turned a smiling face to her and confirmed her remark. 'That's right, ma'am. We're travelling with our brethren to Salt Lake City, the city of saints. We're following in the footsteps of our great prophet.' He sounded Welsh, Georgiana thought, his voice sing-song and melodic.

'Good luck to you,' she said. 'I understand you'll have a long journey across the plains of America?'

'We do, ma'am,' he confirmed. 'But we have our belief to sustain us. Come with us,' he cried heartily, including them both in his enthusiasm. 'You will find true love and happiness.'

'Did you say you were walking?' Kitty asked in astonishment. When he nodded, she grinned and said, 'My boots are onny fit for town streets. Not for trekking!'

He laughed and said that his boots were unsuitable, too. 'But our faith will carry us onwards,' he declared, and with a great burst of energy joined in the hymn-singing as he moved down the line towards the ship.

Georgiana looked around at the passengers waiting on the wharfside for other ships. Some were sitting on crates and packing cases, and were wearing an air of resignation as if they had been there a long time. Others were pacing about, anxious to be on their way. Mostly they were shabbily dressed, country people some of them, the women with worried expressions, wearing hand-knitted shawls and home-made bonnets and carrying babies in their arms. The men were in rough twill trousers, thick wool jackets and heavy boots.

But there were others, better dressed, and come to view the scene and these she guessed, like herself, had paid for a first-class ticket and a little more comfort on board.

Georgiana took a deep breath. We are all taking a chance, she thought. Every single one of us, regardless of wealth or status. Like those Mormons we must have faith that it will turn out well, but I wish I could be as sure as they are.

They boarded the *Paragon* the next day and their luggage was brought on board. Georgiana's cabin was on the upper deck and Kitty's on the second, where bunks were placed around the sides and partitioned off with curtains for privacy.

'I'm glad I'm not down below on 'bottom deck, miss.' Kitty had returned after exploring. 'It's so dark down there, even though most folk have got a lantern.'

Georgiana also went to look around the ship and was horrified to see where Kitty would be sleeping. The second deck was crowded with women and children, all quite respectable, but the atmosphere was claustrophobic with only a trapdoor in the ceiling to let in light and air. On the lower deck, the steerage quarters, men were drinking or playing cards and the women sat in desultory fashion with children about their knees.

'You must come up on the top deck, Kitty,' Georgiana declared and immediately made arrangements for another cabin, which, though not premier class as hers was, was more comfortable.

'When we arrive in America, we'll stay in New York for a while,' Georgiana told Kitty as she unpacked the bags. 'We'll have a look around. The state is very big, I believe, but not all of it is civilized, so we must take care. But we will enquire and find out what opportunities are available to us.'

'You're not thinking of working for a living, Miss Gregory?' Kitty's voice was shocked. 'You'll take a house, won't you, and entertain?' Her words drifted away. 'I mean – a lady like you?'

'I don't know yet, Kitty.' Georgiana decided to confide in her. After all, she had brought the girl away from a secure, comfortable position. 'I have enough money to last us for a while, but I must look to improve our situation.'

'Well, I can get a job of work, miss, cleaning houses or in a shop. I could even sing in 'streets if necessary,' Kitty added cheerfully. 'My da allus said, "Sure and you have the voice of an angel."'

'Well, if the worst comes to the worst, that's what we'll do.' Georgiana sounded more confident than she actually was. 'You can sing and I'll play the piano for our supper.'

The voyage was set to be long and tedious. It was now March and they expected to be in New York by the first or second week in May. The weather was fair for the first fortnight, with a stiff breeze, and they made good progress. Then rough weather got up and though the wind was in their favour, the sea was running high with massive waves and many passengers became sick.

Georgiana staggered to her cabin door for some air and looked out at the spectacle in front of her. The sea was mountainous, towering high above the ship. The sun shone brilliantly, catching every great wave, each billowing swell and tossing white horse with its flashing intensity, so that she had to shield her eyes from its brightness.

'How wonderful,' she murmured, then dashed back inside to be sick.

The wind and sea eventually calmed and Georgiana and Kitty were able to take a walk each day and mingle with some of the other first-class passengers. The ship's Master invited Georgiana to take supper with him, his officers and an elderly lady. Mrs Burrows was, he informed her, a former resident of Beverley, the shire town of the

East Riding of Yorkshire, noted for its fine Minster and horse racing.

'Mrs Burrows, I would like you to meet Miss Gregory who is also from your area.' Captain Parkes made the introductions and invited them to be seated at a long oak table in the low-ceilinged dining area, which was adjacent to the Master's cabin. The table was set with pewter plates, fine glassware and crisp white table linen. 'As you are both travelling alone, I thought perhaps you might care to be acquainted. Most of our other passengers are in families or groups—'

'Are you one of the Hessle Gregorys?' Mrs Burrows boomed, cutting the captain off in his verbal flow. 'Montague Gregory?'

'My uncle.' Georgiana began to explain her relationship but was interrupted by Mrs Burrows who asked in a loud voice, 'Travelling alone? No gentleman to escort you?'

'Exactly so, Mrs Burrows. Apart from my maid.' Georgiana was tight-lipped, certain that this tall, rather formidable woman dressed in an old-fashioned black gown with leg-o'-mutton sleeves, a lace cap pinned to her grey hair, was about to lecture her on such indecorous and foolish behaviour.

'Glad to hear it!' Mrs Burrows exclaimed. 'If I can do it so can you. It's about time you young women stood up for your entitlements.'

Georgiana gave a small gasp. Such an unexpected statement coming from a woman who must be nearly sixty years of age!

'Shocked you, have I?' Mrs Burrows gave a cackle. 'Thought I might. I usually do. Most young

27

people think that I should be in my bath chair – or in a wooden box!' she added, giving a further cackle. 'But I'm not, and don't intend to be, not just yet at any rate.'

'I'm delighted to hear it,' Georgiana said warmly. 'So very pleased. One of the reasons for my leaving England is because I know I will be old before equality comes to English women.'

'And what's the other reason?' Mrs Burrows demanded, glancing up and nodding at the officers as they arrived and Captain Parkes introduced them one by one. She watched as the cabin boy dished up the soup with an unsteady hand. 'You're new, are you not?' she asked him, conducting two conversations at the same time, then told him he would eventually get used to the motion of the ship before he had time to answer.

'Not looking for a husband?' She continued her conversation with Georgiana with hardly a pause and gazed at her with an unflinching eye.

'No, that is not on the list of my priorities,' Georgiana murmured, conscious that the attentions of the officers were on her. 'I want to build a life of my own.'

'Rich, then, are you?' Mrs Burrows asked. 'For there's not much open to single women even in the bright New World. Well, not for young women such as you. You'll not want to be chasing after the *forty-niners* like some foolish young women did!'

Georgiana stared blankly. What was she talking about?

'Gold miners!' Mrs Burrows expounded. 'You'll find New York almost empty. All the men rushed off to California two years ago when they heard of

28

the gold. And half the females in New York went after them. Not gentlewomen, of course,' she added and broke her bread into pieces.

'Were none of you gentlemen tempted to jump ship and look for gold?' Mrs Burrows addressed the officers quite informally and in a loud voice.

One or two of the officers shook their heads and answered, 'No, ma'am.'

The captain spoke up hurriedly, as if he had been waiting for a chance to say something. 'I lost some of my crew last year,' he said. 'The cook went and a couple of the apprentice lads. They were swayed by the lure of gold.'

'All they'll get is dirty fingernails,' Mrs Burrows said tetchily, 'and an aching back. My son lost half of his employees, but they're drifting back, one by one.'

'What is the purpose of your trip, Mrs Burrows? Are you visiting family?' Georgiana was curious about her: she was either very brave or very foolhardy to be travelling so far at her age.

'I've upped sticks now.' Mrs Burrows took a sip of wine from a crystal glass. 'I've been twice before to New York to visit my son, but this will be the last time. I shall stay. Shan't return to England again. I've nobody there any more. All my friends are dying. Got no backbone.' She took another drink. 'No, I'll stay in New York and set off a few crackers, wake some of them New York gels up a bit.' She turned and gave Georgiana a wicked grin which creased her face into wrinkles. 'They think I'm an eccentric old Englishwoman,' she said. 'Can't think why!'

They met frequently after that and, wrapped in

29

cloaks and shawls, took walks together along the deck. Georgiana told Mrs Burrows of her involvement with the Women's Rights group which she had belonged to, and how she hoped that women in America had more equality with men than they had in England.

'Don't be disappointed when you find that they don't,' Mrs Burrows harrumphed. 'Men make the rules just as they do at home! And though there are some women who are very committed to equality, I have found that the majority are very lethargic. Did you hear of that northern tour with the young woman who made a great impact by speaking on poverty and child labour?' she asked abruptly. 'Grace something? Miss Grace? The newspapers said that she was very poor, but I don't suppose she was as poor as they made out!'

'Indeed she was, Mrs Burrows! I know that for a fact for I was there. But she has now pulled herself up from poverty.'

As they walked, Mrs Burrows hung onto her bonnet as the wind threatened to tear it off. 'So it is possible,' she murmured. 'All you need is determination, and maybe a helping hand. Of course,' she went on, 'in America it is possible to overcome adversity. There is a ruling class as in England, but that class is made up from wealth and not from aristocracy, and if you become wealthy through hard work and endeavour, no-one is going to look down upon you because you are from the labouring classes.'

Georgiana sighed. 'But women are still ex-cluded. They do not have the same freedom as men!'

30

Mrs Burrows shook her head. 'What you could do,' she said, 'is find yourself a rich amenable husband and succeed in your ambitions through him. Many political wives do so.' She glanced at Georgiana. 'But I don't suppose you would want to do that? It wouldn't suit?'

Georgiana considered. What is the point of travelling so far and tying myself to some man whose ideals are not the same as mine and who makes decisions for me? I could have stayed in England and done that. 'No,' she said firmly. 'I wouldn't want to do that. It wouldn't suit at all.'

'Then good luck to you, my dear,' Mrs Burrows said wryly. 'You're going to need it!'

CHAPTER TWO

Mrs Burrows had recommended an hotel in New York, close to the park which was being created in the centre, an area of gardens, pleasant walks, lakes and arbours. 'Not finished yet,' she said. 'But ask them for a room with a window overlooking it,' she added. 'Just in case you get homesick for the greenness of England.' She had given a wistful smile. 'As you will.'

Georgiana was enthralled by the lovely harbour as they sailed towards Manhattan Island and saw, bathed in the warm sunlight of spring, the panorama of tall buildings of New York. Living as she had, near to the Yorkshire town of Hull with its narrow medieval streets, she was most impressed by the wide roads, carriageways and boulevards, and the handsome mansions built upon them. Kitty gazed out of the hackney-carriage window, amazed at the magnificent hotels and the shopping plazas as they travelled along Broadway, the long broad avenue which ran through the centre.

They both drew in a breath when the carriage pulled up outside the Portland Hotel, Georgiana in dismay as she wondered how she would afford such luxury, and Kitty in delight as she saw the uniformed bellboys and commissionaires waiting on the wide steps to open the carriage doors and lead them through the central glass lobby into the reception hall.

'Two rooms, if you please,' Georgiana asked the reception clerk. 'For myself and my maid.'

'For yourself and your help, madam? You're just in from England, I can tell!' he said, and glanced at his register. 'I'm not sure if we can accommodate you,' he murmured. 'We're so very busy just now.' He tapped his fingers on his mouth as he considered.

'The hotel is recommended by Mrs Burrows,' Georgiana said firmly, thinking that no matter the cost, all she wanted to do was climb into a bed which didn't rock. 'She particularly said to mention her name.'

'Mrs Burrows! The English lady. Is she a friend of yours, madam?' he said enthusiastically. 'I just adore her, she is so quaint!'

Georgiana raised her eyebrows but made no rejoinder on his comment and after turning over a page in his register, he nodded, asked her to sign, snapped his fingers at a passing bellboy and told him to take Miss Gregory and Miss Kitty Kelly up to their rooms on the fourth floor. 'Your luggage will follow shortly, Miss Gregory. Welcome to the Portland. I hope you enjoy your stay.'

A bed with muslin drapes dominated Georgiana's large and luxurious room, but as well as a wardrobe and chests of drawers, there was a writing desk and comfortable chairs placed by the window which overlooked the new park. She saw men digging and planting trees in the grass and strangely, she thought, there were pigs snuffling in the newly dug area. On opening another door at the other side of the room, Georgiana discovered a bathroom with a bathtub, a washstand and a mahogany towel rail draped with thick white towels.

'Oh, miss. It's lovely,' Kitty said. 'A proper bathroom.'

'Don't get too fond of it, Kitty,' Georgiana told her. 'We'll stay for a week or two until we find our way around and then look about for something a little smaller and less expensive.' And I must try to remember that Kitty is my *help* and not my servant!

They both had a rest, then Georgiana put on her shoulder cape and her hat and they went down into the foyer. Kitty carried an umbrella, for the blue skies were clouding over, and they strolled out of the hotel to explore the streets of New York.

'Folks is very friendly, Miss Gregory,' Kitty remarked. She was very bright and chirpy and very excited at the newness of it all.

33

Georgiana agreed. Men touched their hats as they passed and ladies inclined their heads. 'I think they must know we have just come off a ship,' she said. 'We must have the stamp of Englishness on us. Though I understand that there are many English people here, in spite of it being a Dutch city originally.'

But, as they explored, they realized that it was not only the English and Dutch who inhabited this city, but people from many nations, German, Italian, Irish and French. As they strayed down side streets, Indian, Mexican and Spanish men leaned in apparent idleness against doorways. There were also tenement buildings crowded together, with children sitting on the doorsteps, and Georgiana was reminded that, as in England, not all of the New York residents were affluent.

'It's a bit like home, Miss Gregory, isn't it?' Kitty said in a subdued voice. 'There's no getting away from poor folks, there's even pigs rooting around amongst the rubbish.'

'You're absolutely right, Kitty,' Georgiana agreed. She found she was rather despondent and maybe even a trifle homesick, as Mrs Burrows had said she might be. 'Come along, we've seen enough for today. Let's go back to the hotel for tea.'

The hotel lounge was large and divided up into smaller areas by stands of exotic plants and flowers and tall Chinese vases. A piano stood in one corner and Georgiana looked at it longingly. One of the things she was missing was her music. She was an accomplished player, though she hadn't a strong melodic voice. After they had tea in the hotel Kitty excused herself and said she would go upstairs and start unpacking the trunks. 'Everything will be creased if I don't. Do you think they'll have an ironing room, Miss Gregory?'

'I'm sure they will, Kitty. Just ask at the reception desk,' and Georgiana smiled to herself over the fact that she had taken tea with her maid, something she would never have done at home in England.

A woman approached her as she was idly watching people arriving and departing through the glass swing doors. She was perhaps in her early thirties and dressed in a yellow silk gown with a voluminous skirt and a wide straw hat trimmed with ribbons and flowers. 'I beg your pardon.' She spoke in a high drawling voice. 'But I haven't seen you here before. Are you newly arrived from England?'

'I am.' Georgiana smiled, glad to talk to someone. 'Just this morning.'

The woman held her gaze. 'Then, welcome. I am Mrs John Charlesworth. My husband and I live here at the Portland.'

'Georgiana Gregory,' Georgiana responded. 'I'm from the east coast of England. Won't you sit down?' She indicated the chair nearest to her.

Mrs Charlesworth sank into the chair and signalled to a bellboy. 'Your husband, Mrs Gregory? He is presumably on business in New York?'

'I have no husband, Mrs Charlesworth.'

'Oh!' Mrs Charlesworth seemed taken aback but recovered enough to order coffee for them both, which Georgiana declined, explaining that she had just had tea. 'Then you have a companion with you? I saw—'

'My maid, or *help* as servants appear to be addressed here.'

'Oh, don't take any notice of that silly nonsense.' Mrs Charlesworth waved a lazy hand in dismissal. 'It's only the clerks and domestics who don't care to be addressed as servants. But *we* still call them that! Or at least the ladies do, I'm not sure about the gentlemen.'

The bellboy brought her coffee and poured it. She took a sip, then asked, 'So you must be visiting family? Is your home near London? It must have been terrible travelling alone on the ship with all those dreadful religious immigrants?'

'I live a long way from London. The east coast of England,' Georgiana repeated and knew her voice had grown sharp. 'And the Mormons, if indeed that is who you mean, travel on separate ships.'

'Well, they don't stay here, thank goodness,' Mrs Charlesworth continued. 'They'll be off on their trek to Utah, I expect. There are thousands of them, you know, and their leader Brigham Young has just been made a Governor!'

'I know little about them,' Georgiana replied briskly, 'except that their faith appears to be genuine.' She was wondering how she could best make her escape from this woman, when Mrs Charlesworth repeated her question of whether she was visiting family.

'I am not,' Georgiana replied. 'I am intending to make a new life for myself in America.'

Mrs Charlesworth stared at her. 'But you must have some protection!' she protested. 'You won't realize, coming from a small country, that you will be at the mercy of every racketeer and swindler in town! I will speak to my husband about what must be done.'

'Please don't, Mrs Charlesworth,' Georgiana said with as much self-control as she could muster, though she was seething at the audacity of this woman, whom she had only just met, preparing to organize her life. 'When these dreadful people of whom you speak hear that I have nothing worth stealing, then they will leave me alone and go on to richer pickings.'

As Georgiana outlined her status, Mrs Charlesworth looked her up and down curiously. 'So perhaps you are looking for a husband? You cannot possibly survive without one. Not here in New York. So what will you do?'

Georgiana rose to her feet. 'I am not looking for a husband, Mrs Charlesworth, and I am perfectly capable of surviving without one! As for what I will do with my life, I wouldn't dream of discussing any ideas I might have with a perfect stranger on my first day in a new country. I wish you good day.'

She swept away from the astonished Mrs Charlesworth and climbed the stairs to her room, her heart beating fast and her cheeks flushed. You've made an enemy already, Georgiana, she told herself. That odious woman has probably got a great deal of influence in this town and you've just insulted her. She paused outside her door to calm herself, not wanting Kitty to suspect that anything was wrong. Have I made a great mistake? she thought. Have I burned my boats? What will I do?

For the next few days she avoided the hotel lounge and she and Kitty explored the city, which was growing at a tremendous pace. The buildings were higher than she had ever seen in England, some of them five storeys, and many of the hotels were enormous and extremely luxurious. She went into the Astor Hotel for coffee and asked the bellboy how many bedrooms there were. 'Over three hundred, ma'am,' he informed her proudly, 'and seventeen bathrooms! There's nowhere else so grand, not in New York at any rate.'

Indeed! So I shan't be staying here, she mused. Though no doubt I would find a rich husband if I did. She earmarked several smaller hotels where, on enquiring their tariffs, she realized she could stay at a cheaper rate than at the Portland. Just a few more days, she determined, and then I'll move out.

The following afternoon she stepped downstairs into the hotel lounge and found it almost empty but for one gentleman sitting by a window reading a newspaper. She glanced across at the piano. Would it be considered an imposition if I should play, I wonder? But why not? It is there, it is not an ornament. I will.

She walked across, seated herself and ran her fingers across the keys. It had been well played and the sound was mellow. There was no music on the stand but she closed her eyes and played from memory snatches of her favourite pieces. Wagner's *Flying Dutchman*, Beethoven, and songs from the music hall of which her Aunt Clarissa disapproved, stating emphatically that they were songs from the devil. She wouldn't allow Georgiana to play them, though she did each time her aunt went out. She played for perhaps fifteen minutes, concentrating and absorbing herself in the music and feeling rather nostalgic. I'm not missing Aunt Clarissa, except in a general way, she thought. Nor Cousin May, though I could perhaps regret Martin Newmarch if I allowed myself, and if he wasn't now married to the lovely Grace.

No, none of those, but I must admit that I am missing the familiarity of my homeland, the choppy brown waters of the river Humber which if I stood on a stool I could see from my bedroom window. And the sweet smell of new-mown grass after it has been scythed. Those are the things I am missing most of all.

She came to the end of the piece and sat with her hands gently on the keys, and was surprised to hear a ripple of applause. Other guests had come into the lounge, had sat down to listen to her and were now clapping. A gentleman, the one who had been reading his newspaper earlier, was hovering nearby and approached her. He bowed, putting his hand on his chest in a foreign manner, and enquired, 'Miss Gregory?'

'Yes.' She was embarrassed at having brought attention to herself and wondered how he knew her name.

'Forgive me,' he apologized, 'but I took the liberty of enquiring of the desk clerk. I came especially to see you.'

'Oh?' She was astonished. 'Why? How do you know of me?'

'It is no great mystery.' The smile he gave her dimpled his plump cheeks. He was a rotund man, perhaps in his early thirties, taller than her with brown hair which flopped over his forehead. 'Mrs Burrows suggested I call on you when I was next in the Portland.'

Georgiana gave a relieved sigh. 'Oh. Mrs Burrows! How kind of her.'

'Permit me to introduce myself.' He took a card from the pocket of his brightly coloured tartan waistcoat and handed it to her. 'Wilhelm Dreumel, at your service, Miss Gregory.'

She rose from the piano as he asked, 'Would you permit me a little time to talk?' and they crossed to a sofa in the corner of the room. He sat opposite her, unfastening the button of his grey coat.

'How are you liking the Portland Hotel, Miss Gregory?'

'It's very pleasant,' she said. 'But I must move soon as it is very expensive and I have only limited capital.'

'Ah! Perhaps then I can help you, for you must be careful to choose somewhere that is respectable. Pardon my curiosity but do you intend staying in New York?'

'I'm not sure.' She hesitated, not wanting to say that her plans were as yet unformed. 'I have come to find a new life in America, Mr Dreumel, but where that life will be I have not yet decided.'

He nodded sagely and settling back in his chair he crossed his legs and tapped his fingers on the chair arm. 'Miss Gregory,' he said after a moment. 'Mrs Burrows suggested that I introduce myself,

40

because she thought I might be of some assistance to you. She said to me that as you were a young lady who is not looking for a husband, and as I am a man not looking for a wife, then we should get on very well together!'

Again came the genial grin, and Georgiana couldn't help but smile back.

'She also told me,' he went on, 'that you were convinced that you could make your way alone in this country, but that perhaps you might accept a little help if that assistance was offered without conditions or demands.'

'But why would you want to assist me, Mr Dreumel? You don't know me or anything about me. I might be a foolish woman here on a whim. I might be looking for riches. Why would you help a stranger?'

He shrugged. 'When my grandfather came to this country from the Netherlands, he had nothing. He brought his wife and son – my father – and always spoke of the help he had received from total strangers. He was lucky, I suppose, he could just as easily have come across others who would have turned their backs on him. But because of that, he brought up my father to do what he could for others, and my father did the same for me.

'Times have changed, of course.' He gazed around the room at the opulent surroundings. 'My grandfather and father never made much money though they worked hard, but they were happy men, content with what their endeavours had brought them.'

'Yes.' Georgiana leaned towards him. 'That is what I want! And I don't see why, just because I

41

am a woman, I shouldn't be able to do that too. I want to be considered a proper person in my own right.'

'I can see why you got on so well with Mrs Burrows.' He smiled. 'She too is a very independent woman. Or she was,' he reflected. 'Regrettably her age is now catching up with her, though I'm quite sure that she will always be very vocal in her beliefs.'

'Then there is hope for me!' Georgiana felt buoyed up by their conversation. Wilhelm Dreumel was a very engaging, candid man, obviously not given to handing out flattery or compliments as some men were, but he spoke to her in a frank and easy manner as if he was talking to another man.

'There is plenty of hope, Miss Gregory. But you will not find it easy: there will be many who will look down upon you for not having a husband in tow, and you will be regarded with suspicion by some ladies if you so much as smile or pass the time of day with their menfolk.'

'So what of you, Mr Dreumel?' She remembered that he had said he was not looking for a wife. 'Do you have an understanding wife or are you a confirmed bachelor?'

A shadow fell across his affable face. 'I did have a beautiful and understanding wife, but sadly she died in childbirth and the child did not survive. We had been married only one year and we were both very young. She was eighteen and I twenty-one. I have not wanted another wife, for she was irreplaceable.'

'I'm so sorry,' Georgiana murmured. 'It must

be very hard to lose someone you love.'

He nodded sombrely. 'It is, it is very hard indeed. I shall never recover from it. So,' he perked up and spoke cheerfully, 'after all these years, twelve in September, no-one tries to find me another wife as they did to begin with. Poor Bill, my friends used to say. We must find him someone to marry. They now know that I am a lost cause, and the women that I know are my friends and not my lovers.'

She gazed at him. He would be a good friend, she mused. Honest and plain-speaking. If I get to know him perhaps he would also be a friend to me. It might be helpful, sometimes, to hear a man's point of view.

'Mr Dreumel,' she said boldly. 'Could I invite you to supper?'

CHAPTER THREE

Wilhelm Dreumel said that although he would be happy to be her guest, if she would permit it he would like to choose the venue. Georgiana was glad of that offer for she did not want to be seen dining in the Portland with a gentleman, in case Mrs Charlesworth might also be taking supper and think the worst. How foolish I am, she thought irritably, as she dressed for the evening. I'm trying to be an independent woman and here I am worrying over someone tittle-tattling about me.

However, when she came down the stairs to meet him at six o'clock in the foyer as they had arranged, she saw that Mr Dreumel was engaged in earnest conversation with another man.

His eyes swept over her as she approached and he smiled admiringly. Kitty had ironed all her gowns and she had chosen to wear a deep blue, which, she had been told, emphasized the colour of her eyes. Over her gown she wore a shoulder cape in a darker shade of blue, as the evening was growing chilly.

'Miss Gregory.' Dreumel held out his hand to include her in their conversation. 'Permit me to introduce a colleague, John Charlesworth.'

Oh, no, she breathed. Not the husband of that dreadful woman! She smiled, however, and inclined her head in greeting.

'Delighted, Miss Gregory.' John Charlesworth bowed. 'Are you newly arrived in New York?'

So his wife hasn't told him of me and how rude I was, she cogitated, beginning to regret her hasty departure from that lady.

'Just a few days ago,' she replied.

'And are you impressed by our fine city? I believe it is comparable with London for its shops and theatres, though not of course for its ancient buildings and heritage,' he added.

'Indeed I am. It's a very handsome city,' she agreed. 'The streets are much wider than our English streets and the colour of the stone buildings is very appealing. The gardens too,' she added and was surprised at her own enthusiasm, 'are lovely.'

'Good. Good,' he said, and, as he took his leave, declared, 'I must introduce you to my wife,

44

Miss Gregory. She likes to meet people from other lands.'

'I believe we have met already, Mr Charlesworth,' she said. 'But I shall be glad to renew her acquaintance.'

'Oh dear,' she remarked to Wilhelm Dreumel as they left the Portland – he had suggested that as it wasn't far they might walk to the hotel where they were to eat. 'I'm afraid I may have insulted his wife when I met her. I was rather discourteous, for she was so very patronizing and wished to organize my life.'

He chuckled. 'Don't worry yourself, Miss Gregory. Mrs Charlesworth would not notice if you were rude to her, for she never listens to anyone's opinion. She thinks only that she knows best, and yet she has no education or discernment. She has lived in the Portland Hotel for the last ten years and goes nowhere but to New York balls, parties and theatres. That is her life.'

'Poor woman,' Georgiana murmured. 'Does her husband not travel either?'

'He does, but she will not go with him, preferring to stay at the Portland where she behaves as if she owns it.'

The Marius Hotel where they were to dine was situated in a small quiet square. It was not as large or as lavish as the Portland, being plainly constructed on the outside with balconies on the first and second floors. It was well furnished with good carpets and curtains, and, like the Portland, had many small tables and comfortable sofas in the main lounge, and although it did not have a grand foyer, there was a wide hall with a piano, paintings on the walls and a welcoming fire in a large hearth.

'Delightful,' Georgiana said as they entered. 'How very pleasant.'

Mr Dreumel nodded at her approval. 'After we have eaten supper – and the food is good and wholesome – you may decide that you would prefer to live here. This is why I brought you.'

She noticed, as they were shown to their places in the dining room, that although several tables were occupied, they were occupied by gentlemen only, and the few ladies who were there were sitting separately and at a distance from the other diners. When she commented on this, her companion said that few ladies dined out with their husbands, and that gentlemen generally dined alone.

'Is this a typical New York custom?' she asked. 'Or a general American one?'

'I can't answer that, Miss Gregory,' he said. 'I can't say I have noticed it elsewhere, but then apart from when I am in New York, the company I keep is generally male.'

'Why is that, Mr Dreumel?' She smiled. 'You are not allergic to the company of ladies or you would not have approached me, nor would you have spoken of Mrs Burrows or accepted my invitation to supper!'

'Certainly not.' He laughed. 'I like the company of ladies. But my business takes me to places where there are few members of the female society. I have a newspaper company,' he explained. 'Penny newspapers in New York and Philadelphia. Ladies tend not to be in that kind of business.'

'I'm sure the women of America read newspapers,' she commented. 'Would they not like to read something written by a woman?'

He took her question seriously and surveyed her as the soup and bread were brought to the table. 'I don't personally know of any woman who writes for a newspaper, though there are of course female writers of novels. I regret to say, though, they are not as a rule approved of by the general public. And,' he added with a grin, 'the writer most disapproved of, though her book is widely read, is the English lady Mrs Fanny Trollope, who was not impressed by American life.'

Georgiana sighed. 'It seems, then, that life for women is not so very different here than in England.'

'No, perhaps not,' he agreed. 'But it will come. In time.'

'But it might be too late for me,' she said passionately. 'I want to make my own decisions about my life.'

'You are young, Miss Gregory. And you can do as you wish. Who is to stop you?'

She looked across at him. 'I'm twenty-three!' she replied.

'In your prime! A perfect age for a woman who does not want the disadvantage of a husband to hold her back! A sensible age for travelling alone with perhaps just a companion.'

'A companion?' she said suspiciously. 'What companion?'

'You have brought a young woman with you, have you not?' he asked. 'I thought that Mrs

Burrows said—'

'Oh,' she breathed. 'You mean Kitty? I thought—'

'No,' he said solemnly, though there was a sparkle of fun in his eyes. 'I did not mean anyone else. I would not presume—'

'I beg your pardon.' She was embarrassed. 'You see how difficult it is for a woman, Mr Dreumel? We are torn between what we have been taught and what we want. Sometimes,' she added softly, 'I think that we don't know *what* we want, only that we want something different. It can be quite bewildering.'

They ate in silence for a while, then Georgiana said, 'So shall we talk about you, Mr Dreumel? Tell me about your newspaper business. How far do you travel?'

'Between New York and Philadelphia. I hope eventually to open a newspaper in Detroit. How is your fowl?' he asked suddenly. 'Tender?'

'Very,' she said. 'Delicious. I would like to move here from the Portland if the rates are reasonable.'

'They are,' he said. 'But you must ask tonight. It is a very popular hotel and there are not many rooms.'

She said that she would. She felt comfortable here, the staff were politely friendly without being too familiar or condescending, as she felt they were at the Portland.

'I am also in other fields.' He returned to the original subject, first taking a drink from his wine glass. 'My father worked as a miner in Philadelphia, and because I have a smattering of knowledge I went off to California in '49 to try my luck.'

48

'You're not going to tell me that you struck gold!'

Sheepishly he nodded. 'I found a placer deposit of free gold.' He saw a question in her face. 'It's called free gold because it's mixed in with sand or gravel and is recovered by washing in a mining pan. It's found mostly in river beds.'

'So has it made you rich?' She smiled. 'Do I set my bonnet at you after all?'

He laughed, then leaned towards her. 'I shall get richer with my newspapers, but I bought the New York newspaper with some of the proceeds.' He hesitated, then said, lowering his voice, 'I want to raise cattle, and someone showed me a perfect place. As an American citizen I was able to buy the land, and then I discovered what I believe to be a gold lode there.'

'A gold lode?' she whispered back. 'What is that?'

'It's gold that is buried in rock. It has to be crushed out of the rock which means using expensive machinery. We've staked a claim and are setting up right now.'

'We? You have a partner?'

'Yes.' He nodded. 'John Charlesworth. He has agreed to put capital into the scheme. The one problem is his wife. If she should hear of it it will be all over New York and we'll have every gold miner in America trailing us.'

'But why are you telling me, Mr Dreumel?' she asked, perturbed by this confidence. 'You don't know me. I could tell everyone too. How do you know I can keep a secret?'

He shrugged. 'I don't know. But I can guess. I

49

can generally tell if someone is honest and trustworthy.' He smiled his dimpled smile. 'I don't really know why I told you, but sometimes it is good to confide, to share. Besides,' he added, 'I haven't told you where the land is and if I did you wouldn't be able to find it. Being only a woman,' he said slyly.

'Ah,' she said gaily. 'I thought there would be a reason. So who is looking after this land?' she asked. 'Shouldn't you be there guarding it?'

'Normally, yes,' he said. 'But I have found a fellow who has been in the mining business – an Englishman, who is there now supervising the machinery which is being assembled. I'm expecting him this week, as a matter of fact. He's travelling to New York to tell us of the work in progress.'

After they had finished eating, Georgiana spoke to the desk clerk and asked to see the rooms. They were smaller than at the other hotel but comfortably furnished and decorated in warm colours. They had two free so she booked them for an indefinite stay. Wilhelm Dreumel kept out of earshot as she negotiated a price, and she was glad that he did not try to interfere or recommend.

They strolled back to the Portland. The evening was cool but dry and there was a salty smell of the sea which made her feel nostalgic for home, but she also felt buoyed up by the fact that she was making progress in her life. I have made a friend, she thought, who has confided in me, and I have made a decision about moving hotels and I have not yet been here one week.

'It has been most pleasant, Miss Gregory,'

Dreumel said as he escorted her into the Portland foyer. 'Very pleasant indeed, and I hope that perhaps we can repeat the evening, only perhaps you would be my guest next time?'

'That would be lovely.' She extended her hand to his. 'Where are you staying, Mr Dreumel?' she asked. 'Here at the Portland?'

'No, at the Marius. I prefer the simplicity. So I will hope to see you again soon. Tomorrow if my man turns up as promised I shall be in discussion with him. Perhaps,' he said, raising a finger as if it had just occurred to him. 'Perhaps you would care to meet him. He is from northern England, as you are.'

'Oh, yes! It would be good to hear how a fellow English person is surviving in this new country.'

He smiled. 'It doesn't seem so very new to me as I have lived here all my life, but yes, I do understand what you mean.'

'What is his name?' Georgiana asked. 'I may know of him or his family.'

'Newmarch,' he replied. 'Edward Newmarch.'

She stared blankly for a moment, then said faintly, 'I do know the Newmarches, but I think not the same family. They are not in mining.'

She took her leave of him and walked unsteadily up the stairs to her room. It isn't possible, she thought. It must be sheer coincidence.

Edward Newmarch, her cousin May's husband, had sailed for America eighteen months before Georgiana had decided also to travel abroad. He had left his new wife a letter saying that he was leaving to begin another life and begging her forgiveness. What he didn't say in the letter and

51

what they had subsequently discovered was that he had booked three tickets for the voyage, one for himself, one for his valet, and one for his mistress, a young mill girl, whom he had been seeing since before his marriage.

May Newmarch had dashed down to the dock with her brother-in-law, Martin, in time to see her husband board the ship. But his mistress had stayed behind, choosing, so it seemed, not to go with him.

They had heard nothing more from him, no communication at all. May's father had tried in vain to put a stop to Edward drawing funds from the bank where May's dowry was deposited, even though the money and various shares deposited there after Edward Newmarch's marriage to May were legally his.

'It can't be him,' Georgiana murmured as Kitty pulled off her boots. He'd never get his hands dirty in such a thing as mining, she mused.

'What, miss?' Kitty said.

'Oh, nothing much,' she said. 'Kitty, let's get packed. We're moving tomorrow.'

As they settled into the Marius the next day, Kitty said, 'I like it better here, Miss Gregory. It's not so snooty as 'Portland, and them desk clerks were always telling me that I should leave you and get a proper job. I told them,' she said vehemently, 'this is a proper job, looking after you, and they just laughed at me and said I was like them black slaves in the South.'

Georgiana was shocked. 'But you don't feel like that, do you, Kitty? I'd be devastated if you left.'

'Oh no, miss, I don't. I know how you depend

52

on me, and besides I depend on you. What would I do on my own?'

Georgiana took a deep breath. 'We need each other, Kitty, and that's a fact. We're two women alone in a foreign land.' She considered for a moment. 'How would it be,' she said, 'seeing as people here have problems with the idea of servants – how would you like to call yourself my companion, whenever anyone asks what you do?'

Kitty beamed and her face went pink. 'It would seem as if I'd gone up in 'world, miss.' She pondered. 'Sounds very nice. Better than a lady's maid. Would you prefer that, Miss Gregory?'

'I think that perhaps I would,' she said. 'And it would mean that we could dine together.' She saw the hesitant expression on Kitty's face. 'I don't always like to dine alone and I would show you which cutlery to use if you were not sure.'

'I do know already, miss, cos didn't I some-times set 'table at your aunt's house?'

'Of course you did, Kitty. I'd forgotten.' Her aunt had a housekeeper, cook and kitchen maid. Kitty, who had started out as a parlour maid, had been elevated to look after her and Georgiana's needs. 'Yes,' she said thoughtfully. 'I think that is what we shall do.'

'Goodness, miss,' Kitty exclaimed. 'It's as if I'm gaining that equality like you're allus talking about.'

'Well, thank goodness someone is,' Georgiana said ruefully. 'Come along, then, let's get ready to go down to supper. You could wear your grey dress tonight and tomorrow we'll buy you some-thing else to wear.'

Kitty followed her, just one step behind as they went down the stairs. In the foyer, waiting near the door, was Wilhelm Dreumel. He turned and saw them. 'Miss Gregory,' he called. 'Newmarch is just collecting his bags from the coach. I remember where he's from now. He's from a place near the port of Hull on the east coast of England. I'm sure you'll know him!'

Behind her, Georgiana heard Kitty draw in a breath and she turned and put her finger to her lips.

The doors swung open and a man came in carrying a bag and shook hands with Dreumel. Dreumel said something to him and they both looked up. A dismayed recognition dawned in the man's eyes as he saw Georgiana.

She took a few more steps down and stood in front of the two men. She knew him all right. Only it wasn't Edward Newmarch.

CHAPTER FOUR

In September 1850, when Edward Newmarch stumbled up the gangboard onto the ship, all he wanted to do was close the cabin door behind him and sink into oblivion. He didn't look back at the crowds who were gathered at the Humber dock basin to watch the ship depart, for if he had he would have seen Ruby walking away. Ruby, his mistress, his love, who had refused to travel with him and had told him that she loved someone else. He had barely given thought to his abandoned wife May, he was simply wrapped in his own misery and humiliation.

'Damn and blast all women,' he muttered as he lay face down on his bunk. 'I gave that girl everything she wanted. Money, clothes, trinkets!' Well, all right, he admitted. I couldn't marry her. But it would have been as good as a marriage if she'd agreed to come! She'd have had to change her manners of course, put on a bit of style so that people wouldn't have guessed that she'd come up from the gutter. But Ruby could have done that if she'd had a mind to, she had it in her.

There was a faint tap on the door. 'Yes! What is it?'

'Can I get you anything, sir?' It was his valet's voice. Allen. Robert Allen, who had agreed to come with him. Hmm, Edward brooded. He hadn't needed to ask twice. Allen had jumped at the chance of a new life.

'No, I don't need anything. Wait, on second thoughts – come in.' He raised himself on one elbow. 'Get me a drink,' he said as Allen came in, bending his head so that he didn't bang it on the door frame. Not a tall man, he was stocky in build, unlike his employer, who was tall and slim, but the cabin ceilings and doors were low.

Allen crouched to open the cupboard door. 'Brandy, sir? Whisky? Port?'

Edward exhaled. 'Port, and leave the bottle here by me. Then don't disturb me until supper.'

'We're about to sail, sir. Don't you want to see us leave?' Allen poured the port into a glass and put the bottle by the bed as instructed.

55

'No, I damn well don't! I'll be glad to be gone.' Edward raised his glass and took a drink. 'Have you left anyone behind, Allen?'

'No, sir.' Allen's expression was impassive. 'Nobody.'

'Good for you. Nobody to mourn you or blacken your name, then?' Edward took another drink.

'No, sir. Will that be all, sir?'

'Yes. Make sure there's plenty of meat for supper. I feel the need for some red meat.'

'Very good, sir.' Allen backed out of the cabin, closed the door firmly and returned to watching the shores of East Yorkshire slide away into the darkness. It was cold and wet in spite of being early autumn and there were few people on deck.

He hadn't been able to believe his luck when Edward Newmarch had approached him and told him, in confidence, that he was thinking of going to America. 'But not a word to Mrs Newmarch,' he had said. 'I don't want to tell her yet. Not until I've thought it through,' and then he had asked if Allen would consider going with him.

Wouldn't I just! Allen had thought, and needed no time to contemplate. He was bored with his job of running around after Newmarch, helping him dress, shave, cleaning his shoes, making sure his shirts and collars were freshly starched and ironed, and when his employer was out, as he frequently was, he had to help clean the household silver, which, he considered, was not the work of a valet.

But then, he had deliberated, the Newmarch family were not top-drawer aristocracy with a

56

mass of servants who knew who did what and when, but wealthy folk who had made their money out of industry and commerce, and employed people to do for them what they didn't want to do for themselves.

I'll be rid of him as soon as I can, he determined as he watched the light of Spurn Point flash in the darkness. Just as soon as I see what's what. There'll be opportunities galore, I shouldn't wonder. I might even pan for gold, though the best sites will have gone by now. Not that I'd go into mining. I vowed that when I left home. I saw what coal mining did to Da and our Jim, coughing their hearts and lungs out. No, that life wasn't for me.

He had known very quickly that what Edward Newmarch was planning didn't include Mrs Newmarch. No-one else in the servants' hall knew anything, and certainly not Mrs Newmarch's maid, Dora, for he had had a mild flirtation with her and she would have told him if her mistress was going away. No, he had quickly deduced that his master was planning on taking his little filly, who was nothing more than a mill girl.

Ironic, he thought, and pulled a small bottle of whisky out of his pocket which he had siphoned off from a larger bottle when he was preparing the cabin, and whilst Newmarch was on the wharfside trying to persuade his paramour to accompany them. And she wouldn't come! He grinned in the darkness and took a drink from the bottle. More fool her! Or maybe not, he reconsidered. Maybe she knew that eventually Newmarch would tire of her and she would be abandoned, just as his wife had been.

It would be a hard life for a woman anyway. He took another drink. Unless there's plenty of money, and Newmarch will keep tight hold of his, or rather his wife's, money. Poor bitch, she'll be left with nothing. His mind had switched to May Newmarch. Still, she's got a rich papa, he'll look after her, I expect.

Yes, I'll move on as soon as I can. That's what folk do in America. They don't stay in one place like we do. They grasp every opportunity and if they don't find what they're looking for in one place, then they move on to the next. That's what I shall do. And I'll be welcomed. The country has opened its doors to folk like me, people willing to work, immigrants, poor or not. As long as they're the right colour of course. He took another drink and wiped his mouth with the back of his hand. Some of them are not so keen on the blacks having their freedom. He stared up into the dark sky and saw the flicker of stars. But that's another issue. Nothing to do with me.

Edward kept to his cabin until they reached London Bridge. Their passage to America was the next day and after staying overnight at the Brunswick Hotel they boarded the *Chelsea* at Brunswick Wharf. Edward had a premier cabin on the top deck, and Allen was in second class, where he had to share with others.

To begin with Edward avoided his fellow passengers as much as possible and leaned morosely over the rails gazing at the swelling Atlantic waters. He brooded on his misfortune in love and anxiously debated whether he had made a

58

mistake in leaving all that he had in England for a chance of a different life in America.

Two weeks into the voyage the captain invited him to take supper with him, where he met other first-class passengers who had come from Hampshire, Dorset and Wiltshire and therefore did not know him or his family. Their company was pleasant and he found that they too were as apprehensive and stimulated at what might be in front of them as he was.

He told them that he was a widower looking for a new life, and following their sympathetic reaction decided that this was the role he would play. He found they were disinclined to enquire or question him after such recent sorrow and understood his need for solitude.

He had no conversation or discourse with the immigrant passengers travelling on the lower decks, for he had nothing in common with them. According to the captain they were mainly agricultural workers, some taking wives and children in a search for a better life.

'I've decided to take another ship and go to New Orleans,' Edward told Robert Allen as they headed on course for New York six weeks later. 'And then to California. The captain says that everybody who is anybody has gone to buy land in California. So that's what I shall do.'

'But won't it be too late, sir? The gold rush was last year, in '49.'

'I'm not thinking of digging for gold,' New-march said drily. 'I'll set up as a supplier. The diggers will need supplies. You know, food, shovels, picks.'

'Won't they be there already? The suppliers will have followed behind the miners.'

'That's what I've decided to do, Allen!' Newmarch said stubbornly, brooking no discourse, though he conceded privately that perhaps his valet might be right. 'I want to take a look. Besides, New York is just another city, bigger and grander probably then what we have at home, but nevertheless it is still a city. I want to see America in the raw, to find out what it has to offer.'

Allen was disappointed. He'd wanted to visit New York and had planned to leave Newmarch's employ. He was convinced that there would be opportunities there, men of business who would employ him until he was ready to set up for himself.

'So where shall we head for, sir? If we got off in New York we could go overland to California.'

He saw Newmarch's cynical sneer. He had noticed that his employer had regained his confidence during the latter part of the voyage. He was no longer sunk in despair as he had been when they had embarked, and he had joined with other passengers as they'd set up card games.

'Don't be ridiculous, Allen! I'm not cut out for roughing it. I don't want to join some damn waggon train. No thank you! I want to have a little comfort, even though it's tedious on board ship. No, we'll change vessels and go on to New Orleans, stay there awhile and then on to California.'

I could tell him I'm leaving, Allen contemplated as he waited in line in the galley for the ship's cook to serve up the soup. Edward

Newmarch had brought his own salted meat though he needn't have done, as the price of the ticket included meat, soup, bread and vegetables.

I don't have my wages yet, he reasoned. And I might not get them in full if I leave. It would be just like Newmarch to take the ticket money out of what he owes me.

'We'll buy extra provisions when we arrive in New York.' Newmarch took the soup bowl from him and dipped in a piece of dry bread to soften it. 'We shall have plenty of time before we get the next ship.'

'Very good, sir.' Allen served the meat and potatoes onto a plate. If he gives me money to buy food I could disappear until the ship has sailed. But then he's tight-fisted, he won't give me much. He won't know the cost of things anyway. His type never do.

When they arrived in New York Edward Newmarch obtained passages on a boat sailing for New Orleans the next day, then booked in at an hotel near the waterfront. 'Righto,' he said to Allen. 'Let's buy what we need for the voyage. I'll come with you.'

He hired a hansom, which bowled along Broadway towards the nearest shopping plaza, and whilst Newmarch waited in the cab, Allen went to buy provisions.

'You just off a ship, mister?' A butcher wrapped a ham shank and a leg of mutton in a muslin cloth. Allen nodded. It would be obvious, he supposed. His trousers and coat were crumpled from lying on his bunk for there was no space for hanging clothes, and although he had washed his shirts along with those of his employer's, there were no facilities for pressing or ironing on board.

'Staying in New York?'

'No. Going on to New Orleans.'

The butcher laughed. 'Then make sure you eat the meat before you get there, mister, or else them danged flies will have it.' He had a round flat face and he grinned again. 'Then the mosquitoes will eat you. If the crocs don't get you first!' He looked towards Newmarch waiting in the hansom outside. 'That your boss?'

Again Allen nodded and murmured that he was.

'Quite a swell, ain't he? He'll do well in New Orleans with all them Creole ladies. They'll want him at their balls and parties.' He gave Allen a wink. 'They'll not want you though, unless it's to serve on table.' He wagged a finger. 'You could do well. They'd like that, having an Englishman waiting on them.'

Allen took a deep breath, paid him with the money Newmarch had given him and walked out seething. Was there still a class system, then? Even here? Did breeding matter? I thought that only money talked. It does, I'm sure of it, and I intend to do plenty of talking.

Next day they boarded the *Mississippi Girl*, a paddle steamer. After Allen had unpacked Newmarch's luggage in his cabin he went below, taking with him the meat he had just bought, labelled with Edward Newmarch's name. A tall, thickset Negro was pulling on a white coat over his cotton shirt and trousers and he looked up as

Allen came down the companionway. 'Yes, sir?' he said.

'I'm looking for the cook,' Allen said briefly. 'I need this meat cooking now.'

'Guess I'm the cook, sir,' the man drawled and gazed at Allen with dark placid eyes. He pointed to the table in the middle of the room where other provisions were laid. 'Put the meat down there. I'll cook it as soon as the boiler is hot.'

Allen was curious. 'Are you from New Orleans?'

The man's face closed up and he looked down his wide nose. 'I ain't from nowhere, sir. I just go where the cap'n tells me.'

'What? Are you not a free man?'

'No, sir, I ain't.' The fellow started to sort out the parcels of food on the table. 'And I shouldn't be talking to you, sir, though I guess if you're from a foreign country you wouldn't know that.'

'But if you're a cook, you'll get a wage? A salary?'

'No, sir. Ah just get my bed, my food and my clothes.'

'But there's no slavery in the North,' Allen insisted. 'Couldn't you just get off the ship here in New York?'

'Then what'd I do? Nobody would give me a job. They don't like niggers in New York. No, sir. Besides, my boss'd come looking for me.'

And I thought I was badly done by, Allen reflected as he went back to the upper deck. But at least if I decided to leave, nobody would chase after me and bring me back. He was sobered by the thought of the big black man who looked so strong that nobody would want to meddle with him, and yet who was captive and weak in that he couldn't be called free.

We've abolished slavery in England, but never having seen a slave, I haven't really thought or cared about it before. And here's one right in front of me. It doesn't seem a fair system, he pondered. This isn't a free country after all.

'I've just met a slave, sir.' Allen took New-march's supper to him as they sailed out of New York harbour towards the Atlantic once again, where they would turn towards the coast of Florida. 'He's the cook.'

'Good God!' Edward looked down at his supper tray. 'Are they allowed to cook? Is he clean?' He sniffed at his plate. 'What can I smell? Something spicy! Is this my meat?'

'Yes, sir, yes, sir, and yes, sir. It's your ham and the spice is cloves, with oregano. The cook told me,' he added as Newmarch looked up sus-piciously. 'It's a Creole dish.'

'What else?' Newmarch poked about in the food with his fork. 'What's this red stuff?'

'Chillies, sir. They'll be hot. And garlic.'

Newmarch took a small bite. 'They use these spicy ingredients to disguise bad meat, you know.'

'Yes, sir. The butcher said we should eat the meat before we get to New Orleans or the heat will rot it.'

Newmarch took another bite and chewed. 'Tastes all right,' he considered. 'Quite good, in fact. Right, we'll eat meat every day for luncheon. Alternate the ham with the mutton until it's finished and I'll take supper with the captain.'

The weather became hotter as they steamed down the coast and the Atlantic became a brighter and more brilliant blue as they headed towards the waters of the Gulf of Mexico. They looked towards the stumpy finger of land which they were told was East Florida, and came into the steamy air of the Gulf of Mexico.

'Permission to take off my jacket, sir?' Allen asked, perspiration running down his face. He'd brought Newmarch a glass of fresh orange juice, having squeezed the oranges which he had bought from the cook.

'I should have brought a cotton jacket, Allen. These European clothes are far too hot. I'll have to buy some more suitable clothes in New Orleans. No,' he said. 'Keep your jacket on. It doesn't do to let standards slip.'

And so Allen sweated in his wool jacket, waistcoat and trousers, whilst Newmarch sat in his shirtsleeves beneath an awning on the deck and watched the colour of the waves change again as the muddy waters of the Mississippi river slewed into the sea.

Their progress up the great river towards the old city of New Orleans was slow and took several days, hampered as they were by the mass of river traffic. Ships laden with foreign passengers steamed laboriously along the river between the flat landscape of the plantations where fields of cotton, sugar cane and the huts of the native workers could be seen above the embankment. As they neared New Orleans, flatboats and trading vessels coming down from Kentucky and Ohio bringing in ham, wheat and corn all vied for space along the levee, where merchants and traders piled high their cotton bales, sugar, and other commodities, ready to do business.

'What does the river remind you of, Allen?' Newmarch asked as they stood at the rails watching the ship dock along the riverbank.

'Nothing, sir,' Allen shook his head. 'I've never seen anything like it, nor felt such heat.'

'Why, the old Humber,' Newmarch replied. 'Doesn't it remind you of that? It's wide and muddy and full of ships just like this, and even the embankment to keep the waters out of the town is the same as along parts of the Humber.'

'It's called the *levee*, sir.' Allen thought his employer had taken leave of his senses. The Humber was nothing like this. The Humber estuary had hidden sandbanks and rushing tides; the Mississippi was slow, had hidden tree roots below the surface of the water, floating branches and swathes of moss and bulrushes, not to mention crocodiles and the swarms of mosquitoes which were already sucking his blood as the butcher in New York had said they would.

'I know what it's called,' Newmarch said impatiently. 'Come on, let's get packed, we shall disembark before nightfall.'

Meaning, Allen grumbled to himself as Newmarch went to join some of the other passengers for a last hand of cards, get packing, Allen, and don't forget anything. He emptied the cupboard which now contained only half a bottle of brandy and one or two books, and started to take his employer's clothes from the drawer beneath his bunk. He carefully folded his jackets and put them in the trunk and did the same with the trousers. He put in his shoes and boots, shirts, handkerchiefs and cravats, leaving out one grey suit which was lighter in weight than the others, one shirt and one cravat. 'He'll probably want one of those that I've already packed,' he muttered, 'but I'll risk it.'

He laid the trousers on the bunk and put the jacket over the back of the single chair, for there was little hanging space in the cabin. As he did so, something fell out of the inside pocket. It was Newmarch's bulging leather pocketbook. He picked it up from the floor and, after a single moment's hesitation, opened it. He reached to put the chair against the cabin door in case Newmarch should return, and quickly flicked through the contents.

It wasn't the first time he had looked through his employer's private things, but there was never much money in his purse. This, however, was packed with notes, bills of credit from the bank, documents and English money.

He gave a soft whistle through his teeth as he contemplated it. There would be enough here to set him up for a long time. But no, he deliberated. I haven't yet stooped so low. I'll get by on my own endeavours. He put the pocketbook on top of the small chest, moved the chair back to its original place and continued packing.

A moment later, Newmarch burst through the door. 'My pocketbook!' he blurted out. 'I must have dropped it somewhere.'

'Here, sir.' Allen, picking it up, waved it at him.

'I found it on the floor. Must have dropped out of your coat.'

'Phew!' Newmarch took it from him. 'Thank God for that, Allen. We'd have been stumped without it. My whole life is in here.'

CHAPTER FIVE

'I have an introduction, Allen.' Edward watched as Allen and the Negro driver loaded their luggage into the open trap. 'We'll book in at the hotel, then I'll change and go calling.'

Allen was already exhausted. The heat beat down, even though the day was drawing on, and the aroma of blossom was overpowering. He wiped the sweat from his forehead. 'Very good, sir.'

They drove to the hotel which the ship's captain had recommended, watching the hustle and bustle of New Orleans as they trotted by. The streets were filled with Negroes, Indians, dark-eyed Creoles, Europeans and Chinese and frontiersmen of every nationality in their leather-skinned jackets, and they could hear French, Spanish and English voices as people greeted each other.

Young slave girls with their dark hair covered by colourful scarves, wicker baskets hooked over their arms, chatted on street corners, and laden pack mules plodded slowly up the road towards the market as the drivers cracked their whips above them and shouted fruitlessly for them to hurry.

The cab driver sang in a rich deep voice as he drove away from the river and towards the interior of the city. Within cool flower-filled courtyards, buildings of sun-dried brick or yellow stucco were festooned with bougainvillea and jasmine, and white shutters enclosed the windows against the heat.

'Quite a city, eh, Allen? Very exotic.' Edward glanced over his shoulder at a graceful ivory-skinned woman carrying a parasol, a young Negress at her side. The woman saw his stare and lowered her parasol so that her face was shielded from his gaze.

He suddenly thought of Ruby and was filled with an impotent desire and melancholy for her. He had first seen her whilst travelling in a chaise with his brother as they were returning home from the Hull cotton mill in which they were shareholders. She had lifted her head and smiled at him in a spontaneous carefree manner. He had immediately fallen in love and wanted her, no matter that she was a poor mill girl and he engaged to be married.

I must be careful, he thought. The ladies here will be kept under lock and key. He had heard that the New Orleans gentlemen with their French or Spanish background would not tolerate any reckless dalliance with their womenfolk.

They obtained rooms at the hotel which Captain Voularis of the *Mississippi Girl* had recommended. It was cool within the white walls and they were shown upstairs by a young black boy in a dark blue jacket and trousers which were edged with red. Edward gave him an English shilling, as he hadn't yet worked out the American currency system.

The boy looked at it in his hand and Edward asked him if it was acceptable.

'Sure thing, sir. My boss will take any kind of money so long as he can spend it.'

'But that's for you,' Edward objected, 'for bringing up the luggage.'

The boy nodded. 'That's mighty kind of you, sir. But Señor Gomez will be waiting when I get down dem stairs, and I ain't got no pockets where I can hide it.'

'In that case I'll have it back.' Edward put out his hand for the boy to return the money. 'I'm not tipping your employer. That's not on at all!'

'There's a lot to learn, Allen,' he remarked as the boy left the room. 'More than I imagined.'

'Yes,' Allen agreed. 'It's a mingling of different cultures. And some of them seem to stick to their old ways, rather like we do in England. Maybe it will be different in California, sir,' he added.

'I hope so,' Edward murmured as he took off his shirt to wash in the cool water that Allen had poured into the porcelain basin. 'I'd like to think that there's more freedom there than at home.' He took a deep breath and hoped, not for the first time, that he had done the right thing in leaving his wife and country. But I couldn't have stayed in England without Ruby. Better that I am in a foreign land with distractions.

He looked in the gilt mirror on the wall and saw his wind-browned skin. His cheeks seemed leaner than they had been. I've lost weight, he thought, which is odd when I have done so much

70

loafing around on the ship. I need some good fresh food, he decided.

'I need a haircut, Allen,' he said as he fastened his cravat, then smoothed his sideburns. 'I'll find somewhere tomorrow, and some new clothes.'

'I'll cut it for you when you get back, sir,' Allen offered.

'Good man.' Edward picked up his cane. He didn't need it, but he was of the opinion that he cut rather a dash when carrying one. 'Call me a cab,' he said. 'And then you'd better get some rest,' he added. 'You look pretty rough.'

Allen lay on the bed in his room when Newmarch had gone, and closed his eyes. What to do? He couldn't leave without money and he debated whether to take his wages out of Newmarch's pocketbook. I'd only take what I'm due or else he'll have the authorities onto me. And if I'm caught and he presses charges I could finish up in a stinking jail and never get out! No, I'll wait for an opportunity, he resolved. I'll know it when it comes.

Captain Voularis had recommended that Edward called on Señor Rodriguez, who was an eminent man in the city of New Orleans. 'He can put opportunities your way, Mr Newmarch,' the captain had said, 'there is no-one better.' Edward, always looking for the easiest route to opportunity, decided he would call.

He told the cab driver the address and they travelled over unmade muddy roads until they came to the wrought-iron gates of the house, where a guard and a dog patrolled inside.

Edward passed his card to the guard, on which

71

he had written the name of the hotel and Captain Voularis' name. 'My compliments to Señor Rodriguez. If I might have the privilege of paying him a visit, at his convenience.'

He climbed back into the chaise and asked the driver to return along the levee. The evening had cooled and the residents were coming out of their houses and businesses and were socializing along the riverbanks. Hundreds of ships for as far as his eyes could see were moored along the Mississippi, with the flatboats and broadhorns slipped between.

He heard music from fiddles and pipes and the sound of drumbeat. On the decks of some of the ships, girls and men were dancing. He tapped the driver on his shoulder. 'Those ladies down there.' He pointed with his cane to where two honey-coloured young women were walking with an elderly Negress. 'What would they be, Spanish? Mexican?'

The driver glanced down towards them, then shrugged. 'Quadroon,' he said. 'Mixed blood. Mebbe Spanish, Mexican or French. Their granddaddy or grandmammy would have been Negro anyway, but they ain't pure black like me!'

'So, will they be free citizens?' Edward asked. 'Or are they servants?' He found he couldn't bring himself to say slaves.

'Could be, sir, if they've been given their freedom. Some Europeans, even in New Orleans, don't keep slaves.' He gave a deep chuckle. 'Time's a coming when we'll all be free, but there'll be a fight all right: North and South will git blood on their hands.'

Edward sat back and contemplated. It was such a perfect evening. The sun was warm, people were laughing and making merry, and the city had the feel and appearance of Spain or southern France with its orange and lemon trees and brightly berried hedges, and the smell of blossom. It also appeared to be thriving, judging by the commodities which were on the levee. A fight, the driver said. That can't be right. There was so much merriment and there didn't appear to be any hardship. None at all.

When he returned to the hotel he found Allen fast asleep in his own room, but he had unpacked the luggage and hung Edward's clothing in the cupboards, so he didn't call him but lay on his bed and closed his eyes. He must have fallen asleep for he was awakened by a light tapping.

The same houseboy was at the door, holding a message. Edward put his hand in his pocket before remembering that any coin he gave to him would go to the hotel owner. The boy saw his hesitation and slightly opening his lips he pointed to the inside of his mouth. Edward nodded and gave him the coin and watched as the boy slipped the silver into his cheek. He touched his cap and silently departed.

'Hope he doesn't swallow it,' Edward muttered, and opened up the envelope. The message was from Señor Rodriguez, who requested that he join him for lunch the following day.

He rose early the next morning and accompanied by Allen went in search of a new suit of clothes, something lighter and more suitable for the climate. He bought a cream linen suit and a wide hat to keep the heat of the day from his head. The hat was made, he was told, from the leaves of the palm tree. He fitted Allen out with a cotton coat and trousers.

'They maybe won't do for California,' he said to him. 'But I like the feel of this place so we'll stay a while before moving on.'

He hired a chaise and presented himself at one o'clock at the gates of Señor Rodriguez' house. The guard, obviously expecting him, unlocked and opened them and advised him to continue up the long drive which divided the wide, lush green lawns where palm trees and the purple-blue jacaranda grew. Mulatto and Negro workers were rolling the clipped grass and trimming the hedges.

He drew up outside the door and looked with admiration at the house in front of him. Wide steps led up to the front door and the cream-coloured brick gave off a sunny warmth. Wrought-iron balconies at the upstairs windows held stone pots and jars of brightly coloured flowers, and white muslin curtains floated gently in the warm breeze.

A young mulatto girl opened the heavy wooden doors. She was bareheaded and barefoot and wore a red cotton skirt and white embroidered blouse. 'Good day, Mr Newmarch, sir,' she said in a sing-song voice. 'Come right in. Señor Rodriguez is expecting you.'

Edward followed her through the entrance hall and up a wide staircase with an elaborate scrolled-iron rail to a landing with double doors. She opened one of them and, holding out her hand, said, 'Go right on in.'

He walked into a large room painted white and

gold and filled with heavy but elegant furniture, the chairs and sofas with carved scrolled frames and richly brocaded cushions. At the furthest end of the room, open glass doors led out onto a balcony where the muslin curtains he had seen from below billowed to and fro. From up here he could see the brown Mississippi and the crowded levee.

Señor Rodriguez rose from a sofa to greet him with outstretched hand. He was tall and slimly built, sharp-featured with a long nose and thin cheeks and well-groomed silver hair. He wore a white linen suit with a narrow black silk cravat tied in a simple knot.

'I am delighted to welcome you to New Orleans, Mr Newmarch.' He glanced keenly at Edward. 'I have had a meeting with Captain Voularis only this morning and he mentioned you.' He spoke in a cultivated voice with just a trace of Spanish accent. 'I understand you are looking for a new life in America?'

'I want something different from what I had,' Edward agreed. 'I need to stretch my horizon.'

'Quite so.' Rodriguez smiled. 'You are still a young man, and ambitious, yes?'

At Edward's nod Rodriguez softened his voice. 'And I understand from Captain Voularis that you are recently widowed?'

Edward cleared his throat and murmured that he was.

'So no commitments? No children? You can do as you please? Good. Come,' he said. 'You must meet my wife Sofia and our family, and then we shall have luncheon.'

He led the way to a door at the other side of the room which seemed to open by itself, until, glancing over his shoulder as he entered another room, Edward noticed the little mulatto girl standing behind it. She repositioned herself at the other side of the door and closed it behind them.

Edward refrained from gasping as he saw the magnificent dining room. A long room, yet it was dominated by the highly polished table set in the centre with at least twenty chairs around it. There were heavy silver candelabra upon it and crystal bowls filled with exotic fruits, melon, oranges, bananas and pineapple.

Edward cast his eye over the table setting and saw that six places were laid with gleaming silver cutlery and crisp white table napkins with pale pink blossom laid upon them.

Another door opened and Edward caught a glimpse of the young girl again, but he took a deep breath as a woman came in. She was, he thought, the most beautiful woman he had ever seen. He guessed that she would be in her early thirties.

She had thick black hair to her shoulders, swept back and secured with a flower and diamond pin. Her complexion was creamy and her large eyes were of the deepest brown, and when she smiled, as she did now to greet him, her mouth was soft and full.

'I am honoured, señora.' He gave a deep bow. 'Thank you for inviting me to your lovely home.'

'You are more than welcome, Meester New-march.' Her voice was low and husky with an attractive accent. 'You must feel a little lonely so far from your own country?'

'Just a little,' he agreed. 'New Orleans is very different from where I come from.'

'And you are a widower, yes?' Her forehead creased in sympathy.

I wish they wouldn't go on about it, Edward thought. I wonder why Captain Voularis chose to tell them?

'It ees not easy, I know,' she said. 'I too was widowed when I was very young.' Then she flashed a brilliant smile at her husband, who was watching her. 'But then I met my Sancho, so it was ordained!'

The door opened once more and an elderly woman, dressed in a black gown with a black lace cap on her white hair, was ushered in by the girl, who held her by the elbow until she reached them. She leaned heavily on an ebony walking stick.

'May I introduce you to my mother?' Rodriguez said. 'She does not speak English although she understands a little, in spite of her deafness.'

Edward bowed again and Señora Rodriguez peered narrowly at him and then inclined her head in a little nod.

'Now we just need our daughters and we may be seated.' Sofia looked towards the door and, as if on cue, two young girls entered. 'This is Sibella.' A girl of about fourteen rushed towards him, dimpled a smile and curtsied. Like her mother she had a creamy skin, fine features and large dark eyes which shone with merriment. How lovely she is, Edward thought as he gave her a bow. She must already have many admirers.

'And this is Elena, my eldest daughter.' Sofia

Rodriguez' voice was bright and brittle. Edward turned to bow to the young woman who stood sullenly before him, and he wondered how it was possible for such a plain creature to be born into this handsome family. She was about seventeen years of age, tall and of heavy build with dark corkscrew-curly hair. Her skin, unlike her mother's and sister's, was swarthy with coarse broad features. The only likeness was in her eyes, which were dark like theirs with long sweeping lashes, and which viewed him with suspicion.

She muttered something in Spanish as she curtsied to him and her father spoke sharply to her in the same language.

'Shall we be seated?' Señor Rodriguez snapped his fingers and a troop of servants appeared. Two of them positioned themselves behind the two ladies and one behind the señoritas and drew back their chairs so they might be seated. Another moved towards Edward to show him his place and one attended Rodriguez, who sat at the head of the table.

Wine was poured into crystal glasses and the food was brought in. Edward, having eaten plainly for so many weeks, found his mouth watering as dish after dish was placed on the table. They were served with a dish of guacamole containing tomato, avocado and chilli, which made him draw in his breath with its fire. Bright red and green peppers decorated a dish of cold spit-roasted quail. Smoked fish, oysters, crayfish, boiled turkey, pastries filled with minced ham and hot black peppercorns were placed before him. Tortilla and rice with ham and olives were offered. A dish of figs and dates mixed with almonds and raisins, capers and spinach, was topped with slices of oranges and lemons and sprinkled with sugar and almond oil.

For dessert he was offered honey corn cakes and a creamy chocolate blancmange flavoured with nutmeg, cinnamon, ginger and malmsey.

His glass was constantly filled, first with a crisp white wine, next a delicate rosé. Then the glasses were changed and he was brought a deep red Portuguese wine, mellow to the tongue, followed by a sweet dessert wine spiced with coriander and cardamom.

After they had finished, the ladies departed to another room and through the closed doors Edward heard the angry tones of Elena, who he had noticed ate greedily and quickly. Her mother answered sharply and then came the raised voice of the older señora, though he couldn't understand what was being said.

'You will take a glass of malmsey, Mr Newmarch?' Rodriguez lifted a crystal decanter enquiringly. 'We will drink a toast to your success in your new country!'

Edward blinked and accepted, though he knew he had had more than enough. He lifted his glass. 'Thank you,' he murmured. 'And may I wish you and your family good health and continuing prosperity.'

What riches, he thought. What sumptuous surroundings! Everything he saw around him spoke of wealth and old money. If I could cultivate this man, would some of his aura rub off on me? Could I acquire such grandeur and splendour?

Edward drained his glass, saw Rodriguez smiling to himself and realized that the Spaniard wanted something from him, equally as much as he wanted from the Spaniard.

CHAPTER SIX

'How do you do?' Georgiana was standing on the stairs, so she had the advantage of being higher than the man who was posing as Edward Newmarch. She recognized him instantly as Edward's valet, for she had seen him many times when calling on her cousin May. His name? she thought. What is his name? She tried to think of Edward's voice as he called to him, as he often did, to fetch him this or that.

Allen! she remembered. That's what it is. So what has happened to Edward? Is he dead and Allen posing as him and spending May's money? Her lips tightened. I cannot condone this, even though I have no regard for Edward Newmarch! But then she saw Wilhelm Dreumel's smiling honest face and wondered how she could tell him that the man he was trusting with his land and gold mine was an impostor. But she must.

'I'm pleased to meet you, Miss Gregory.' Allen's voice was nervous and his eyes had an appeal in them. 'I believe we come from the same district?'

Such nerve, she bristled. 'I am related to the Newmarch family by marriage,' she said coldly. 'You must be from another branch of the family?'

80

'Yes, ma'am, my family came originally from the west of Yorkshire. They were – in the mining business.'

Perhaps they were. She continued to watch him. But as coal workers, not as owners. 'And so you decided to take a chance in America? Did you come alone?' she asked pertinently.

Could this be true? But why is Allen using Edward Newmarch's name? I must find out before I challenge him.

'No.' He appeared to hesitate. 'I came with a – friend, but we went our separate ways. He – we were staying in New Orleans, then he moved to California.'

One of the staff came up to Wilhelm Dreumel. 'Beg your pardon, Mr Dreumel, but your table is ready.'

Wilhelm Dreumel turned to Georgiana and asked if she would care to join them for supper.

'Thank you, no,' she said. 'I'm sure you and Mr *Newmarch*,' she emphasized the name, 'have much to discuss. Miss Kelly and I have a table in the corner.' She indicated a table already set for two. 'And we need to make plans.'

'Of course.' Dreumel bowed and Allen backed away, a grim expression on his face. 'I trust that we will meet again soon.'

He's such a nice man, Georgiana mused, thinking of Wilhelm Dreumel. I can't let him be taken in by that impostor. And what has happened to Edward? She thought of her cousin May, totally without means of her own and dependent on her father. I must write and tell her. If Edward is dead, for that blackguard could have

81

disposed of him, then she might be able to get her dowry back. If there's anything left of it.

'Miss Gregory!' Kitty whispered. Her blue eyes were wide as they sat down at the table and waited to be served. 'That's Robert Allen! Mr Newmarch's valet! I met him once when I went with you to see Mrs Newmarch. He was cleaning his shoes! Mr Newmarch's shoes, I mean!'

'I know,' Georgiana answered in a low voice. 'And he knows that we know. But what to do? That's the question.'

Kitty's eyes grew even wider and her red hair seemed to stand on end. 'Suppose – do you suppose that he's done something dreadful to Mr Newmarch?'

'I do hope not,' Georgiana said, then as their food was brought to the table, murmured, 'Kitty, get on with your supper. We must act as if there is nothing untoward until I have had time to think.' She began her soup. 'I don't think he's wearing his own clothes: they don't seem to fit well.'

'He's mebbe had to buy more,' Kitty whispered hoarsely. 'Mebbe the others got bloodstained and he had to get rid of them!'

'Kitty!' she admonished, though the same thought had crossed her own mind. 'We must remain calm until we find out the truth.'

The truth, or what was deemed to be the truth, came later that evening. They finished their supper, took a short walk into one of the nearby gardens and then returned to the Marius. Robert Allen was sitting by himself in the hotel lounge with a glass of ale on the table in front of him. He rose from his seat when he saw them enter, obviously intending to speak.

'Go on up, Kitty. I mean to have a few words with Robert Allen,' Georgiana said in a tight voice.

'Are you sure, miss?' Kitty was alarmed. 'He might be dangerous.'

'He's hardly likely to attack me in full view of the hotel staff!' Georgiana asserted. 'Off you go. I shall be perfectly all right.'

With several backward glances Kitty mounted the stairs and Georgiana moved towards Allen, whose expression was pinched and nervous.

'So, Allen.' She refused to afford him the dignity of a prefix to his name and saw him flinch. 'You have assumed another name, and one which does not rightly belong to you!'

'Miss Gregory! It is not what it might seem. Won't you sit down and I will try to explain?'

'It is not what it might seem!' she said coldly. '*What* is not as it might seem? It appears to me that you are masquerading as someone else. That is perfectly obvious from where I am standing, no matter what it might *seem* to be!' She didn't sit down as he had requested but remained standing firmly in front of him. 'What has happened to Mr Newmarch?'

He pressed his lips together and shuffled his feet. 'We parted company,' he muttered. 'He, erm – he became acquainted with a Spaniard in New Orleans. They had a disagreement over something and Mr Newmarch went into hiding. He didn't come back, so I set off for New York. That was well over a year ago. I've not heard of him since.'

She gave a thin smile. 'So you're using his name, wearing his clothes and spending his money?' Or May's money, she thought, for she still held that charge against Edward Newmarch, even though in the eyes of English law a wife's possessions belonged to her husband.

'*Not* his money,' he insisted. 'I haven't used his money. I only drew what was due to me. His name, yes. I thought I would stand a better chance of success by using his name and background.'

'And what if he should want to use his own name?' She sank down into a chair. 'Or is he not in a position to need it?'

He didn't seem to grasp the implication of her words for he replied, a trifle arrogantly, 'This is a big country, Miss Gregory. There are many men with similar names.'

'Who come from the north of England?' she said derisively. 'Come, come, Allen. You can surely do better than that!'

'I never thought–' he began.

'You never thought that you would be found out! Well, I can tell you that you are found out and that I shall inform Mr Dreumel at the earliest opportunity! I shall also write to my cousin, Mrs Newmarch, to tell her that her husband has disappeared, and an impostor has taken on his identity.'

She stared Allen in the face. His cheeks had become quite ashen. 'If you have any decency left in you at all, will you tell me whether I can inform her if her husband is dead or alive?'

He shrugged. 'He was alive when I last saw him,' he said. 'I swear that he was.'

'Is there proof of that apart from your word?' she asked bitingly. 'Is there anyone else who can

84

verify it?'

'No,' he muttered. 'He said he needed to hide away for a couple of weeks.'

'Why didn't you go with him if he was in trouble? Why did you come to New York?'

'He told me to wait, that he would come back when things had died down. I don't know what kind of trouble it was except that there was a woman involved. I was ill in New Orleans. The climate didn't suit me at all. I had malaria. So – when he didn't return, I decided to leave and come back to New York.'

'Come back?' she asked.

'Yes, we had a few hours here on first arriving in America. I liked the feel of it. On the journey back I met Dreumel.'

'It still doesn't account for your using Edward Newmarch's name instead of your own!'

'It doesn't, does it?' His face became devoid of expression. 'But whatever I tell you, Miss Gregory, you're not going to believe me.' He lifted his chin and gazed back at her. 'So believe whatever you want. But I'll tell you this. Wilhelm Dreumel depends on me and if you tell him who I really am, he'll probably dismiss me and all the work we've done will come to nothing. He'll lose money and so will his partner.'

She was stunned. Whatever should she do? She rose to her feet and he did also, so that they stood facing each other. 'I shall think about telling Mr Dreumel,' she said at last, and saw a flicker of relief on his face. 'Though I shall definitely write to my cousin,' she added. 'She must be informed.'

'As you wish, Miss Gregory.' He gave her a

brief bow and left, speaking first to the desk clerk then striding swiftly upstairs.

She followed more slowly and on entering her room found Kitty sitting by the fire, sewing a button onto one of her gloves. 'Did you get any sense out of him, Miss Gregory? Did he tell you what's happened to Mr Newmarch?'

Georgiana sat down. 'No, not really. Allen said he was alive when he left him. That was in New Orleans. Allen's up to something, no doubt about that. But what?'

'Poor Mrs Newmarch,' Kitty said, biting off a piece of thread. 'It's bad enough her husband going off and leaving her, without somebody else spending his money.'

'He said he hasn't,' Georgiana murmured. 'But I'm not sure that I believe him. I must write to May immediately.' Having made the decision she rose quickly, going across to the table which also served as a writing desk. 'He said, Allen, I mean, that he last saw Edward in New Orleans over a year ago. So–' She tapped her finger on her lip. 'Good heavens,' she said. 'He could be anywhere.'

Kitty looked up. 'Why – you wasn't thinking of going to look for him, Miss Gregory? Was you?'

'*Were you*, Kitty,' she answered vaguely. 'Not wasn't. No, I wasn't. Edward Newmarch means nothing to me, though I'd like to track him down for May's sake and give him a piece of my mind.'

Kitty looked confused over the corrected grammar but simply asked if it was far to New Orleans, because if it wasn't, perhaps they could go and see if he was still there.

'It would take weeks, Kitty, and I've other more

important things to think of.'

She thought of them all night long, tossing and turning in her bed as she deliberated whether or not to tell Wilhelm Dreumel about Robert Allen. Finally, as a rosy dawn was breaking, she decided what she must do and promptly fell into a deep sleep, not waking until nine o'clock when Kitty knocked on her door and asked if she wanted breakfast.

She struggled to a sitting position. 'Yes,' she croaked, 'but I'll have it up here, Kitty. Would you go down and ask them to send up coffee and toast and marmalade?'

Ten minutes later, Kitty returned carrying a tray laid for breakfast. 'They were busy downstairs, miss, so I brought it up,' she said. 'Folk just arriving on 'morning coach and other folks leaving.' She put down the tray and opened the curtains. 'I've just seen that nice Mr Dreumel leaving with Robert Allen.'

'What? Oh no!' Georgiana had decided during the night that she would tell Wilhelm Dreumel about Allen after all. It wasn't something that should be hidden. She got out of bed and rushed to the window, but the street was empty.

'Did they get on the coach?' she asked.

'Yes, miss. That one that goes to catch the river boat.'

Confound it! This is Allen's doing, she thought. He's persuaded Dreumel to go back to the mine before I get a chance to talk to him! She finished her breakfast, washed and dressed and went downstairs to the reception desk.

'Could you tell me when Mr Dreumel will be

returning?' she asked. 'Has he rebooked his room?'

'Mr Dreumel has a permanent room, Miss Gregory,' the clerk said. 'He doesn't need to book.' He reached under the desk. 'He asked if I would give you this letter.'

She took it from him and went to sit by a window to read it. 'Dear Miss Gregory,' he wrote. 'I'm sorry that I have had to rush away, but Newmarch brought news of importance and it is imperative that we leave immediately. I shall be away for several weeks, I fear, but trust that I shall still find you at the Marius on my return. You must ask the staff for anything that you require and they will do their best to oblige you. Should you have any difficulties or problems during your stay in New York, John Charlesworth would most certainly be able to help you for he knows many people.

'I send you my very best regards,

'Wilhelm Dreumel.'

Bother. Bother. Bother! Now what do I do? I must do something! She sat fuming. I didn't expect to have to deal with complications like this! I came to find a new life, for heaven's sake! A life for myself, and here I am, running around after everyone else. She knew that she couldn't let the matter drop. She owed it to May and also to May's father, who had been responsible for her when she was a child. She could not just ignore the problem.

Kitty came down the stairs and stood beside her. 'What are we going to do today, Miss Gregory? I'm at a loose end not having any jobs to do.'

'How would you like to go on a journey, Kitty?'

88

'That would be nice, miss.' Kitty beamed at her. 'Very nice. Where to?'

Georgiana look a deep breath. 'I don't know yet. But somewhere.'

CHAPTER SEVEN

Edward and Rodriguez chatted well into the afternoon, Rodriguez topping up Edward's glass with malmsey and then ordering coffee to be brought in. The coffee was strong, sweet and spicy and Edward felt his heart thumping.

'Perhaps you would like to take a siesta, Mr Newmarch?' Rodriguez proposed. 'It is our custom after luncheon, though we are a little later than usual. I suggest,' he said with a smile, 'that you might prefer to rest before driving back to your hotel – unless, of course, I send one of my boys to drive you, though they too will be sleeping now.'

'No, please, don't trouble, señor. I will just close my eyes for ten minutes before leaving.' Edward did not want to overstay his welcome.

'Then, come!' Rodriguez clapped his hands and a black boy appeared. 'Take Mr Newmarch to a guest room. Make sure he has everything he requires.'

'Yes, señor. If you would come this way, sir.' The boy led Edward out of the room, along the landing and opened a door into a bedroom. The curtains were drawn, making the room cool and dim. A large draped bed with a mosquito net over it had the sheets laid back ready for occupancy. On a rail near a marble washstand were soft white towels and a white cotton robe.

'If you'd sit down, sir, I'll unfasten your boots,' the boy said. Edward obeyed, holding up first one foot and then the other. He took off his jacket, which the boy hung up. He handed him the robe.

'There's fresh orange juice and water on the table, sir, but if you want anything else just ring.' He showed him a silver handbell placed on the table beside the bed. 'I'll be right outside.'

Edward took off his trousers and shirt, put on the robe and slipped beneath the mosquito net. Within minutes he was asleep.

When he awoke it was evening. The bright sunlight had dimmed and a cooling breeze was blowing the curtains. He sat up. Good God! What time was it? He looked at his fob watch, which he had placed on the table. Six o'clock!

He quickly dressed, first washing his hands and face with scented water which was in a bowl on the washstand. He poured a glass of orange juice and drank thirstily. His head was throbbing, the effect of too much wine.

There came a discreet tap on the door and he called, 'Come in.' The boy entered holding a tray with a silver teapot, milk jug and sugar bowl and a china cup and saucer.

'Señora Sofia said to bring you English tea.' He grinned, his teeth white in his dark skin. 'She said it was what all English people have at this time of day.'

'How kind of her,' he said, relaxing a little. I

must thank them, he thought, and take my leave or they might not ask me again.

Señora Sofia, however, did not appear to be in a hurry for his departure when he presented himself, but asked him to sit down with her in the drawing room. 'Are you rested, Meester Newmarch?' she asked. 'I think that our ways are not the same as yours. You do not take – what you call it? – a nap – in the afternoon?'

'Only the elderly.' He laughed. 'But then our climate is not so hot that it makes us tired, and our evenings are cold so that we don't walk out, or *promenade* as you do here, but tend to stay indoors at home; or perhaps the gentlemen might go to their clubs.'

She made little tutting noises. 'So, you think you will like it here when it is so different?'

He gazed at her. She really was very beautiful. Rodriguez was a very lucky fellow to have such a wife. 'I'm sure that I will,' he said softly. 'There is much that I find very attractive.'

She lowered her lashes, then lifted them to gaze at him from fathomless eyes. 'You must of course be careful that you mix with the right people. There are some ruffians here who might take advantage of you, being new to the country.'

He nodded. 'Have you always lived in New Orleans, señora?'

'Since my marriage to Sancho,' she said. 'I am – was – Mexican. There was much fighting between the Mexicans and the Americans and then the Spaniards. It was difficult to know who to follow and it was very dangerous for a woman, especially a woman with a young child.'

'What happened to your husband?' he asked. 'Your first husband, I mean?'

'He died,' she said simply. 'Sancho killed him.'

Edward felt a cold shiver down his spine. There had been, he thought, an iciness running through Rodriguez. Not a man to cross.

'Brown was not a good man,' she said, 'but it was not all his fault. He had bad blood. His mother was a slave and his father was a cotton farmer. His father used to beat all his slave children so Brown ran away when he was only a boy and that is when I met him.'

Edward was fascinated. He owned shares in a cotton mill in Hull. Who would have thought that so much could happen before the cotton reached the mill?

'He was not a good 'usband, he used to beat me and so I ran away with my child, Elena.' She smiled. 'And I met Sancho. He was a soldier and he protected me from the other soldiers.' She shrugged. 'It is easy for a soldier to take a woman but 'e was 'onourable and kept me safe. Then Brown found out where I was. He was taking me back wiz 'im but Sancho found out and came after us. He killed Brown with a single shot.'

Edward swallowed hard and determined that not under any circumstances would he flirt with Señora Rodriguez.

'So I was a widow,' she said softly, gazing at Edward. 'But then Sancho and I were married. Now of course,' she went on, in an almost absent-minded way, 'we must find a suitable 'usband for Elena. She is not beautiful like her sister Sibella, but she has many qualities. She is intelligent and she has a sense of humour which is sometimes rare in a woman.'

She lifted her eyes to his and to his amazement she put her small hand over one of his. 'She will make a good wife for someone, do you not think so, Meester Newmarch?' She gave him a soft beguiling smile. 'And she will be very rich.'

Edward cleared his throat and wondered how he could withdraw his hand without offending. He gently squeezed her fingers and murmured, 'I'm quite sure that there will be many suitors enchanted by her, señora.'

There came a tap on the door and Edward rose to his feet as Rodriguez came in. 'Ah, señor.' Edward greeted him. 'I am about to depart.' He gave a small bow. 'May I thank you for your very generous hospitality. I trust that I have not stayed overlong?'

'Not at all.' Rodriguez held his gaze for a second, then it flickered to his wife. 'You are more than welcome. In fact, tomorrow we are holding a supper party for a few guests and we would be delighted if you would join us. At about eight o'clock?'

Edward thanked him, accepted and took his leave, finding his hired chaise waiting at the door and a boy holding the reins of the mare. He tipped him an English sixpence and vowed to visit a bank and exchange some money. English currency is no longer any use to me, he thought. I'm in America to stay. It suits me very well.

His thoughts turned to Ruby as he drove back to the hotel. How would she have fitted in here? Would she have been able to talk to these wealthy people and visit them in their splendid opulent houses? Or would she have been overcome with embarrassment? Dear, darling Ruby. How I miss you.

He had realized how much he yearned for Ruby as he sat with the beautiful, desirable, but unattainable Sofia. How he longed to have Ruby's soft and yielding body next to his, but no, dear girl, he sighed as he pulled into the front of his hotel. You wouldn't have fitted in at all. If I am going to get anywhere in this country, then I am going to have to do it alone, at least until I get established.

'Allen! Allen! Where the devil are you?' Edward threw down his coat and called. Though his bed had been made by the hotel servants, his clothes had not been put away and there was no sign of Allen. He opened the communicating door into his valet's room and found him lying on his bed. His face was flushed and the hair around his forehead and neck was wet.

'Are you ill?' Edward asked sharply. 'What's the matter with you?'

Allen turned towards him on hearing his voice. 'Sorry, sir.' He attempted to rise but fell back on his pillow. 'I – I feel terrible, sir. My throat,' he rasped, 'and my head.'

Edward backed away. 'I hope it isn't contagious! I don't want to catch it. I have a supper engagement tomorrow. Who's going to press my shirt?'

Allen shook his head. 'I just need a couple of hours' rest, Mr Newmarch,' he croaked. 'I'll be all right by the morning.'

But he wasn't and Edward sent down for

94

someone to clean his shoes and wash and press a shirt and trousers, and to bring Allen a jug of cold water to assuage his thirst.

'This is not on,' he muttered. 'The fellow is supposed to be looking after me.' He breakfasted alone in the dining room, any other hotel guests evidently having risen early and gone about their business. I'll take a walk, he thought, familiarize myself with the surroundings. If I like it I might stay here for a while. I'm sure that Rodriguez will have good contacts. He could perhaps guide me into some kind of profitable line without too much demand on my time.

He wandered on foot towards the levee, admiring the ivy-clad stately houses which were half hidden at the top of long gravel drives, their classic marble pillars guarding entrances to a splendour he could only dream about. But also, as he wandered, he found shanty housing along muddy lanes and alleys where he dared not proceed. He clutched his watch and chain and hurried on to a more amenable area.

A large man of indiscriminate race approached him and offered to take him for a boat ride along the river. 'Show you the crocs, sir, and the swamps. Ain't like anything you've seen before. You'll be quite safe, ain't no worry 'bout that.'

'Thank you, no.' Edward backed away. 'I have an appointment. Just killing time. Must be off!'

The man grinned and turned away. 'Get you another time? Yes, sir.'

Edward hurried off and followed the road down towards the river. A ship had just docked and passengers were coming down the gangboard on unsteady legs. He was reminded of the time when he had watched a ship in the Hull docks unloading passengers so that they might stretch their legs before continuing their journey to America. It was this very scene which had implanted the idea that he too would like to sail to a new life, away from the petty restrictions and conventions of England.

But he had not reckoned on Ruby refusing to travel with him. She was not willing to trade her familiar life, poor though it was, to go with him to new adventures. She didn't trust me, he mused, as he gazed at the activity on board ship. That was what it was. She probably thought that I would abandon her. Take your wife, she said. He gave a grim inward laugh. Take your wife! As if May would travel to a foreign land! She's so rooted in tradition that the very idea would be abhorrent to her. Pah! I know not one single Englishwoman who would leave home and family to travel abroad and seek a new life. Not one. Not even those who profess to want their freedom and independence.

He turned away and headed back for the hotel, trying to dismiss the sensation of loneliness which was washing over him.

Allen had made an effort to get up but he looked ill. He could hardly stand and he clutched his hand to his sweating forehead. Edward berated him and told him to go back to bed. 'For God's sake, Allen. I'll manage.' The washed and ironed shirt and trousers were hanging neatly on the wardrobe door and his black books had been polished. 'You're not indispensable, you know! Get some rest.'

He turned to go downstairs for luncheon. 'Shall

I send up some food?'

Allen shook his head and tried to speak. 'Water,' he croaked. 'I'm on fire.'

Edward studied him thoughtfully. 'I think we'd better have a doctor look at you.'

The doctor, a Frenchman, when he finally came late afternoon, pronounced that Allen had malaria. 'He is lucky that it is not yellow fever,' he said to Edward. 'Otherwise it is *mort* for him. Give 'im this quinine; it is bitter but 'e must take it or he die.'

'Will I get it?' Edward asked in alarm.

The doctor raised his hands in a Gallic gesture at the futile question. ''Ow do I know? The mosquito, 'e is everywhere. Wear your 'at, keep under the net at night.' He gave a pinched smile. 'The mosquito, 'e likes English blood: it is thin and very tasty. Much better than Creole or Indian blood.'

He gave Edward his bill and waited. 'You may pay me now, please,' he said. 'Foreigners do not always stay 'ere; they go on to look for gold and forget to pay their bills before they leave.'

Edward, rather huffy at having his honesty questioned, opened his pocketbook. 'I only have English money,' he said. 'I haven't been to the bank yet.'

'It ees better than nothing.' The Frenchman took a sovereign from him and looked at it disdainfully. 'But be advised. Change your money. You are not in England now.'

Edward left Allen sleeping and asked the hotel clerk for directions to the nearest bank. He had bills of credit with him and various papers for proof of identity.

'Glad to welcome you to New Orleans, Mr Newmarch.' The manager of the bank was most effusive when he realized how much money Edward was changing. 'Are you planning on staying awhile?'

'No plans made as yet.' Edward put some of the money in his inside coat pocket, some in his trouser pocket and the rest in his pocketbook. 'Just having a look around, you know.'

'You do right to separate your money.' The manager nodded approvingly. 'Can't be too careful. There are some blackguards about. Take my advice. If you're playing cards or dice, only use the money in your pocket, don't bring out your pocketbook.'

This was the second warning Edward had had, but he was inclined to dismiss it. Apart from the shady-looking fellow who had offered him a boat ride, everyone else had seemed very friendly and honest. Even people just passing by had wished him good day with a smile or a nod. Nevertheless, he walked swiftly back to the hotel, jauntily swinging his cane and keeping his coat buttoned.

Allen was up when he returned and said he felt a little better. The shivering had subsided and his face had taken on a more normal colour than the flushed complexion he had had previously. He was still weak, however, and Edward suggested that after he had gone out, Allen might as well go back to bed.

'I've been invited out to supper at the Rodriguez' house,' he said, as he buttoned up his shirt and Allen gave a desultory polish to his shoes, 'so I might be late.'

'Is this a social occasion, sir?' Allen asked. 'Or are you hoping to come across some venture to interest you?'

'I must admit that I am looking for something of the sort.' He held up his chin as Allen fastened his cravat. 'At the luncheon yesterday I met Rodriguez' family. His beautiful wife, his mother and two daughters. The younger daughter is as lovely as her mother, the other plain as can be and utterly graceless, and they're looking for a husband for her.'

He glanced in the mirror and brushed his fingers over his sideburns. 'I doubt they'll find one, even though she apparently will come with a large dowry. She's not Rodriguez' daughter. She's quadroon, but she hasn't got that lovely skin colour which they often have. She's got her grandmother's blood, I reckon. But apart from that, she's sulky, arrogant and quite without any decent manners.'

'Perhaps she's been compared too often with her mother and sister, sir?' Allen suggested.

'Maybe so.' Edward shrugged into his coat. 'But I pity some poor fellow who is persuaded to marry her.'

Allen glanced at him. 'That's not why you've been invited, sir?'

Edward turned sharply. 'What? What do you mean?'

Allen bit his lip. 'Well, you're eligible, sir. Or – at least they think you are.' He picked up a clothes brush and started to brush the back of Edward's coat.

Edward put up his hand to stay him. 'Captain

Voularis told them I was a widower,' he muttered. 'And I didn't correct that impression.' He stared at Allen. 'Is that why he told them? Does Voularis get a fee for introducing suitable bachelors?'

He sat down suddenly on the bed. 'My God! She's mine if I want her. And I don't! No matter how much money she brings with her.'

'And you are a married man, sir,' Allen reminded him.

Edward nodded. 'I am, that is true. But I can't tell them that now, can I? My reputation would be ruined!'

Allen held back a weary sigh. All he wanted was to go back to bed. Newmarch had a habit of getting himself into a fix. First with the girl Ruby, and now with this Rodriguez family.

'You'll have to be careful, sir,' he suggested. 'These people maybe won't take kindly to being told – erm,' he almost said lies, but decided against it, 'erm – embellishments.'

'You're absolutely right, Allen.' Edward's face had paled. 'Rodriguez certainly wouldn't. He's already killed one man.'

CHAPTER EIGHT

Edward arrived at the Rodriguez' house to find many guests already there. Fine carriages were parked outside and black drivers were standing in groups, talking. His hired cabriolet dropped him at the door and a liveried servant greeted him and invited him to enter. Edward followed him into the drawing room, which was lit by a myriad of candles held in sparkling crystal chandeliers.

A drifting scent of orange blossom permeated the air and young black girls walked around the room with baskets of fruit balanced on their heads, so that the guests could help themselves to slices of melon, black grapes, peaches and oranges, dates and figs.

Other servants carried silver trays of cut-crystal wine glasses, and as Edward drank he relaxed and his fears of being invited only as a possible suitor for Elena began to diminish.

'Good evening.' He was approached by a man of around his own age, a short portly man with a look of the Mediterranean about him. 'It is Mr Newmarch, I think.'

'Indeed.' Edward gave a small bow. 'Edward Newmarch, lately from England.'

'Carlos de Lassus. I am American, my forebears were Spanish. How do you like our country?'

'I like it very well,' Edward replied and wondered how this stranger knew his name.

'Rodriguez told me that he was expecting an Englishman to join us,' de Lassus said, his dark eyes gazing at Edward. 'We can always recognize the new English arrivals: they are so very pale-skinned.'

Edward nodded. 'Are you a friend of the Rodriguez family?' He looked around and realized that there were no ladies present, only men. 'Or a business associate?'

'Both. Rodriguez and I have known each other

since childhood. We are sort of cousins. Our families came from Spanish Florida to New Orleans. They have lived through the rule of Spain, France and Britain. Now we belong to America.'

He gazed across to where Rodriguez was in earnest discussion with a white-haired elderly man with drooping tobacco-stained whiskers, dressed in an old-fashioned black frock coat. 'Of course,' he said thoughtfully, 'some Spaniards, even men like Sancho, do still follow the old ways. They do not embrace the American life. They feel some resentment that they are expected to change.'

'But you, sir?' Edward enquired. 'You consider yourself to be an American?'

'Absolutely,' he drawled. 'It's the only way to prosper.'

Edward considered. Could he ever think of himself as being other than English? He had been steeped in tradition by his family, though he had often rebelled, unlike his brother Martin who had always followed the rules. But isn't that why I am here? he pondered. To escape the constraints of England? Yes, up to a point, he admitted to himself. It was. But he also wanted to leave to escape the restrictions of married life. He had wanted to bring Ruby and for them to enjoy the adventure and romanticism of another country.

'I beg your pardon,' he said, as he realized de Lassus was speaking. 'I didn't quite catch–?'

'I said, I believe you are a widower?' De Lassus eyed him keenly. 'That makes you a contender.'

'A contender?' Edward stared back, then took another glass of wine from a passing servant. 'What? – I don't understand!'

Carlos de Lassus gave a sudden grin and Edward thought how different he was from his sombre cousin Rodriguez. 'For the hand of the delightful Elena. Sancho enquires of every new eligible male passenger who arrives in New Orleans. He has an *arrangement* with the ships' captains to tell him who might be suitable.'

Edward felt himself grow cold. 'But I'm – I'm not over the death of my wife,' he stammered. 'I can't possibly consider–'

'Sancho will wait. He respects protocol,' de Lassus explained. 'But he wants her married. You realize she is not his child?'

Edward nodded, his face immobile with tension.

'He will settle a large sum on her of course; it would be the honourable thing to do.' De Lassus dropped his voice. 'But he has never liked her, and he wants her gone so that he can make a good marriage for his own daughter.'

Edward remained silent. How could he wriggle out of this situation? He should never have said he was a widower. But then, neither could he have said that he had abandoned his wife. Inwardly he groaned. What a shambles!

'If someone did marry her though,' de Lassus continued, 'I think she might make a good wife. Once she is away from here where she is considered inferior, she would change, I am convinced of it. And she is clever and bright and–' He ran out of praise and added, 'Though I like her well enough, I confess she is not attractive.'

Edward swallowed and thankfully heard the dinner bell. 'I fear,' he said solemnly, 'I made a vow on my wife's deathbed that I would never love or marry again.'

'Phew!' De Lassus dismissed his remark. 'How would she know?' he said irreverently. 'Come. Let us join the ladies.'

The ladies were waiting in line in the dining room for the gentlemen to appear and as they did, they paired off. Edward noticed that Sofia took the arm of the elderly man who had been speaking to her husband, young Sibella rushed to the side of de Lassus and embraced him in a way in which only a very young girl could, and he in turn planted a kiss on the top of her forehead. Rodriguez took his mother's arm, and, to Edward's alarm, he saw Elena bearing down towards him.

She gave him a deep curtsy, in a derisory manner, he considered, for she also fixed him with a malevolent glare. He gave a bow. 'Señorita,' he greeted her, taking her proffered hand, and followed a servant to their places at the table. When the senior Señora Rodriguez and Sofia were seated, everyone else also sat down.

Elena stared straight in front of her and Edward glanced at her out of the corner of his eye. She was wearing a gown of white silk which, on anyone slender, would have been charming, making the wearer look ethereal and sylph-like, but on Elena's robust figure reminded him of a ship in full sail. Her unruly black hair was dressed with white flowers which she pulled at constantly, as if they were irritating her.

She turned to him. 'You do realize why you are here, Meester Newmarch?' she said in a tight whispered voice. 'You do understand that you 'ave been chosen?'

He stared at her and shook his head. Nothing would have induced him to marry her, even if he had been single. 'Your father invited me,' he said in a low voice. 'He is most hospitable.'

'He is not 'ospitable and 'e is *not* my father,' she grated and looked across at Rodriguez with such hatred that Edward was filled with anxious foreboding. 'We do not like each other, señor, and he wants rid of me.'

She waited whilst they were served with chicken soup and then said with her mouth turned down, 'He wants me to marry you.'

'But – but, I can't!' Edward grew hot then cold. 'I'm married! At least I was married – my wife–'

'I know.' She broke bread into her soup and ate noisily. 'But that doesn't matter. 'E says if we are betrothed we can wait until after your mourning period.' She glanced up at Edward. There was no pleasure on her face as she continued, 'I said that I would, but I must tell you, señor, that I will make conditions.'

He gazed at her. Words failed him. His soup went cold, his appetite completely gone. He opened his mouth to protest but nothing came out.

'He 'as worn me down, you see. I 'ave refused everyone else that he 'as brought.' She shrugged her shoulders almost to her ears. 'But now – 'e gives me only two options.'

'What are they?' Edward whispered.

'I can marry you if you will ask of me–'

'But– You don't know me,' he interrupted. 'We have only just met. You know nothing of me– I could be a criminal or anybody!'

She laughed cynically at that. 'I don't think so, señor: 'e will 'ave asked questions and found out. Rodriguez knows all the criminals.' She glanced towards where her mother was sitting next to the elderly gentleman whose head and whiskers were bent over his soup. 'Or else I must marry that old billy goat who is sitting next to my mother.'

Surely not. Rodriguez couldn't be so cruel! The man was old enough to be her grandfather! He began to feel some sympathy for the girl, though not enough to give her any encouragement.

His bowl was taken away, the soup untouched, and the next course of lobster served with side dishes of sliced eggs, prawns and anchovies brought in. 'Do you not wish to 'ear my conditions, Meester Newmarch?' she asked. 'It is as well that you do.'

He tried to gather his senses and speak in a friendly way without giving offence. 'I regret that I cannot–' he began.

'I would wish to 'ave my own 'ouse. Not here in New Orleans but elsewhere.' She spoke into his ear, and, repulsed, he eased his head away from hers. 'I would not wish to live wiz you and neither must you expect to sleep wiz me.'

He gazed in shock. For a young woman to speak so bluntly!

'I will sleep wiz someone else, you see.' She looked at him frankly and defiantly. 'You would 'ave plenty of money. You can choose some other woman, or women, if you wish.'

'Is there someone else you want to marry?' he asked.

She glanced again at Rodriguez. 'Yes, but Rodriguez won't let me. The man is quadroon like me and just a servant. He isn't good enough for a man like Rodriguez. 'E says I must have someone with breeding.'

Edward picked at his lobster, then said in a low voice, 'I'm sorry, señorita. But it can't happen. I can't possibly marry you.'

She looked at him in dismay. 'But it 'as been decided. I 'ave agreed.' She pointed with her finger at the old man and her mother glanced across at her, a questioning look on her face. 'You can't let me marry 'im. 'E would want to sleep in my bed. 'E has said so already!'

Edward felt sick. I need to get out. I need some air. But there was no chance of that. His plate was taken away and another brought, along with a dish of sliced turkey, goose, capon and spicy forcemeat balls, and his glass refilled with wine. He looked across at Rodriguez and found that he was watching him. Rodriguez raised his glass in a toast, a smile on his face, and Edward responded with his own glass though he found it difficult to smile.

After the meal was over, the men moved to the drawing room and the ladies elsewhere. Port was served, malmsey and cigars offered. Rodriguez sought out Edward. 'So very pleased that you could come to our little supper, Mr Newmarch.' He shook Edward's hand. 'You seem to be getting on very well with our daughter. I haven't seen her so animated in a long time.'

'For such a young woman she is very lively,' Edward agreed. 'They have a great deal of energy at that age, do they not?' He gave a weak laugh. 'I remember I was much the same when I was young.'

'Oh, but you are not so old!' Rodriguez remonstrated. 'Under thirty? Yes? A good age for a man.'

'Maybe, but I have had such sorrow and adversity in my life to make me feel old,' Edward asserted. 'My wife–'

'Yes. Yes. I do understand. But by coming to a new country you are already putting your old life behind you, are you not?' Rodriguez leant his head back, drew on his cigar and blew smoke rings in the air. 'What you need, Mr Newmarch, is a helping hand.' He gazed thoughtfully up at the ceiling. 'Perhaps a leetle business coming your way? Some good connections. A new lady in your life?' He smiled at Newmarch. 'All of this can be arranged.'

The doors to the dining room were opened and the gentlemen were invited back in. The table and chairs had been cleared and the room transformed into a ballroom. A small orchestra was in place and playing a soft air, and as the gentlemen entered through one door and the ladies through another they struck up with music for dancing.

Sofia appeared at Edward's side. He gazed at her. She was so breathtakingly beautiful. He gave a deep bow. Her skin was flawless. A touch of carmine on her lips gave them a moist seductiveness and her eyes gleamed beneath dark lashes. She was dressed in a rose-coloured gown which emphasized her small waist and revealed her bare shoulders. In her dark hair she wore a glittering comb and he could smell her perfume. She drew her fan to her face and leant to whisper to him.

'Elena speaks very well of you, señor. She does not often approve of the gentlemen she meets.' She almost touched his ear with her lips as she spoke and he caught his breath and didn't answer, but turned to hold her eyes with his. Are there other women like her in this country? he wondered. Eligible women, of course. If there are, then I will surely succumb to their charm and beauty. I'm a mere man. I cannot possibly resist.

'Would you care to ask me to dance, Meester Newmarch, or shall we sit and talk?'

Not talk, he decided. The conversation will inevitably drift towards the subject of Elena and I must avoid that at all costs. 'I would be delighted if you would care to dance, señora.' And I can put my hand on her waist and breathe in her perfume. It will be so good to feel a woman next to me again.

He looked down into her eyes. He desperately wanted to flirt with her, to whisper to her how beautiful she was, but he held back. He was so sure that he could feel Rodriguez' penetrating eyes on him and he could not, dared not, risk his displeasure.

'We would like to know you better, Meester Newmarch,' she said softly. 'Would you care to visit with us at our plantation in the country? We 'ave a nice 'ouse there. Sometimes we like to get away from the city. Otherwise, it is always business, business, business.' She tapped his arm with her fan. 'I will travel with our daughters on Thursday and Sancho,' she barely breathed his name, ''e will come on Saturday with his mother. Perhaps you would come on Friday and I will show you

109

the sugar cane and the cotton fields?' She smiled and he felt that there was a hidden invitation there. 'You ride, of course, señor?'

'Ride?' he croaked. 'Yes, of course.'

'We have good riding country and some fine horses. The best.' She smiled. 'It would give me great pleasure if you would come.'

How could he refuse when it was put so charmingly? Yet it was with misgivings that on the Friday morning he stepped into the carriage which Rodriguez had sent to collect him and drive him away from the bustling and colourful city, taking him east to the lowlands, to the fields of cotton and sugar cane, to Sofia and to– He drew in a breath as the driver urged on the horses. To Elena! I'm a fool, he thought. I am a fool!

CHAPTER NINE

Georgiana asked the desk clerk if he had a forwarding address for Mr Dreumel. She thought he hesitated for a moment before answering. 'I regret not, Miss Gregory, but Mr Charlesworth might know it. If he's in New York I guess you'll find him at the Portland Hotel.'

'Thank you,' she said. 'I will enquire if he is there.'

She slipped back upstairs and put on her shoulder wrap and her wide-brimmed bonnet, and took her parasol for the sun was bright. 'I won't be long, Kitty,' she said. 'I'm just going to

110

the Portland. Whilst I'm gone perhaps you'd pack a change of clothing for both of us. Something sensible,' she added. 'Suitable for a journey.'

'But where are we going, Miss Gregory?' Kitty asked plaintively. 'How can I pack if I don't know where we're going?'

Georgiana raised an eyebrow. 'Well, don't pack dancing slippers, that's for certain.'

Mr Charlesworth was in and would be down in just a moment, the bellboy informed her after going up to his room. He asked if he could get her anything whilst she waited. A glass of orange juice or coffee?

She declined and took a seat in the foyer with a view of the stairs and the door, where she watched people coming and going. This is a much smarter hotel than the Marius, she decided, much richer residents judging by the elegant clothes they are wearing, but, she pondered, I do prefer the Marius. It is well run and comfortable without being pompous or pretentious.

John Charlesworth came down the stairs. He was wearing a double-breasted frock coat and carried a silk top hat as if he was on his way out somewhere. She considered that he was rather handsome and that he probably knew it. He was tall and slim, with long sideburns and well-groomed dark hair flecked with silver. He oozed confidence and panache.

'Miss Gregory.' He bowed over her hand and she invited him to be seated. 'I am delighted to see you again. Regrettably my wife is out this morning or she would have been pleased to meet you.'

'I'm sure we shall catch up with each other

soon, Mr Charlesworth, but in fact this isn't a social call. I was wondering if you had a forwarding address for Mr Dreumel?'

She saw the same hesitation in his face that she had seen in the desk clerk's. They both know, she considered, but don't want to tell. It must be because of the mine. 'I realize that you might be breaking a confidence, Mr Charlesworth,' she said. 'But I have some rather disturbing news which I feel I should impart to Mr Dreumel.'

She saw the question in his eyes and added, 'Unfortunately there was not the opportunity to speak to him last night as I would have wished, and this morning I discovered that he had departed in rather a hurry.'

'Indeed yes. Something has cropped up. We were brought news of it by Newmarch.'

She decided to confide, at least partially. 'It is of Edward Newmarch that I wished to speak,' she said in a low voice. 'I know him. I am related to the Newmarch family by marriage.'

'Really?' He seemed astonished, then said, 'Of course England is a small country. It is inevitable that you would know most people, of your circle at least.'

She took a deep breath. 'The man who calls himself Newmarch is not of my circle, Mr Charlesworth, not that that matters. What matters is that he is not Edward Newmarch! He is an impostor. His real name is Robert Allen and he formerly worked for Edward Newmarch as his valet and came with him to America eighteen months ago.'

Charlesworth's eyes flickered over her face.

'This has very serious implications, Miss Gregory. Are you absolutely sure?'

'Yes. Edward Newmarch is married to my cousin. Mr Charlesworth, Mr Dreumel confided in me of his interest in a particular mine, though he didn't say where. Robert Allen's family, I believe, were coal miners, which is probably where he acquired some knowledge. You will understand why I am concerned that his activities may not be honest.'

Charlesworth ran his hand over his chin. 'Have you confronted him? Is he aware that you know of this duplicity?'

'I have and yes he does. He recognized me instantly, as I recognized him. Even my maid – my companion, Kitty, knew who he was. What bothers me, Mr Charlesworth, is where is the real Edward Newmarch? Allen claims that he left him in New Orleans!'

'This is most unfortunate.' Charlesworth got up from his chair and began to pace up and down. 'It couldn't have come at a worse time. There is a lot at stake here, Miss Gregory. I personally have put a considerable amount of capital into this venture and I know that Dreumel has mortgaged the Marius.'

'Mortgaged the Marius?' she asked. 'What? Do you mean that–'

He nodded. 'Dreumel owns the Marius. He didn't want to use his newspapers to back the mine project, so he took out a loan on the hotel.' He glanced quickly at her. 'I speak in confidence, Miss Gregory, I perhaps should not–'

'I am not a woman who gossips, Mr Charlesworth.' She remembered what Wilhelm Dreumel had said about Mrs Charlesworth, if she should find out about the mine. 'My concern is that Allen shouldn't commit fraud on Mr Dreumel, or yourself of course,' she added.

'Mm. It is of no use writing,' he muttered. 'A letter might take weeks to reach him. Yet I cannot travel there for at least a week.' He stared out of the window. 'So what best to do?'

'Allen told me that Mr Dreumel depends on him,' Georgiana said. 'He said that he might be dismissed if he found out about him, and that Mr Dreumel would lose money if he left.'

'This is perfectly true.' Charlesworth turned to face her. 'We have trusted him to manage the mine and the men who work there. But how do we know that he knows what he is doing if he is only a valet? I am not an engineer and neither is Dreumel. He must be told.' His face creased with frustration. 'Suppose they strike gold! This fellow might claim it. Yet I have commitments here that I cannot break.'

'I could go,' she offered. 'If you tell me where.'

'Miss Gregory!' He gave a short astonished laugh. 'I don't think so! You are not familiar with the territory and, besides, you are a–'

'A woman?' she suggested. 'I can ride a horse and drive a trap!'

'I beg your pardon, Miss Gregory,' he had an amused condescending expression on his face, 'but riding around a park, or down a country lane in England, would not equip you for travelling cross-country along rough tracks in America! The place where Dreumel has gone is out of the New

114

York State. It is true that part of the journey can be made by railroad or canal but after that the roads are bad. Some of this country is still wild and raw.' He shook his head. 'I could not allow it.'

'You cannot disallow it, Mr Charlesworth,' she said stiffly. 'I am not your wife. I wish to find Mr Dreumel and I am asking you if you will please tell me where he has gone. You don't have to tell me where the mine is,' she persisted. 'Just tell me the nearest town and I will enquire further once I am there and perhaps he could come to me.'

'Town!' He laughed heartily. 'A collection of shacks, that's all there is.' He sat down beside her again. 'Miss Gregory. You cannot conceive of the dangers for a woman travelling alone. It just cannot be done! There are rough pioneers, fighting men, Chinese, Indians even, whom you might encounter on the road to Duquesne.'

'Women do travel,' she argued, and made a mental note of the name he had unintentionally mentioned. 'Pioneer women who travel with their husbands and build up a homestead. I have read of them, I admire them immensely! I saw women in England,' she added, 'Mormons, prepared to walk across America to get to their destination.'

He nodded and gazed at her. 'It is true, there are such women. But they are not like you, Miss Gregory. You, if I am not mistaken, have lived a life of comparative ease. You have had servants to attend you, ridden in carriages and always had someone to escort you.' His voice was soft, and she felt his eyes embracing her face, her silk dress and bonnet. 'I think that a civilized life is probably what suits you best. I cannot see you

115

wearing homespun or drawing water from a well!'

She lifted her chin and gazed squarely at him. 'So you are not going to tell me? Very well.' She rose from the chair. 'Then I must find out for myself.'

He stood up beside her. 'No,' he said quickly. 'If you are determined to go, then I will tell you. But it is against my better judgement. And I must ask why? What does it mean to you? Can you not wait another week when I can escort you?'

And what would you tell your wife? she mused. Or perhaps you wouldn't tell her, and then suppose she found out! 'It is, I feel, the first stage of a longer journey,' she told him. 'I would like to find out what has happened to the real Edward Newmarch. I want to know if he is dead or alive and then I can inform my cousin – his wife. Edward Newmarch,' she said bluntly, 'left his newly married wife to come to America and she has not heard a word from him since. If he is dead then his money should revert to her. It was rightly hers anyway. I don't like to think that an impostor is spending it when she has nothing but what her father can give her.' But also I'm determined on this because I am stubborn, she thought. I won't be told that I cannot do something because I am a woman.

'Very well,' he said. 'Then in that case you must travel first by the Erie Canal to Trenton and Philadelphia. Then change boats for Harrisburg. When you reach there take a coach and travel to Duquesne. From there you will need to hire transport. I'll give you a map to show you the

116

way to the nearest settlement. It has no name,' he added. 'When you arrive there, enquire of a man called Lake. He's a trapper, half Indian – from the Iroquois tribe, I believe. He'll take you on to Dreumel.'

Georgiana's voice was husky and nervous as she asked, 'What about the road? Wouldn't that be quicker than by waterway?'

'Not at the moment, it wouldn't. The national roads are good, but the transport is not always reliable and many of the smaller roads are pot-holed, making a journey extremely uncomfortable. When will you go? Tomorrow?'

'If we can get a berth, then perhaps today. I might even catch up with Mr Dreumel,' she said brightly. 'He won't be too far ahead.'

He shook his head. 'I don't think so. You will be careful?' he cautioned. 'I wouldn't let my wife go on such a journey.'

'It's as well then that I'm not your wife, Mr Charlesworth,' she replied, 'for I would lead you a merry dance.'

'I'm sure that you would.' She saw admiration in his eyes, but then he urged her again to take care and said that he would come to the Marius within the hour with a map of the route.

'Quick, Kitty.' She rushed into her room to find Kitty with one iron on the fire, and with a thick blanket on the table carefully pressing the skirt of a gown with another. 'We're leaving in an hour.'

Kitty's face was flushed from the heat of the iron. 'Are we coming back?'

'Oh yes, but we'll have to vacate the rooms, otherwise I'll have to pay for them. We'll just take

117

the essentials with us and I'll ask the hotel to store the rest. I have just found out...' she had taken to confiding in Kitty more and more, '...that Mr Dreumel owns this hotel,' but she stopped short of saying that John Charlesworth had told her that Dreumel had mortgaged it.

'Really?' Kitty said. 'So where are we going, miss?' She dragged a carpet bag from beneath the bed. 'Are we going on a tour?'

'In a manner of speaking.' Georgiana slipped out of her gown and into another plainer one with a fitted jacket, then took off her shoes and put on her laced boots, which were more comfortable. 'We're going on a river boat to Philadelphia. We're going to look for Mr Dreumel and Robert Allen.'

'Oh! Is that where they are?'

'I don't know where they are.' She took a thick paisley shawl out of the cupboard, one she had brought for the voyage on the ship. 'Come on, be quick, put away the ironing – I'll know when Mr Charlesworth gets here.'

Kitty put the irons on the hearth to cool and hung up the dress she had been ironing. 'I've already packed one bag with washing things and bed gowns, Miss Gregory. And what about food?' she asked. 'Will we need to take some like we did on 'ship?'

'I don't know, Kitty.' Georgiana stopped in her rushing around, sat on the bed and pondered. Mr Charlesworth is quite right. I'm not prepared for this at all.

Perhaps there will be food on the boat, she considered. Travelling on the ship to America was the first time she had ever had to think of how food was conveyed to the table. And then Kitty organized it for me. I didn't go out and buy it myself. Her self-confidence slipped. What am I doing? What am I thinking of? Why don't I find a nice man to take care of me, settle down and live a life of ease?

She looked at Kitty, who was humming softly as she placed stockings and gloves into the bag. I've to take care of Kitty too, she thought. She depends on me. 'Don't take extra gloves, Kitty, or petticoats,' she said, 'and just one more pair of stockings, and a plain bonnet. And just this gown. I won't need another.'

Kitty turned to her in astonishment. 'But suppose you're invited out to supper, Miss Gregory! You can't wear the same gown and dirty gloves and stockings! You must have a change so that I can wash them.'

Georgiana suddenly remembered the tour she had been on with the Women's Rights group, when they had invited Grace, a mill girl, to go with them. Grace hadn't had any clothes but those she was wearing, yet she had made the biggest impact of all on the community who had come to hear them. Do our clothes make us what we are? she thought. Am I only as good as the gowns that I wear?

'Then if I am invited out,' she said, 'people will just have to take me as I am, dirty gloves and all.'

It was a more civilized journey than she had been led to expect from John Charlesworth when he brought her the map and again told her to take great care. The packet boat was small but quite comfortable and they enjoyed the pleasure of watching the scenery as the boat steamed slowly along the canal. Freight was carried below deck and here male passengers drank ale and played cards, or lay down to sleep on the planking. The upper deck cabins were reserved for the female passengers and there was a small dining room where they could eat and food was provided.

Georgiana chatted to some of the other passengers and heard of the millions of tons of freight which were carried by the river and canal boats, cheaper and quicker, said one businessman, than conveying it along muddy and hazardous roads.

'Pretty soon,' he said, 'when the canal network is fully opened up, we shall be able to cross the whole of America by waterway. No worry over tired horses or broken-down waggons.'

He drew on a large cigar and smoke circled into the air. 'Last year we opened up Ohio. Three canals from Lake Erie to major towns in the state. Yes, ma'am. This country will be wide open and when the politics are sorted out and we get some good engineers, the railroads will take over. Tell your husband, if you have one, that that's the place to put his money. Canals and railroads.'

She nodded and agreed that she would, and moved away to join Kitty who was leaning on the rail looking towards the outlying hills. In the near distance gangs of men were working with pick and shovel on the new railroads.

'It's incredible, Miss Gregory,' Kitty said. 'This canal has been hewn out of the rock, and we shall be going through some locks,' she added excitedly. 'I've never done that in my life before!'

'Nor I.' Georgiana smiled. 'We are having quite an adventure already, aren't we, Kitty?'

They stopped from time to time on their two-day journey whilst timber was brought on board for the boilers. Gangs of men on the bank hauled on wood stacks piled high at the riverside and threw the timber onto the decks. As they drew nearer to their destination the fuel changed and sackloads of coal from the mines of Philadelphia were carried on board.

It was evening when they arrived in Philadelphia and Georgiana exclaimed, 'I don't understand why John Charlesworth made such a fuss about us travelling alone. This is a lovely city, most civilized, and I wish we had time to explore. But I think, Kitty, if we can get a boat tonight then we must get on it.'

'If you say so, Miss Gregory, though it would be nice to sleep in a proper bed!'

Georgiana hesitated. Should they stay over-night? There were some fine buildings and wide boulevards from what she could see, just as there were in New York, and no doubt there would be some good hotels where they could stay the night. But no, she decided. 'I think we'll press on. We can rest when we reach our destination. I don't feel the journey will be as bad as Mr Charlesworth made out.'

'Perhaps he just didn't want us to come, miss. Perhaps he thinks that women should stay at home.'

'Yes.' Georgiana nodded. 'I'm sure you're right.' She laughed. She had enjoyed the freedom of travelling alone and hadn't felt in the least threatened. 'He hadn't reckoned on two intrepid Englishwomen, had he, Kitty? This journey is no different from travelling on the waterways of Yorkshire.'

CHAPTER TEN

When they disembarked at Harrisburg they were very weary. The boat had been packed with people and produce and there wasn't a berth available. They sat below deck huddled beneath a blanket which Kitty had had the foresight to bring, but they had little chance of rest, for the other passengers chatted and laughed and many of the men played noisy games of cards. They also smoked and spat which Georgiana found extremely trying. They had tried sitting on the outer deck, but a wind had risen and it was bitterly cold.

By day they had tried to snatch some sleep but found they were the objects of curiosity, as the other passengers questioned their motives for travelling and were most intrigued that they were English.

'You going far, ma'am?' A rough-looking man dressed in a hide jacket had approached them.

'Not far,' Georgiana said, but didn't volunteer information on their destination.

'That's sure a pity.' He'd blown smoke across them from his evil-smelling cheroot. 'I was going to offer to escort you ladies. Look after your bags and suchlike.'

'Thank you, most kind,' Georgiana had answered, then added, 'but we are being met.'

'Ah!' He'd nodded and moved away towards another family group, sitting down beside them and entering into their conversation.

'I'm glad to be off that old boat.' Kitty looked from the quayside towards the small city of Harrisburg. 'How much further, Miss Gregory?'

'The next stage of our journey we take a coach to Duquesne,' she answered, 'and I could almost hope that there won't be one until tomorrow so that we can go to an hotel and rest.'

But the coach for Duquesne was about to depart, and as they hesitated they were told to hurry along as there wouldn't be any other transport for two days. Hastily they handed their luggage to the driver and climbed aboard.

'Ain't much left of the fort, if that's what you be going to look at,' they were informed by a man, sitting with a woman opposite them and dressed in rough country clothes.

'I beg your pardon? The fort?' Georgiana asked. 'Which fort is that?'

The man gave a snigger. 'You don't know about Fort Duquesne?'

'I'm afraid not,' she said. 'We have only newly arrived from England.'

Another man spoke up brusquely. 'They would hardly be expected to know. It was a long time ago, getting on for a hundred years.'

The first man looked silently at him and then at Georgiana and Kitty. After a moment he said, 'My grandpappy remembered it. Leastways he was

123

always talking 'bout it. Belonged to the French.' He nodded solemnly. 'Then the British took it. Got the Indians to help them. It's ours now.'

There then followed a long discourse from the passengers on where the other forts had been situated and the battles that had taken place, and Georgiana felt her eyes closing, though sleep was almost impossible as the coach bumped and rattled towards Duquesne.

'All change at Duquesne.' They were awakened abruptly by the driver opening the coach door and the other passengers climbing over their feet to get out.

They blinked and looked around them. They were in mountain country. The air smelt different, of wood fires and pine needles, and though there was a settlement, it was small with the buildings mostly built of wood.

'Can you face another journey, Kitty?' Georgiana said wearily as they stood amongst piles of timber and merchandise at the roadside. 'We could stay here today and travel on tomorrow.'

Kitty looked around her at the stores and taverns and the church. 'Do you think there will be an hotel, miss? Doesn't look to me as if there will be.'

'There'll be some accommodation, I expect,' Georgiana said. 'Perhaps only plain and simple, but yes, let's try. We need some sleep.'

She asked the driver if he knew of an hotel or accommodation where they could stay. 'There are hostelries, ma'am,' he said, 'but I only know Mrs Smith's guest house. Waggon drivers stay there,' he said. 'It's clean and comfortable but

124

it'll probably be full.'

And it was. 'Mighty sorry,' Mrs Smith said. 'Everybody's busy right now. Try Bertram's beer parlour. They take visitors.'

But they decided against that establishment when they saw the number of men gathered around the door and no women. 'Perhaps we could manage a short drive.' Georgiana studied the map that John Charlesworth had given her. 'It doesn't look too far from here.' Charlesworth had marked a cross where the settlement was, the settlement with no name.

Kitty put her hand above her eyes and stared along the road towards the foothills of the mountains. 'The road looks all right,' she said. 'A bit bumpy but probably no worse than the one we have just driven on. Let's go, miss, if we can find a trap for hire.'

They enquired again and were sent to a wheelwright's workshop. 'A trap?' he said. 'Ain't much call for them round here. Got a waggon or a cart if that would do?'

'All right. Can I have a look at them?' Georgiana asked.

'You driven a waggon afore?' He got up from his work bench and ambled towards the yard at the back of the building with Georgiana and Kitty following behind.

'No, I haven't,' she confessed. 'Only a trap.'

He gave a grin. 'And what'll you do, little lady, if a wheel comes off?'

'Well, I would hope,' she said severely, 'if I am hiring it from you that you will make sure it is fit for the road.'

'Depends where you'm going,' he said, walking towards a massive waggon covered with a thick canvas which would take a team of horses to pull it. 'This un'd take you to Californy if you wanted to go. But I can't guarantee it won't fall into a mud hole.'

'I don't,' she said sharply. 'No more than half a day's journey. We expect to be at our destination before nightfall.'

He stood with his chin in his hands for a moment whilst he meditated. Then he muttered, 'Best take old Henry then. She'll get you where you want to go.'

He put blackened fingers between his teeth and gave a shrill whistle which pierced their ears. A horse whinnied, the sound of hooves clattered across the yard and a shaggy grey mare trotted towards them.

'Why is she called Henry if she's a she?' Kitty asked.

The wheelwright looked at her from under thick eyebrows. 'Henrietta!' he said, as if she should have known. 'Called after my ma. It was her favourite horse. Followed her everywhere.'

'So – what will she pull? A waggonette or–?' Georgiana wished he would hurry up; the day was getting on, she was tired and hungry and wanted to be on her way.

'Best take this.' He pointed to a dilapidated dog cart with two large wheels. 'If you ain't got much luggage and there's just the two of you.'

'Is that the best you have?' Georgiana was dismayed.

'Yip.' He spat on the ground and Kitty jumped

back. "'Cept the waggon and I guess that's too big just for two ladies.'

'All right.' Georgiana sighed. 'We'll take it and I assume the horse is reliable?'

He nodded. 'She'll get you where you want to be and find her way home if you get lost.'

'We won't get lost,' she said abruptly. 'We have a map!'

He laughed and whistled another stream of spittle through his teeth. This time they both jumped back. 'Well, I hope it's a good un.' He grinned. 'Cos some of these tracks have a habit of movin'! Hog-drovers' roads, some of 'em, or bullock tracks. They don't take no notice of maps.'

He hitched up Henry to the cart and put in a sack of hay and another of oats. 'Give her this,' he said. 'She'll tell you when she wants it, else she'll go off and graze.'

Georgiana cast a glance at Kitty and hid a smile. The man was plainly mad. 'How much do I owe you?' she asked.

'Well, I don't rightly know.' He rubbed his chin. 'Best pay me when you come back.'

'You're very trusting,' she said lightly. 'I might run off with Henry.'

'Reckon not,' he said slowly. 'She'll give you a nip in the backside if you take her where she don't want to go.'

They drove towards a store and bought bread and fruit and a large slice of cheese, and then set off towards the mountain road. Henry stepped out smartly and Georgiana started to relax. It was good to be out and she enjoyed the rush of air as they bowled along.

127

They passed several small settlements in the next two hours where fields were planted with crops, and men, women and children were working on the land. Houses, workshops and warehousing had been built as immigrants, seeking another homeland away from the cities of New England and Europe, followed the canals, tracks and national road system which ran between east and west, found a place they could settle, unhitched their waggons and built their homes.

'Why Mr Charlesworth thought this would be difficult, I can't imagine,' Georgiana remarked. 'The road is good so far, and although I'm tired, it isn't so difficult.'

Kitty nodded in agreement. 'It's getting dark though, Miss Gregory. I hope it's not much further.'

Georgiana pulled on the reins to halt. 'The mountains are blocking out the light.' She consulted the map. 'It looks to me as if the road veers left, then right. Hmm. He's drawn some squiggles here and I'm not sure what they mean.'

Kitty looked over her shoulder. 'Is it water?' she asked. 'Perhaps it's a stream.'

'Perhaps so.' Georgiana gathered up the reins, shook them and clicked her tongue. Henry lifted her head from where she had been grazing on the grass verge and half turned towards them. 'Come on then, Henry,' she said. 'Let's go.'

Henry bent her head and continued to graze. Georgiana shook the reins again. 'Come on,' she called. 'You can have a feed when we get there.'

The mare lifted her head again and shook it, giving a little whinny in response, and slowly set off once more. 'Maybe she's hungry,' Kitty said. 'I know I am.'

'Tear off a piece of bread,' Georgiana suggested. 'And a piece for me. I don't want to stop again – the darkness seems to be falling fast.'

Coming from the flatland of east Yorkshire, she was used to the slow onset of dusk, when the wide skies of that county changed from blue or grey and became tinged with red and yellow, orange or purple, depending on the season, as the sun gradually set and disappeared below the low horizon.

Here the golden sun was only half visible above the mountain tops and she guessed that in no more than half an hour it would be gone, leaving them in darkness.

'We haven't got a lantern!' she said suddenly. 'Why didn't I think of bringing one?'

'Oh, miss!' Kitty exclaimed. 'I should have thought of it. Why didn't I?'

'We were not to know that we would be travelling in the dark. I should have stopped in Duquesne and enquired further about accommodation. How very foolish of me.'

And so they continued for another quarter of an hour, munching on the bread and blaming themselves for not preparing for the journey better. Finally, Kitty said, 'It's Mr Charlesworth's fault, Miss Gregory. He should have said how long a journey it would be, and how many miles. If we'd known, then we wouldn't have set off when we did but would have stopped overnight. It seems to me, beggin' his pardon for I know he's a gentleman, miss, but I don't think he's very good at drawing maps.'

'You're right. I quite agree and I wonder if he has actually travelled this route.' Georgiana narrowed her eyes as she saw that the road branched off left. 'Here it is. At least – I think this is it. It's very narrow, not much more than a track! Do you think this is it, Kitty?'

'Doesn't seem to go anywhere, miss, but it might be. Oh!' she said as Henry veered to the left. 'Henry thinks it is. Perhaps she knows the way.'

'It seems she does.' Georgiana peered down the track. 'There have been vehicles along here anyway. Look, those are wheel marks.'

Henry trotted briskly on down the track, which was lined on either side with trees, further blotting out the little remaining light.

'And there's a track on the right, miss. Just there, by that old hut.'

Henry, without any signal from the rein, turned down the right-hand track and trotted on. They came upon a clearing where the track petered out and the mare came to a full stop.

'It's the wrong road!' Georgiana could have wept. 'Now what shall we do?'

Kitty shivered. 'We'll have to stay here till morning, miss. We can't drive in 'dark.'

Henry whinnied and pawed the ground, half turning her head towards them.

'We promised her some food when we arrived,' Kitty said. 'She must think we've got there. I'll give her some hay, shall I?'

Georgiana nodded, too dispirited to speak. She sat with her shoulders drooping and the reins

130

held loosely in her hands as Kitty jumped down from the cart and gathered up the sack of hay.

'Should I unhitch her, Miss Gregory, or do you think she'll run away?'

'She won't run away if we show her the hay.' Georgiana climbed wearily down. 'But keep hold of the reins just in case. We don't want her to go back home and leave us stranded.'

They unhitched the mare from the cart and scattered some of the hay on the ground, but once she was free from the shafts Henry started to move off with Georgiana and Kitty in tow.

'Whoa! Whoa! Come back.' Vainly they held on, the reins cutting into their hands, but Henry was determined to be off, through the clearing, through some sparse trees and onto a downward path.

'I can't see where we're going!' Kitty shrieked. 'It's pitch black.'

'Hold on,' Georgiana shouted. 'Don't let go. We might never get her back.'

Henry came to a dead stop and bent her head. Kitty almost fell over as the momentum ceased. 'There's water, miss! It's a stream. I can hear it gurgling. She's onny come for a drink. Ooh,' she whined. 'It's boggy. My boots are wet!'

When the mare had finished drinking, she shook her head and about turned and set off back to the cart and the mound of hay, where she started to graze. Georgiana fastened the reins to one of the shafts where the horse had freedom of movement but couldn't escape without taking the dog cart with her.

'That hut back there,' she said. 'I think it might

be a cabin which the waggon drivers use for shelter. Let's take a look and maybe we can spend the night in there. Otherwise we'll have to sleep in the dog cart and it will be cold and very uncomfortable.'

'And we can't sleep on the grass,' Kitty declared. 'Cos it's wet and stony and there might be wild animals,' she added. 'Miss Gregory,' she murmured. 'Are you scared? I am. I don't like being in 'dark.'

'I don't mind it if I know there's a candle or a lamp within reach. But I don't like it when I can't see my hand in front of me as now.'

But as they spoke, their voices having involuntarily dropped to whispers, a moon appeared from behind the mountains, lighting up their immediate surroundings.

'Oh hurrah!' Georgiana cheered. 'Thank goodness.' She gazed up into the night sky. 'It's clear, not much cloud, though it's cold. We shall be all right, Kitty. Let's take the blanket and the food with us so we don't have to come back again.'

They both jumped as an eerie shriek came from beyond the belt of trees. The mare lifted her head as if listening, but then dropped it and continued grazing.

'It's all right!' Georgiana tried not to panic. 'It's just a bird or an animal. Come on,' she urged, 'quickly,' and with a rush they gathered up their belongings, bags and blanket and stumbled out of the clearing and up the path towards the cabin.

It was staunchly built from logs with a thick wooden bolt drawn across the door, so they knew at least that there was no-one inside. They heaved

132

at the bolt and cautiously opened the door. 'Might there be rats, do you think?' Kitty shuddered. 'I hate rats! There used to be rats where we lived in Hull. Dirty nasty creatures.'

'I shouldn't think so.' Georgiana blinked, accustoming her eyes to the blackness of the interior. 'I think they prefer to live in holes outside.'

'What about snakes?' Kitty peered into the hut. 'Might there be snakes?'

Georgiana took a deep breath. There was every possibility that there might be snakes, she thought. 'See if there's a piece of brushwood lying around,' she said. 'And we can waft it around to clear anything out.' She sounded braver than she was. I've always been considered sensible, she thought. I must behave as if I really am.

They found a fallen branch with dead leaves clinging to it and as Kitty held the door open to let in the moonlight, Georgiana swept around the hut, along the walls and corners, along the two rows of wooden double bunks and around the floor.

'No snakes!' she announced. 'And look what's here!' On a shelf was a tinderbox complete with flint and steel, and a candle beside it. 'If I can get a spark we can have a light for a little while, but we mustn't use all the candle in case someone else needs it after us.'

She managed to strike a spark and lit the candle wick which lit up the hut to show it in all its bareness. But they didn't mind – they could close the door and bolt it from the inside and know that they could sleep safely.

Except that they didn't sleep. The bunks were

133

hard and they were cold as they had only one blanket between them. As Kitty had an extra shawl, she insisted that Georgiana should have it. They heard too all kinds of strange noises, howling and shrieking and bumps against the walls of the cabin.

'Are there bears, do you think, Miss Gregory?' Kitty whispered through the darkness. 'If there's one outside how will we get out? And will it attack Henry?'

'I don't know,' she whispered back. 'There might be. But it will be gone by daylight,' she assured Kitty. 'Whatever is out there will go off to look for food.'

At dawn a chink of light appeared through a gap in the wall and achingly they roused themselves and stretched. 'It must be very early,' Georgiana said. 'But we'll start moving. There's no sense in staying around here as we're awake.'

'I hope the bears have gone,' Kitty said and put her ear to the door. 'Can't hear anything.'

Cautiously they slid back the bolt and opened the door a crack. A great draught of clear air entered the cabin and they saw sparkling dew on the grass.

Kitty crept outside and looked up and down the track. 'We're all right, Miss Gregory,' she said. 'There are no bears. We can go and get Henry.'

Georgiana leaned against the door frame and looked up into the blue sky and at the mountain tops, which were shrouded with silver mist. A large bird, maybe an eagle, she thought, hovered above them and she could hear the rushing of the stream.

Her spirits soared and she took a deep breath of mountain air. It's strange, she reflected. Just a few months ago I would never have dreamed that I would spend a cold night in a wooden hut on a mountainside with no conveniences, and still be happy.

They gathered together their belongings, bolted the cabin door and walked on the wet grass towards the clearing, but they stopped simultaneously as they reached it. The dog cart was there as they had left it, but not Henry.

CHAPTER ELEVEN

'Oh, miss!' Kitty wailed. 'She can't surely have run away home? Whatever will we do?'

What did I just think about being happy? Georgiana leaned against the dog cart. So what do we do? 'Perhaps she's by the stream,' she said, none too hopefully. 'We'll take a look.'

The daylight showed that the stream was wide and the waters rushed headlong over stones and boulders. Higher upstream a small waterfall gushed and splashed over a rocky outcrop, the source of the sound reaching the cabin. A wide grassy track led towards it.

'Look, Miss Gregory! There she is!' Kitty spotted the horse splashing in the middle of the stream with her reins trailing. 'Come on, Henry,' she called. 'Come on.'

But the mare whinnied, and turning the other

way she retreated further downstream.

'She might trip on the stones and break a leg,' Georgiana said anxiously. 'I'll fetch the hay bag,' and she rushed back to get it from the dog cart.

'Here Henry, come for breakfast.' She scrambled amongst the rocks, her skirts trailing in the water, and held out a handful of hay in the mare's direction. Henry whinnied, but stopped her cavorting and stood looking at Georgiana. 'Come on,' she said soothingly. 'Come on!'

The horse moved slowly towards her. 'Good girl,' she said softly. 'Good girl. That's it. Come on.' Georgiana edged backwards to bring Henry closer to the bank of the stream. 'Stay still, Kitty!' From the corner of her eye she saw Kitty moving towards her. 'Don't disturb her.'

Henry stretched her neck towards the hay, which was just out of reach, took a step forward, leaned again and Georgiana opened up her palm to give her the hay. 'Good girl,' she said again, and gently, so as not to unsettle her, fumbled in the hay bag for another handful. 'Here you are!' She held out her hand again and as Henry reached for it she bent for the trailing rein and grabbed it.

She let out a gasping breath and gently pulled the horse towards her. 'Naughty girl, running away!' She stroked Henry on the nose as she nuzzled towards the hay bag which was in her other hand. 'Come on.' She let out a laugh. 'You can have some more breakfast when we've tied you up again.'

After they had hitched the mare back to the cart, they swilled their hands and faces in the cold sparkling water and took a long drink, which refreshed them. Georgiana consulted the map again. 'I'm sure this is the right way, yet there's no road out of here.'

'Do we drive through the water, miss? Those squiggles might mean the stream.'

'But how do we get the cart over the stones? It'll get smashed!' She looked towards the stream. 'Wait here with Henry,' she said. 'I'll go and see if there is another way.'

The clearing sloped down towards the stream, with a regular track through it where other creatures had made their way to the water. Georgiana looked to where the waterfall cascaded down, and saw hoof and wheel marks leading to it. The track was wide enough to take a horse and even a small waggon, but where did it go? Only to the edge of the waterfall? She walked towards it and as she came to the end of the track saw that, where the water fell into a pool, there were no stones or rocks, but a gravel bed which led to the other side of the stream.

'This is where Henry came into the water,' she said to herself. 'She didn't come over the rocks. Then she wandered downstream.'

She looked across to the other bank and perceived that the gravel bed came out in shallow water. As her eyes followed upwards she saw a track leading to another clearing. 'That's it,' she breathed. 'That must be the way.'

They set off once more after a breakfast of bread and cheese and Henry automatically turned right as they reached the stream, trotted along the track and entered the water without any urging, pulling briskly up the other side. As they reached the top they saw a wide track running beside the foothills of the mountains and a vast expanse of rocky land below them.

'I can't see any settlement, miss,' Kitty said in a small voice. 'And we've no bread or cheese left!'

'I can't understand it,' Georgiana murmured. 'I thought that the country was teeming with settlers. Why has no-one built here?'

They drove on for over an hour, the morning sun getting ever hotter as they reached the lower plain, the heat bouncing off the rocks as they passed through outcrops and narrow gorges.

'Look, miss.' Kitty's eyesight was keen. 'Two people on horseback just in front of those rocks. Over there, to the left.'

The riders were now coming nearer, and both women drew in a breath. 'Oh, miss,' Kitty said fearfully. 'They look a bit fierce, don't they?'

Georgiana tried to stay calm. The two men did indeed look wild and menacing. They had long black hair and were dressed in loose cotton shirts and narrow fringed trousers. One had a coloured band tied around his forehead, the other wore a wide round hat. They rode swift spotted Appaloosa horses. 'You can't expect people to dress in their best out here, Kitty,' she began lamely.

'They're Indians, miss!' Kitty's voice was breathless. 'They've got rifles! Oh, what shall we do?'

'Hush!' Georgiana was sharp with nervous tension. 'They're harmless. The Indians live side by side with the settlers now. We'll ask them if they know Lake or Mr Dreumel.'

As the men drew level she called out, 'Good

morning,' as pleasantly as if they were out for a drive on a sunny day. 'We're looking for a Mr Lake at a settlement which has no name. Are we on the right road?'

The two men glanced at each other, then at her and Kitty. 'Where's your man?' said one.

'We – erm, we don't have one,' Georgiana admitted. 'We wish to find Mr Lake to take us to Mr Dreumel.' She added a lie. 'He's expecting us.'

The men conferred in a language they didn't understand, then stared unsmiling at them. 'You come with us,' said the one who had spoken previously.

'Oh no. We can't!' Georgiana was alarmed. 'Mr Dreumel is waiting for us.'

The man nodded, then they both wheeled around and took a place on either side of the dog cart. Henry whinnied and nuzzled at the other horses, then, as one of the Indians slapped her rump, set off at a fast pace, with Georgiana and Kitty hanging on as if for their lives.

'I object!' Georgiana shouted to the men. 'Slow down! We don't wish to go with you. Who are you?'

'Iroquois!' The Indian in the headband riding nearest to her turned towards her and slowed his pace. 'We Iroquois.' He suddenly gave an ear-splitting whoop. 'You be my squaw!' he announced.

'Certainly not!' she began heatedly, then she saw a glance and the beginnings of a grin pass between the two of them. They're fooling with us! They think we're fresh from the city and frightened of Indians. Whereas I know for a fact that treaties have been signed!

139

'Oh very well then,' she said, as if resigned to the idea. 'I'll be your squaw.' She saw Kitty's mouth drop open. 'But you must marry me in church or I won't agree to it.'

The Indian in the hat began to laugh and said something incomprehensible. 'What did he say?' Georgiana asked. 'Can he not speak English?'

'He can.' The other Indian glanced at her and she saw the humour in his eyes. 'He say – what will my wife say if I take another woman home!'

'And what will she say?' Georgiana raised her eyebrows, still going along with the play-acting. 'Will she object to you marrying an English-woman?'

He nodded solemnly. 'I think she'll go crazy and get the hatchet out!'

Georgiana smiled. 'Shall we call the wedding off, then? I don't care for the sight of spilt blood. Besides, I don't know your name.'

'Dekan.' He pointed to his companion and said, 'This is Horse. He's looking for a wife. He's so ugly that no woman will marry him.'

She turned to look at Horse, who swept off his hat and placed it over his heart. He was young, about seventeen or eighteen, and she thought him the most handsome man she had ever seen. His skin was light and smooth with high cheek-bones and a narrow nose, his dark hair was sleek and his eyes almost black.

She sighed. 'Alas, I'm too old for you, Horse,' she said. 'And my companion, Kitty, is too young to be married.'

'I'm not, Miss Gregory,' Kitty whispered. 'But would I have to live in a tipi?'

140

'I think you would need to know him a little better, Kitty, before we discussed that,' Georgiana murmured. 'Where are you taking us?' she asked the men.

'To see Lake. That's what you want, isn't it?'

'Yes. Thank you.'

'You shouldn't be out here alone,' Dekan said severely. 'It's not safe for women. There are Indians—'

Georgiana started to smile but then realized he was serious.

'Not all Indians are peaceable,' he went on. 'And there are gunmen and trappers who haven't seen a woman in a long time. You have no weapon?'

'Er – no, we haven't.' Perhaps I was foolhardy, Georgiana thought. I suppose I didn't expect to have to travel such a long way or under such wild conditions. She looked into the far distance. Ahead of them the track, what there was of it, snaked on beyond rocks and scrub, through crevices and narrow creeks, but she thought that beyond the furthermost rocky outcrop there was a wisp of smoke, and she hoped, oh how she hoped, that it meant habitation.

'How much further before we get to the settlement?' she asked. 'The one with no name.'

'Two more hours,' Horse said. 'And it has a name. It's called No-Name. It belongs to the Iroquois. It is our reservation.'

No-Name was a settlement of only a handful of small cabins and two longhouses set within a woodland. Much of the woodland had been cleared and the surrounding land was planted

141

with corn or had cattle grazing on lush green grass.

'You're farmers!' Georgiana said, as they approached later in the afternoon. She was surprised. 'I hadn't realized.'

'Our women have always grown crops and the men were hunters,' Dekan explained. 'Our forefathers hunted buffalo, bison, elk, but the Iroquois lost their hunting grounds many years ago. We have had to adapt to live with the whites, or else we die.' He held his rifle aloft as they approached the settlement. 'Many of our old people resent the loss of freedom. We were forest people – hunters. Now great cities are being built on our hunting ground and we have been given land on which to grow crops.'

'I'm sorry,' she murmured. 'It doesn't seem fair.'

He shrugged. 'I have only known this. But the old people tell us stories of how it used to be in our forefathers' time.'

'And Lake?' she said. 'Who is he?'

'He's a guide and a trapper. He says he won't ever grow crops, that it is woman's work. He's a descendant of Handsome Lake, who, in our history, brought together the white man and the Iroquois to live in peace.'

They approached the front of one of the wooden cabins, and Georgiana and Kitty climbed stiffly out of the dog cart.

'Oh, miss,' Kitty said. 'I don't think I'll ever walk again!' She was almost crying with tiredness. 'And I'm so hungry and gasping for a drink.'

'Come with me.' Dekan motioned them

142

towards the cabin. 'Horse will look after Henry.'

'Oh! You know Henry?' Georgiana said.

'Mr Dreumel sometimes borrows her,' he said. 'She knows her own way here.'

Dekan took them into his cabin where a dog sat outside the door. He introduced them to his wife, Little Bear. Her dark hair was covered by a shawl and she wore a long-sleeved elkskin jerkin over a fringed skirt. She viewed them gravely and bid them welcome to her home, and Kitty, uncertain as to what was expected of her, dipped her knee.

'You will sleep here tonight,' Little Bear told them. She spoke haltingly in a low husky voice. 'Tomorrow Lake will come and take you on your journey.'

'Thank you.' Georgiana was extremely grateful. Her body ached and like Kitty she was hungry and thirsty. They were asked to sit down and Little Bear went out of the cabin, returning quickly with a bowl of water for them to wash. When they had finished she took the bowl away and then came back with two bowls of something like gruel made from cornmeal, and a dish containing pale and tender meat and a round root like a potato.

'You are very kind,' Georgiana said. 'Thank you, this is delicious.'

'It is antelope,' she seemed pleased with the compliment, 'and wild yam. It will give you strength.'

There was a low bed in the corner of the cabin, but Little Bear brought in two mattresses and laid them on the floor. They were made of straw with a cotton covering, over which she threw colourful wool blankets and skin rugs.

'You may sleep whenever you wish,' she said. 'Dekan will sleep in his brother's cabin tonight.'

Georgiana thanked her again and said that they would like first of all to take a walk to stretch their legs. As she and Kitty walked around the settlement they were followed by giggling children and a straggle of dogs.

The cabins were neat and built from logs, some with wooden fences around them to separate them from their neighbours, which Georgiana found curious and unexpected. Dekan joined them and shooed the children away. 'They don't often see white women,' he said. 'Only sometimes when the pioneers pass in their waggons.'

'I thought there would be more travellers,' Georgiana remarked. 'We have seen virtually no-one since leaving Duquesne.'

'There have been many,' Dekan said. 'Everyone is journeying west to look for gold. They go by sea and canal and across country, but do not often come up here.' He put his hand to his forehead and gazed towards the darkening mountain range to the north. 'They do not yet know of the riches in this land and beyond.'

She followed his gaze. 'Do you mean that there is gold up there?'

'Perhaps. The earth holds many treasures.' He looked down at her. 'She will not release it without a price.'

'A price! What do you mean?'

'Land is being swallowed up by the white man's greed. They want to make roads over the land which has been allocated to us.' He nodded sombrely. 'If they do this they must pay. There will be much bloodshed.'

'I hope not,' she said uneasily.

'It is coming. Some white men cannot be trusted,' he continued. 'They make promises and then break them. Our ancestors warned us of this.'

'And do you believe that is true of all white men?' She had to give herself a shake, for she found it incredible that she was having such a conversation with a native American Indian.

'No, not all white men,' he admitted. 'There are some with good intentions who can be trusted, but our ancestor Red Jacket, when he died, left a warning that because of the white man's greed the Iroquois would one day be scattered across the land.'

He stopped outside a longhouse. 'This is where our children go to school. They learn the language of the settlers, English and French, but they also learn of their own history. They are taught Christianity but they also pray to the spirits of our fathers, to Red Jacket and Handsome Lake. We listen also to our own protectors.'

'Your protectors!' Georgiana exclaimed. 'Who are they?'

'Different families have their own spirits who protect them. There is the Beaver Clan, the Wolf, the Deer and the Bear. Sometimes we are named after them.'

'Like Little Bear?' she said.

He nodded. 'Yes. She is honoured by that name and is on the council of women. They make many decisions within the community.'

And here are we, women of the so-called

145

civilized world, Georgiana thought wryly, still trying for equality.

He continued, 'But times are changing. When the white man lies and steals, the Iroquois and their brothers from other tribes will put on their warrior paint and fight for what is theirs.'

She had watched him closely as he was speaking. He was tall and muscular with a determined expression on his face, and as he stood with his moccasin-clad feet planted apart, she thought that even though he spoke with an English tongue, she could see in him the unvanquished spirit of his forefathers.

CHAPTER TWELVE

The next morning they were awakened by the sound of dogs barking, children squealing and men laughing. Kitty sat up. 'I've overslept, Miss Gregory,' she said. 'I'm sorry.' Then she added, 'But what do I do? I've no breakfast to bring in, no tea to make!'

Georgiana stretched and laughed softly. 'We are having a most extraordinary time, Kitty, are we not? How is it we are lying here in an Indian's cabin, wrapped in animal skins, when only a few months ago we were living a genteel existence in England?'

She included Kitty in her description of gentility, for she thought that Kitty would never have believed how her life would alter in so short a time. 'I slept well, but had the strangest dreams,' she went on. 'Of Indians and trappers.'

She had dreamed that Red Jacket, the long-dead Indian chief, had come to tell her to leave, the cabin at once or suffer the consequences. He wore a red blanket over deerskin trousers and had feathers in his black hair. In his hands he carried a bow and arrow. Behind him a white man sat on his horse, with a rifle pointing at Red Jacket. She hadn't been afraid in the dream, for Dekan was there. His face was painted and he stood in front of her to protect her and his chief.

'I dreamed of wild animals coming to get us, Miss Gregory,' Kitty said. 'Did you hear them howling in the night?'

They were interrupted in their conversation by Little Bear coming in with breakfast, which again was two bowls of cornmeal, only this time with a scattering of seed and grain and sweetened with wild honey.

'Lake is here,' she said in her husky tones. 'He will greet you when you are ready.'

They finished breakfast and dressed, which didn't take long for they had only removed their top garments and boots for sleeping. They stepped outside and found Dekan in conversation with a fierce-looking man. His face was weathered, with a scar across his right cheekbone. He was dressed in a buckskin shirt and trousers and a cracked leather coat. A string of beads hung around his neck and a belt containing various pieces of equipment, a powder horn and bullet pouch, a knife in a sheath, was slung across his shoulder. On his head he wore a battered leather hat with a feather

147

stuck through a hole in the brim.

'Good morning,' Georgiana said, and for the first time in her life was not in the least concerned about her dishevelled appearance or that her hair was not dressed, but hung loosely around her shoulders. 'I am Georgiana Gregory. I understand from Mr Charlesworth that you could take me – us,' she indicated Kitty standing behind her, 'to Mr Dreumel.'

Lake gazed at her from piercing eyes without speaking for a few moments, then said, 'Expecting you?'

'Erm–' She glanced at Dekan, caught out in her lie. 'I have important news for him.'

Lake continued to scrutinize her and she felt slightly unnerved. Then he asked, 'Can you ride?'

'Yes, I'm a good horsewoman.' Georgiana glanced at Kitty, who shook her head. 'Can we not take the cart?' she asked.

'No. The trail is rough. The girl will ride behind me.'

Kitty took in a nervous breath, but the expression on Lake's face brooked no argument.

'And our luggage?' Georgiana asked. 'We have one bag each.'

'No.' Again that indomitable expression. 'Bring necessities only and put them in the pack.'

'So, no extra stockings, Kitty!' Georgiana said, as quickly they pushed the bare essentials into the leather pack which he had offered them. 'And as for gloves! I think this is not going to be the jolliest of expeditions.'

She was trying her best to be cheerful, for Kitty was clearly anxious at the prospect of riding

148

behind Lake.

'He smells, Miss Gregory! I don't think he washes all that often,' she whispered.

'He probably doesn't get the opportunity,' Georgiana murmured. 'Remember what he does, he's a trapper and a guide, and he's probably been wearing those clothes for a long time. Put up with it, there's a dear.'

As she spoke in such a familiar manner, they glanced at each other. Their roles were changing. Although Kitty was now Georgiana's companion rather than her maid, the old divisions had to an extent still been there, but as each day passed Georgiana felt more and more responsible for Kitty, and was becoming fond of her. In their new environment they supported and reassured each other.

'I'm sorry, Kitty,' she said, seeing the girl's nervous expression. 'Would you rather be back home with my aunt?'

'Oh, no, miss.' Kitty was quick to deny it. 'I wouldn't want to think you were out here on your own. It's just, well, I've never ridden on a horse before. At least, only on coal carrier's carthorse when I was a bairn.' She gave a sudden grin. 'He lifted me up and put me on and gave me a ride. I think I was seven,' she said wistfully.

'This will be quite different,' Georgiana started to say, when Little Bear came in carrying a bundle of clothing which she handed to Georgiana.

'You wear these?' she said. 'We look after your clothes until you return.'

Georgiana held up the garments. There were two divided skirts and smock-like shirts, made

149

from thick bleached cotton.

'Your clothes not suitable for where you are going. These will be easier for you to ride in.' Little Bear added softly, 'You must ride astride like a man.'

'You are most thoughtful.' Georgiana had been wondering how she would manage to ride wearing a bustled skirt and without a side saddle, though she had deliberately left several petticoats behind at the Marius. 'These will be much more comfortable.'

They put them on and smiled at the spectacle of each other. 'Hardly the height of fashion, Kitty, but Little Bear is right, we will be more at ease especially if it is going to be a long journey.'

'Four hours,' Lake announced when they came outside. 'Maybe five,' he added, looking at Kitty. 'We go up into the mountains.'

'So be it,' Georgiana said. 'Where is Henry?' she asked Dekan, for he had taken the mare away to feed her when they arrived the previous evening.

'Take Indian horse,' Dekan said. 'Henry is no good for that region.'

But Henry came trotting towards them, her reins trailing, having escaped from the corral where she had been left. She whinnied on seeing Georgiana and nuzzled up to her, bumping her with her nose.

'She wants to come,' Georgiana said. 'Wouldn't she be all right?'

Lake put his head back and opened his mouth in a silent protest, then spluttered. 'Wants to come! She's a horse, lady! She don't have any wants. Only food and water. Those are her wants.

We don't ask for her opinion!'

'But I told her owner I would look after her,' Georgiana protested. 'I'd like to take her.'

Lake shrugged his shoulders and looked at Dekan, who grinned and made a comment, which Georgiana guessed was tantamount to saying that women would have their own way.

'Take her and another horse.' Dekan suggested a compromise. 'Then Henry can carry the packs.'

Lake reluctantly agreed and Henry was fitted with the packs, water bottles and food. Georgiana wondered vaguely about shelter for the night, if they didn't reach their destination before dark.

Dekan offered her his outstretched hand and she put her foot into it to mount the sleek pony they had given her to ride. She hazarded a guess that it belonged to one of the Indian women, for it was smaller than the horses that the men had been riding.

Kitty stood at the side of Dekan and looked nervously up at Lake sitting astride his mount. He put out his hand, but she hesitated, not knowing what to do. Dekan, in a swift movement, put his hands on her waist and, as if she was no more weight than thistledown, swung her up and placed her behind Lake. He gave her a smile and said softly, 'Don't worry. You will be safe.'

They set off, Lake leading, Georgiana following and leading Henry. A group of Indians came to see them off: Horse, who put up his hand in farewell; Dekan's wife, brothers and their wives and a host of children. Kitty looked back at Georgiana. 'I'm scared, Miss Gregory,' she said in a small voice. 'I don't know what to hold onto.'

151

Georgiana held back a gurgle of laughter. 'His shoulder belt, Kitty,' she said. 'The one holding his knife, or else put your arms around his waist!'

They rode along the main track for an hour and passed several waggon trains travelling in both directions, then turned off onto a narrower trail which led to several small settlements with wooden shacks and cabins, and fields laid out for cultivation. Another hour and they were starting to climb. Lake drew on the reins and suggested they get down to stretch their legs, as the next hour would be more difficult.

Georgiana swung off without assistance and secured her mount, then turned to help Kitty down. 'That wasn't so bad, was it, Kitty?' she said, 'and look at that for a view!' She heard Lake give a derisory snort, though he said nothing and after dismounting turned away.

Below them the hillside ran down into a wide scrubby plain for as far as they could see. From up here the settlements looked like mere dots on the ground and they were astounded, not only at the distance they had come, but at how vast the landscape was.

'This can never be filled,' Georgiana murmured. 'No matter how many settlers come, and there are thousands already. This country is so huge it can never be fully populated.'

'Not true.' Lake's voice came from behind them. 'One hundred years ago, the Iroquois hunted in the lake country. Now it is filled with foreigners and the buildings of New York rise high into the sky.'

They turned to look at him as he stood on a

rock surveying the landscape. He had taken off his leather coat and hat. He was tall and sinewy and his dark sleek hair caught in the breeze. He looked younger than Georgiana had first considered him to be, and appealing, she considered, in a dark brooding kind of way.

'You are from that tribe?' she ventured.

'My mother!' he said abruptly. 'She was from the family of Handsome Lake. My father was a French trapper who took her as his squaw.' He spat as he mentioned his father. 'I do not take his name.' He turned away and, gathering up his coat and putting on his hat, said roughly, 'We must go.'

This time, Kitty managed to scramble on behind Lake unaided and they moved off along the stony path. They climbed steadily upwards and Georgiana began to wonder how Wilhelm Dreumel had come to be up here.

'Where are we?' she called to Lake. 'What part of the country?'

'States of New York and Pennsylvania.' He pointed north. 'Up there is Cleveland and Lake Erie. Below us is the Ohio river. This is the back country. No man's land.'

They came down into another valley and the air was hot. The women fanned themselves with their hands and pulled their shawls over their heads. Georgiana asked if they might stop for a drink of water.

'Half an hour,' Lake said. 'Then we stop.'

They resigned themselves and in roughly that time they came to a narrow rushing boulder-strewn stream within a sheltering belt of trees. Stiffly they got down and stretched their aching limbs, then bent to swill their hands and faces and take a drink from the ice-cold water.

'Lake Erie water,' Lake commented. 'Goes down to the Erie Canal.'

'We travelled on it,' Georgiana said. 'And now we are near its source!'

He gave a dry laugh, which for a second lightened his sombre expression. 'No. We are hundreds of miles from it, but there are many tributaries. This is one of them.'

I cannot comprehend the size of this country, Georgiana reflected. We have been travelling for over three hours and there is still no habitation. But she consoled herself that if Lake was correct they would be at their destination in two more hours.

But darkness began to draw on and when she called to Lake to ask how much longer the journey would take, he turned in his saddle and said, 'We ride until dark, then in the morning we go on.'

'Wh– do you mean that we won't be there before nightfall?'

'Noon tomorrow,' he said.

She was aghast, weary and angry. John Charlesworth didn't tell me of this, she agitated. Why didn't he? We could have been better prepared. Has he been on this journey himself? Perhaps he thought we would turn back! But then she reasoned that he did say the journey would be hazardous. What was it he said? Riding around a park in England would not equip her for travelling across this country. Well, he was certainly right there!

She was overwhelmed by the immensity of the

154

landscape and although she knew that the states of Pennsylvania and Ohio which lay below them were developed, their towns, cities and industries constantly increasing in size, up here amongst the mountain ranges there was not a single sign of population.

They began to descend the slopes into a forested valley which in the shadowy dusk looked mystically and breathtakingly beautiful. As darkness finally fell and they could no longer see what was beneath the horses' feet, they came to a halt by a fast-running creek.

'We rest here,' Lake said. Kitty slid down from the horse and fell to her knees. He bent to help her up. He gazed at her and nodded. 'You did well, miss. Tomorrow you feel better.' He turned to Georgiana and pointed towards the tree line. 'You sleep in here.'

She narrowed her eyes. It was so black she could hardly see a hand in front of her, but as she stared into the trees she could make out a clearing and the dark shape of a wooden structure. 'A cabin,' she breathed. 'Thank heavens. I thought we'd have to sleep outdoors!'

She and Kitty felt their way to the creek, and cupping their hands in the cool water drank deeply. When she looked up she felt dizzy, for the sky was filled with thousands of stars and the air was as sharp and cold as the water they had drunk.

Lake took two blankets which had been laid over Henry's back and one of the packs, and handed them to her. 'Wrap up and keep very still. That way you'll keep warm.'

'Thank you.' She took the blankets from him. 'What is this place?'

'Settlers built it. They were going to farm but the land didn't want them.'

Lake didn't seem to have any trouble finding his way in the darkness and led the horses to the creek for them to drink. He moved silently and merged into the shadows and as Georgiana and Kitty made their way to the cabin, Georgiana looked back to where he had been and could no longer see him.

'Where will he sleep, do you think, Miss Gregory?' Kitty seemed nervous. 'Will he want to come in here with us?'

'I shouldn't think so.' Georgiana felt her way around the cabin, which was smaller than the waggon hut they had slept in previously. She was searching for a shelf or cupboard, hoping to find a tinderbox and candle as before. She ran her hands along the walls and then gave a soft exclamation as she found a shelf and beneath it an aperture from where came a cold draught.

'A hearth!' she said. 'If we'd arrived in daylight we could have collected wood to light a fire!'

The door was suddenly kicked open, and the dark shape of Lake entered. Kitty drew in her breath, but Georgiana said calmly, 'Come in, Lake. I've found a tinderbox and a candle, so we can have light.'

'Save it for the next traveller,' he said abruptly. 'I've brought wood for a fire.' He knelt down and they could hear him breaking up twigs, then saw the spark from his flint. Within a few minutes, scraps of dried grass had caught fire which carried to the twigs, and the cabin was lit up by firelight and permeated with the scent of pine.

'Thank you so very much.' Georgiana suddenly felt emotional. 'That is so comforting!'

He nodded. 'I shall be outside. Eat and then sleep. We have an early start at dawn.'

'Eat? What do we eat?' Kitty asked, and opened the pack expectantly. Inside was a parcel wrapped in a large leaf and inside that were slices of meat. 'Antelope!' she said. 'Dekan's wife must have given it to Lake.'

'Oh, they are so very kind,' Georgiana murmured, as hungrily they ate. 'We shall sleep well tonight.'

'Yes,' Kitty agreed. 'Not like when we slept alone in that other cabin. I was very scared.'

There were two bunks raised from the floor and they lay down and wrapped the blankets around them. 'Lake said we have to keep very still to keep warm.' Georgiana looked towards the fire. They had put on more wood which Lake had left and it was burning merrily.

'Miss Gregory!' Kitty's voice was sleepy. 'Why was it so important that we came to see Mr Dreumel?'

Georgiana breathed in deeply. She had almost forgotten the point of her mission. Was it because of her cousin May? Because of Robert Allen being an impostor? Or because Wilhelm Dreumel was being deceived? 'I think it's because I'm an interfering busybody, Kitty.' She received no answer, only the sound of Kitty's soft breathing.

And has it been worth the effort of travelling on rough tracks in a dilapidated dog cart with a horse

157

that knows its own mind? she thought. And trekking through mountainous country with a half-breed Indian who barely speaks to us, yet makes a fire to keep us warm! She snuggled under her blanket. Yes, she decided. On the whole, I think it has.

CHAPTER THIRTEEN

Georgiana woke as dawn was beginning to break. A sliver of white light touched her face and she realized that there was a small window in the cabin. She rose and stretched and grimaced at the ache in her back, then looked at Kitty who was still sleeping soundly. Kitty hadn't made a sound throughout the night, not even when there was a crack of gunshot and Georgiana had sat up and spoken to her. Georgiana had listened for a moment but heard nothing more than the murmur of the wind in the trees. The cabin was in darkness as the fire had gone out, and she lay down and within seconds had fallen asleep again.

The insides of her knees and thighs were red and sore where they had rubbed against the saddle, and she felt very stiff, but she put on her boots, bodice and split skirt and wrapping a shawl around her shoulders opened the door and stepped outside. The air was sharp and cold but smelt clean and fresh, and the eastern sky glinted with the promise of a bright day.

Lake was sitting on a log by the river and as she

approached he turned swiftly, putting his hand to his waist, where she saw the glint of a knife.

'Sorry,' she said. 'I didn't mean to startle you.'

He stood up. 'Don't ever come up behind a man like that, lady. Not out here. Not without warning.'

'I'm sorry.' Again she apologized. 'It's so different, you see. From what I'm used to. But I will learn.'

He nodded. 'You want to eat?' He had a handful of berries in his hand which he offered to her. His fingers were long and thin and stained with what looked like blood.

She shook her head. 'No, thank you. We still have some meat left. But I'll have water.'

She turned to go to the creek and he handed her a water pouch and asked her to fill it for the journey. She did so, then rinsed her face and dried it on her shawl. 'I heard gunshot last night,' she said, when she returned.

'Wolf,' he said briefly. 'Must have got wind of us, or the smoke from the fire.'

'Did you kill it?' she asked nervously.

'Yip. It came too close. You want the skin?'

'No. Thank you.' She glanced around for sight of the animal's body. 'I wouldn't know what to do with it.'

Kitty came to the door of the cabin. She was fully dressed and looked very refreshed after her night's sleep. 'Good morning,' she said cheerfully. 'Are you waiting for me? I'm ready.'

'Eat first,' Lake told them. 'Then we'll move off. We'll arrive by midday.'

He went to see to the horses and they saw him

running his hands down their legs and examining their feet. He straightened up after looking at the pony which had carried Georgiana. 'You ride the other horse,' he called to her. 'This one has gone lame.'

When they had finished the remains of the meat and packed their few belongings, the packs were fastened to the pony and Georgiana mounted Henry, who whinnied when she saw her and again bumped her with her head.

'That horse likes you,' Lake said. 'You should keep her.'

'I've only hired her,' she said. 'I have to take her back.'

He shook his head. 'Buy her. She needs a woman's hands.'

'Perhaps I should,' she considered. 'If her owner will sell.'

She felt comfortable on Henry. The Indian pony was swift and Georgiana felt that should she ever need speed he would be the faster. But Henry's pace was steady and constant as she followed down the forest trail behind Lake and Kitty.

They travelled for an hour through thick forest and Georgiana wondered how Lake knew his way, for there were times when it seemed as if the trail disappeared altogether. They crossed over narrow rushing streams and picked their way through dried-up boulder-strewn creeks, ducked beneath overhanging tree branches and skirted rock slides, and just as they were starting to feel chilled because of the dimness and shelter of the pine trees, they began to climb. In a short time they reached a clearing and were able to look down at the landscape below.

'I can see a settlement!' Georgiana said. 'Over there. Below the forest. And a road!'

'And waggons!' Kitty exclaimed.

They had been beginning to think that they would never see habitation or population again.

Lake nodded. 'A waggon trail.'

'But–' Georgiana began. 'Why–?'

'Why couldn't we have come that way?' Lake finished for her.

'Yes. Wouldn't it have been a better road?'

He wheeled his mount around and prepared to ride up the mountainside again. 'No. That's not the way we go.' Then he glanced at her. 'This is Indian trail. Faster. Safer. Down there is for settlers and waggons. Not long now,' he said, which gave them hope, which was dashed as he added, 'to the head of the valley.'

The trees were not so dense now as they climbed, though the trail was steep and hazardous with huge boulders which they had to skirt, the horses skittering on loose stones which clattered down the mountain. They grew hotter as the sun rose higher and the women pulled their shawls over their heads to protect them. Georgiana started to wish, not for the first time, that she had brought her hat instead of leaving it at the Indian settlement.

'There it is.' Lake drew to a halt as they came out of the tree line to a rocky clearing, and pointed down the mountainside. The trees thinned towards the base, being replaced by thick scrub which then petered out into lush green pastureland.

'It's beautiful,' Georgiana murmured and cast her eyes around it. She glanced to the left of the wide valley where the green uplands rose towards a high escarpment of rock, then over to the right where the meadowland was confined by the mountain range. Down the valley bottom a wide creek flowed through the grassland to the end of the vale, where it disappeared beneath a rocky hillside.

She narrowed her eyes to stare southwards above the escarpment where from this height she could see the waggon trail, now as slim as a pencil line, snaking across a rocky plain. Then she turned back to the valley below. There were shacks or cabins in the distance and cattle grazing at the side of the creek, but she couldn't see any people.

She turned towards Kitty and Lake, who had dismounted. 'So,' she deliberated, and saw Lake looking at her. 'Is this the only way in?'

He raised his eyebrows and shrugged with a slight ironic smile on his lips.

She glanced down again. Was there a break in the rock escarpment? From here there didn't appear to be. So how did Wilhelm Dreumel bring in waggons and equipment?

She dismounted and stood beside him. 'It's a secret valley, isn't it?' she said. 'Nobody else, except the Indians and Mr Dreumel and his men, knows that it is here.'

Lake too looked down into the valley. 'And the buzzards and the eagles. Anything that flies. Once, many years ago, it belonged to the Indians, but they moved on to better hunting ground.' His lips turned down. 'That was before the white man decreed that they should exchange the land of their fathers and live in settlements and become farmers.'

'How did Mr Dreumel find this land?' Kitty asked curiously.

'He didn't find it,' he said abruptly. 'He saved someone's life. A half-breed. He told him of the valley and brought him here.'

'Why would he do that?' Georgiana gazed at him intently.

'A return for a life.' He half turned from her so that she couldn't see his face. 'Dreumel was looking for land to breed cattle. This is fertile land, fed by the streams and the creek and protected by the mountains and the escarpment. He will look after it. For as long as he can,' he added.

And then he unexpectedly found gold, Georgiana considered. And that's where Robert Allen came into the picture.

'Come.' Lake abruptly turned away and mounted his horse, leaving a stirrup free and putting out his hand to help Kitty up. 'We shall be there by noon.'

The mountainside was steep but the horses were sure-footed, and Georgiana made encouraging sounds to Henry as she negotiated the slope. 'I would call you Hetty if you were mine,' she murmured to her. 'Why should you be called Henry? That's not a suitable name for a young mare of independent spirit. Hetty is much more appropriate.'

Henry or Hetty gave a snicker, but Georgiana was not to know if it was in response to her murmurings or because they were down at last and pushing their way through the scrub to reach the grassland, with the promise of a cooling drink from the gurgling waters of the creek.

Georgiana and Kitty were hot, hungry, tired and sore by the time they splashed across the creek and reached the few shacks halfway along the valley. The track was dusty and potholed, and if they had been expecting a structured settlement they were to be disappointed. There were half a dozen log cabins, thrown up, it seemed, for they were ramshackle affairs. One was larger than the others and Lake led them towards it.

A man with a grizzled beard sat outside the doorway on a wooden chair, his feet resting on planks of wood which had been laid as a board-walk. He removed a clay pipe from his mouth. 'How do, Lake. Weren't expecting you!'

He seized the chair arms and pushed himself up. 'Pleased to meet you, ladies.' He grabbed his hat, lifting it to reveal a bald head with sprouting wisps of white hair, then replaced it.

'Is Mr Dreumel here?' Georgiana asked.

'Nope.' He sat down again.

'Edward Newmarch?' She assumed Robert Allen would be using that name.

The old man spat into the road. 'Nope.'

'So where would we find them?'

'Don't rightly know, ma'am.' He ran his tongue around his gums. 'Could be anywhere.'

Georgiana dismounted, glad to have her feet on the ground, though her legs ached. 'They'll be up at the mine, I suppose?'

'Mebbe so.' His eyes surveyed her, then he

glanced towards Kitty. 'Can either of you gals cook?'

'Cook?' Georgiana was disconcerted by their title and the question. 'Why?'

'Fellow who called himself a cook has gone. Left. Skedaddled. We're eating dry tack. Ain't easy when you've onny a few teeth.'

'I'm sure it's not,' she agreed. 'But I'm afraid I haven't come as a cook.'

'What have you come for, lady?'

'I've come to see Mr Dreumel.'

'He ain't here.'

Georgiana fought back her frustration and behind her Kitty gave a slightly hysterical laugh.

'We'll wait,' she said, and turning to Lake asked, 'Will it be all right if we go inside? It's so hot out here.'

There was a hitching post outside the building and Lake fastened up the horses. 'You can rest inside,' he said. 'The men will be down this evening. Isaac is here as a guard, though he's not much use.'

He led them into a large room where chairs, tables, packing cases, boxes, and barrels of ale were crammed together. A long counter ran down one side. On it were glass jars with the crumbly remains of biscuits, an opened tin of sardines and a dish of honey with a fly struggling in it. A half-eaten loaf of bread lay mouldering on a tin plate and there was a sour smell of stale ale and tobacco.

'I can't believe that this is how Wilhelm Dreumel lives,' Georgiana muttered. 'He is so very neat and well turned out.'

'He doesn't.' Lake overheard her. 'This is the

165

men's doing.' He wrinkled his nose and turned to go out. 'The place stinks.'

'It's very odd, Miss Gregory,' Kitty whispered as he went out of the door. 'But you know when I said that Lake smelled? Well, I haven't noticed it lately.'

Georgiana grimaced. 'Probably because we don't smell very sweet either, Kitty! Oh what I wouldn't give for a soak in a hot tub! This is not what I expected at all.'

They made themselves as comfortable as possible, putting chairs together so that they might stretch out their weary legs. Lake brought them water and offered them beer, which Georgiana refused though Kitty accepted, then searched through some of the boxes and found a bag of biscuits, which he gave them.

'I have to leave now.' He stood and looked down at them, his face inscrutable. 'I have brought you to your destination. You will be safe enough when Dreumel returns.'

Georgiana considered, then asked quietly, 'Will we be safe *before* he returns?'

He stared at her for a moment before putting his hand inside his jacket to the back of his belt. 'Take this.' He handed her a knife in a leather sheath. 'Stay in the camp. Then you'll be safe.'

'Thank you.' Gingerly she took it. The knife handle was bleached bone and protruded above the sheath, which was scrolled with symbols. She reflected that she would never have the courage to use it. 'Do I–?' She wondered how to bring up the matter of payment for his services. 'Can I – I mean, do anything for you in return for you

166

bringing us here?'

He looked down at her for a moment without speaking, then a flicker of a smile passed over his lips, vanishing in a second. 'You are in my debt,' he said softly. 'One day perhaps you will repay me?'

'I'll be glad to,' she said, slightly unnerved by the intensity of his glance. 'Thank you.'

He turned and left, not lifting his hat or saying goodbye, and the two women glanced at each other.

'Well,' Kitty said. 'What a strange man!' She got up from her chair and went to the door of the hut, watching him mount and wheel around to go back in the direction from which they had come. The Indian pony was tethered behind him. Georgiana stood behind Kitty in the doorway. 'Goodbye, Lake,' Kitty called. 'Thank you.'

He turned in his saddle and looked at them, then raised his hand in acknowledgement and trotted away.

Kitty came back inside and stood looking at the jumble around them. 'Would it be all right if I had a little sort-out, Miss Gregory? A bit of a tidy-up? If this is where we're going to stay.'

'I don't know,' Georgiana said. 'We could ask Isaac, I suppose.'

As she spoke, Isaac entered. 'Make yourselves comfortable,' he grunted. 'Though it ain't really fit for wimmin.' He chewed on his lip. 'There's a cabin free if you're stopping awhile. Fellow who called himself a cook had it but as he's gone–'

'We'll have it,' Georgiana said quickly. Like Kitty, she didn't relish staying in this building, for

167

it was obviously used by the men as a saloon for drinking and eating. There were iron pans on the floor which looked suspiciously like spittoons. 'Will you show us which it is?'

Isaac led them down the boardwalk to one of the cabins. 'It ain't very clean,' he said. 'He weren't no good at housekeeping.'

'And he was the cook?' Georgiana said incredulously as they went inside. The cabin, like the other hut, hadn't been cleaned in a long time.

'He didn't cook in here,' Isaac said. 'He cooked in the longhouse where you've just been.' He rubbed a rough hand over his whiskers. 'There's a cooking stove in there. Hasn't been lit since he went.'

'How long has he been gone?' Kitty asked. She hadn't noticed a stove amongst the clutter. It must have had boxes piled on top of it.

'Bin a while,' he said. 'Just before Bill Dreumel left for New York. We ain't had a decent meal since.'

'If you'll light the stove,' Kitty said, 'I'll try and cook something. Will there be anything worth eating in those boxes?'

'Reckon so.' Isaac's eyes lit up at the prospect of food. 'Beans, cornmeal, barley. Could catch you some fish! Plenty in the creek.'

Kitty went back with Isaac to the longhouse to investigate the prospect of lighting the stove and cooking, whilst Georgiana started to unpack their few belongings. There were four bunk beds in the room but only one had been slept in, judging by the rough blanket laid on it. The other bunks had storage boxes, lengths of timber, a spade, a pan, an axe and various other pieces of equipment piled on them. There were two wooden chairs stacked one upon the other, and a free-standing stove with an iron chimney going through the roof in the centre of the room. She put her hand near it. It was stone cold.

Where should I start? she thought. My former life hasn't prepared me for this! Turning her back on the disorder she went to the door of the cabin and looked out. The sun was setting, but had not yet reached the top of the tree line at the end of the valley. The sky was suffused with red and yellow, and its advancing dazzling colour appeared to set the mountains on fire and turn the rippling water of the creek into liquid gold.

If I was in England now, she pondered as she surveyed the vista, Aunt Clarissa and I would be taking tea and I would be contemplating, as I was wont to do, the long evening in front of us, and debating whether to play the piano after supper or read a report on Women's Rights. My aunt would be playing patience or nodding over her embroidery. Dear Aunt Clarissa, she thought, with sudden nostalgia. I wonder if I will ever see you again.

As it is, she glanced up the forested hillside, I wonder what I am doing here, waiting to confront a man who is an impostor. Who might even be a murderer! I have acted on a whim, which is not like me at all. Is it justice I am seeking? Justice for my cousin May, or for Wilhelm Dreumel, who might be unaware that he is being deceived?

She turned back into the cabin and stood with her hands on her hips. In the corner of the room she saw a broom leaning against the wall and a bucket at the side of it. She gave a wry self-deprecating smile. I didn't at any rate, not by any stretch of imagination, envisage that I should have to clean out a room before I could live in it!

An hour later smoke was issuing from both chimney stoves. Isaac had cleared the ash, brought in wood and lit the fires. The prospect of a proper meal seemed to have galvanized him into action. He'd moved boxes and packing cases around the longhouse so that Kitty had room to cook, found a sack of flour, dried beans and barley, and had been promised soup and dumplings.

He brought an oil lamp to the cabin for the evening was closing in, and as Georgiana was putting another log into the stove the door opened again. 'Isaac–' she started to say. 'Could we–'

'Not Isaac,' another man's voice told her. 'How the devil–?'

'Did I get here?' she answered, observing Robert Allen caustically. 'I suppose you thought you'd seen the last of me, *Mr Newmarch?*'

Allen came towards her. 'Yes,' he admitted. 'I really thought that I had.' He looked exhausted. His clothes, his face and hands were spattered with mud. 'I should have known better,' he gibed. 'Your sort never gives up.'

'My sort?' She bristled. 'What exactly is *my sort?*'

'Your class, Miss Gregory.' He faced her, his eyes defiant. 'Determined to keep lesser folk down. Oppress them. Prevent them taking the advantage of an opportunity when it presents itself.'

She lifted her head and stared coldly at him. 'You know nothing of me. Not a thing! You are

170

judging everyone by your own standards which, from what I have observed, are totally reprehensible.'

He put his hand to his eyes. 'Then you know nothing of me, either! I admit,' he said, sighing and glancing away from her, 'that it doesn't look good. And my conscience has bothered me over Newmarch. But the man was a fool! An utter fool.'

'Was?' she breathed. 'Then, he's–'

'Might I sit down?' He glanced towards the chairs which Georgiana had placed near the stove.

She nodded, and as he sat down she stood over him. 'Don't you think it's time I knew the truth? I told you that I would inform Mr Dreumel. And I will. That is why I am here. That is why I have travelled all this way and at great inconvenience, I might tell you! But I am determined to find out about Edward Newmarch.'

He picked up a piece of wood from the floor and manoeuvred the door of the stove open with it. Staring into the flames, he murmured, 'It's good to have a fire in the evening. Relaxing after an honest day's work. My da and my brothers were miners, you know. Though of course you wouldn't know, how would you? But they couldn't always afford a fire, even though they were working in coal all day.'

He looked up at her. 'But I won't bore you with all of that, Miss Gregory. I wouldn't want to upset your finer feelings.'

She said nothing, but continued to stare at him.

'Sit down, Miss Gregory,' he said. 'If you don't, then as you are a lady, I must stand, and I really am so very tired.'

She sat down and, folding her hands in her lap, she waited.

'You're right of course. You do need to know about Edward Newmarch.' Allen took a deep breath. 'So I'll tell you. Even though he made me swear not to breathe a word. We were in New Orleans and he'd been invited by a rich Spanish family to visit them at their country house—'

CHAPTER FOURTEEN

The Rodriguez country house was even more magnificent than the one they owned in New Orleans. Marble pillars flanked the entrance and as the carriage pulled up, three black servants descended the wide steps to greet Edward. One to assist him from the carriage, one to take his overnight bag and one to take him through the cool hall and into a sunny drawing room, where the floor was laid with polished marble chips and scattered with Chinese carpets.

Sofia rose from her chair to welcome him. 'I am delighted that you were able to come, Meester Newmarch,' she said huskily. 'So very pleased.'

She invited him to sit down and rang a handbell to order refreshments. 'Bring wine,' she said to the mulatto girl who came in answer. 'And orange juice. Figs too, cherries—' She made a circling clicking motion with her fingers to indicate other items.

Within minutes the door opened and more

servants arrived carrying trays with glasses of white wine, dishes of grapes, figs, dark red cherries, almonds, olives, and plates containing slivers of smoked meat and fish and tiny pastry cases filled with potted chicken.

Sofia picked up a piece of smoked chicken with her fingers. 'This is cooked on what we call a *barbacoa*. The Spaniards first saw it in Mexico.' Edward watched her, fascinated. Her lips were soft and full, and he caught a glimpse of her pink tongue as she placed the meat in her mouth. 'The food is cooked outside,' she continued. 'In ze open air.'

Edward took a sip of wine. It was cool and dry with an aftertaste of apple and spice.

'You must rest after your journey, Meester Newmarch.' Sofia smiled at him. 'And then I will take you to see the estate. Today we will have just a short ride and then tomorrow we will take a peecnic for lunch, yes? We will take wine, and chicken, and wine.' Her eyes sparkled. 'And turkey and wine.' She laughed. 'We will cook on ze *barbacoa*, yes?'

'Yes,' he croaked as he considered the prospect of her company. She hadn't mentioned her husband, and she had previously said that he wouldn't be arriving until Saturday, which was the next day. 'That sounds wonderful, señora.'

She lightly touched his arm. 'You must call me Sofia if we are to be friends.' Her voice was low and seductive. 'And what shall I call you, Meester Newmarch? You are not a stuffy Englishman, I think?'

'No! No, absolutely not! Edward,' he flustered.

173

'I would be honoured if you would call me Edward.'

'Ed-ward,' she breathed, her tongue trilling around the letter *r*. 'It is a very English name, I think?'

'Yes.' He felt totally tongue-tied. 'It is.'

When he had finished his glass of wine she poured him another and insisted that he ate some food before going to rest. 'We will take a short *reposo*,' she said, 'and then when it is cooler we will ride.'

'And will your daughters accompany us, señ– Sofia?' he asked. 'They are well, I trust?'

'Sibella is resting, and then she must study. Elena,' she shrugged expressively, 'she has gone somewhere, I don't know. She is very restless.' She gave him a beguiling smile. 'She needs to be tamed.'

'Tamed?' he queried. 'Is that possible?'

'Perhaps not.' She gazed at him from her dark eyes, then lowered her lashes. 'Not all women can be tamed, though often men think that they are.'

He had no answer to give her, but simply murmured platitudes. She rang the bell again and a boy came to take him to his room, which was on the first floor, where the shuttered windows overlooked a green lawn. At the furthest edge of the lawn was a belt of trees and beyond that as far as he could see were acres of sugar cane.

'What must it be like to own so much?' he murmured as he lay beneath a mosquito net and between crisp cotton sheets. 'I'm poor in comparison.' He breathed deeply and considered. If I could marry Elena I would have a share in all of

174

this. But I would always be tempted by the lovely Sofia. But I can't! I'm a married man, goddamn it! I swear I would marry Elena if I wasn't.

He fell asleep and dreamed of May and Ruby. Ruby was walking away from him but May was pursuing him. She had a whip in her hand and was lashing furiously around his head, calling him all manner of names, though he couldn't hear what she was saying.

Someone knocked softly on the door. '*Señor*,' they called. '*Señor!*'

'Coming!' He sat up. 'Yes. I'm coming.' He rubbed his eyes. Would anyone find out if I married Elena? he wondered. Nobody knows anything about me. Only Allen, and I could pay him off. But no. I couldn't. It wouldn't be the thing. Not the English way. Not gentlemanly!

A tray of tea was brought to him and he thanked the maid for her thoughtfulness. I hardly ever drank tea at home, he mused, but I suppose they think that all English people do. I'd much rather have coffee.

Sofia was waiting for him and led him outside, where a groom was waiting with two horses. A dun-coloured criollo with a side saddle for her and a sturdy black mustang for him. Sofia wore a green riding habit and a matching hat with a veil which partially hid her eyes. They rode, followed by the groom, down the long drive and headed towards a narrow creek where she pointed out the extent of their land. 'All that you can see across the water,' she pointed, 'belongs to Sancho. And up 'ere.' She raised her arm to her right, and then to her left. 'And as far as the

175

'orizon. That is sugar cane,' she said. 'And where you cannot see, he grows cotton.'

He was very impressed. I must buy land, he thought. That is the thing to have in this country. 'I have shares in a cotton mill,' he began. 'In England.'

'Oh!' She turned to him. 'You own a cotton mill?'

'Well, not exactly own it, but I own part of it!' That's almost true, he thought defensively. I do own a number of shares.

He saw a gleam in her eyes. 'That is good. So you are rich, yes? Like Sancho?'

He smiled and shook his head, though he didn't deny it. 'I have a private income,' he said modestly. 'My father left me an annuity when he died.' Though not enough, he deliberated. Martin got the estate. If it wasn't for May's money I wouldn't be able to manage.

'Ah!' she said thoughtfully. 'And you will have your poor wife's money, of course?'

'Wh-what?' He was startled by her question. 'My – wife?'

'Yes.' She showed concern and solicitude. 'Your poor wife who died!'

'Oh! Yes!' He broke into a sweat. For a moment he had thought he was found out. He put his hand across his face. 'Forgive me,' he murmured. 'Sometimes I can't bear to think of it.'

She leaned across and touched his arm. 'You must learn to love again,' she said softly. 'It is the only way to recover.' She searched his face as he put his hand over hers. 'You must learn to love and you must marry for a second time.' She gave

176

a slight shrug of her shoulders. 'And you do not 'ave to do the two things at the same time or wiz ze same person!'

What is she saying? A pulse hammered in his throat. Is she suggesting something?

She gathered up the reins and kicked in her heels. 'I am telling you of this, Ed-ward.' Once more her tongue purred seductively around his name. The mare started to trot on. 'Because I know it.'

That evening they dined alone, though there was always a servant hovering in the background. Sibella came in after they had finished eating to kiss her mother goodnight, and greeted Edward charmingly, but Elena did not appear.

'She is busy wiz her horses, I think,' Sofia said when Edward nervously asked about her. 'She likes to ride. She is a good horsewoman. She knows also about cotton and cane. She would be able to run a plantation if she should marry someone with land.'

He nodded and wished he hadn't mentioned Elena's name.

'They will come with us tomorrow,' Sofia continued. 'Elena and Sibella, on our peecnic.'

He was disappointed, for he had thought that he was going to have Sofia all to himself. He felt reckless and heard, in every word that Sofia uttered, a hint or suggestion that their relationship could be more than just sociable. She was not coquettish or provocative, but she gazed at him in such a beguiling manner and spoke so seductively that he was enraptured and captivated by her.

A host of servants accompanied them the following morning, as well as Sibella and Elena. Some of the servants rode or walked ahead with mules which were laden with baskets, and others walked behind carrying branches of green wood, iron cooking pots and pans.

Elena was as fine a horsewoman as her mother had described, and she took on a different persona when on horseback. She looked confident and even quite handsome in her dark maroon habit, and unlike her mother and sister did not wear a hat or veil but caught up her thick hair in a crocheted snood.

'You come and ride with me, Meester Newmarch,' she called, wheeling her horse in front of Edward. 'I will show you where we go.'

He hesitated, but to refuse would seem churlish, so with an apologetic smile at Sofia, he trotted off after her.

The trail they were following ran between acres of cotton fields which widened out, then dropped into a gentle green valley. 'There,' Elena pointed as they came to a halt at the top of the hillside. 'Down by the trees. You see the river? Here is where we stop.'

She turned to him. 'You have decided to marry me? Yes?' she said. 'That is why you have come?'

'I – no! I cannot. My wife!' What am I to do? he worried. How can I get out of this?

'Then why you come?' Her eyes flashed.

'I was invited,' he insisted. 'Your mother—'

'Tst,' she said impatiently. 'It was Sancho who invited you.' She gazed at him scornfully. 'Do not think it was for friendship, señor. Sancho does

178

not have time for friendship, 'e only has time for business.' She rubbed the tips of her fingers together. 'And for money.'

She kicked her horse on and rode down the valley, and he followed reluctantly. He could hear the voices of the servants behind as they laughed and chattered.

''Ere is where we would live.' She went on as if there had been no break in the conversation and no refusal on his part. 'At the top of the valley.' She pointed upwards to a bank of trees. 'There we would build a ranch 'ouse and grow cotton. It is good land beyond the trees. Flat land where we could watch the cotton grow.'

'But, Elena,' he said in desperation. 'Why me? There must be other men you would rather marry. A farmer perhaps who knows about growing things? I'm not a countryman!'

She smiled then and nodded. 'That is why! I would grow the cotton, with Zac. 'E would be the one, and we can ship it to your mill in England and make you rich!'

'Zac?' he said, stupefied, and couldn't remember telling her about the cotton mill. 'Who is Zac?'

'Zachariah. My man.'

He exhaled. 'The man you want to marry?'

'Sancho will not let me.' She turned her lips down. 'But if I marry you, Sancho will be 'appy. You are an Eenglish gentleman. It will bring 'im – what you call it? Presteem?'

'Esteem – prestige! But why will it?'

'He will not let me marry a quadroon.' She gave a derisory grimace. 'Nor a Spaniard. I would taint ze blood. But a Frenchman is all right or an

179

Englishman. Eenglish is good, you 'ave a castle, yes? And once we are married Sancho has no control over me. Only you 'ave that, Meester Newmarch.'

Fat chance of that! Edward thought. If anyone was to have control it would be Elena, and he resented the fact that she was not allowed to marry a Spaniard but could marry an Englishman or Frenchman. Damned foreigners, he grumbled to himself. How dare Rodriguez compare the French with the English!

The others caught them up and the servants proceeded to erect the *barbacoa* frame. They first prepared a fire of twigs and branches, then around it they hammered four stout wooden uprights into the ground, split the tops into a fork to take parallel bars, and criss-crossed these with green wood which would not burn but only singe. They set light to the fire, and from this they made another fire for hot water and to cook beans and corn.

Elena went with some of the men and girls to catch fish from the river. The young servant girls babbled and giggled and ran ahead to jump into the shallows, laughing and screeching in their excitement. Edward watched Elena as she moved towards a young male servant. He was much taller than her and heavily built, his wide shoulders bulging beneath his cotton shirt. They briefly touched hands before drifting apart. So that is Zac, Edward thought uneasily. Elena looks petite at the side of him. What a formidable pair.

Chicken and turkey were put on the roasting frame and the fatty juices sizzled and spat onto the flames, sending up a delicious aroma. Then the first of the freshly caught fish wrapped in green leaves was added, cooking quickly as the fire grew hotter.

'Ed-ward.' Sofia held out her hand to him. A blanket and cushions were laid out beneath a tree on the ground behind her. 'Come and sit by me.'

A girl brought a jug of wine and a dish of almonds and grapes. Sofia poured the wine and handed a glass to Edward. She raised her glass in a toast. 'To friendship,' she said softly, before taking a sip, then leaned towards him and kissed him gently on the lips.

He gave a small gasp and put out his hand to draw her closer, but she gave a slight shake of her head and moved away. 'No,' she whispered. 'Just a leetle aperitif.'

He took a large gulp of wine, then lay back on the cushions and closed his eyes. The sun warmed his face, the wine warmed his blood, he could smell Sofia's perfume and he wanted to take her in his arms and make love to her, to kiss her soft mouth and feel her yielding body next to his. Ruby, he groaned. I'm forgetting you already.

'Ed-ward, are you all right?' Sofia bent over him.

'No, I'm not all right,' he murmured and clutched her hand. 'I want you. You are the most beautiful woman in the world and I am mad with desire for you.'

CHAPTER FIFTEEN

Sofia stroked his cheek, seeming not to mind that the servants were around. 'Sancho is frequently away,' she said softly. 'We would see each other often if you were part of the family. If you married my Elena.'

It doesn't seem quite right, he thought. Though I find her most desirable, this is Elena's *mother* suggesting infidelity if I marry her daughter! I'm used to the reserve and formality of English-women. English *gentle*women, at least, he mused as he gazed at Sofia. Not young women such as my darling Ruby. No, she was quite different. Sofia is Mexican of course, and probably hot-blooded. He started to sweat and became quite agitated as he thought of what making love to an uninhibited Sofia might be like.

He cleared his throat. 'I will give it some thought, Sofia,' he said, 'about marrying Elena, I mean. She is very young and perhaps might fall in love with someone else–'

'*Tst, tst,*' she said. 'She has already, but she can-not marry him. Sancho will not allow it.' She smiled sweetly and seductively. 'You would be the perfect 'usband for her. She would be good to you, and you would become much richer from cotton in New Orleans than in England.' She ran slender fingers along his thigh. 'And also have much pleasure.'

Then, though his senses flared and he caught his breath, he remembered that it was Sofia he had told of the cotton-mill shares he held in England, and realized that it was she who must have told Elena. They are setting a snare, he deduced, as he played with Sofia's fingers. Sofia is arousing me, enticing me, *promising* me her favours, so that I will marry her daughter. But will she keep her promise? And what of Sancho? What would he do if he found out?

They ate and drank and when the younger servants had finished serving the food, they, with Elena and Sibella, ran towards the river and played games. Edward was bewildered by the lack of formality between the Rodriguez family and their servants. If I had brought Allen along, I couldn't see him cavorting around in front of me as they are doing.

'This is not like England, I think?' Sofia said softly. 'Your slaves do not have such fun?'

'Slaves!' He was horrified. 'We don't have slaves in England! Though I know that once we did.'

She gave a little shrug. 'Our slaves are 'appy. They are fed and clothed and 'ave a little cabin to live in, and as long as they do not misbehave, they stay with us for ever. We look after them and they look after us.'

'And what abut Zac?' he asked. 'Is he a slave?'

'No,' she said sharply. 'He is not. 'E is a servant. A free man. He would not be tolerated near Elena if 'e was a slave.'

'I don't understand,' he said. 'Your first husband was a slave, yet you married him.'

'Yes, he was his father's slave,' she admitted.

183

'But now is different. I was very poor when I met Brown, but Elena is a daughter of rich parents so she must marry well.' She leaned towards him and whispered. 'Sancho would kill Zac if he thought they were 'aving a liaison.'

Edward thought it unlikely. He had seen the size of Zac. Rodriguez was slimly built and older, but, he pondered, he probably has plenty of people who would willingly put Zac out of reach.

'They will be found out. We must save them, Ed-ward.' Sofia's eyes were moist and appealing. 'Please 'elp us. Sometimes Sancho can be so cruel.'

A sudden low cry was uttered by one of the servants and he pointed along the valley to the top of the hillside. A man on horseback could be seen looking down on them, his figure and that of his horse etched on the skyline.

'Sancho,' Sofia said softly, and she clapped her hands and said something in Spanish. Immediately everyone moved into action. More wood was put on the low fire, the servants down by the river raced back, as did Elena and Sibella, and Sibella skipped and ran along the valley to greet her father and ride up behind him.

Rodriguez kissed his wife and shook Edward's hand and accepted a glass of wine from one of the young girls, who dimpled and curtsied when he spoke to her.

More meat was put over the fire and Sancho sat on the blanket beside Edward and lazily popped almonds into his mouth.

'So, Newmarch,' he began formally. 'How do you like our country house?' He swept a hand

184

around to encompass the surroundings. 'And our garden?' he joked.

'It's wonderful,' Edward replied quite truthfully. 'And do you know that in England, it is probably raining and people will be preparing for the winter?'

'Hah!' Rodriguez said. 'I do not wonder that so many people come here. It is a good place to live, yes?'

'Yes, indeed. Very good indeed.' Edward felt safer now that Rodriguez was here, even though he might try to persuade him to marry Elena and offer incentives to do so. I can resist money, he thought, but I cannot resist the temptation of Sofia. I am bound to fall.

That evening, as it became cooler, fires were lit in all the rooms of the house. They ate in the dining room by the glow of a wood fire and the flames of dozens of candles which were placed on the table, in alcoves, in front of mirrors and windows, so that they were reflected from the glass into shimmering, scintillating dozens more.

Edward drank more wine as it was offered, though he knew that he shouldn't. He was feeling quite heady as he had drunk wine steadily during the day, but he was lulled into a sense of ease as Sancho's mother was at the supper table as well as Elena and Sibella, and he was sure that the conversation would be general rather than personal. When they had finished eating, the ladies excused themselves and he and Rodriguez withdrew into a small library where there were comfortable leather chairs and a fire blazing in the hearth.

'Port, Newmarch? Or perhaps you would prefer

185

cognac?' Rodriguez indicated the decanters on a side table.

'Port, please.' Edward sank back into the comfort of his chair and thought how very pleasant this was. Beautiful home, beautiful wife, lovely countryside. How lucky Rodriguez was to have all this, and he wondered vaguely if it all came from sugar cane and cotton.

'Do you have other interests, Rodriguez?' he asked. 'Or does cotton and cane keep you busy?'

His host sat across from him. 'I have managers for the fields, but yes, I have other interests. I deal in merchandise which comes in on the ships.' He narrowed his eyes slightly and his mouth turned up at the corners, but it wasn't quite a smile. 'There is always something that someone wants, and I can get it. Silks. Precious stones. Wine. Opium. Anything!'

He took a sip from his glass, then putting it down on a side table he perused Edward, tapping his fingers together as he did so, and Edward noticed the heavy gold rings on his third and little fingers. 'What would you like, Newmarch?' he asked softly. 'What would make you happy? A house? A ship? Money? We would like to see you living here in our country. We do not welcome everyone, be assured of that. But you would fit in.' He nodded. 'I can see that you would be comfortable with riches.'

Edward was flattered by the blandishments. It was true, he concurred. Being rich would suit me very well. Father always insisted that Martin and I work for a living just so that we would know how the less well-off managed. But I always

186

thought that absolute tosh. I've never really cared about the poor or how they fared. It's every man for himself as far as I'm concerned.

'What would I like?' he responded. 'Well, of course, I came to this country to start afresh. I am not without fortune,' he added, not wanting Rodriguez to think him a pauper. 'I have considerable assets, but I was stifled in England, feeling the need to look further afield. To discover the strength of my ability which was being wasted.'

It was patently untrue as he well knew, but if Rodriguez could put him in the way of a fortune without him having to expend too much effort, then he would sit back and enjoy the fruits of it.

Rodriguez handed him a cigar and a neat gold clipper to take off the end. He then lit it for him and sat back in his chair and lit one for himself. 'You came to the right place, my friend,' he said. 'It was fortuitous that Captain Voularis mentioned my name to you.'

Edward gave a little smirk behind his fingers as he smoked. He doesn't guess that I know the reason why, he thought. 'Voularis must be quite a judge of character,' he commented, 'meeting so many people on his ship.'

Rodriguez nodded and gazed at him with an inscrutable expression. 'My ship, actually,' he said in his suave manner. 'Voularis works for me.'

'Ah!' Edward wafted the smoke away from his eyes. 'I see.'

'I have two ships,' Rodriguez continued. 'They carry merchandise and passengers. I would like to buy a third, but it might be prudent of me to take a partner, if I can find the right man.'

Edward felt a tingle of excitement. He remembered seeing the ships in the Hull docks and thinking that shipping might be the business to be in. 'How very coincidental,' he said fervently. 'I have often considered that shipping might be rewarding. In England the railways are making great strides with transportation of goods across country, but we can never be without our ships for worldwide trade.'

'Quite right,' Rodriguez agreed, looking at him from beneath lowered eyelids. He drew heavily on his cigar, then exhaled slowly, leaning his head backwards so that the smoke drifted towards the ceiling. 'So, perhaps you might be interested in a little venture?'

'I might be,' Edward said complacently. 'Depends on the terms. I have only just got here, of course. Haven't had time to look around, you know. But I am interested.'

Don't be too eager, he thought. Play him along for a while. He's obviously keen to have me as a partner or he wouldn't have invited me here. And not once has he mentioned Elena. A doubt about Rodriguez' motives disturbed his satisfaction, but he instantly dismissed it. A man like Rodriguez would never mix business with personal affairs.

'Yes.' He took another sip of port. 'We must talk again. I think I might be very interested indeed.'

'Good.' Rodriguez reached out and rang a handbell which was on the table. 'Enough now of business matters. Shall we rejoin the ladies?'

'*Momia!* Sancho has offered Newmarch shares in a ship!' Elena rushed towards Sofia, who was

188

sitting with Rodriguez' mother, and whispered in her ear. 'I listened at the door.'

'Tst!' The senior Señora Rodriguez was not so deaf that she did not hear her remark. 'This girl has no manners. She would have had a beating for such behaviour in my day.'

Sofia ignored her mother-in-law, and murmured to Elena, 'Be careful, you will make Sancho angry if he catches you.'

'What? What did you say?' Señora Rodriguez glared at Sofia.

'I said you were an old busybody,' Sofia muttered, her mouth hidden behind her fan, which she put up to her face. She lowered it and smiled sweetly at the older woman and raised her voice. 'I told her that she must be grateful to Sancho for all he does for her and to be pleasant to the Englishman.'

Señora Rodriguez harrumphed and bellowed, 'Get him to marry her and take her back to England with him!'

'I will try to speak to Newmarch alone.' Sofia spoke to her daughter in an undertone. She glanced towards the window. 'It is a fine night. Perhaps I will show him the garden.'

She cast her eyes over to her mother-in-law, who was eyeing them both suspiciously, then told Elena, 'Go now and tell Maria that her mistress is tired and wants to go to bed.'

Elena grinned and, giving a condescending bob of her knee to Señora Rodriguez, left the room on her mission.

Sancho and Edward returned as a protesting Señora Rodriguez was being shepherded out of the room by her maid. 'Goodnight, *Momia*,' Rodriguez said and kissed her cheeks. 'Sleep well.'

'She is retiring early?' He spoke in English to Sofia out of respect to their guest.

'Poor *Momia*. It is a strain for her when she cannot 'ear,' Sofia replied. 'And she is tired after her journey. She said to please excuse her, Meester Newmarch. She will see you in the morning.'

'Of course,' Edward graciously assented. 'I shall look forward to that. And your daughters? Have they retired also? They will be tired after the hectic day, I expect?'

'Sibella will be reading in her room,' Rodriguez said. 'She is constantly improving herself. Always a book in her hand. She reads in English as well as French and Spanish,' he added proudly.

He made no mention of Elena and Edward gave a small sigh of reprieve, though he found it odd that Rodriguez did not remark on Elena's accomplishments if he wanted to marry her off.

'Newmarch!' Rodriguez appeared to hesitate. 'Would you think me very inhospitable if I excused myself and left you to be entertained by my wife? I have brought much paperwork with me and if I work on it tonight I shall be free tomorrow to entertain you and show you the rest of the estate.'

'Oh, Sancho! You are so naughty,' Sofia pouted. 'Meester Newmarch doesn't want to talk only wiz me!'

'On the contrary.' Edward smiled. If Rodriguez was foolish enough to leave his lovely wife with him then he must suffer the consequences. His previous fears of being tempted by Sofia and

190

found out by Rodriguez had dissipated and melted away. The lure of Sofia, the seduction of her, was what he wanted more than anything else. 'I would be delighted, señora.'

'It is a beautiful night, Ed-ward,' Sofia murmured after Rodriguez had left them. 'There is a moon. Would you like to look at ze garden by its light?'

'Yes,' he breathed and could feel a pulse hammering in his throat. 'I would.'

'Come then.' She picked up a shawl and placed it around her shoulders. 'Just for a few moments as it is quite cold tonight.'

Edward wasn't cold. Quite the opposite. But where was Rodriguez? Upstairs or down? Was he near a window where he might look out and see them?

Sofia led him out of the house by a side door rather than the front, explaining that it was quicker to the garden that way. 'The front is green, what you say – lawn? Out 'ere is my garden where I might walk privately with no-one to disturb me. It is my secret arbour. You like the lovely smells, yes?'

'Yes!' The perfume of exotic blossom lingered on the air. And this is winter, he mused as he breathed in the sweetness. The moon cast its light over the shrubs and flowers which clambered over the arched trelliswork and bowers, turning them to silver.

'In the summer, when it is 'ot during ze day, I stay indoors. But at night I come out 'ere. Sometimes I even sleep outside.' She laughed. 'You see, I am just a peasant at 'eart! Sancho doesn't

191

understand that.'

But I do, he thought. That is her attraction. That is why I loved Ruby, who was a peasant too. The common people have a zest for life, love and passion that their betters do not have, or else keep hidden. But I have it, he thought fiercely, and reached for Sofia.

'I would like to sleep out here with you, Sofia,' he whispered urgently and pulled her towards him. 'But there would not be much sleeping.' Hungrily he sought her mouth, cradling her head in his hands.

'Oh! No!' she gasped, pulling away. 'Not yet. It is too soon.'

'Yes,' he pleaded. 'It is not too soon. I want you, Sofia. Desperately. And I want you now.' He lowered his hands to her shoulders, brushing away her shawl and clasping her bare flesh with flexing fingers. 'Please! Don't make me wait.'

'We must.' Her breathing was fast and her words tumbled out. 'We cannot. Not when Sancho is 'ere! If 'e should find us!' She pulled at his hands, which were unbuttoning her bodice. 'Please. Calm yourself. Come and sit down.'

He allowed her to lead him towards a wooden seat beneath an arch which was covered in trailing greenery, but he grasped her once more when they were seated and ran exploring hands over her breasts.

'No. You must not!' She removed his hands.

'Yes,' he murmured, holding her two hands with his one and keeping her fast whilst he slid the fingers of his other hand beneath her bodice to touch her lissom flesh and search out her

192

nipples. 'I must.' He had lowered his head to take her in his mouth when he felt her suddenly freeze.

'Stop!' she whispered. 'It is Sancho!'

He drew away and Sofia quickly adjusted her bodice. 'My shawl!' she exclaimed softly. 'I 'ave lost it.'

He got up from the seat and slowly moved towards the shawl on the ground where he had carelessly dropped it. His eyes moved about the arbour. The moon threw shadows making pockets of darkness and he hoped that Sancho had not seen them embracing beneath the bower. He retrieved the shawl and crept back to the bench.

'I can't see him,' he whispered. 'But I can smell his cigar.'

She nodded. 'Yes,' she said hoarsely. 'That is what I noticed. Come.' She flickered her fingers, indicating that he should follow her. 'We must walk down ze garden into the open. Then 'e will not suspect anything if 'e sees us.'

He reeled after her, his mind in turmoil, his body quivering and frustrated. Damn and blast Rodriguez. He said he was going to do some work! Does he suspect something? Did my desire for Sofia show?

'We are all right now,' Sofia whispered. 'He will not come down 'ere.' They were in a little orchard where the grass was long beneath the trees and where a wooden cabin stood with its doors wide open. 'If he does I will tell him I am showing you my doll's 'ouse.'

'Your doll's house?' he grunted. 'What do you mean?'

'I told you that I sometimes sleep outside! 'Ere is where I sleep. I 'ave a little bed inside and I keep the door open so that I can smell ze grass and blossom.'

She took his arm and moved close to him. She seemed to have got over the shock of being almost caught out by her husband. 'I will show it to you sometime, Ed-ward,' she whispered. 'When Sancho is not 'ere.'

'When?' he demanded, his desire for her returning. 'Tell me!'

'Perhaps you will stay a little longer after Sancho returns 'ome? Sibella will return with her father for she must study, but Elena and I can stay.' She lifted her face up to him and he kissed her lips. 'We must find a reason for you to stay too.'

CHAPTER SIXTEEN

'*Idiota*,' Sofia hissed at Elena. 'Why did you not come sooner? That Newmarch, 'e is not ze usual Eenglishman. He is very passionate. Phew!' Sofia wafted her hand in front of her nose. 'You stink of *cigarro*.'

Elena grinned. 'It worked, *si*? 'E want to make love to you?'

'*Tst*. Like your grandmother says, you 'ave no manners!' Sofia said angrily. 'Where is your respect? I do this for you, so that you can have your Zac and a dowry.'

'She is not my grandmother,' Elena said sulkily, then added, 'sorry, *Momia*. I was held up by Sancho. 'E wanted to know where I was going,' she grinned, 'and I had one of his *cigarros* hidden behind my back! I told him that if Meester Newmarch asked me to marry him, I would pray that I would make him an obedient wife.'

'What did he say?' Sofia asked anxiously.

Elena shrugged. 'He just laughed.'

Edward rode out with Rodriguez the following morning and covered most of the estate. He was tired when they got back, being unused to riding all day, but had found his talk with Rodriguez most enlightening. His host had told him of the acreage he held, how many servants and slaves he had working for him, of the merchandise which he shipped not only through the American States but also to China, Spain and England.

'This country is becoming more developed day by day, month by month. Men are coming in to search for gold.' Rodriguez had given a dry laugh. 'They do not realize that you do not have to dig for it. What must be done is supply the settlers and their wives with what they need. Ordinary things like wheat and sugar so that their women can cook, cotton so they can make clothes, timber that is already felled and ready for building homes.'

Edward had felt an excitement in the pit of his stomach. That is exactly what I said to Robert Allen! That the men who came to dig would want wheelbarrows, picks and shovels. And yes, he allowed, they would want all the commodities that Rodriguez mentioned too.

'So, have you given further thought to my offer? About the ship?' Rodriguez had asked. 'I must leave first thing in the morning. My banker is coming to see me and he will want to know if I am going ahead. I can, of course, bring in someone else. One of my cousins has expressed an interest. But,' he raised a hand, 'I am rushing you. Of course you need more time to consider. To write to your banker and ask his advice. Stay a few days longer,' he had urged. 'Sofia will look after you, and my mother will stay for propriety's sake.' He raised his eyebrows. 'We must observe cold caution.

'Speaking of which,' he continued, 'Elena will also stay with her mother. She has intimated to me that she looks on you very favourably.' He appeared to hesitate. 'She is young and passionate, Mr Newmarch. I must ask you to respect her naivety if you are swayed by anything other than marriage.'

Edward drew in a breath and said stiffly, 'Be assured, señor, that I would never take advantage of her innocence.' Not if she was the last woman on earth, he vowed.

'I never thought that you would, but she is hot-blooded – like her mother once was,' Rodriguez added. 'But if you have given consideration on the matter of marriage, then,' again came the thin smile, 'our business partnership would have to be reassessed.'

'In what way?' Edward asked.

'It could be part of Elena's settlement, along with the house that she says she wants, and the stables with thoroughbreds.' He spoke genially, as if he was an indulgent father, which Edward knew he wasn't.

A ship. A house. Stables and horses! Edward's thoughts whirled as he bathed and then changed for supper later. His head buzzed. And if I could have Sofia too! How can I possibly refuse?

He was pleasant to Elena during supper and she joined in the conversation, asking him questions about England, the countryside, people and customs, but he was constantly aware of Sofia's arousing presence and Rodriguez' probing gaze.

The next morning after Rodriguez' departure, Elena announced that she would be out all morning. 'I am riding,' she said. 'I will take a servant with me, *Momia*, so you need not be afraid for me.'

Edward saw a shadow of alarm on Sofia's face as she replied, 'You must take care where you go, Elena. There are bandits. You could be kidnapped.'

'Hah!' Elena flashed a disdainful smile. 'Sibella might be kidnapped, but not me.' She lifted her chin and seemed to be about to say something more, when she remembered Edward's presence. 'I shall be well cared for,' she added. 'Besides, who would cross Rodriguez?'

Who indeed, Edward thought as he sipped his coffee. Am I brave enough to risk his wrath by indulging in a liaison with his wife?

'What would you like to do today Ed-ward?' Sofia said softly after Elena had left and there were just the two of them in the sunny drawing room.

Edward put down his cup and saucer. 'Anything,' he said, grasping her hand. 'Anything as long as it is done with you.'

197

'We must be careful,' she whispered. 'The servants! Sancho's mother.'

'Show me your doll's house,' he urged. 'That's what I'd like to see. Would that be possible?'

She held his eyes for a second and then moistened her lips with her tongue. 'It would,' she said huskily. 'But you must promise that you will be good. You must remember that I am a married woman. Sancho is a very important man.'

He kissed the palm of her hand. 'If I have to be good then there is no point in being with you. I might as well go back to New Orleans now.'

'No!' she responded. 'No. Please don't. We want you to stay.'

'We?' he queried.

She shrugged. 'I! You know my English is not good. And Elena too. She will be disappointed if you leave.'

'Will she?' He trailed his fingers down her throat. 'Well, that would never do. Fetch your wrap, Sofia. Come and show me your doll's house.'

The door to the little cabin in the garden was closed and Sofia opened it. 'Someone has been in 'ere!' She glanced around and stamped her foot. 'It is not as I left it. I will find out! Someone will get a beating for this.'

'You can hardly blame them,' Edward said. 'It's very cosy, and private.'

'But it is mine! No-one else must come 'ere. Only when I tell the servants to clean it. No-one! Not Sancho, not Sibella or Elena. Elena!' she breathed. 'It is she!'

'And Zac?' Edward was amused. So the girl really was infatuated by the servant if she would

198

risk coming here. He turned to close the door, shutting out the sunlight. 'Come,' he said softly, drawing Sofia towards him. 'Don't think about Elena. Think on other matters which will please you – and me.'

He unfastened the ribbons on her bodice. 'I want you, Sofia,' he whispered. 'Say you want me too.'

'No!' She stayed his hand. 'You are too quick for me, Ed-ward. I don't know you. You are attractive man, but you are a stranger.' She gazed up at him. There was a flush on her cheeks and, he thought, desire in her eyes.

'How do I know that you won't make love wiz me and then leave?' Her fingers sensuously stroked his wrist.

'I won't. I promise.' He pleaded with her. 'Please, Sofia. You are so lovely.' Gently he propelled her towards the bed. 'I won't leave. I want to be with you.'

She lay down on the bed and let him take off her shoes, lifting one small foot and then the other. 'If I could be sure,' she whispered. 'If you were going to be part of our family – then I would say to you, make love to me, Ed-ward.'

He knelt beside the bed. 'Would you?' he said hoarsely. 'If I married Elena, could I come to you? Could we be lovers?'

She put her arms around him and drew him towards her so that his face was close to hers. 'Yes. We could come 'ere when Sancho was in New Orleans. You would be living up on the hill with Elena. It would be very easy.'

He traced her mouth with his fingers and

groaned softly. 'Elena mustn't find out.'

She gave a hint of a smile. 'She would not care. She would 'ave Zac. But Sancho must not know. He must never know. He would kill you if 'e found out.'

He breathed in. I'm not the bravest of men, but how would he find out? He couldn't. Sofia wouldn't tell him, nor Elena. 'I want you so much, Sofia,' he groaned. 'I would risk anything, even Sancho's anger.'

'Then you will ask 'er? You will ask Elena to marry you? You may ask her first if you wish, as Sancho is not 'ere. I will tell 'im that you asked me also.' She took his hand and laid it on her breast. 'Shall you do this for me?'

'Yes. Yes,' he said urgently. 'I will.'

She let him stroke and caress her, fondling her breasts, stroking her feet and calves and softly kissing her face and throat, but she stopped him short of doing more. 'We must wait.' Her words were breathless. 'I must be sure. I am desirous of you, Ed-ward. But I must be careful. Sancho is cold. He is – *remoto*, yes? He would know if I come to 'is bed full of fire like I used to be.'

'But, Sofia! He's not here!' He could have wept with frustration. 'How can he possibly know? Please. I beg you!'

'He would know.'

She would not surrender and he needed all his will power not to take her forcibly. Goddamn it! He sat on the bed with his head in his hands whilst she put on her shoes. If this had been Ruby! She wouldn't have refused me. Never once did she turn me away! He thought despairingly of

200

his young mistress in England.

'Ed-ward!' Sofia said coaxingly and stroked his hair. 'It will be better for waiting.'

He nodded, then stood up. 'Perhaps we should get back. Could I borrow a horse? I'll go out for an hour.'

'You are angry wiz me?' she said plaintively.

'No. Not angry. Just disappointed.'

He felt like a small boy deprived of a treat. He opened the door and the sunlight streamed in. He looked down the orchard towards the arbour. Sofia came and stood beside him and put her hand on his arm. 'It is lovely, yes? It will be our secret place, Ed-ward. Do not be impatient. There will be other days when we will get to know each other better. And,' she said, 'you could build your own little 'ouse where I could come to you. Not a doll's 'ouse.' She laughed. 'What would it be? A fort, like soldiers have? A hideaway?'

'A den!' he said. 'I had one when I was a boy. Nobody knew about it. It was hidden in the shrubbery at the bottom of the garden. I'd forgotten about that,' he said pensively. 'Quite forgotten.'

'Then you must build another when you are married and have your own 'ouse and land. Sancho will give you land.' She patted his arm. 'I will make sure that 'e does. But be quick, 'e is an impatient man, we don't want him to change his mind about you.' She reached up to kiss his cheek. 'We have much to look forward to.'

Elena returned in the afternoon, cantering up the drive, jumping down and throwing the reins to a boy. There was no sign of Zac, but another servant rode up a few minutes later. Sofia excused

201

herself to Edward and said she must speak to her daughter. 'I will tell 'er that she is found out! She must not use my little 'ouse again,' she said. She turned at the door. 'Will I tell 'er that you wish to speak wiz her?'

'Yes.' Edward had been mollified by Sofia's attention after he had returned from his ride. She had been charming and provocative and at lunch she had fed him, placing pieces of fruit into his mouth, letting her fingers linger on his lips, tasting her wine and then kissing him so that he could taste it too. 'You are a she-devil,' he had groaned and grabbed her fiercely, then hastily pulled away as a servant knocked on the door and brought in more delicacies for them to eat.

I'd better get it over and done with, he thought. I can't back out now. And who's to know? I shan't be going back to England. Only Allen knows my circumstances, of my marriage to May. The thought of Allen gave him some reason for disquiet and he wondered whether he should pay him off. I could tell him that I don't need him any more. Give him extra so that he doesn't feel let down. Then no-one will know anything about me. I'll have a new life. Rodriguez will know of someone reliable that I could employ as a valet. A paid servant of course. I won't have a slave. Definitely not. That really goes against the grain.

'He is ready,' Sofia said to Elena, and sat on a couch in her daughter's room whilst she took off her riding outfit. 'Wear something pretty,' she suggested. 'And take him into the garden for a walk. Only not the orchard, and,' she said sharply, 'not near my little 'ouse. I am cross with you. You know I won't have anyone in there.'

Elena shrugged and held up a plain linen dress. 'I don't suit pretty clothes,' she murmured. 'Anyway there was nowhere else. I needed to see Zac.' She glanced at her mother. 'To tell him something.'

'What? Oh my God! What?'

'I'm not absolutely sure.' Elena pulled the dress over her head. 'But if Newmarch will marry me he had better be quick.'

'Ah! *Dios!* You are so hot-headed, Elena! Why did you not wait?'

Elena smiled. 'I am like you were, *Momia*. Did you not get caught too, wiz me?'

'Yes,' Sofia said thoughtfully. 'And I must be careful not to get caught again. Sancho would not tolerate an English bastard.'

Elena grunted. 'Any more than he tolerates a black one.'

'You are not black,' her mother objected. 'You are quadroon!'

'It's the same thing to Sancho.' Elena brushed her unruly hair and Sofia came to pin it up for her. 'If I had been pretty like you, then he might have accepted me. But I'm not. I suppose I am like my father?'

'Yes,' Sofia sighed. 'You are just like 'im.'

'Meester Newmarch, would you like to take a walk?' Elena met Edward in the hallway and smiled in her most beguiling manner, and Edward inwardly cringed. Thank heavens she has said she doesn't want me to share her bed.

'You 'ave agreed to marry me, yes?' she said without any preamble as they walked down the

203

steps to the lawn. 'You remember that I said you cannot sleep wiz me?'

'Yes, I remember. It's a business arrangement only.'

'And if I 'ave children, you must swear they are yours even if they are not white!'

Edward stared at her. 'But–'

'Sometimes black children are born to parents who 'ave white and Negro blood,' she said. 'It is a – throwback. My father's mother was black.' She stared back defiantly. 'That is all right by me. I am not ashamed, nor will I be!'

'Of course not.' He felt sorry that she had even to say it, that throughout her life Rodriguez had defined her as inferior. 'Why do you want to be married to someone other than Zac?' he asked, as he had asked once before. 'I know that you have said that Sancho won't allow you to marry Zac, but why can't you wait until you are of age and then marry him?'

'We would 'ave no money. No 'ouse, nothing.' Her eyes gleamed. 'Besides, one day Sancho will guess that I have tricked him and I will laugh in 'is face. Ah! Do not be troubled, Meester Newmarch. 'E will not find out about you. 'E will think that you 'ave been tricked too.'

The games we play, Edward mused. Elena will think she is married to me, whereas I already have a wife in England. Rodriguez will pay me for marrying Elena, yet Zac will be sleeping in her bed. And I will become Sofia's lover. What a tangled web! A small doubt gnawed away at his insides. It's like a Shakespearean play. There will be a comeuppance before the final curtain falls.

CHAPTER SEVENTEEN

A messenger was sent to Rodriguez to tell of Elena and Edward's betrothal. He responded immediately, offering congratulations and stating that he would put everything in hand for the marriage to take place in New Orleans.

I must do something about Allen, Edward deliberated, else he might betray me. 'I need to return to New Orleans,' he told Sofia. 'I have things to arrange, the bank – er, a suit of clothes, you know. It will be a quiet wedding, won't it?' he added anxiously. 'In view of my – er, late wife.'

She gave a peal of laughter. 'Oh, Ed-ward. You don't know Sancho. 'E doesn't do anything quietly. 'E must be seen to be generous to Elena. And do not worry about your suit of clothes. Sancho will take you to his tailor. There will be no expense spared. We will come wiz you to the city. We must order Elena's gown and somesing beautiful for me also.'

'You need nothing to make you more beautiful,' he declared fervently. 'You are quite perfect.'

They travelled back the following day, the three women and Edward, and some of the servants on top of the carriage with the driver. I haven't had a chance to be alone with Sofia since the announcement, Edward pondered. Rodriguez' mother had always been there, or else Elena, or one of the servants. There had been a hustle and bustle around the house and even the servants and slaves were always in attendance on him, following him wherever he went and assuring him of their attention and service.

When he arrived back at his hotel, Allen wasn't there. He enquired at the desk and the clerk said he had seen him go out that morning. Edward was annoyed, for he had been rehearsing what he would say to Allen regarding his dismissal. He waited around for a while then hailed a cab to take him to the bank, and on to Rodriguez' house as arranged, for Sofia insisted that he should stay with them whilst plans were being made for the wedding.

Elena was very excited at the prospect of marriage, and her animation made her look quite attractive. It is probably true, as Carlos de Lassus said, mused Edward, observing her, that Elena will change when away from Rodriguez' influence.

'We must hold 'ands sometimes,' she whispered to him. 'So that people will see. Only not when Zac is around for 'e will be very jealous.'

I'm between the devil and the deep blue sea, Edward pondered. I seem to be getting deeper and deeper into deception and intrigue, and I fear I am losing my wit and my reason. He sighed. And all for Sofia. I want her. I must have her. And, if I am honest, which I am not always, I want the riches that Rodriguez is offering. I am greedy for them. So damn the consequences.

He went back to the hotel the following day and found Allen in his room. Edward asked him where he had been the previous afternoon, and he explained that he had been to see the doctor.

'I'm sorry I missed you, sir, but I felt ill. I would have gone to visit him before except that I was expecting you back.'

'Yes – well, I was asked to stay on,' Edward said vaguely. 'So what's wrong with you?'

'It's the malaria again. The doctor said it's bound to flare up from time to time.'

'But it's winter!' Edward protested. 'There can't be so many mosquitoes around now.'

'It's because I had a bad dose of it. I haven't properly recovered. He says to go and see him again in another month.'

'Look here, Allen,' Edward began. 'I'm going to be away for a few weeks. I, er, I've been invited to a wedding.'

'You'll want extra clothes packing then, Mr Newmarch,' Allen said. 'I'll make sure they're all pressed and ready. You could do with some more shoes, lighter-weight ones, sir. Yours are too heavy for this climate. Cravats, lawn shirts, stockings.' Allen ticked off on his fingers what he thought Edward would require. 'I'll get them for you on approval.'

Edward was shamed into silence. Damn it, I do need him for a while longer. I'll give him notice later.

'You must come to see our ship,' Rodriguez said one evening as they were dining. 'She is moored along the levee.' He made an expressive gesture with his fingers and mouth. 'She is *magnifico!* Made in your country. In Bristol. All iron with six masts. We shall change her name to *Sofia* in honour of my wife.'

'Wonderful,' Edward exclaimed. 'I shall look

forward to seeing her. Cargo weight?' he enquired.

'Eight hundred tons. And cabins for three hundred passengers!' Rodriguez allowed himself a smile of satisfaction.

Edward was impressed. To be part owner of so fine a vessel! It must surely be worth a little disquiet and uneasy conscience for such a venture?

'We must go back to the country soon,' Elena said. 'I want to show Ed-ward where we build my – his 'ouse.'

'Yes. Yes,' Rodriguez said tetchily. 'But your mother has to arrange the ceremony, see the priest, send out invitations and a hundred other things. There is much to do here.'

The priest! Edward drew in a breath of alarm. That means vows. Declarations! His wedding to May had been fairly quiet and decorous with only family and close friends attending. But this ceremony is apparently going to be a very grand affair. What will I do if Allen should hear of it and announces that I am still married?

'Are you not well, Meester Newmarch?' Sofia asked. 'You have gone quite pale.'

'No! Yes! I am quite all right. A touch of malaria, that's all,' he lied. 'I got a dose of it on the ship.'

'You must always sleep beneath a net,' she tutted, then gave him a little smile. 'At all times.'

The thought of sleeping beneath a net with Sofia made him grow hot so that his face flushed.

'You see, Sancho,' Elena said, observing Edward's discomfort. 'The climate in New Orleans does not suit Ed-ward. We must go back to the country. The air is much better there.'

'Would it not be simpler to be married in the

208

country?' Edward ventured. 'A quiet wedding ceremony?'

There was a sudden stillness and they all stared at him. Then Rodriguez broke the silence. 'I have my position to think of, Mr Newmarch. Business associates will expect to be invited. And all of my family.' His voice was cold. 'And although Elena is not my natural daughter she will be accorded the same honour as if she were.'

Edward cleared his throat. He had obviously made a grave blunder. 'I beg your pardon,' he apologized. 'It is at a time like this I realize that I am a foreigner in another land.'

Rodriguez relaxed. 'We are all foreigners, Mr Newmarch. And we do not always follow the ways of this country, though we obey its rules. Elena will have a Spanish wedding, even though she is not Spanish, but we shall observe the customs of *my* country, *my* family. When you are married, you may, if you so wish, follow your own desires or embrace the new life of an American.'

'Two more days.' Sofia chose to intercede. 'That is all I need. I 'ave seen the priest. The seamstress knows what to do. We shall take a few days' 'oliday in the country, Sancho, so that we are refreshed and ready.'

'You have only just come back,' Rodriguez grumbled. 'But go if you must. I shall stay here. I have work to do.'

Rodriguez and Edward rode out the next day to see the new ship, which was lying further downriver waiting for restoration. 'She has had a little damage in the storms, but nothing much,' Rodriguez said. They stood on the levee and gazed at her. 'The Mississippi is not deep enough for her. She has been towed here for repair. She needs new sails and I've ordered a four-bladed propeller to give her more speed.'

Edward had expected a paddle steamer such as the one which had brought him to New Orleans, but this was a big vessel capable of voyaging in any deep seas. 'She's a fine ship,' he declared. 'What do you intend to carry?'

'Mormons!' Rodriguez replied. 'They hire a whole ship to carry only them. They sail from Liverpool or London to New York. They pay their fares and are no trouble. They pray constantly for their deliverance, which means that the ship will arrive safely back in harbour.'

He stood with his arms folded and watched as another ship, a paddle steamer, came upriver. 'Then,' he said, 'they change ships and some come to New Orleans, as you did.'

'And they use your other ships!' Edward said.

'One of them,' Rodriguez agreed. 'Not the one you used, but the other one. They prefer to have it to themselves so that they do not disturb anyone else with their praying.' He nodded. 'They are good well-meaning people,' he commented. 'Confident in their belief. But I regret to say that they are following the wrong religion!'

This man, is immovable, Edward thought. He would not budge one inch on custom, religion or business matters if he thought he was right. God only knows what he would do if someone crossed him. I suspect he would not care too much if he found out about Elena and Zac once she was safely married, but if he found out about Sofia and me! Phew! Perhaps I should escape whilst I can! Pack my bags and go. He would never find me, not in this vast country.

But Sofia was waiting for them when they got back and announced that they could go to the country, that she had made all arrangements and could not do more for the moment. He succumbed to the fascination, the lure of her and the promise of fulfilment now that he was officially betrothed to Elena. The vows he had made to his wife on their wedding day meant no more to him now than they had when he had taken a mistress in England. And it escaped his reasoning that in going through a marriage with Elena, he would be breaking the law.

'Meet me tonight at your doll's house,' he whispered to Sofia on the first evening back in the country. 'You promised.'

'I cannot,' she hedged. 'It is not the right time for me. I am of child-bearing age, you know!'

'When?' he said. 'When?'

'Soon, a few days only.' She seemed anxious, her hands fluttering, her manner nervy. 'Will you ride wiz Elena? She wants to show you the land where you will build your 'ouse.'

'Will you come?' He couldn't bear not to be with her.

'No.' She gave a little sigh. 'I 'ave a 'eadache. I must rest. It is the worry of so many things to do.'

Elena was waiting for him with a horse already saddled. He was rather perturbed to find Zac there too on a powerful stallion. 'Is he afraid I might take advantage of you?' he gibed.

'Yes, I sink so,' she said cheerfully. 'I told him

that you would not, but 'e did not believe me.'

Incredible, Edward thought moodily. That Zac should be so jealous. She's the last woman that I would want to take to my bed.

They rode along the valley where they had had the *barbacoa*, then followed a track to the top of the grassy hill towards the tree line. From there they looked over acres of cotton and cane fields and in the distance could see the wide brown ribbon of the Mississippi.

'Here would be the ranch 'ouse,' Elena said and rode her horse in a wide arc. 'There will be windows on all sides so that we can look out over the cotton fields. There,' she pointed with her whip, 'will be the stables for our 'orses. And here,' she indicated a bank of trees, 'Zac will have his 'ouse.'

Edward glanced at Zac who was sitting quite still, listening and looking. We'll see about that, he thought. Zac needn't think he's going to be master just because he's sleeping with Elena. Oh dear no! It will be *my* house, *my* land and, although I don't mind turning a blind eye on occasions if they indulge in a little intrigue, *I'll* make the rules, whether Elena likes it or not!

By the end of the third day he was bored. The weather was as warm as the month of June in England. He had enjoyed the luxury of lazing in the sunshine, though Sofia had laughed at him from beneath her parasol, saying that only Englishmen would do that, and he had relished being waited upon by servants who brought him cool drinks, hot spicy coffee, titbits to nibble and cigars to smoke. But now he was restless: his nearness to Sofia, breathing in her perfume, watching her lips as she spoke, filled him with an urgent desire.

'I must take a walk,' he said, getting up. 'To stretch my legs.' He held out his hand. 'Come with me.'

'It will soon be time for supper,' she demurred.

'They won't start without us,' he insisted. 'Come.'

She smiled and gave him her hand to help her up from the cushioned cane chair. 'Just a short walk, then,' she agreed. 'To the arbour.'

She grumbled, for the grass was wet. There had been torrential rain the night before, and although the day had been sunny a warm haze clung to the trees and the bowers, so that as they brushed past them they were showered with droplets of fine mist.

'I am wet,' she complained. 'My shoes!'

'Then I will carry you,' he said, and before she could dissent he picked her up and carried her towards the orchard and the cabin.

'No, Ed-ward, we must not! It is too danger-ous,' she protested.

'It is not.' He held her firmly. 'You said that no-one ever came here.'

He pushed the door of the cabin wider with his foot and went inside. It was quite dark and smelt slightly damp and steamy, but somehow this increased his desire for her. He kicked the door closed and, placing her on the bed, unbuttoned his jacket. He knelt at the side of the bed. 'I have been very patient, Sofia,' he murmured. 'You know that I have, and you did promise.'

She gazed at him and he saw uncertainty on her face. She bit her lips together. 'I don't know if it is right,' she began. 'If Sancho should find out.'

'But you said,' he began unfastening her gown, 'you said that when I am married to Elena we can meet whenever Sancho is in New Orleans.' He slipped her bodice off her shoulders, revealing her smooth pale breasts. He bent to kiss them. 'And he is in New Orleans now.'

'But,' she objected breathlessly, 'you are not yet married to Elena.'

'But I will be.' He gently pushed her down onto the pillow. 'In no time at all, so why wait? I can't wait, Sofia. I want you. Must have you. Now.'

CHAPTER EIGHTEEN

Though she fought him to begin with, her objections eventually gave way and she responded. 'You are a good lover, Ed-ward,' she whispered. 'I did not expect it from an Englishman. You 'ave roused me as I 'aven't been roused in a long time. Not since Brown,' she admitted. 'He was a good lover, though impatient.'

'And Sancho?' he asked. 'You said that he'd rescued you from Brown!'

'So he did. But 'e treats me always as a lady.' She smiled seductively. 'And now you know that I am not a lady.'

He nodded and heaved a sigh of satisfaction. She was not. She was a tigress. Once she had succumbed to his advances she had surprised him by her passion. It was as if it had been bottled up,

214

waiting for someone to spring the cork, and she had taken his breath away.

'Will you come back later?' he asked. 'Tonight when everyone is in bed? Please!'

She hesitated, then said, 'Yes, all right. You must use the side door, but be careful, the night servants don't sleep. They are on watch until sunrise.'

He crept downstairs at one o'clock as arranged, but found his way barred by a young black boy sitting by the door. 'I can't sleep,' Edward said brusquely. 'Let me out, please. I'm going for a walk.'

'You want me come wid you, Meester Newmarch?' the boy asked.

He can't be more than twelve, Edward thought. How can he be on guard? Though I suppose he would be able to run fast to fetch help if there were intruders. 'No,' he said. 'But don't lock me out.'

He walked down through the arbour and into the orchard and wondered how Sofia could come out without being seen. He waited for a few minutes within the shadows of the cabin and then saw someone approaching. It was not the dainty form of Sofia, but the plodding figure of Elena.

'What–! What are you doing here?' Then he saw the young boy behind her.

'Ssh!' She put her finger to her lips and entered the cabin. 'It is all right. The boy comes with me for protection. 'E thinks I come to meet you secretly. My mother will slip out of the door whilst he is 'ere wiz me.'

Edward was astonished and not a little alarmed. Why did Sofia tell her daughter that she

215

had arranged to meet him? What on earth was she thinking of?

Elena waited ten minutes, sitting on the bed and breathing heavily. Then she stood up. 'It is enough time I think for us to 'ave – what you call it? Coupled? Yes? The boy, 'e will remember. I go now. Then my mother comes.'

What's happening? What game are they playing? He peered down the orchard towards the arbour as Elena and the boy returned to the house, then was suddenly startled by Sofia coming round the corner of the cabin.

'We must not be found out,' she whispered. 'Elena will give the boy somesing to do, to keep 'im busy until we return.'

'Sofia!' he said, taking her in his arms. 'There must be some other way without telling Elena.'

'It is all right,' she murmured. 'I tell 'er that we only talk.'

'Hah! I'm sure she'll believe that!' But he was distracted by her sensuous fingers exploring beneath his shirt and unfastening his buttons, and with a groan he sank onto the bed and pulled her on top of him.

'Your wife?' she said, moving her body slowly across his. 'Was she good lover? Better than me?'

'May? No!' He ran his hands over her smooth skin, over her breasts and belly, and down to her frizzy bush. 'She isn't. Not like this.'

'She was cold English woman? So you take a mistress, yes?'

'Yes,' he breathed, consumed with craving. 'I did. She's beautiful just like you.'

'Why you not bring 'er wiz you?' She slid off

216

him so that he could come on top of her.

'She wouldn't come,' he grunted. 'Don't talk. It's past. Enjoy now.'

But she persisted as later they lay on the narrow bed with their arms entwined about each other. 'And your wife, she know about your lover? But she not angry wiz you?'

'Oh, yes.' He laughed softly as he remembered. 'She was angry all right. Furious!'

'Even though she not want to make love wiz you herself? I not understand!'

'It's the way she has been brought up.' He put his hands behind his head and considered. 'She hadn't been told what to expect, so I suppose she was shocked. And I suppose she might have been jealous of Ruby when she found out. She called her all kinds of names.'

'Perhaps you should have tried 'arder wiz her. Though not everyone 'as this passion inside.' She clutched at her breastbone in emphasis. 'Sancho 'as not got it, except for business,' she added.

'Oh, May definitely hasn't got any passion,' he said thoughtlessly. 'Not like you – or Ruby. She never will have. Not in a million years!'

She studied him in the half-light. 'What you say? I sink your Eenglish is not right!'

'What?' He turned to her, smiling, but saw the concern on her face. 'What do you mean?'

She half sat up, leaning on her elbow and staring at him. 'You say, she 'as not got any passion. You should say, she 'ad not, yes?'

He was startled. What a fool to make such a mistake. 'It – it was a slip of the tongue only,' he said with a half-laugh.

217

'No.' She moved away from him. 'It was not! You say also that it ees the way she 'as been brought up. And, she *isn't*. It is, er–' She struggled to find the right words. 'The present! You speak of your wife as if she is alive. But she is dead, no? You say that you are in mourning.'

He saw perception dawning on her face and he knew that he could not deny it. Besides, his conscience churned, he had stated that his wife was dead. He had never given her a name. Could he now, after talking of May and naming her, could he coldly deny her existence? Am I so hard and calculating that I can do that?

'Sofia!' He reached out in an attempt to pacify her, but her brown eyes flashed with sparks of amber.

'No,' she snapped. 'You tell me! Is your wife dead, or do you tell lie to me?'

'She is not dead,' he admitted. 'She's alive in England. I left her.'

'*Bastardo!*' She slapped his face. 'You Eenglish bastard. You trick me!'

'Ow! Sofia! It wasn't like that. I didn't mean to trick you!' His face smarted. 'It just got out of hand.'

She curled her fingers into a claw and struck out again but he caught hold of her. 'Listen to me!'

'No,' she screeched. 'You listen to me. You promise to marry Elena but you are not a widower like you say!'

'No-one would know.' He struggled to hold her fast for she was lashing out like a wildcat. 'How would anyone find out? Nobody knows me.'

She gasped. 'You would marry in church?

218

Before God and the priest? In front of everyone? You not care about that?' She stopped her assault and stared at him. 'What kind of man are you?'

He stared back and let go of her. 'The kind that you wanted for your daughter! Why did you want me, Sofia? Why, on such a short acquaintance, was I persuaded to marry her? It wasn't just so that you and I could become lovers!' he taunted.

'I will tell Sancho,' she hissed. 'He will kill you.'

'Oh, yes!' he said with a pretence of irony. 'Does he kill everyone who crosses him? Will he kill you when he finds out you've been here with me?'

She hit out again and caught him on his chin, scratching him with her nails. 'He will not find out. I tell 'im you tried to seduce me!'

'You didn't take much seducing,' he said with sarcasm. 'You were quite willing.'

'I did it for Elena.' She raised her head and glared at him. 'Sancho says we must find a 'usband for her. She is difficult wiz 'im. He want her to go. He will give a dowry if she marries well, but not if she marries a servant.'

'Well then,' he said. 'You tricked me, didn't you? You came to my bed to persuade me to marry Elena. Would you have continued the affair once we were married?'

She gave a little shrug. 'Per'aps. Per'aps not. I don't know,' she pouted. 'But now you 'ave spoilt it.' Then she raised her hands to her mouth in alarm. '*Dios!* What will we do?'

Hurriedly she slipped on her gown and shoes and snatched up her shawl. 'I will ride to New Orleans in the morning and tell Sancho! You 'ad

219

better hide, Meester Englishman.'

'No. Wait. Sofia!' he pleaded. 'Can we not resolve this? Let Elena decide. She must be the one to say she will not marry me.'

'She is foolish girl,' she said bitterly. 'She will say we will not tell that you are still married. I know her, you see.'

'Well then–!' he began, when they heard a sound outside the cabin.

'*Momia.*' Elena's whispered voice came from outside. 'You must be quick. The boy, 'e wants to lock the door. I tell him I can't sleep, I must walk in the garden.'

Sofia spoke in rapid Spanish to Elena and although Edward couldn't understand, he knew full well what she was saying.

'You are still married, yes?' Elena came into the cabin. 'Your wife is not dead?'

He shook his head.

'You cannot marry me like you said?'

'I'm sorry, Elena. I just got carried away by the thought of living here, and,' he added defensively, 'you both did your best to persuade me.'

'He must marry me.' Elena turned to her mother. 'No-one will know about 'im and if they find out afterwards there is no shame on me.'

'You heathen,' Sofia spat out. 'It is not possible.'

'*Si*,' Elena said eagerly. 'Then I will 'ave my 'ouse and my land and he can leave if 'e is found out, and the child will 'ave his name.'

'Child? What child?' Edward stared from one to the other. 'Don't tell me–!' He put his hand to his head. 'That's why you needed a husband! You were going to say the child was mine! And I

220

thought I was devious. What a farce!'

'I am going to bed!' Sofia stormed to the door. 'I will think what to do in the morning.'

'Señor – Meester Newmarch,' Elena said as her mother flung out of the door. 'I don't care that you are still married, though it was better that you did not tell me. I must 'ave my 'ouse for when my child is born. Sancho will not give it to me if 'e thinks that it is Zac's child.'

She raised her hands in an expressive gesture. 'I must say that you 'ave your way wiz me otherwise. The boy saw us come 'ere,' she added. 'Sancho will be very angry.'

Edward recoiled in horror at the threat. Things were getting worse and worse. He was sinking ever deeper. Whatever should he do?

'Tomorrow we speak again,' she said. 'If we both tell my mother that we shall be married, she will not do anything. She will not tell Sancho.' She gave a sly smile. 'I know that she will not. I see 'er come here to you. She will not tell.'

'My God! What a kettle of fish,' Edward muttered as he got back to his room. He sat on the bed for a moment whilst he attempted to put his thoughts in order. *I must have been crazy to contemplate marriage.* Suddenly everything came into focus. *If I marry Elena I shall be a bigamist! I wonder what the punishment is for that in America. But if I don't marry her she will say that I have seduced her and given her a child! Sofia may say that I attempted to seduce her too, which will add weight to their story.*

He took a deep breath. *There's only one thing to do. Escape! But how?* The doors were guarded both front and side. The door at the back was the servants' entrance and he was sure that there would be staff there. The window! He got up and drew back the curtains, opened the casement and looked down. His room was at the side of the house, facing the arbour and orchard, and although it was a long drop, the walls were smothered in creeper with thick and sinewy old stems.

Quickly he gathered up his belongings and stuffed them into his bag. 'It's now or never,' he muttered. 'I'm damned if I go and damned if I stay. So I'll go.' He moved a chair to the window and placed his bag on it, then gingerly, for he had never been very athletic, he put one leg over the window sill, reached for his bag, lowered his head and shoulders and started to heave himself out of the window.

He paused halfway. Why am I bringing the bag? It's cumbersome and contains only clothes. Nothing that I can't do without. He thrust it back through the window again, then, with both hands free, began his precarious descent. He managed to cling on fairly easily until he got to the last few feet, when a thin whippy branch pulled away from the main stem, snapping beneath his weight and plummeting him down onto the gravel below.

He paused for only a second to get his breath back, then scrambled to his feet and, with aching and jarred legs from the fall, stumbled round to the stables. The horses within the loose boxes snickered at his arrival but he clacked his tongue and spoke quietly, trying to see the mount he had ridden when out with Sofia.

'Good fellow,' he whispered on finding him, and looked about for a saddle. He found several, neatly hanging on the wall with bridles, stirrup irons and a shelf of leathers, whips and grooming brushes. He chose the high pommelled saddle he had used previously, which Sofia had told him was the most comfortable for long journeys.

The sky was light though it was the middle of the night. Soothing the horse, he led him down the drive, anticipating constantly that there would be a shout for him to stop. He reached the gate and to his relief there was no guard on duty. He lifted the iron bar securing it, swung open the gate and, still murmuring to the horse, walked out, carefully closing it behind him.

A vivid dawn was breaking as sweating and saddle-sore he reached New Orleans, though thick black clouds were rolling in from the Gulf of Mexico and towards the Mississippi. He rode towards a hostelry close to the Rodriguez' house and called to a stable boy. 'Do you know Señor Rodriguez?'

'Sure.' The boy gave a grin. 'Everyone knows him.'

'This is his horse.' Edward slid stiffly down, his knees buckling beneath him. 'He lent it to me. Keep it here until he comes for it. It's too early to go to the house,' he added, seeing the question on the boy's face. 'Give him a good rub down, will you?' He gave the boy a coin. 'If no-one comes for him by tomorrow, take him up to the house.'

Don't want to be charged with horse stealing as well as everything else, he deliberated as he hurried on his way. Now I just hope that the hotel doesn't lock its doors.

The hotel door was open and there was no-one at the desk as he sidled in. He ran upstairs to his room, throwing off his coat and unbuttoning his shirt as he entered.

'Who's there?' Allen, in his nightshirt, burst in from the adjoining room. 'Oh, sir! You startled me. I thought it was an intruder.'

'Get dressed, Allen, we're leaving.' Edward opened his wardrobe door to take out another shirt.

'Leaving, sir? Has something happened? I thought you were going to a wedding?'

'Changed my mind. Things didn't turn out as expected.' He suddenly felt exhausted and plumped down on the bed. 'God, Allen! I've had such a terrible time.' He bent down and put his head in his hands. 'I'm a fool. I've got myself into such a scrape. There was this woman, you see—'

He proceeded to give Allen a sketchy outline of what had happened, missing out the affair with Sofia and emphasizing that Elena wanted to marry him so that she could give her child his name. 'She's going to say the child is mine, which it isn't, so I left. By a window! And Rodriguez is sure to come after me, so we have to leave immediately. I'll pay the bill and we'll go. Get your things. Come on, start packing!'

'Could I just think about this, sir?' Allen said slowly. 'Does Rodriguez know what has happened?'

'No, not yet, but he will before the day is out.' Edward gazed at Allen. 'I've just had an idea too.

He'll expect that I'll come back here to collect you and my belongings. I wonder–?'

'Yes, sir?'

'Would it be better if I travelled alone rather than two of us travelling with several trunks? Yes,' he decided. 'I think it would. If I go now before he knows anything about this shambles, I could be miles away. And if he comes looking for me you can say that you don't know where I am.'

Allen agreed that this would be a better idea. One man and his servant, plus several pieces of luggage, would be easily recognizable. Besides which, he had no desire to be caught up in Newmarch's shenanigans.

'And,' Edward warmed to his theme, 'I'll borrow your clothes.' He quickly shed his fine cotton shirt and linen trousers. 'Lend me yours, there's a good fellow. They'll be looking for a gentleman, won't they? Not someone dressed as a valet.'

Allen silently handed over a shirt, jacket and trousers, which Edward put on. 'Bit short in the leg,' he said, viewing himself in the mirror. 'But never mind. Right – money in my pocket. Enough for about a couple of weeks or so. Shouldn't be any longer than that. They'll soon get tired of searching. You keep my papers with you. For heaven's sake don't lose them or we're sunk. There. Now I have no identification on me. Nothing to say I'm Edward Newmarch. To all intents and purposes I'm Robert Allen.'

'One moment, sir.' Allen left the room and went into his, coming back with a ticket in his hand. 'The ticket from the voyage. Second class. It has my name on it.' He couldn't help the sarcasm in

225

his voice but Newmarch didn't seem to notice as he postured in front of the mirror.

'I'll wait here, then, shall I?' Allen asked.

'Yes. I don't know what you'll do with your time. Look at the ships maybe?' He paused. 'I was nearly the owner of a ship,' he said regretfully. 'Ah well!'

He slipped down the stairs, keeping his head lowered as he saw the clerk coming out of his cubbyhole behind the desk. He had no clear idea where he would go but hurried along the road towards the river. A boat. I'll catch a boat and move out of New Orleans for a few days. He patted his pocket where his money was. I hope I've brought enough with me. Still, if I travel second class...

The rain started to fall as he scurried along and looking up he saw the dark clouds directly overhead. Should have brought an umbrella, he thought, but then, do servants carry umbrellas? I've never seen Allen with one, except when he's brought one for me.

'Morning!' A deep voice greeted him. 'You're out early this morning, sir.'

He glanced up and recognized the swarthy fellow who had once offered him a ride in a boat.

'Yes,' he said, not stopping. 'I'm trying to catch an early boat.'

'Going anywhere special?' The man caught up with him.

'Erm, just upriver,' he answered nervously, not liking the stranger's close presence.

'I've got a friend with a boat. Cap'n Mac. Take you anywhere you want, mister. No questions asked and take you fast if you in big hurry.'

'Oh!' Edward pondered. I shouldn't accept people at face value. He can't help looking so ugly and dangerous. He's probably a good family man. 'Well, yes, I am in a bit of a hurry.'

The man nodded and held Edward's elbow in a firm grip as the clouds opened up and torrential rain pelted down. 'Come with me. Better run, she'll be pulling off any time now.' He hurried him, not towards the wharfside, but further along the levee where there was a cluster of broken-down cabins within a sparse wood of spindly trees and several piles of felled timber. 'You got some cash?' he asked.

'Yes,' Edward shouted above the sound of the storm. 'Only enough for second class.'

The fellow roared with laughter. 'There's only one class on this boat, mister. There she is.'

Edward peered ahead. A dilapidated paddle-wheel barge with peeling paintwork on its hull and deck lay where his companion was pointing. The embankment was high at this point and the boat's stern was low in the water. 'Is she sea-worthy?' he yelled. 'She doesn't look very safe.'

'She ain't going to sea,' was the answer and he was pushed from behind whilst a rough-looking man on board, wearing oil-stained twill dungarees and peaked cap, grabbed his arm to pull him down on the deck. 'Get below if anyone's chasing after you,' he directed. 'I'll say you're not on board.'

Edward wiped the rain from his face as the boat scraped and creaked, and, with much grinding and clanking and clouds of steam, pulled away from the levee towards the middle of the river.

'Thanks,' he said. 'How far are you going?'

'Depends,' said the man.

'Well, I don't have a great deal of money.' He put his hand into his jacket pocket, and finding it empty put it in the other one. That too was empty apart from the ticket which Allen had given him. 'I've been robbed!' he gasped. 'That fellow!' He stared back at the levee, but the man had gone from sight. 'Do you know him? Is he a friend of yours?'

'Nope. Ain't never seen him before. You lost your money, mister? Or did you get on my boat under false pretences?'

'No. No, I didn't. I had money until that fellow asked me if I wanted a boat! You'd better take me back to shore and let me off.'

'Can't do that, mister. Can't turn this old girl around. You've got to travel along whether you want to or not. Unless you want to swim with the crocs.' He grinned malevolently. 'And if you can't pay for your passage, then you'll have to work for it. So git bailing, mister.'

CHAPTER NINETEEN

'And that's the last time I saw him.' Allen finished his tale of Edward Newmarch's disappearance. 'I waited for over a month but he didn't come back. Rodriguez came looking for him. Oh, not himself of course, but two of his men, and villainous characters they were. I tried to convince them

228

that I didn't know where Newmarch was, but they were hanging around the hotel every day waiting for him to come back, and the management were getting jittery and asked me to leave. I was glad to go in any case, as the bills were getting bigger and bigger, so I paid from out of the money Mr Newmarch had left, found some rooms and moved in there.'

'He might have come back and not been able to find you,' Georgiana commented.

Allen shook his head. 'I left a forwarding address at the hotel and I went in several times to ask if they'd heard from him. But there was nothing. I took a job as a porter to pay for my rooms, but the Negroes and quadroons made life very difficult. They said I was taking their livelihood, so after another month I decided to move on.' He shrugged and said defensively, 'I had no identification of my own, only the papers belonging to Newmarch, and I reckoned that if he was playing at being a valet, then I could pretend to be him.

'I wanted to travel light so I sold some of his things. I've still got the money,' he added, 'but as he owed me my year's wages I felt this was within my right. I dressed in his clothes as he'd taken mine and set off back to New York.'

'How very extraordinary,' Georgiana said. 'It's so preposterous that it could be true!'

'Oh, it's true all right, but as to what happened to him, I can't tell you. I asked around New Orleans. I went down to the wharf to ask if he'd taken a boat passage. But no-one had seen him, or said they hadn't, and he hadn't booked a ticket, not in my name or his own.'

'Well,' Georgiana said reluctantly. 'Perhaps I owe you an apology, and I give it. I beg your pardon if I doubted your integrity, but you must see how it appeared?'

'I do! But just to ease your mind further, I've told Bill Dreumel about it,' he said. 'He guessed there was something wrong when you and I met at the Marius. He's an astute man and asked me if I knew you. I gave him the story as far as I knew it on our journey here.'

'Except that he's not here!' She raised her eyebrows questioningly.

'No. We parted company at Trenton. He has a newspaper company in Philadelphia and needed to go there first. He'll be back here within the week, I expect. Now, if you'll excuse me, Miss Gregory.' He eased himself up from the chair as if he was aching. 'I need to wash and eat and go to my bed. I've had a hard day.'

'There's something cooking on the stove,' she told him. 'If you can stay awake long enough perhaps you'd like to eat with us? Kitty is making soup and dumplings.'

He stopped in his tracks and his eyes grew large. 'Soup and dumplings!' He licked his lips. 'You mean, real food? Not dry tack?'

'Yes. I don't know how she's managing it but she says that she can!'

When Georgiana next looked out of the cabin door, she saw him swimming in the creek, dipping and diving, disappearing beneath the water, then reappearing. She glanced again and saw, to her great amusement, two other men jump in. Both were quite naked, their white bodies gleaming in the half-light.

Kitty had made a cauldron of onion and barley soup with dumplings floating on top. Isaac had caught a fish, a large one with sharp silver scales, which he cleaned and gutted and which Kitty then floured and fried. She had also made a batch of bread. "'Tis Irish soda bread,' she said proudly. 'I found baking soda and I remembered my mammy making this when I was just a little bairn.'

'Just the other day, then, was it?' Jason grinned. He was one of the men Georgiana had seen swimming in the creek. The other man was Ellis. Both had been working at the mine with Robert Allen, or Ted as they knew him, for as he had explained to Georgiana earlier, he had not felt comfortable with the pseudonym of Edward and had decided to shorten it.

'Well, ladies.' Isaac looked up from his dish and wiped his bearded mouth with the back of his hand. 'If it was up to me, you can stay for good and need never go home, wherever home might be.'

'It was in England,' Georgiana said. 'Now it's wherever we happen to be. So right now it's here, wherever this is,' she added.

'It's Dreumel Creek,' Robert Allen replied, and Georgiana tried her best to think of him as Ted. 'Though there's a big question mark as to how much longer we stay. The mine has just about run out,' he explained. 'Most of the men who were working here have left. There's just me, Jason, Ellis and Pike, who's up there now on guard.'

'So what's he guarding if the mine has run out?' Kitty asked perceptively.

'Equipment.' Ted glanced at her. 'Bill Dreumel and Charlesworth have spent a deal of money on laying the claim, buying pumping machinery – sinking a shaft and timbering it. And paying the men. Then we've put up these shanties. We only had canvas tents to begin with but it was so cold in winter. But we've to guard the claim in case somebody else comes along.'

'So all of that will be dead money if the gold's run out.' Jason's words were thick as he munched a mouthful of bread.

'Why are you still here?' Georgiana asked him. 'Why didn't you leave like the other men?'

'Don't know!' Jason dipped a crust of bread into his tin bowl and wiped around it, soaking up the last of the soup. 'Just a feeling, I guess.' He was a young man, maybe nineteen or so, with thick dark hair and a merry grin. 'I suppose I just want it to succeed. Dreumel's a great guy. He has – well, vision, I suppose, so I'll stay until he says it's all over.'

'And I've nowhere else to go,' Isaac said, and feeling in his waistcoat pocket he brought out a blackened clay pipe.

Georgiana and Kitty glanced at each other. The longhouse was warm and smelled of wholesome bread and barley. It was now about to be filled with the odour of tobacco.

'Isaac!' Kitty got up from the table to serve the fish. 'How would you like it if I made some sweet bread tomorrow? Sweet honey bread?'

Isaac's mouth dropped open and he drooled. 'Oh, Miss Kitty! I ain't tasted a piece o' sweet stuff in I don't know how long.'

Kitty gave him a big smile. 'Well, all right then. There's plenty of flour. I'd make a cake only there's no butter.'

'There's a can of corn oil, miss,' Ellis, who had said very little so far, chipped in. 'Would that do?'

'I don't know,' Kitty said dubiously. 'But I could try it. There's just one thing though.' She raised a finger and shook it at all of them. 'I don't allow smoking in my kitchen – or spitting,' she added. 'So if you want to eat cake you'll have to smoke outside.'

Isaac stared at her. 'No pipe?'

She shook her head. 'And no spitting,' she repeated. 'Not inside.'

Georgiana hid a smile. She was amazed at Kitty. Everything they had done or been through since leaving England, the girl had taken in her stride. No complaints or moaning. She'd just got on with whatever she had to do. And now, within hours of arriving here, she had taken charge and was giving out orders to these men.

When they had finished eating, all the men except for Ted went outside and Georgiana and Kitty started to clear away, though each man took his own bowl and tin plate to wash in the creek. 'I'll give you a hand,' Ted said, and filling a pan with water from a bucket he put it on the stove.

'I wanted to ask you something,' he said to Georgiana. 'Although Dreumel knows my story, the other men know me as Ted Newmarch, an immigrant from England. A miner. They've no reason to doubt who I am and I'd rather they didn't know. If they heard I was just a valet, I'd never hear the last of it and they wouldn't trust

233

me up at the mine.'

'So you want us to call you by the name of Newmarch?' Georgiana said. 'It won't be easy, considering that the real Edward Newmarch is married to my cousin!'

'You could try calling me Ted.' He looked at her with an anxious appeal in his eyes. 'Otherwise I might as well pack up and leave. And I've worked hard on this project.' He suddenly sounded bitter. 'For the first time in my life I've done something that *I* wanted to do, not just to earn a living, but because I felt it worthwhile. And,' he went on, 'I don't want to let Bill Dreumel down. He's given me a chance, you see. He's trusted me, even when he found out I wasn't who I said I was.'

Georgiana studied him and it was then that she realized that he was only young, maybe twenty-one or -two, younger than her, and as she looked at him in his working clothes and with a rough scrubby beard, he seemed vulnerable. And his present life was in her hands.

'Well,' she said. 'There's no advantage to me in the men knowing who you are. I came here because I thought you were depriving someone else of their identity, my cousin of her rights, and even betraying Mr Dreumel.' She saw him bite his lip and take a deep breath. 'So unless you are a consummate storyteller, I'm quite satisfied on all of those points,' she continued. 'And Edward Newmarch has apparently gone to where we can't find him.'

Relief flooded his face. 'Thank you, Miss Gregory. I do appreciate that. I'll be honest with you. I had no intention of staying on with

Newmarch. I took advantage of his offer to come to America but I was going to leave as soon as the time was right.' He gazed keenly at her. 'He's an arrogant swaggering fool and a philanderer, but I don't wish him harm. If ever you write to your cousin, you can say quite honestly that her husband seems to have disappeared off the face of the earth.'

'Mm.' Georgiana was thoughtful. 'I don't think so. This is such a vast country, he could be anywhere, and there is no knowing whether he's alive or dead. You say you've still got his papers and pocketbook?'

'Yes, he'd been to the bank just before he disappeared, but I've used most of that money on my wages and paying the hotel bill. There's not much left. There are notes of credit – you can have those,' he offered, 'though I'd rather keep the papers as proof of identity.'

'I don't want them,' she said. 'If there had been anything worth having I would have written to his wife to tell her. As it is,' she added, 'I think we'll forget about him for the time being. He was always going to be trouble. I suspected that from the first time of meeting him.'

Would I have been so open back in England? she thought. Would I have had such a conversation with a former valet? I am amazed at myself. 'We'd better just get on with our lives, I think,' she advised. 'What mine or Kitty's will be I don't know. We'll just take each day as it comes.'

'If you don't mind my saying so, Miss Gregory,' he said awkwardly, 'I think that you're very brave.' His face flushed at the acknowledgement.

'I was wrong about you,' he admitted. 'I didn't think that a lady such as yourself would have had the courage or determination to set off on such a journey with only a maid for company.'

'Oh, Kitty's not a maid any more,' she said. 'She's a companion! And I must confess that I had underestimated her worth when I asked her to come with me. I knew her to be reliable but I hadn't realized how dependable she would turn out to be. I wouldn't have got so far without her. She's been my strength, she's cheered me up and not once has she said that she wants to go home.'

'How much we've all changed,' he murmured. 'Out here I feel the equal of any man.' He gave her a fleeting grin. 'And I never thought that I'd be speaking to a lady of your class in such a manner.'

'You didn't know me, that's why,' she answered. 'I haven't changed all that much but I was as restricted by convention as you were. You may not have known it, but in England I was an active campaigner for the rights of women.'

'I'd heard something,' he admitted. 'But I thought that you were only amusing yourself with the latest fancy! I'm sorry.'

The next morning, when Georgiana and Kitty awoke, the three men had already left for the mine, Isaac remaining behind to guard the camp. 'Pike will be down later,' he said. 'He'll be coming for breakfast and a sleep.'

'I'll make some gruel, shall I?' Kitty asked. 'And some more bread?'

When Isaac eagerly nodded, she said, 'You'd best keep the stove in, then, Isaac. Could you

236

make that your job? See that it doesn't go out?'

'I'd sure be glad to! I get darned fed up here on my own with nothing to do all day. Nobody to talk to. It'll be mighty good to have some company.'

Whilst Kitty organized Isaac and the kitchen, Georgiana saddled up Hetty and rode towards the mountain which led to the mine. The meadowland on either side of the creek was lush and green, with the scent of wild sage. As the slopes rose higher, the terrain changed from bracken to a covering of fir and pine trees. At the end of the valley a trail which had been made by the miners led up the mountain and, although it looked easy at the base, higher up were large boulders which appeared to block the way.

The creek was narrower at this end, its flow coming from a gap beneath the rocks. So what is at the other side of the mountain? she pondered. Where is the creek's source? And where does it go to at the other end of the valley?

She would have to cross the creek to peer beneath the gap to find out where the waters were coming from. The waters rushed and frothed as they escaped, and, reluctant to get wet as she hadn't a change of clothes, she decided that she would leave the exploring for another day.

Such a beautiful valley, she considered as she cantered back, letting Hetty have her head. It seems almost a pity that it is hidden away.

Pike appeared a little later in the morning. He was a thickset man with bulging muscles and a scarred face. On Georgiana enquiring if he had had a quiet night up at the mine, he replied that the only thing that had disturbed him was a lone wolf. 'He nodded a greeting to me,' he said laconically, 'and I did the same. Then he went on his way.'

'You didn't try to kill him?' Kitty asked fearfully.

'Nope,' he said. 'We just let each other be.'

'Hope you don't regret it,' Isaac rumbled. 'Danged critter will probably come back for you!'

'Guess I'll be ready for him if he does.' Pike tucked into his gruel. 'He'll know that. I ain't a woodsman fer nuthin'.'

As the sun began to sink that evening, Isaac woke Pike from his sleep to go back to his shift at the mine. It was his week to do the night shift. Kitty had cooked rice which she had discovered in a sack beneath some boxes when she and Georgiana were sorting out in the longhouse. Isaac had caught another fish, which she'd cooked, flaked and added to the rice.

'It's rather plain. It would be good to have vegetables to go with it,' she said. 'But the only way we can have them is to grow our own.' She glanced at Georgiana. 'And I don't know if we're staying that long.'

'Wish you were, little lady.' Pike licked his lips. 'Folks would come flocking here just to sample your cooking.'

Kitty went pink with pleasure at the compliment and Georgiana, who was leaning on the door watching the skies turn red and orange over the mountains, turned and said, 'Well, we'll soon know if we're staying or not. Someone is driving a waggon down the valley, and I think it's Wilhelm Dreumel.'

CHAPTER TWENTY

Dreumel's expression was one of astonishment and disbelief on seeing Georgiana and Kitty. He took off his wide-brimmed hat and ran his fingers through his hair. His face was dusty from travelling. 'But how–? It is impossible. I cannot believe it! Someone brought you? Was it Lake?'

'Yes.' Georgiana started to explain as Kitty went off to make a pot of coffee. 'But we came part of the way alone. Mr Charlesworth gave me a map–'

'What! Charlesworth suggested that you should come alone?'

Georgiana saw that he was more than a little annoyed by that, so she hastily reassured him that Mr Charlesworth hadn't had any option. 'I intended to come anyway,' she said. 'I will explain why in a moment.' They sat on a wooden bench outside the longhouse and she continued. 'We travelled by canal boat and then by coach to Duquesne, then quite by chance called on a wheelwright to ask if we could hire a horse and trap. Except that he didn't have a trap, just an old dog cart, and a horse called Henry.'

'Ah! I see now! So Henry brought you! But not all of the way?' His pleasant face had a crease of anxiety above his nose.

'No, we met with some Iroquois Indians, Dekan and Horse, and they took us to No-Name, where we waited for Lake. He brought us on the last part of the journey,' she said. Then, seeing the look of disquiet on his face, she apologized. 'I'm so sorry if I have blundered into your private affairs, Mr Dreumel, but I felt at the time that it was very important to speak to you.'

'No! No.' He brushed aside her apology. 'It is not that. I am only thinking how very perilous it was for you and the young lady to travel alone. This can be a very dangerous country.'

'Perhaps we were fortunate,' she said. 'Our only frightening experience was when we had to spend the night in a drivers' cabin and the next day we thought that the mare had escaped. After that we were in good hands, though we were very tired.'

'I am surprised that Lake agreed to bring you,' he murmured.

'He didn't make any objections,' she said, 'though he wasn't very happy about my bringing Henry. But may I ask how you came into the valley? Not over the mountains? Ted said that you have been to Philadelphia.'

'Yes. I have,' he agreed. He didn't give her any details and raised his eyebrows in enquiry at her use of Allen's pseudonym of Ted. She explained. 'We have spoken at some length. He has told me that he has given you the truth of himself. I came to warn you of him.' She dropped her voice as Isaac went past with wood for the stove. 'I thought you were being deceived by an impostor.'

He leaned towards her. 'Are you telling me that you travelled here because of that? For no other reason?'

'What other reason would there be?' She was vexed and spoke rather sharply. 'I thought he was

240

taking advantage, not only of you, but of my cousin who is married to the real Edward Newmarch. I had to stop him!'

'Of course. Of course!' he said hastily. 'But he has explained the circumstances and I believe him. I want to believe him,' he added, and she realized that he was a most trusting person and would probably expect everyone to be as honest as he was.

'Yes,' she agreed. 'I think that I do too. I suppose taking Edward Newmarch's identity was the only option open to him, if what he says is true, even though it was wrong.'

'And what will you do now, Miss Gregory? Now that you have fulfilled your mission and found that the blackguard has not taken advantage of me?' He smiled as he spoke and she thought he was laughing at her.

She straightened her shoulders and looked directly at him. 'It was potentially a very serious situation,' she said coolly. 'You could have been swindled.'

'Ah!' As if realizing his error, he was contrite. 'I do not doubt it and I am more than grateful for your concern, but apart from giving me a false name and background, he has, I believe, been honest about everything else.'

'His mining background?' She was still slightly put out.

'An exaggeration, I agree. But he has more than made up for it with the hard work he has done on my behalf. Without pay,' he added. 'Only his board. I have promised him only a share in the venture if we succeed.'

'I see,' she said, prepared to be mollified. 'He obviously believes in what you are doing.'

'And he has stayed,' he said seriously, 'in spite of the news.'

'About the mine running out?' she said. 'You must be very disappointed.'

'Not just the mine.' He gave her a questioning glance. 'Do you remember that I left you a letter at the Marius telling you that I had heard some disturbing news and must leave New York?'

She said that she did and thought that it was news of the mine.

'No. Whilst I was staying in New York,' he went on, 'Ted had driven to Philadelphia to collect supplies and pieces of machinery that I had ordered. It takes several days from the valley to reach the Philadelphia road. When he arrived in Philadelphia, which is a big city, the whole place was buzzing with the news that the Pennsylvania Rail Road Company is planning to cross the plain linking New York Central with the Ohio and Mississippi valleys, right up to the Erie Canal.'

He ran his hand over his face, then looked up as Kitty came out with a lantern, for it was now getting quite dark. She also brought coffee and a piece of honey cake. 'Ah,' he said, taking a bite. 'This is like my mother used to make.'

He took a sip of coffee. 'This is good,' he said appreciatively. 'Very good. Anyhow. Ted went to enquire at the railroad office and to ask if he could see a map. When he saw it he realized that the railroad would come right alongside the mountains.' He indicated with his hand over to the eastern end. 'Perhaps even through the moun-

242

tains, opening up the whole of the territory.'

'That would ruin the valley!' she said.

'It would; the area would be flooded with railroad workers. I realize that there are plans to cross the whole country by railroad, but I wanted to breed cattle here. I can't do that with a railroad running through!'

He sighed. 'It's another blow. First the mine drying up and now this. I never expected to make a big strike from gold, but I'd hoped that what we got from it would pay for the cattle. Charlesworth, though, has put money into the mine and I'm sure he'll pull out when he hears this latest news and buy railroad shares.'

'There must be a way around this,' Georgiana said. 'If you own the land, surely the railroad company can't come onto it?'

'If it's in the way, they can. If it's only a small community, then they'll ride roughshod over whoever owns it. The only hope I have,' he said, 'is that federal law states that a railroad connection must be completed within six years, and eastern railroad builders don't have much capital and need government subsidy.'

'Have there been surveys?' she asked. 'Does anyone know that you are here?'

'Someone must have been up here, otherwise there would be no plan of the proposed route, but maybe they didn't find this valley, only the mountains surrounding it. And the only people who know we are here are the Land Registry officers from when we made our claim and bought the land.' He laughed. 'It could be anywhere. I simply stuck a pin into a map and said this is where it is!'

'Couldn't you open it up?' Georgiana said thoughtfully. 'Open up the road where you came through from the plain and turn this hidden valley into a place where people want to live?' She saw the doubt on his face and pointed across the creek, which was now just a darkly shimmering streak. 'Build a bridge across to the other side. You could still have your cattle; there's plenty of pastureland.'

He looked at her with interest. 'Sometimes, you know, it is not possible to see what is in front of you. You have vision, Miss Gregory!'

'I'm simply seeing it from a different point of view.' She smiled. 'It's such a beautiful place it seems a pity not to share it. You could build cabins here.' Her voice rose in enthusiasm as the idea took hold. 'Not like you have now, but better ones where families could come to start a new life! There could be shops – stores as you call them – an hotel, a saloon bar. If there was a thriving settled community here, then the railroad company would have to divert their tracks.'

'Yes,' he agreed. 'I am following you. And if the railroad was nearby, people and freight would travel by rail instead of waggon. But,' he grew despondent again, 'I don't have any spare money to build cabins.'

'You've got the timber,' she said, looking up the hillside at the dark tree line. 'You just need the men to build them. Advertise,' she said eagerly. 'You've got a newspaper! Sell parcels of land and the timber and let people build their own home-steads.'

'We will talk again tomorrow,' he said. 'Come.

You must be getting chilled, and,' he sniffed, his head in the air, 'I can smell food cooking. The cook must have returned!'

'No, he hasn't,' she replied. 'That's Kitty's cooking that you can smell. It will be something simple as there are hardly any provisions.'

'Ah!' he exclaimed, banging his forehead with his hand. 'I am a *dunderhead*. I've brought supplies! Meat, flour, tea, sugar, corn oil, cookies. Isaac,' he shouted. 'Unload the waggon. We'll have a foodfest!'

When Ted Newmarch, as Allen called himself, came down from the mine, he told Dreumel that there had been no more than five dollars' worth of gold that day. 'We need to sink another shaft,' he said. 'This present one is useless. If you'd blast open the little canyon further up, I'm sure we'd get a strike.'

'Charlesworth will be here soon,' Dreumel said. 'When he arrives, we'll talk about that, but we'll need more men and more money. If Charlesworth doesn't want to go ahead, then we'll have to wind up.'

Kitty had made more barley and onion soup for supper, and had sliced up some of the salt beef that Dreumel had brought and cooked sweet potatoes and beans.

'You're a good cook, Kitty,' Ted remarked. 'You must have been watching Cook in the kitchen.' He stopped in confusion as he remembered who he was supposed to be. He had almost let slip that he already knew Kitty and Miss Gregory. Jason, Ellis and Isaac were seated at the table and none knew his real background.

Kitty smiled and blushed. 'My ma used to make a meal out of practically nothing,' she said. 'There was never much money coming in. I used to send my wages home once I'd gone into service.'

'I heer'd times is bad in England.' Isaac gulped on a tankard of beer. Dreumel had brought a cask and also a bottle of Dutch gin. 'I heer'd as poor folks is starving and beggin' in the streets.'

'It's true that there are many poor people in England,' Georgiana interspersed quickly; she'd seen Ted open his mouth to speak and wanted to get in her views first, not to contradict but to compare. 'But we saw people begging in the streets of New York when we arrived. It seems that there is no answer to the problem of poverty.'

'And no-one understands the poor unless they've been poor themselves,' Ted chipped in, glancing at her. 'No amount of reading on the subject could prepare anybody for experiencing it. There was a British poet – a woman, Letitia Landon – who said, "Few, save the poor, feel for the poor," and she was right.'

What misconceptions we have of people, Georgiana thought as she returned his gaze. I would not have considered him a thinking man. How wrong I was.

'Larnin', that's the answer.' Isaac nodded his head knowledgeably. 'If you have edication, you can do anythin' at all. Why, if I'd had it, by now I'd have had my own little cabin with a rockin' chair on the porch, 'stead of being here scratching out a livin' in the middle of the wilderness.'

'Why did you come, Isaac?' Kitty asked. 'Did you come for gold?'

'Sure I did. Bin all over lookin' fer it. Trekked over mountains and through river beds. Took a waggon one time, stocked it with tools, biscuits and meat, then one of my horses died on the trail. Fair wore out she was. I joined a pack train. Took up claims, pitched my tent, dug and panned, lived on bread 'n' beans, but never earned more'n a hundred dollars.' He coughed and cleared his throat as if to spit, but then thought better of it. 'Went to Californy in '49, but every strike I got to had just run out. Thousands of men, there were, all lookin' fer the yeller stuff.' He shook his head and sighed. 'I'm gittin' too old fer diggin' anyway. Then I met young Ted here on the trail and he said they wanted somebody smart to keep guard on a camp. I reckoned I could do that well enough.' He gave a yellow-toothed grin at Dreumel. 'And Bill here says I'll git a percent' of whatever they bring out.'

'Might not be much, Isaac,' Dreumel warned. 'We told you that there's been nothing much for weeks. Now with the news of the railroad–'

'Better git blastin', then,' the old man said. 'Afore them railroad folk come and do it for you.'

The next day Wilhelm Dreumel asked Georgiana if she'd like to go with him up to the mine. The other men had already gone ahead. They started at dawn and didn't finish until dusk. 'Yes, please,' she said. 'I would like to see it.'

Kitty didn't want to go. She said she would rather stay at the camp and sort through the groceries. Dreumel laughed and said he would make her *kwartier-meester*.

'What does that mean?' she asked.

'You are in charge,' he explained. 'You are the officer who looks after the provisions and feeds the men. I regret, however, that I cannot pay you,' he added.

'Oh, I don't want paying,' she answered cheerfully. 'I'm enjoying myself and what would I buy if you did? Besides,' she said, 'Miss Gregory pays my wages.'

'You could buy a piece o' dirt and start diggin'.' Isaac had overheard the conversation. 'You jest might find gold.'

'I'd be better off planting potatoes,' she told him. 'Come on, Isaac. Will you give me a hand with these sacks?'

'She's a good girl, that one,' Dreumel said as they saddled up the horses and prepared to leave. Georgiana agreed that she was. Kitty had cleaned out their cabin, washed the grubby blankets that had been left and hung them out to dry in the sun. Isaac had removed the tools which the previous occupant had left lying around, and the cabin was now habitable even though they couldn't quite call it home.

The sky was a brilliant blue and the creek sparkled as it rushed along. 'Where is the creek's source?' Georgiana asked as they cantered by its banks. 'And where does it fall?'

'It's a tributary,' he said. 'And eventually falls into the Ohio river. But its source,' he pointed ahead to the mountains, 'the head waters, are somewhere beyond these mountains. But you will see when we come to the end of the valley that in fact it isn't the end.'

'I rode down here,' Georgiana said. 'But I could

248

only see where the waters ran in through the gap beneath the rocks.'

'You have to ride into the water to trace it. Don't worry.' He smiled. 'It isn't deep at that point! But that is for another day. Today we'll go to the mine so we must climb a mountain.' He looked across at her. 'I hope that Henry is capable of it.'

'She's called Hetty now.' Georgiana patted the mare's neck. 'And I trust her to climb anything.'

When they reached the end of the valley, Dreumel said, 'You will see as we climb where the creek comes through the rock. That is the canyon which Ted mentioned yesterday when he said we should blast through. If we do, we will alter the water flow and it will run swifter, maybe even flood the valley.'

'Unless you open up the rocks at the other end to let it out,' Georgiana said. 'But that would be major work!'

'Oh, we can do it,' he said. 'The men are experienced in explosives, but it's a big undertaking.'

They climbed upwards on the track which Georgiana had previously seen. Dreumel pointed out blackened areas where small explosions had been set to clear some of the bigger rocks, to make the route easier. The trail wound upwards, then curved back when the sheer face of the mountain wall made it impossible to climb. Then it wound back again to become a more accessible terrain.

Georgiana grew hotter and hotter and Dreumel, seeing her discomfort, passed his hat for her to wear. 'We have been up here in the winter, when the snow was so thick and the air so cold that we couldn't feel our frozen feet,' he said. 'And sometimes we had to stay at the mine for weeks when we couldn't get down.'

They reached a plateau and halted to look back and give the horses a rest. Behind them was the valley and the camp alongside the creek. Georgiana could see figures moving about which had to be Kitty and Isaac, but from up here were so small as to be unrecognisable. She looked down to where the creek flowed into the valley, filtering through a narrow canyon, splashing and gurgling as it forced its way through the rocky outcrop. Her gaze followed its course back down the ravine to trace its wellspring, and she opened her eyes in astonishment as she saw another wide valley with elk grazing on the grassland and a river running through it.

She gasped and looked at Dreumel. 'But this is as big as your valley! This is another secret place, enclosed by the mountains!'

He nodded. 'I don't know why it hasn't been found. There are land speculators all over the region, and have been for half a century, but somehow this has been missed.'

'And Lake showed it to you,' she murmured, taking in the lonely splendour.

'How did you know it was Lake?' Surprise showed on his face. 'Did he tell you?'

'No,' she confessed. 'He only said that a half-breed had shown you the valley in return for his life. I guessed that it was his life he was meaning.'

'It was,' he agreed. 'But I don't talk about it. I did nothing more than any other man would do.

250

Let's move on.' It was as if he was embarrassed and wanted to change the subject, and Georgiana reluctantly withdrew her gaze from the vale below. Looking up to the rugged mountain above them, she urged Hetty onwards.

CHAPTER TWENTY-ONE

They climbed for another half-hour and then began the slow descent down a track which wound round the other side of the mountain to lead them towards the second valley. From their high vantage point, Georgiana could see a shaft with a windlass over it and at its side a towering pile of broken rock. The area was strewn with mining equipment: troughs, sluice boxes, rocker frames, picks and shovels. Water ran in streams from the surface of the hillside down into the creek. To one side, away from the working area, a canvas tent was pitched and a small fire burned beside it.

Dreumel cupped his hands around his mouth and hailed. A man's head popped out of the tent, then the rest of him emerged. It was Ted. He waved an arm in response. In his other hand he held a beaker from which he took a drink. Jason appeared from behind a rock, buttoning up his trousers, and Ellis was half hidden by the windlass wheel.

'You amaze me, Miss Gregory,' Ted said in a low voice as they arrived, and she guessed that he

251

was conscious of the other men's presence. 'You're quite an intrepid woman.'

She slid off Hetty's back, hot and sticky but glad of the loose cotton garments which Dekan's wife had loaned her and which she was still wearing. They were stained and creased but very comfortable.

'Yes,' she admitted. 'This is not how I would normally have spent my day had I been in England! But then yours too would have been very different,' she couldn't help slyly commenting. 'I imagine,' she added, for the benefit of the other men.

'Sure, we'd all have been doing somep'n else,' Jason chipped in. 'I'd have been on the farm helping out my pa. He was right mad at me when I said I was setting out to look fer gold. Intended going to California but I ran out of money afore I was two days out of Virginia!'

'Why didn't you go back home?' Georgiana questioned, and gratefully accepted a scalding hot cup of coffee from Ted.

'And have my mammy and pappy laugh and say told you so? No, ma'am! I lived rough fer a while and then met up with Pike and we travelled together. Then we came across Mr Dreumel, who asked if we'd like to join him and Ted in a mining exploration, and we came on up here.'

Georgiana leaned against a rock and watched the men as they discussed the day's activities. They gazed into the shaft, scratching their heads, and then looked down into the valley. Dreumel came across to her. 'I'm going down with Ted to look at the canyon. It's difficult, we can't take the

252

horses, but if you think you can manage it–?'

'Yes,' she said without hesitation. 'I'm sure I can.'

There was no regular path, only a rough trail made by the men on previous journeys down to the creek. She slipped and slithered, for it was mainly scree on this side of the mountain, with many sharp rocks which cut into her boots. Her hands were scratched and bleeding as she clambered after the men, but she insisted she was all right as Dreumel constantly looked back enquiring after her. She was determined to make the descent on her own, without asking for assistance.

The creek, wider in this vale, foamed and swirled around the rocks which formed the canyon, its undertow spinning into a whirlpool before gushing through the narrow opening and into the next valley. Dreumel and Ted ventured into the water, balancing precariously on the rocks in the deep current.

'There's barely room for a man to get through,' Dreumel called as he peered into the gorge. 'But I can see to the other side.'

Ted joined him and after a moment's hesitation Georgiana took off her boots and followed them. The water was ice cold, which at first was refreshing but then numbed her toes. Ted put out his hand to help her across and this time she didn't refuse assistance. As she joined them, close to the whirling vortex, she bent to look through the canyon where the water was surging, splashing great plumes of spray high up the rocky walls. Its exit opening up, it fell into the other valley in a bubbling, sparkling cascade.

Dreumel waited for her as she sat down on the hillside and put her boots back on. Ted started the climb back up to the mine. 'Ted wants to sink another shaft but also blast through this canyon, so that it will be easier for us to get to the mine. It wastes time climbing up and down the mountain and it's difficult carrying supplies,' Dreumel told her.

'He really believes in this, doesn't he?' Georgiana said as she pulled her boots onto her cold wet feet. 'Why is he so convinced that there is gold here?'

Dreumel shook his head. 'He thinks it's right down below the bedrock. He can't give a rational explanation; just a feeling he has. Believe me,' he said, 'I would have given up by now, but he's so sure, I feel I would be letting him and the men down by abandoning it. But,' he took a deep lingering breath and put out his hand to help her up, 'if Charlesworth isn't willing to go ahead, and we'll need more money for explosives and equipment, then I can't carry on. I am a cautious man, Miss Gregory. I have mortgaged the Marius. I dare not mortgage my newspaper business, for I shall have nothing left.'

The following day when the men, including Wilhelm Dreumel, but not Isaac, had gone up to the mine, Georgiana decided to wash her clothes. 'I don't think I am nice to be near, Kitty.' She laughed. 'So I will wrap one of those clean blankets around me and wash this shirt and skirt.'

'I was thinking 'same, Miss Georgiana,' Kitty said. 'About myself, I mean,' she added hurriedly. 'So give them to me and I'll give all our clothes a

254

dip in the creek. There's some soap, so I'll give 'em a scrub.'

'Do you think–?' Georgiana spoke thoughtfully. 'Do you think we could get rid of Isaac for an hour and take a dip ourselves? Wouldn't that be nice?' she added with a wide smile.

'Ooh, miss.' Kitty put her hand to her mouth. 'Could we? Dare we? Would anyone be able to see – the men, I mean, up the mountain?'

'No!' Georgiana assured her. 'Not from up there. Besides, they're on the other side of the mountain and won't be coming down until this evening.'

'All right,' Kitty said. 'I'll send Isaac off fishing. He'll be glad to go because I'm allus finding him jobs to do. He grumbled yesterday after Mr Dreumel made me his *kwartier-meester!*'

Isaac went off happily with a wooden rod and a line fashioned out of twine, a piece of rotten beef and sardines for bait, and a net. 'I'll do what I can,' he said. 'I ain't promising nuthin'. I'll go upstream anyhow, away from you chattering wimmin.'

'He'll have a sleep in the sun as well, I expect.' Kitty laughed as she watched him go, and they both turned back into the cabin to undress.

Georgiana kept on her underdrawers and chemise and carried her clothes for washing under her arm, but Kitty, on reaching the creek, pulled her shift over her head and impulsively jumped naked into the water, then came up shrieking and spluttering, her eyes tight shut and her arms and legs flailing.

'Oh!' Georgiana gasped softly. Dare I do that? She looked warily around. When she had assured

Kitty that no-one would be watching, she hadn't thought of being stark naked.

Oh, heavens, she thought. Why ever not? She pulled off her chemise and unfastened her drawers, and with a swift backward glance slipped them down and plunged into the creek.

The freedom she felt as the water slid over her bare flesh was something she had never before experienced. A warm bath in a tub, with a maid holding a bath sheet at the ready to cover her nakedness, was not the same. Not in the least, she thought, as she submerged completely and the cool water floated over her head. I now feel totally liberated.

'Miss – miss!' Kitty called as Georgiana rose up gasping. 'Oh, I thought we were going to drown!' She was doing a frantic doggy-paddle, thrashing the water with the flat of her hands and kicking wildly with her feet. 'Can you swim?'

'I can, after a fashion.' Georgiana breaststroked to the side of the creek. 'We were at Scarborough one year and I went into the sea in a bathing machine and someone taught me.' She laughed and ducked her head under again. 'But it wasn't like this,' she spluttered, coming up for air. 'We were fully clothed in our bathing dresses.'

'I've never swum before.' Kitty doggy-paddled to the bank, where she pulled their clothes into the water and proceeded to rub them. 'Some of 'bairns used to swim in river Hull, but my da said I hadn't to. Full of disease, he said, and besides,' she pulled a face, 'there was all sorts of stuff floating in it. I wouldn't want to tell you what, miss.'

'I can guess, Kitty,' Georgiana interrupted. 'You

don't need to explain!' She rolled over onto her back and floated, wondering vaguely what Kitty would think of her apparent abandonment, but Kitty seemed quite unperturbed and continued chattering as she, as naked as Georgiana, dubbed and rubbed at their garments.

Georgiana looked up at the blue sky and the mountains as she floated and pondered on how she had changed since coming to America. Or have I? she mused. Am I the same person that I was, but taking advantage of the opportunities that have arisen? Certainly if I was still in New York, then I would have to behave with more decorum than I do out here in the wilderness. But in this vastness there seems no point in being particular about niceties.

She rolled over and looked down the creek towards the mountain where they had had their first glimpse of the valley. Part of it was in shadow as the sun rose higher in the sky, but close to its base she thought she could see movement. She trod water and narrowed her eyes. A wolf? No. Not in daylight. A horse! Two horses! And people riding them. She gave a shriek. 'Kitty! Someone's coming! Quick. Quick!'

Her sense of liberation fled from her as they both splashed and hauled themselves out of the creek. 'The blankets!' she shrilled. 'Where are the blankets?'

'Oh, miss. We've left them back at the cabin! I'll run.'

Kitty, naked and pink as the day she was born, scuttled back to fetch the blankets to cover them, whilst Georgiana slipped back into the water.

257

The riders, still a good way off, had crossed the creek and were heading down the grassland towards the cabins.

'Here, miss.' Kitty clutched her blanket around her and held out another. 'Quick. Quick. They won't see anything. Look, I'll hold the blanket out like when you get out of the bath.' But Kitty found that impossible as she wrestled to keep her nude form covered, and Georgiana grabbed the blanket as she leapt out of the water and wrapped it around her.

'It's Lake,' Kitty said, 'and another gentleman! And we've no more clothes to put on!'

'Mr Charlesworth, I think,' Georgiana replied, glancing towards the approaching riders. 'And our clothes will soon dry if we spread them out. But not where they can see them,' she said hastily. 'I do not want them to see my underdrawers!'

Kitty started to giggle and picking up the bundle of wet clothing dashed away behind the cabin, leaving Georgiana to hurry, in as dignified a manner as was possible, to untangle her wet hair and adjust her blanket ready to meet the visitors.

'I beg your pardon, gentlemen.' She stood at the cabin door as they rode up. 'I'm afraid you have caught me at a disadvantage. If you would care to go to the longhouse, Isaac will be back soon and will offer you refreshments.'

She was aware of how fatuous her greeting sounded and of how both men were staring at her. Charlesworth's eyebrows were raised in astonishment, whilst Lake's eyes, wide with undisguised amusement, coolly roved over her, from her hair hanging in wet tendrils around her

258

face, to her bare shoulders and down to her feet.

Kitty suddenly appeared at her side. She had acquired a long shirt from somewhere which covered her completely and hung around her ankles. 'Gentlemen,' she said, her voice wobbling as she tried to contain her laughter. 'If you will come with me, I'll make you a pot of coffee,' and she marched purposefully on bare feet, red wet curls bobbing, towards the longhouse.

Mr Charlesworth tapped his leather hat at Georgiana as he moved away, but Lake sat still on his mount for a moment longer, just staring at her. Then he nodded. 'You look good, lady,' he said in a low voice, 'a fine woman.' As he rode off he added laconically, 'That blanket suits you.'

'Do you think they saw us from up the mountain, Kitty?' she asked when the girl came back after giving the men coffee.

'They'd have to have good eyesight, Miss Georgiana.' Kitty laughed. 'Maybe Lake did, but Mr Charlesworth's a gentleman so he'd never admit to it.'

'Mm.' Georgiana brushed her damp hair and pinned it up. 'I'm not too sure about that. Charlesworth had a gleam in his eye that I didn't care for. I hope they don't laugh about it with the other men,' she said crossly.

Kitty shrugged. 'Well, we're covered up now, and, miss, you're not showing any more than if you were wearing one of those ballgowns that you sometimes wore.'

'No,' she replied. 'That is perfectly true. But I was never afraid of a ballgown falling down as I am with this blanket.' Georgiana hitched it up.

259

'Where did you find the shirt?'

'I think it's Isaac's.' Kitty giggled. 'I remembered that I'd seen it the other day when I was tidying up. It is clean,' she added. 'Well, almost.'

By the time Dreumel and the other men came down the mountain, Georgiana had put on her newly washed clothes. They were still damp and clung to her body, but she felt more comfortable and less embarrassed as she again greeted Charlesworth and Lake, apologizing for her previous appearance.

'Apologies are not necessary, Miss Gregory.' Charlesworth bent over her hand. 'Rather it is we who should regret coming upon you so suddenly. Certainly you would not have expected company.'

'Indeed not.' Georgiana glanced at Lake, who was honing a knife as he sat on the bench outside the longhouse door. He cast a brief look at her and she saw a touch of humour around his mouth.

Damn him! He did see us from the mountain. He must have eyes like a hawk! She felt a flush rise to her face and, embarrassed, she excused herself and went off to speak to Dreumel.

Kitty and Isaac cooked supper. He'd caught fish and she persuaded him to help her fry it. He grumbled constantly. 'I nivver thought I'd be doing wimmin's work,' he complained. 'I came here to guard the camp.'

'But the other cook was a man, wasn't he?' Kitty asked him. 'And if I show you how to do it now, when Miss Georgiana and I move on, then you'll be able to do it yourself.'

'Move on?' He blinked at her. 'Move on where? Shucks, I thought you were staying on here!'

'Well, we can't stay here for ever.' She flipped the fish over. 'Miss Georgiana will want to go to other places, I expect.'

Isaac went to the door and called out to where Georgiana was sitting on a bench with Dreumel, Charlesworth and Ted. 'Miz Gianna. I just heard from this gel of your'n that you'll be movin' on pretty soon!'

'Probably.' She turned towards him. 'There's nothing to keep us here.' She gave a little shrug of her shoulders. 'In fact, I was wondering, Lake, if you would accompany us back to No-Name when you return?' She looked up at him as he leaned against the cabin wall, but lowered her eyes in confusion as she realized that he had been watching her with his dark unfathomable gaze.

'Two days,' he grunted. 'If Mr Charlesworth is ready we go back in two days.'

CHAPTER TWENTY-TWO

Dreumel, Charlesworth and Ted went off early to the mine the following morning. They had talked well into the night, as Georgiana discovered when, unable to sleep, she had risen from the hard bunk and gone to the cabin door and looked out. She had at first smelt the aroma of tobacco, and glancing towards the longhouse she saw the shadowy figures of the men in deep conversation.

They returned down the mountain in the evening and she saw from the expression on each

261

face that the discussions had not gone well. Wilhelm Dreumel's face was impassive, Charlesworth's set as if in stone, whilst Ted wore a look of pure fury. He stormed off to the cabin he shared with the other men, appearing a moment later clad only in a pair of flannel breeches. He raced down to the creek and flung himself into the water.

Georgiana was curious to know what had been the outcome. Would Charlesworth pull out of the venture or not? But she was not at liberty to ask, for, as she quietly said to Kitty, it was really nothing to do with her. 'We'll move back to New York, Kitty,' she said solemnly. 'There is no reason to stay here, which is a pity, for I do rather like it.'

'Oh so do I, Miss Georgiana. But what will we do in New York?' Kitty asked. 'I suppose it will be luncheon parties and supper parties and such-like?' Her mouth turned down at the probability, showing that she was as dispirited by the prospect as Georgiana was herself.

Georgiana sighed. The thought of attending social functions did not appeal, especially if there were people like Mrs Charlesworth in attendance, and poor Kitty, what will she do apart from press my gowns and make sure I have clean gloves and stockings? She looked down at the boots she was wearing on her bare feet, and turned over her hands to examine her fingernails. They were chipped and torn, and her hands were scratched from carrying wood to the stove.

She gave a wry smile. Mr Charlesworth had said to her that he could not see her wearing home-spun or carrying water from a well when she had argued that pioneer women travelled across the country, as she wanted to do. Perhaps it is just a novelty at the moment, she conceded, and I suppose I do like my creature comforts. I cannot say that I am enamoured of having to take a spade to the furthest tree to dig a latrine. She paused in her reverie as she remembered that Kitty had told her what she should do. Kitty seemed to know how to manage these personal matters. She gave another sigh and, turning to the cabin door, she looked out. These last few days had opened her eyes to so many issues, not least of all about herself.

'Miss Gregory!' Mr Charlesworth greeted her. 'I have decided to leave tomorrow. So if we are to travel together perhaps you would be ready?'

'Oh! So soon?' She was disappointed. 'I thought – have you finished your discussions with Mr Dreumel?' she was emboldened to ask.

'Oh yes, there is nothing more to discuss. Dreumel wants to sink another shaft, but in view of what we now know about that fellow Ted, or whatever he calls himself, I am not prepared to take the risk! He plainly does not have the experience as he claims, so I shall pull out.' He lifted his head and looked down the valley. 'I might put my money in the railroads. That seems to be the thing to do.'

Georgiana was aghast. It was her fault! If she hadn't blurted out to Charlesworth about the real Edward Newmarch, he would have stayed in partnership with Wilhelm Dreumel. Ted and Mr Dreumel probably thought of her as an interfering busybody of a woman.

'We will be ready. Will you excuse me, Mr Charlesworth,' she said abruptly. 'I need to speak to Mr Dreumel.'

She walked along the boardwalk to where Dreumel was seated outside the longhouse. He was puffing steadily and contemplatively on a pipe, the smoke curling lazily above him. He took it out of his mouth as she approached, and started to rise.

'No, please don't get up,' she said. 'I – er, I wanted to apologize, Mr Dreumel. I'm so sorry that Mr Charlesworth is pulling out of your venture. I feel that I am to blame for telling him about Ted.'

'Not at all, Miss Gregory. You acted in good faith. It is to your credit that you wanted to see justice done. I was just thinking,' he said, drawing on his pipe again. 'Or debating, perhaps I should say, on whether to borrow against my newspaper and sink another shaft, or whether–' He pulled a sardonic face. 'Or whether I should be blowing up my newspaper as well as the chances of success with another shaft! I must also try to buy Charlesworth's claim or he will sell it to someone else.'

'You must be very sure of finding gold,' she cautioned. 'And can you be? One hundred per cent sure?'

'No,' he admitted. 'I cannot.'

'Kitty and I are leaving tomorrow,' she said. 'Mr Charlesworth says he is going, so we will travel with him and Lake. There is no reason for us to stay,' she added reluctantly.

He nodded. 'I shall be sorry to see you go. It was good to have you here.' He smiled at her. 'To discuss my problems with you.'

'Some of which you would not have had if I

hadn't appeared on the scene,' she said, a little shamefaced.

'Ah!' He made a protesting gesture. 'We would still have had trouble, with the mine, with the railroads. You did not cause those problems!'

'I wish I could help,' she said. 'I really do.'

They were ready for their journey by daybreak. Georgiana and Kitty had nothing much to pack, for they had brought little, but Mr Charlesworth had two packs loaded onto the spare horse. 'Bet he's brought his shaving tackle and a spare nightshirt,' Kitty whispered and Georgiana smiled.

Mr Charlesworth had not lost his spruce and elegant manner of dress. His cord breeches and boots looked clean in spite of the long journey to Dreumel's Creek, and the wide-brimmed hat he was wearing to keep the sun from his face was of the softest leather, unlike the other men's battered and cracked headgear.

Everyone came to see them off. Isaac lifted his hat as he had done on their arrival and said he was mighty sorry that they were leaving. 'It's bin good to have wimmin about the place,' he declared. 'Specially them as can cook,' he said to Kitty.

'No hard feelings, Miss Gregory?' Ted said. 'I'm sorry you've had a wasted journey.' He added quietly, 'I don't know what to say about Mrs Newmarch, I really don't. I could say she's well shot of her husband. He left her and he's a bad lot. But who knows.' He shrugged. 'Maybe she cares for him.'

'Not a wasted journey,' Georgiana replied. 'I shall think of it as an experience.' But about her cousin May Newmarch she made no comment.

May, she decided, must do what she will with her life, as I have done with mine. Her gaze followed the former valet as he went to speak to Kitty. And I suppose you too, Robert Allen or Ted Newmarch, only took the opportunity which presented itself when there was no other.

Wilhelm Dreumel bowed over her hand with an old-world courtesy, which even in this isolated place didn't seem amiss coming from him. 'I hope we will meet again, Miss Gregory,' he said. 'Shall you stay at the Marius when in New York?'

'Oh, yes, indeed I shall. Besides,' she said with a laugh, 'I have left some of my belongings there.' She looked down at the borrowed clothes she was wearing, which were extremely crumpled and stained in spite of being washed in the creek.

'They will be perfectly safe,' he said. 'The staff were instructed to attend you. Goodbye.' His eyes gazed warmly at her. 'Lake will take care of you.'

Georgiana mounted Hetty, who frisked and skittered as if she realized she was journeying home, whilst Kitty got up behind Lake. Charlesworth sat straight-backed on his horse and didn't seem at ease. He's not used to horses, she surmised, and realized that he had said very little to Wilhelm Dreumel this morning and nothing at all to the men. This has been only a business venture for him, she thought as she gathered up the reins in her hand. Charlesworth does not have a feeling for this valley in the same way that Wilhelm Dreumel has. He has sunk money into the shaft only to make more money.

'Goodbye, everybody,' Kitty cried as Lake dug

his heels into his mount. She waved her hand. 'Goodbye, Ted.' She looked back to where Ted was standing apart from the others. 'Don't give up!'

He raised his hand. 'I won't.'

What does she mean? Georgiana pondered as she too waved a last goodbye, feeling sad as she saw Wilhelm Dreumel standing forlornly, one hand hanging listlessly by his side, the other clutched to his chin as if deliberating on a problem.

They had to dismount and lead the horses part of the way up the steep side of the mountain, and as they sweated and strained, Georgiana realized why Lake had said they must leave at daybreak. To come up during the heat of day would have been impossible. Eventually they reached the rocky clearing below the tree line where they had first looked down on the valley, and they stopped and gazed down again. 'It is so lovely,' Georgiana murmured. 'I feel honoured to have been here.'

Beside her, Charlesworth harrumphed. 'I'm not sure that the panorama justifies the difficulty of getting here. As far as I'm concerned the whole effort has been a waste of time and money.'

'But surely,' Georgiana looked at him, 'you must have believed in the venture at the beginning?'

'When Dreumel told me that he was risking the Marius to look for gold so he could buy cattle, I did believe that it was worthwhile. I speculated that no-one would take that kind of risk unless it was a one hundred per cent sure thing.'

That's just what I said to Mr Dreumel, Georgiana thought. And he *was* sure. But now he is not!

'However, they've been weeks and not brought out enough gold to buy a decent supper, let alone cattle. No,' Charlesworth gazed down into the valley, 'it's not for me. I'll sell my interest in the claim for the best offer and think I'm well rid of it.'

Georgiana saw Lake give a derisory glance at Charlesworth, but his only remark was that they must get on. They should ride whilst the morning was cool and stop again at noon. Lake led the way along the track, with the packhorse behind him, Georgiana following and Charlesworth at the rear. But the going was slow as, within an hour, Charlesworth complained that his saddle was loose and he was uncomfortable. They stopped whilst it was adjusted and a little later he said that he must stop to have water, and again they waited whilst he unfastened his water bottle and took a drink. Eventually, Lake insisted that Charlesworth rode behind him, leaving Georgiana to take up the rear position.

Their stop for rest was at the cabin where they had spent the night on their outward journey, and they were glad of the respite and the chance to quench their thirst from the stream. Kitty had brought slices of meat, soda bread and dry biscuits. Charlesworth greedily took more than his share. Lake refused all food but drank deeply from the stream. Fifteen minutes later he urged them on.

'Good heavens, man,' Charlesworth objected. 'These ladies need more time to rest.'

'There is no more time,' Lake insisted. 'We have only one more rest before nightfall. And a storm is gathering.'

Georgiana was happy to continue, wanting the journey over as soon as possible. Charlesworth in front of her was constantly grumbling. About the heat, about his horse, about banging his head on the overhanging branches and about the futility of his excursion. She yearned to tell him to be quiet for she needed time to think, and to savour the experience of travelling in a country which was still wild, as yet untamed by man's hand.

Mr Dreumel will take care of his valley, she deliberated. If he gets the chance. But there will be others who would not. Men like Charlesworth who want only to make money for their own use and not for the common good. I wonder how much his share of the mine is worth, she mused. Mr Dreumel hasn't the funds to buy Charlesworth's share and sink another shaft. She thought of Ted, so committed to the mine, yet without the money to put into it. How strange, she suddenly realized, he said he has Edward Newmarch's letters of credit, yet he hasn't attempted to use them. She gave a silent derisory laugh at herself. And I thought he was a rogue!

But he could use it, she reflected. It's of no use to anyone, left in his pocket. And May doesn't know of it. Then she felt guilty at such an improper notion and dismissed it.

She was still thinking on the matter when Lake called a halt at the end of the day. It had been a difficult journey with fallen trees across their path which had to be negotiated, and a heat which became more and more sultry and intolerable. 'We must make shelter quickly,' Lake said. 'Before the storm breaks.'

269

They had been steadily descending the forest trail and had come out into a clearing where a stream gathered into a pool then cascaded over the edge of the crest. A clap of thunder sounded loud over their heads. Lake dismounted and lifted Kitty down. 'Hurry,' he said to her as he unbuckled the packs and released whippy poles which had been strapped to the pony's side, and set them down. 'Unfasten the packs and take the canvas over there.'

He indicated towards a hollow set into the mountain wall. It was almost a cave yet not deep enough to be called one, and it was here that Lake unrolled the canvas which Kitty had shaken from one of the packs. He fastened the poles together with twine from his deep pocket, and quickly placed the canvas over them to make a tent.

Georgiana led Hetty, Lake's horse and the packhorse to the pool to drink and expected Charlesworth to do the same, but he sat astride his mount and looked around him. 'I don't think this is a very good place,' he pronounced. 'We should stay in the forest.'

'You stay in the forest if you want to,' Lake muttered without turning round. 'But this is the best place to camp. We can't light a fire in the forest.'

'I'll get kindling, shall I?' Georgiana asked him as she tethered the horses.

Lake looked up and nodded and she went back into the forest, bringing out short dead branches, dry pine needles and cones. 'Good,' he said, when she came back and piled them into a pyramid in front of the tent. 'You bin a trapper's bride?'

'No!' she laughed. 'I saw you do it when you brought us here.'

'Ah!' Again he nodded. A man of few words, she thought, yet she was aware of a warm sense of approval tinged with something which she couldn't quite define. Then she flushed as she realized it was admiration she saw in his glance.

'There won't be room for all of us in there,' Charlesworth interrupted.

'That's right,' Lake replied. 'This is for the women. We sleep outside.'

'But we'll get soaked if it rains!' he spluttered and Georgiana and Kitty both turned away to hide their amusement at his red-faced annoyance.

'Isn't there a cabin nearby?' Charlesworth asked angrily. 'I cannot stay outside all night. What about wolves?'

'We'll stay by the fire. Wolves won't come near. And I've got a gun. Water your horse,' Lake said abruptly, 'and tether her safely. They don't like thunder.'

The fire was no sooner lit and sending up spirals of smoke than the rain started and they dashed for shelter. 'Please. Do come into the tent!' Georgiana called. The two men had crawled into the hollow beneath the cleft and were sheltering under another piece of canvas. 'At least until it stops raining.'

'It won't stop raining, lady,' Lake answered. 'Not until morning.'

'I shall certainly come in, if you will allow me,' Charlesworth said, rushing towards the tent. 'He's not much of a scout, if you ask me,' he grumbled as he crawled in under the canvas. 'I'm

271

sure there'll be another cabin along the route.'

'But we'd get wet going to it,' Georgiana said, moving up to make room for him. 'I'm quite sure that Lake knows what he's doing.'

'This is another reason why I'm glad to be out of this mining business,' Charlesworth said irritably. 'I'm out of my depth here. There's got to be another trail through to the valley! This fellow told me that this is the only one, but I'm not sure that I believe him. I know that Dreumel goes in from Philadelphia, but I can't work out which route he takes.'

Georgiana was silent. When she had asked Lake if there was another trail he had raised his eyebrows in a noncommittal manner, but he hadn't said that there wasn't. And she had the feeling that this return journey was over more formidable terrain than when they had come. Certainly she hadn't remembered this particular clearing. Was Lake making it more difficult for them?

'I'd like to ask you a question, Mr Charlesworth,' she ventured, and had to raise her voice as the noise of the rain increased.

'Yes, my dear Miss Gregory.' He shuffled around to make himself comfortable, which meant that Georgiana and Kitty had to move up even more to accommodate him. 'I will answer it if I can.'

'I only wondered. How much are you asking for your stake in the mine?'

CHAPTER TWENTY-THREE

Charlesworth laughed and patted her knee in a patronizing and overfamiliar manner, then let his hand linger. She smiled as if she didn't mind, then slowly placed her hand over his and removed it.

'I like a little gamble now and again,' she said in a girlish voice. 'I'm sure Mrs Charlesworth does too.'

He cleared his throat at the reminder that he had a wife. 'Occasionally,' he admitted. 'On the horses. But never in business matters.'

'Of course,' she said sweetly. 'We women couldn't be expected to know of such things.' She heard Kitty give a snort and turn over in her blanket. 'But in fact, Mr Charlesworth, I would like to buy into a gold mine, just to say I have done it, you know! But I would have no idea how to find another such as Mr Dreumel's, unless I went to California of course.'

'Preposterous!' he exclaimed. 'A young woman such as you? Why, the place is swarming with thieves and roughnecks, you'd lose all you had within days of arriving.'

'I couldn't afford a great deal, you understand,' she continued, as if she hadn't been listening to him. 'But I have some ready money. Sovereigns and American eagles. I believe they are better than paper money?' She put on an innocent expression and was pleased to see a glimmer of interest. 'Perhaps we could speak of it in the morning?'

He didn't make any attempt to move out of the tent when Georgiana wrapped her blanket around her and lay down to sleep, and she reconsidered her imprudence in suggesting that he and Lake should shelter with them. Though I can hardly blame Charlesworth, she thought. The rain was coming down in torrents and the forked lightning lit up the tent. As the thunder cracked over them, Kitty drew deeper into her blanket and made little whimpering sounds.

'It's all right, Kitty,' Georgiana murmured. 'It's only noise. It can't hurt.'

'But suppose the mountain falls down, or some of the trees get hit by lightning?' Kitty peered out of the blanket, her face red and her eyes frightened. 'We might get killed.'

'I'm sure this is why Lake chose this place,' Georgiana said. 'We're well sheltered here.'

She slept fitfully, aware always of Mr Charlesworth's presence. He snored and shuffled and turned so constantly that eventually she gave up trying to sleep and lay with her eyes wide open, thinking still of Wilhelm Dreumel and his shattered dreams.

Presently the rain eased and the only sounds were the drip drip of raindrops and the gush of the stream. Then she heard the solitary call of a bird, and slipping out of her blanket she stepped over Charlesworth and crawled out of the tent. Lake was standing at the edge of the clearing, looking down the mountainside, and she saw that at some stage of the night he had brought the

274

four horses into the hollow under the shelter of the cleft.

He saw her looking at them and signalled her to come. 'They were frightened of the thunder,' he said softly, 'so I brought them in with me.'

She smiled. So he wasn't such a hard man as he had appeared to be.

'Not sentiment, lady,' he said curtly. 'Without the horses we travel on foot.'

Her smile faded. How foolish of her. A man like him must be aware of all possibilities at all times. But his abrupt manner disappeared as he again beckoned her near.

'Watch,' he said softly, pointing towards the east. A slim finger of gold was rising in the sky behind a mountain range. It touched the rain-spattered needles of pine and fir trees which covered the slopes, making them sparkle and shimmer. As the finger grew wider and broader and the gold transformed to flame-red and orange, it flushed and illuminated the green valley, turning the fast-running babbling streams into liquid gold.

'Beautiful,' she breathed, hardly daring to speak lest she break the moment.

'This is the best place in the world to see the sunrise,' he murmured. 'And I have seen many.'

'And you never tire of them?' she asked.

'Never.' He shook his head. 'You're cold?' he said as she shivered.

'I left my shawl in the tent. But no matter, I wouldn't miss this.' She let her gaze follow the changing kaleidoscope of colour.

He unbuttoned his leather coat. 'Come.' He put out his hand and drew her towards him. He opened the garment and wrapped it around her, enclosing her within his arms. She stood perfectly still, hardly daring to move or breathe, a flush suffusing her cheeks. She had never been so close to a man before. Never been so close to anyone, not even her parents when she was a child. She was facing away from him and felt the heat of his body warming her back and shoulders, and his arms encircling her waist.

'I have never shared this view before,' he said softly. 'Always I have watched it alone.'

She swallowed. 'Sometimes – it is good to share,' she murmured huskily. 'Sometimes words cannot convey such a scene.'

'No,' he breathed, close to her ear. 'Some things are impossible to describe.'

And it is not possible to describe how I am feeling now, she thought, with him so close and intimate. She closed her eyes for a second. She could feel his steady breathing through her body, feel his heart beat, smell the sweat on him, and the pungent odour of leather and horses, and she felt her own heart hammering.

Slowly she turned within his coat so that she was facing and looking up at him. They neither of them spoke, then he bent his head and kissed her on the mouth. 'Gianna! You are a good woman,' he whispered. 'A strong woman. You are right for this country.'

Her lips parted. 'Why do you give me that name?'

'The old man – Isaac.' He touched her cheek with his rough fingers. 'That's what he called you.'

She smiled and was about to reply, when a sudden stamping and snorting of the horses alerted her. She glanced over his shoulder and froze.

'What is it?' He was instantly alert.

'Wolf,' she breathed, her legs turning to jelly as she saw the pacing animal.

Slowly, his movements measured and unhurried, Lake turned, releasing her and pushing her behind him. His hand slid to his belt and as the wolf sprang, its jaws wide, exposing sharp yellow fangs, the knife flashed in his hand, aiming at the unprotected belly of the animal as it leapt. Lake's sharp cry and the anguished howl of the wolf as its blood gushed forth, spattering them both, echoed around the mountains.

Georgiana fell to her knees, her body shaking. How suddenly death could come in this wilderness. They could have perished if it hadn't been for Lake's swift action.

Kitty's head and that of Charlesworth's appeared at the tent opening. 'What's happened? Oh, Miss Georgiana, are you all right?' Kitty asked. Then she saw the body of the wolf as Lake dragged it to the edge of the clearing and threw it over the side, where it crashed down into the trees. She gave a muted cry. 'Oh, God save us! Did it attack you?'

'No! No! It's all right, Kitty. We're not hurt. Lake has killed it.' Georgiana went back to Lake, who was staring down into the valley. 'Thank you,' she whispered. 'I was so frightened.'

His eyes continued to stare into the distance. 'It shouldn't have happened,' he said harshly. 'I was unprepared.' He turned to look at her. 'I was distracted.' His mouth pressed into a thin line.

277

'This is not a place for women.'

'But you said–!'

'I was wrong.' He was abrupt and turned away. 'We must move on. Lead the horses to the stream,' he commanded. 'Eat and then we'll be on our way.'

When they stopped for a rest at midday, she went over to speak to him. 'That wolf–' she began.

'Timber wolf. Was out of place,' he said gruffly. 'Usually they travel in packs but don't often attack people, except in winter when they are hungry and looking for food. He must have become separated from the others. He only attacked us because he was nervous and thought he was under threat. I wouldn't normally have killed him.'

'You killed the other one,' she commented. 'On our journey here.'

He nodded. 'Sometimes I have to. He was rabid so he had to die. I'm a trapper. I trap beaver. Mink. Raccoon.' His eyes glanced over her. 'I sell the pelts so you ladies can cover your shoulders with fur. I kill for a living. Not for the fun of it.'

As they started out on the final part of the journey she felt jittery and unnerved at the result of the incident and his change of attitude towards her. Why had he kissed her? Was it simply because of an emotional moment? She wouldn't have guessed that he was an emotional man, yet obviously he was if he could take pleasure in a sunrise. And why then did he become brusque after he had killed the wolf? Was it because he had been caught off guard?

The trail began to drop lower into the valley, leaving the steep mountainside behind. She was able to recognize familiar landmarks and isolated settlements, and her tension eased as she realized they were almost at the Indian settlement of No-Name.

'How much longer?' Charlesworth bellowed from the position he had taken at the rear. 'Surely we must be almost there?'

Lake turned in his saddle. 'An hour,' he called. 'If we keep up this pace. Don't lag behind.' Georgiana saw him glance at Kitty and his face crinkle as if he had winked or smiled at her. 'Watch out for wolves,' he hollered. 'They may be following us.'

Charlesworth urged his horse on and came closer to Georgiana. 'I shan't come out here again,' he muttered. 'And if you've any sense, Miss Gregory, you won't either.'

'Will you sell me your interest in the mine?' Lake shouted back to Charlesworth and Georgiana looked up in some surprise and not a little irritation. 'I'll give you the value in pelt.'

'Ah!' Charlesworth considered. 'Perhaps I might. Yes, perhaps I might! We'll talk when we get to the place that has no name.'

'It has a name,' Georgiana told him curtly. 'It's called No-Name! And I asked you first if you'd sell the share to me!'

'I wouldn't sell to you, Miss Gregory.' He drew as near as he could without the horses clashing. 'This is not women's work. Besides, it's played out,' he said in an undertone. 'But I want what I gave for it. And if this fellow wants it, I'll trade for skins and my wife will get a fur wrap to keep her happy.'

Dekan and Horse rode out from the settlement

279

to greet them and escort them in. Charlesworth cantered on ahead whilst Lake and Georgiana slowed their pace now they were at their destination.

'Any trouble, brother?' Dekan asked Lake, who hesitated for a moment, glancing at Georgiana before saying that there wasn't.

'Lake killed a wolf,' Kitty piped up from behind Lake's back. 'It was about to attack. He saved Miss Gregory's life.'

'Then you are in his debt,' Dekan said to Georgiana in such a solemn tone that she couldn't be certain if he was serious or not.

'I'm sure that I am,' she replied, tight-lipped. 'But I doubt he would allow me to repay him.'

As they dismounted and the horses were taken away to be fed and watered, Kitty went into the cabin with Little Bear, and Charlesworth went to the men's cabin, where he said he would lie down and rest. Georgiana approached Lake. 'I was going to buy Charlesworth's interest in the mine,' she said crisply. 'Now he's going to sell to you! Even though he told me it's played out,' she added.

He gave a half-grin. 'What would he know about it? Anyway, you can buy it from me if you really want it.'

'What's the point in that?' She could feel her irritation rising. 'Why would you buy it in the first place? You wouldn't work it, you're a trapper!'

'And you're a woman,' he said slowly. 'So why would you?' His eyes didn't leave her face. 'I heard you asking him to sell it–' he continued.

'You heard–?' He must have been right outside the tent to hear any conversation!

He nodded. 'Got kinda wet.' Still his eyes remained on hers. 'Don't trust him,' he said. 'Not with Dreumel's mine or sharing a woman's tent.'

She was silenced for a moment. He must have stayed outside the tent until he heard Charlesworth's snores and knew that she and Kitty were safe. 'So why did you ask him to sell the share to you when you knew I wanted it?' she persisted.

'I knew he wouldn't sell it to you. Not to a woman. And not to Dreumel, in case it's worth something after all. But he'd trade for pelts because he thinks he'll make money on them.' He gave another lopsided grin. 'And he knows nothing about fur either.'

'You haven't answered my question,' she said. 'Why do you want it?'

'I don't,' he said softly. 'But Dreumel does.'

She was silenced once more by him. What a strange man he was. He had already repaid Wilhelm Dreumel for a favour, and now he was bestowing something more. She stared back at him for a moment, then turned away to go into the cabin. He caught hold of her arm. 'I said you can have it if you want it.'

'Instead of Dreumel?' she asked. 'Maybe I would sell it to the highest bidder!'

He pursed his lips and shrugged. 'Maybe you would but whoever bought it would never find their way up there.' His hand was still on her arm. He stroked her skin with his thumb. 'Perhaps it's best if I keep it,' he said softly. 'Dreumel will be up there until the fall and I'll see him when I get back.'

'Get back? From where?' She felt mesmerized

by the pressure of his hand on her flesh.

He pointed north. 'Lake Huron. For beaver. I'm late, I should have been there already.'

'Late? For what?'

'For trading. The trappers meet up at an old fort trading centre. They sell their furs, buy knives, food, coffee, whisky. Some of them drink away the whole season's skins.'

The hard Adam's apple in his throat moved as he swallowed. 'Some of them will even trade their squaws for whisky.'

'There are Indians there too?'

He shook his head. 'Some trappers have Indian women as their squaws.'

'Do you?' she whispered.

He clasped both her hands, cradling them between his. 'No.' His dark eyes locked into hers in such a penetrating gaze that she couldn't look away. 'I travel alone. Just my horses and pack mules.'

Fear suddenly struck her. 'Are you not afraid of being attacked?'

He shrugged. 'If it happens, it happens. I have my gun and my knife.' His eyes flickered momentarily and a small grin played around his mouth. 'If I am not distracted, I shall be safe.'

'I hope so,' she breathed. 'I do hope so.'

'Miss Georgiana!' Kitty called from the cabin. 'There's supper here for us.'

'Yes. I'm coming.' Her voice cracked hoarsely as she called back. Her mind seemed to be blank and she couldn't think or concentrate. Reality was non-existent. Only her physical senses were working, the stuff of flesh and blood, pounding so vigorously that she had no control over them. The cause, she knew, was Lake standing so close to her, and the effect so consuming that no matter what the future held, she felt she would never be the same again.

'I leave before dawn,' he said quietly. 'I may not see you again.'

She licked her lips. 'Perhaps not.' She gazed up at him. 'Unless you come to New York?'

He smiled and shook his head, dropping her hands. 'No likelihood of that. The Iroquois no longer live there.'

It was not yet light when she rose from her bed the next morning and went outside. Lake was fixing his high pommel saddle to his mount. He'd one other horse and two mules, all three of which were laden with fur packs hanging from either side of the saddle with a further pack on top. Dekan was with him but with a murmur to Lake as he saw her coming towards them, and a brief touch on his shoulder, he melted away into the darkness.

Lake turned to her as she approached. He held out his hand, which she took, drew her towards him and enfolded her in a swift embrace. 'You don't belong in a city,' he murmured, and kissed her long and fervently.

'I know,' she answered, her breath taken away, and, putting her arms around his neck, returned his kiss with a passion that she had only ever dreamed of. 'But I no longer know where I belong.'

'Only with me,' he said, gently pushing her away and mounting his horse. 'And I forever with you.'

CHAPTER TWENTY-FOUR

Georgiana and Kitty were accompanied by Dekan and Horse across the rocky plain towards the foothills of the mountains where they had first met the Iroquois on their outward journey to No-Name. The two women were again travelling in the dog cart pulled by Hetty. They were wearing their own gowns and petticoats and feeling very restricted after the freedom of Indian clothes. Charlesworth rode alongside. In the cart was a pack of pelts which Lake had traded for the share in the mine. He had insisted that Charlesworth gave him a signed written note to say that the bearer was entitled to the claim.

'You know the trail to Duquesne?' Dekan said.

'Yes.' Georgiana managed a smile, though she felt sad at the parting. 'And if we forget, Hetty knows it.'

'The ladies will be quite safe with me,' Charlesworth said to the two Indians. 'I have a gun.' He patted his thigh. 'They need have no fear.'

'I have no fear of man or beast, Mr Charlesworth,' Georgiana said calmly. 'I have my blade,' and she lifted her skirt to show Lake's knife strapped around her ankle. Though whether I should be able to use it, she thought, is a different matter altogether.

Kitty too lifted her skirt hem. 'I have one as well,' she said. 'Ted gave it to me.'

Dekan and Horse glanced at each other, then at Charlesworth. 'Don't cross them,' Dekan told him gravely. 'Women and knives don't go together unless they're slicing elk!'

They reversed their previous journey, pulling up the mountain track, then down towards the stream which led to the clearing and the drivers' cabin, where they had formerly spent a night. They allowed the horses a drink and took one themselves, and ate sparingly of the food which Dekan's wife had once more provided. It was now late afternoon, but Georgiana reckoned that they could reach Duquesne before nightfall. One thing she didn't want was to spend a night in the cabin with Charlesworth.

He grumbled that they would be too tired to undertake the rest of the journey, but Georgiana and Kitty insisted, saying that they would rather spend the night in accommodation at Duquesne. Finally he reluctantly agreed to continue after Georgiana suggested that if he preferred to spend the night in the cabin alone, she and Kitty would travel on.

'I must first of all return Hetty,' Georgiana murmured to Kitty as they approached the town. 'I shall be so sorry to leave her behind. I've become very attached to her.' Her sense of loss since Lake had departed was made worse by now having to bid farewell to Hetty. She's just a horse, she kept reminding herself, but after paying the wheelwright for the hire of her and walking away across the square, she looked back and saw Hetty watching from over the fence with what Georgiana considered was a reproachful demeanour.

They stayed at Mrs Smith's guest house, which this time had rooms available, basic but clean. The beds were comfortable, but Georgiana lay with her eyes wide open for most of the night and sleep didn't come. She spoke little the following day when they boarded the coach to Harrisburg and didn't respond to Charlesworth's constant moans of protest regarding the state of the road, the carriage and the coachman's unsuitability to the task of getting them back to civilization without breaking all their bones. She sat staring out of the window cocooned in her own desolation, and in the certain knowledge that the one man she could ever love was lost to her.

The journey by river and canal was an unremembered void and she changed boats in an unconscious manner, accepting seats, bunks, food and drink as an instinctive reflex. She would, if not prompted by Kitty, just as easily have done without and not even noticed.

'Thank you,' she responded to Charlesworth as he handed her down from the hired chaise at the door of the Marius. It had taken them almost a week of travelling to arrive back in New York. 'I trust that Mrs Charlesworth will be pleased with her furs and that it was worth the effort of bringing them.' He had kept the packs by his side constantly and had slept with them beneath his head.

He put his finger to his lips. 'I shall have them treated and made up,' he said. 'But they are not all for Mrs Charlesworth. Oh dear, no! She will have her beaver cape and I hope to get a good price for the rest at market.' He gave a self-satisfied smile. 'I reckon I did well on the deal.

Better than that half-breed trapper anyway.'

Georgiana bristled at that. 'You mean Lake!' she said curtly.

'Why, yes, of course,' he said in an astonished tone. 'Who else?'

She and Kitty spent the next week relaxing, bathing, washing their hair and cleaning their clothes. They walked along the streets of New York glancing in the fashionable shops. New boots and shoes were essential purchases, for their own were quite ruined by their having constantly worn only one pair.

Georgiana received a card from the Charlesworths inviting her to a supper party at the Portland Hotel. She remembered Wilhelm Dreumel saying that the Charlesworths lived there and that Mrs Charlesworth behaved as if she owned it. 'What will you do, Kitty, whilst I am out?' she asked, for she had been unable to think up a reason to decline the invitation.

'Don't know, miss.' Kitty had seemed rather lethargic over the last few days. 'I've done all the mending and the ironing. Perhaps I'll go for a walk, if that's all right?'

'Of course.' Georgiana gazed at her. 'Feel free to do whatever you want. Do you need money?'

'Not at the moment, thank you.' Kitty swallowed. She looked as if she was going to cry. 'Are we staying here, Miss Georgiana? Or are we going on somewhere else?'

'Have you got a taste for travel, Kitty?' Georgiana asked. 'Were you not exhausted by the journey?'

Kitty pressed her lips together. 'I'm more

287

exhausted staying here, miss. The streets are hot and 'pavements – sidewalks are hard, and the days seem to drag.'

'They do!' Georgiana agreed. Then, sighing, she picked up her parasol. 'Well, as I don't want to stay in New York either, we must think of what we shall do next.'

When Georgiana arrived at the Portland the other guests were already gathered in the Charlesworths' suite of rooms. Some of the ladies turned to stare as she entered, then turned away, hiding their mouths behind their fans as they spoke.

'Miss Gregory.' Mrs Charlesworth greeted her and both women inclined their heads. 'We were just speaking of you.' She waved her hand in the direction of the other guests. 'Do come and be introduced. Mr Charlesworth has been telling us of your hazardous journey across country and through the forests. And of the wolf!' Her eyes grew wide. 'Of how you were all almost torn to pieces by the brute.'

'A slight exaggeration, Mrs Charlesworth!' Georgiana said solemnly. 'Some of our party were still asleep in the tent and quite out of danger.'

'Oh, you had a tent?' a male guest interrupted. 'I thought you said you were out in the open, Charlesworth!'

'Well, we were, in a manner of speaking,' Charlesworth blustered. 'Out on this ridge. Great danger of being blown off in the storm. My word, never seen rain like it. Torrential! We could easily have been washed over the edge. As it was, I said to this tracker fellow, best build a fire within the shelter of the mountain, to stave off the wild animals, you know.'

'But the wolf still came?' A woman in a satin gown with a bustle, wearing a lace cap on top of her curls, flapped her fan vigorously. 'You must have been very frightened, Miss Gregory? I wouldn't have been able to go on any further.'

'Then you would have had to stay on the mountain,' Georgiana replied sweetly. 'But wolves don't normally attack. This one had become separated from its pack and was therefore vulnerable.'

'Oh, nasty creatures!' Mrs Charlesworth exclaimed. 'I'm so glad that I don't have to go amongst them. And neither will Mr Charlesworth any more, for he says he has quite finished with that kind of thing. You would do well to take our advice, Miss Gregory, and stay in the city.' She looked around her guests. 'Shall we go in to supper?'

'You're very brown, Miss Gregory,' one of the women commented, as they were seated at table. 'Did you not take a parasol or hat with you on your journey?'

'I had noticed it too,' said another. 'I have an excellent lotion I can recommend to you, but you must stay indoors for at least a week for it to be effective.'

'I suppose that in England you do not have such heat as here in America,' Mrs Charlesworth observed. 'I believe you get a great deal of rain? If you stay in America you must keep indoors during the summer months or your skin will be ruined.'

Georgiana was astonished that they should discuss her so personally. She heard from down the supper table one or two thinly veiled references indicating that the travels of women alone were not entirely approved of by the ladies in the company.

She listened half-heartedly to the conversation going on around her, and came to the conclusion that it would not matter if she didn't join in the discourse, for no-one appeared to be listening to anyone else in any case. Is this going to be my life if I stay here? she wondered. Swapping stories with a company of people who are probably as bored as I am? She pricked up her ears only once, and that was when Charlesworth remarked in an undertone to a man sitting nearby that if he wanted to buy a fur for his wife, then he should come to see him. 'I did a good deal,' he murmured. 'Sold on a share in a mine that's worked out, for a pack of pelts. Poor old Dreumel,' he added. 'He really believed in that mine.'

'Dreumel did?' the man exclaimed. 'Why – doggone it, Charlesworth! Dreumel isn't the kind of man to take a chance! You sure it's worked out? Where is it, this mine?'

Charlesworth shook his head. 'I really couldn't tell you. Somewhere between the State of New York and State of Pennsylvania,' he muttered. 'In the middle of the wilderness anyway. Nobody will find it, not till they run the railroad through it. I wouldn't be able to find it again at any rate.'

Georgiana took a deep breath, then sipped some wine to steady herself. But I could, she thought. I'm sure that I could.

Charlesworth insisted on escorting her to the Marius when she stated her intention of walking back after supper, rather than taking a hackney carriage. 'Can't be too careful, Miss Gregory,' he said, tucking his hand in a familiar manner beneath her elbow.

'By the way.' He leaned heavily and confidentially towards her and she pulled away, murmuring, 'Excuse me!'

'Beg pardon.' He gave her an indulgent smile. 'But I was about to impart a confidentiality.'

'Please don't, Mr Charlesworth,' she said in alarm. 'It would be most improper!'

'Don't be alarmed, my dear.' He once more took her by the elbow. 'All I was going to say was that our little secret is quite safe!'

'Our little secret!' She stopped suddenly in her tracks. 'Whatever do you mean, Mr Charlesworth? You and I do not have any secrets, little or not!'

He shushed her, making a show of putting his fingers to his lips. 'I mean about the tent!' He nodded his head and raised his eyebrows significantly at the same time.

'I have no idea what you are talking about!' Irritated, Georgiana raised her voice. 'Please be more specific.'

'Being in the same tent, I mean.' He spoke in a whisper and glanced around. 'On our journey across the mountains!'

She was horrified. How could he be so ungentlemanly as even to mention it? She recalled Lake saying that he didn't trust him.

'I wouldn't want Mrs Charlesworth to hear of it,' he said, and the expression on his face seemed to invite her to join in some duplicity. 'She's not a woman of the world, you know. She wouldn't understand at all! She couldn't begin to comprehend the dangers of our journey or the need for companionship when facing such hardship.'

'Companionship! What nonsense, Mr Charlesworth,' she said briskly. 'You were asleep instantly. Kitty and I both remarked on it,' she lied. 'And there was no danger whilst Lake was there to guard us *and* he sat outside the tent all night,' she added significantly. 'Just to be sure!'

'I did?' Charlesworth's self-esteem seemed to droop. 'He did! Oh! I see.'

What did bother her, however, she ruminated as he left her at the door of the Marius, was that he was quite the sort of man who might brag of his exploits to his gentlemen friends. They would hoot bawdily if he told them he had shared the tent with Miss Gregory and her companion, ignoring the fact that an armed guide was guarding them. If he could exaggerate the tale of the wolf, he could certainly boast, with a wink and a nod, of a night on a mountain top.

And where does that leave my reputation? she wondered as she climbed the stairs to her room. To be talked about all over New York!

'Kitty, I need to speak to you,' she said during breakfast the following morning.

Kitty pressed her lips together and looked at her anxiously.

'It's all right,' Georgiana soothed. 'It's nothing dreadful. But I must discuss an issue with you and gauge your opinion. I have come to a decision. At least,' she wavered, 'I think I have, but I must give you the option of saying yes or no, for your future is as important to me as it is to you, and you may not wish to share in what I

292

want to do. You may have ideas of your own.'

'Oh, Miss Gregory.' Kitty started to weep over her coffee cup and hastily put it down in order to blow her nose. 'I've something to say to you too. I've been trying to pluck up courage for days and I haven't been able to.'

'Good heavens, Kitty. Don't cry. You'll make *me* want to cry and I haven't done that in a long time.' Though I've wanted to, she pondered miserably and blinked her eyes rapidly.

'Fact is, miss.' Kitty's mouth trembled. 'And I don't want you to be angry with me, cos I value your good opinion above anything else.' She sniffed and Georgiana waited uneasily for her to unburden herself. 'But I'd better tell you before you tell me what you were going to say–'

'Go on then, Kitty, don't keep me in suspense. I'm not going to bite you!'

'Fact is, miss, I don't want to stay in New York.' Kitty lifted moist eyes to Georgiana. 'I want to go back to Dreumel's Creek.'

'Oh, Kitty!' To her chagrin, an uncalled-for tear ran down Georgiana's cheek and she hastily brushed it away. 'So do I!'

CHAPTER TWENTY-FIVE

Any doubts the two women may have had about their decision to return to Dreumel's Creek after only a short time back in New York were dissolved that same morning, when Georgiana had an unexpected visit from Mrs Burrows.

'I am meeting a friend for luncheon,' she said. 'And thought I would drop in on the off chance that you might be here. I do hope you don't mind.'

'Mrs Burrows, I could not be more delighted to see you,' Georgiana greeted the older woman warmly. 'You are perhaps the only person I know in New York who can give me advice and tell me whether or not I am about to act foolishly.'

'My dear young woman.' Mrs Burrows seated herself comfortably in a chair in the Marius lounge and snapped her fingers at a boy to bring coffee. 'I cannot conceive that you would ever be foolish. It is not in your nature.'

How very little you know of me, Georgiana thought. I could be on the verge of being very witless indeed. She briefly outlined the journey she and Kitty had undertaken to Dreumel's Creek, and their return. She sketched in details of the mine and the valley and of Wilhelm Dreumel's disappointment at not being able to sink another shaft, and of Mr Charlesworth pulling out of the venture. She didn't mention Lake, for fear her manner would betray her.

'You travelled so far and back and are now considering returning! Mm.' Mrs Burrows considered, and when the boy had brought their coffee said in a positive tone, 'Wilhelm is well rid of Charlesworth anyway. He wouldn't know how to set about a day's work, though his money would have been useful. What Wilhelm needs is some practical help as well as an input of money.' She pondered for a moment. 'How much does he need, do you think?'

Georgiana gazed at her in astonishment. 'I – I wasn't suggesting that you–!'

'Oh, I know you were not,' Mrs Burrows replied briskly. 'But if Wilhelm Dreumel thinks sinking this other shaft is worthwhile, then it will be. He doesn't take unnecessary risks.'

That's what the man at the Charlesworths' supper party said, Georgiana recalled. So it must be true. 'Do you think, then, Mrs Burrows,' she said hesitantly, 'that if I was to use my inheritance to put into this venture, I would be acting irresponsibly?'

Mrs Burrows' smile creased her face into a dozen wrinkles. 'Others might, my dear, but I would say, nothing venture nothing gain. What would you do with your inheritance if you didn't use it in this way?'

'Why, nothing! Only live on it! I had no other definite plans.'

'And if this project should fail, and if *I* am to be sensible I should warn you that it might, what then? Would you scurry back to England and fall on the mercy of your relatives and hope that they would support you?'

'They did not approve of my coming out here, Mrs Burrows. I would not under any circumstances crawl back and tell them that they were right in their judgement and I was wrong! No,' Georgiana said determinedly. 'I would work. I'd teach or – or anything. And I am aware,' she added, in case Mrs Burrows should remind her, 'that I have not been prepared for earning a living.' She raised her head defiantly. 'But that will not stop me!'

'Well then! Use your money,' Mrs Burrows declared. 'And if you lose everything, come back and see me and I'll fix you up with a rich husband. I remember you saying on the ship that that is what you wanted above all!'

'Oh, Mrs Burrows.' Georgiana laughed, shaking her head. 'You know that I did not.'

'Mmm.' Mrs Burrows scrutinized her. 'You look so very fit and well that I was certain you had fallen in love already! I felt sure you had given your heart to some rich and handsome fellow in New York!'

'You would have heard of it if I had.' Georgiana smiled wistfully. 'I can put my hand on my heart and say truthfully that I have not!'

Kitty asked Georgiana if she would pay her her wages now instead of at the end of the year. 'I know it's not usual, Miss Georgiana, but I want to be independent,' she said earnestly. 'If we're going back to Dreumel's Creek, then I want to work. You won't need a maid, and I can be your companion without you paying me.'

Georgiana was astounded. Kitty, it seemed, had thought through her plans quite carefully. 'What will you work at, Kitty?' she asked.

'Well, I can't really do it without you, miss. Because if you didn't want to go back, then–' She hesitated. 'I'd have to make another plan, and I'm not totally sure of that one yet. But if we can find our way back over the mountains, then I'd go and be cook at Dreumel's Creek. I'd ask Mr Dreumel if he'd let me buy supplies from him and then I'd charge the men for their breakfast and supper.'

'You know that the men haven't found gold,

and that they might not? It isn't a certainty.'

Kitty looked rather sheepish. 'Ted says it is – practically, anyway.'

'Ted!'

Kitty nodded. 'We've talked,' she said. 'And he's convinced that they'll find gold if they sink another shaft.' She pursed her lips and her cheeks flushed. 'I quite fancy him, miss,' she admitted. 'And he feels 'same about me. We're from 'similar background, you see. We understand each other, though I've told him I don't approve of him taking Mr Newmarch's name.'

Georgiana was stunned into silence as Kitty told of how she and Ted had talked, and he'd outlined his plans to make something of his life which had begun to take shape after he had met Wilhelm Dreumel.

'Mr Dreumel trusts him, Miss Georgiana, and Ted says he won't ever let him down, and,' she blushed even more, 'he says, Ted I mean, that if he strikes it rich, then he wants to marry me.'

'And is that what you want, Kitty?' Georgiana asked quietly. 'Riches are not everything!'

'I know that, miss,' Kitty said cheerfully. 'But I'll probably marry him anyway. That was my other plan. He needs a good woman to help him settle down.'

Lake said I was a good woman, Georgiana reflected when she was alone. But he didn't mean it in the same sense as Kitty does. There would be no possibility of settling down with Lake. Not ever. She swallowed a lump in her throat. I might as well get used to that right now. But there is nothing to stop me loving him, and I feel that I

297

do, so I must be content with that.

They went shopping for suitable clothes, plain skirts and cotton shirts and divided skirts for riding. 'You will have to ride, Kitty. I will try to buy Hetty and we must get a suitable mount for you,' Georgiana said.

Kitty put her hand to her mouth in dismay, not only at having to ride a horse alone but also because she knew that her wages wouldn't stretch to buying one.

'You can pay me back when we are rich,' Georgiana said with a smile, 'and if we don't get rich I'll give it to you as a wedding present!'

Along with the belongings they didn't need, Georgiana left a note with the desk clerk for Wilhelm Dreumel, in case he should travel to New York and by some chance they missed him. She wrote that they were travelling back to Dreumel's Creek, put in the date and said that she expected it would take them approximately seven days to travel. She then wrote a note to the Charlesworths telling them she was going away, but not saying where.

Georgiana consulted the map which Charlesworth had originally given to her. 'It's not completely accurate, Kitty. I don't think that Mr Charlesworth had ever travelled there before. Perhaps this is just a sketch which Mr Dreumel had given him to show where the mine was. What we'll do,' she said, 'is travel as last time to No-Name, and then ask Dekan or Horse to put us on the right mountain track. Lake won't be there,' she added. 'He's gone up country.'

'I shall feel scared, miss,' Kitty admitted.

'Specially going through the forests. Suppose we meet up with wolves again?'

'A tinderbox!' Georgiana exclaimed suddenly. 'That's what we need. And a box of lucifers. We shall have to light a fire at some stage. And we'll try not to worry about wolves,' she stated firmly. 'Lake said they don't usually attack.'

Two days later they were ready. Their berths were reserved on the packet boats to Trenton and Philadelphia, the weather was fine and hot and Georgiana looked forward to the journey and the cool breezes on the canal.

'Goodbye, New York,' Kitty cried excitedly as they departed from the Marius. 'You're a splendid city, apart from the pigs, but we're off to the wilderness to find our fortune!'

The boat on which they had booked to travel had unexpectedly been withdrawn, and the smaller replacement boat was packed with travellers. The upper berths which were reserved for ladies only were crowded, and many of the ladies were complaining vociferously that someone else had taken their places.

The berths themselves were narrow and hidden behind thin flowered curtains which were barely wide enough to provide privacy for the occupants. 'Here, Miss Georgiana.' Kitty had rushed towards two vacant bunks, throwing her shawl and bonnet on the lower one to reserve it, and climbing into the top one she looked defiantly down at a young woman who had raced her to it.

'This doesn't bode well, Kitty,' Georgiana murmured. 'This is a very old boat!'

'Never mind, miss,' Kitty reassured her. 'As

299

long as it's watertight.'

They had been under way no more than an hour when the blue sky darkened, a clap of thunder startled them and the rain pelted down, causing them to scurry from the deck and shelter within the ladies' cabin. Other women did the same and they sat on their bunks or stood and chatted to one another until the rain began to drip through the roof, landing on the top bunks and wetting the blankets.

There was nothing to do during the day. It was impossible even to read in the dim light, and the crowd of women sitting in the small cabin made it hot and airless. Many of them turned pale and some dashed out onto the wet deck to relieve themselves of the lunch which they had only recently eaten.

No-one slept very much that night, for the little boat pitched unsteadily. Georgiana held tightly to the mattress, fearing if she didn't she would be flung out onto the floor.

The next morning the weather was fine and dry and the female passengers, having walked the deck and breathed in the fresh air, became more companionable. They asked Georgiana and Kitty a dozen questions at a time – where they hailed from, where they were going and which was their husband or young man.

'They're meeting us,' Kitty answered for Georgiana and herself. 'And we're from England, though we've lived in New York.'

Georgiana hid a smile as Kitty airily discussed her journeyings in America by boat, coach and horse, across canals and mountains, as if she was a most experienced wayfarer.

They changed boats in Trenton but were a day late arriving in Harrisburg and, although the coach was waiting, they elected to stay overnight in an hotel in order to sleep, for they were both very tired. They caught the mail coach to Duquesne the next morning, and it, like the former vehicle on which they had travelled, rattled and crashed along the rough road, the driver cracking his whip and urging on the horses as if the devil himself was after them. The passengers were shaken and jostled into each other, the coach was filled with dust and tobacco fumes and the male passengers chewed and spat, until Georgiana was at last forced to complain.

'Beg pardon, ma'am.' One of the men lifted his hat, which had been fixed firmly on his head since he had boarded the coach. 'I reckon you're English?'

'We are,' Georgiana assented.

'They're English,' another passenger informed the others as if they hadn't heard.

'English!'

'From England!' They nodded at one another and all turned their eyes on Georgiana and Kitty, nodding and smiling and discussing them for another hour or so, until the driver drew to a halt by a roadside shack to water his horses, and the passengers got down to stretch their limbs and buy a few comforts before the final part of the journey.

'All change for Duquesne!' Georgiana was awakened from an uneasy doze and stumbled out of the coach with an aching body.

'I'll never walk again!' Kitty said and promptly

sat on the ground. 'I used to think when I was just a little bairn that I'd like to be a lady and travel in a carriage. But give me my two legs and a good pair of boots any time.'

Georgiana groaned in agreement. 'Let's find a porter for our luggage and somewhere to stay. Then we'll go and see the wheelwright about Hetty and another horse. We'll set off early tomorrow,' she said, 'and not risk travelling in the dark.'

'But we'd better get some canvas for a tent, miss,' Kitty said practically. 'Just in case!'

The wheelwright looked up as Georgiana knocked on the open door of his workshop. 'Well, you'm come back! I don't know what you done with old Henry but I ain't been able to do a darned thing with her since she came home.' He spat a stream of yellow spittle across the dirt floor. 'Not a darned thing.'

'Can I see her?' Georgiana asked.

'Reckon so. Do you want to hire her agin, cos nobody else will have her?'

Georgiana glanced at Kitty. Perhaps he might be willing to sell Hetty for a reasonable charge if he wasn't able to hire her out. 'What's the matter with her? She hasn't gone lame or been wounded in some way?'

'Nope.' He led them across the yard. 'I reckoned at first she had the 'fluenza when she was off her food. I was ready for putting her down, but she weren't sweating and she'd no cough and her coat looked good.' He put his fingers to his lips and then, taking them out, added, 'Reckon she was frettin', just like she did when my old ma died.'

302

He put his fingers to his lips again and whistled. Then he whistled again and they heard the slow clip-clop of hooves at the back of the building. Hetty plodded around the corner. Her head was bent and she came as if reluctantly to the call.

'Buck up, old gal,' the wheelwright hailed her. 'Come and see the pretty lady.'

'Hetty!' Georgiana called. 'Hetty, come on!'

The mare lifted her head at Georgiana's voice. She snorted and bobbed her head up and down, then with a whinny picked up her feet and trotted towards them. Georgiana put out her hand to greet her, but Hetty nudged it out of the way and butted her on the shoulder.

'Guess she's pleased to see you, lady.' The wheelwright chewed on a wad of tobacco and Kitty watched him warily. 'She's been missing you, I reckon.'

'And I've missed her.' Georgiana stroked Hetty's neck. 'Will you sell her to me?'

'Reckon I'll have to,' he said. 'She ain't no use to me moping around the way she does.'

'Have you another horse to sell? We need one for my companion.'

The man sized up Kitty. 'I ain't a horse dealer, lady. Just keep one or two for hire, but I'll git you one for tomorrow. I'll do a deal with you. Buy Henry from me and I'll throw in the saddle and bridle, and git you a nice little mare for the young gal here.'

'Something quiet,' Kitty said. 'And steady!'

He nodded. 'You taking baggage?'

'Erm – yes,' Georgiana said. 'Of course – we'll

303

need packs!'

'I'll find you a packhorse or a mule.' He eyed her narrowly. 'Travelling far?'

'Just like last time,' she said brightly. 'No distance at all.'

The next morning they arrived back at the wheelwright's after a good supper and a night's rest, and found Hetty looking over the fence, waiting for them. She was saddled up and ready. They stowed their belongings into packs, which the wheelwright lifted onto a sturdy mule.

Kitty was introduced to her mount, a handsome chestnut mare. 'A Missouri Fox Trotter,' the wheelwright pronounced. 'That's what she is. Got a touch of Spanish, and a bit of Morgan, so she'll ride well, little lady. No need to be feared of her.'

'No!' Kitty said in a timid voice. 'I'm not.' She patted the horse on the nose and gave her a sugar lump which she'd taken from the breakfast table. She took hold of the reins, put her foot in the stirrup iron and hoisted herself up. 'Thank you, she's lovely.'

Georgiana settled the payment. 'Thank you for your help,' she said to the wheelwright as she mounted Hetty. 'It is very much appreciated.'

He nodded. 'You're welcome, lady. Where do I say you're heading fer if anybody asks?'

'No-one will ask,' she said. 'But we're going to No-Name.'

'Good luck, then.' He waved a hand in farewell and stood by the gate to watch them.

'Are you ready, Kitty?' she asked and Kitty said nervously that she was as ready as she would ever be. They looked along the long dusty track and up towards the mountain range which lay beyond.

Georgiana took a deep breath. 'Come on then,' she said. 'Let's be on our way.'

CHAPTER TWENTY-SIX

'I said, get bailing, mister,' Cap'n Mac repeated. 'Otherwise we'll end up in this ole river and I couldn't begin to tell you what's floating in there.'

'But,' Edward began heatedly, 'that fellow's robbed me! I don't have any more money. I have to tell the police...' His voice faded away as he realized the consequences of doing that. The police would no doubt ask why he was in a hurry to leave New Orleans at such an early hour. And, he thought, it wouldn't surprise me if they were in the pay of Rodriguez. A man like him knows many people.

Reluctantly he picked up a bucket and started to bail. I've been snared, he thought. Duped. This old tub wasn't going anywhere! Where's the crew? Where are the other passengers? He glanced around at the peeling paintwork, the creaking paddles without a safety guard, the blackened smoking chimney. Though I daresay there might be a few blackguards who use this way out when they're in a hurry.

He straightened his back. Robert Allen's trousers and jacket, which he was wearing, were of thin cotton and he was soaked through to his skin. The water swilling around his feet was thick and slimy and the rain was pouring down in torrents. 'How long before it stops?' he called to Cap'n Mac, and wondered if that was his real name and title. 'The rain, I mean.'

The man shrugged. 'Tomorrow! Maybe the day after. Who knows?' The rain was running down his face but he didn't seem to notice.

'Where did you say you were going?' Edward shouted.

He gave a malevolent grin. 'I didn't.'

Edward bent again to the bailing and started to think furiously. So what does he intend to do with me? His crony back there has my money. Nobody knows I'm here on this old tub. He's probably thinking of tipping me overboard as soon as we're out of sight of anybody on the bank!

The banks were lower here and they were passing small shanty settlements with dilapidated shacks, a goat or cow tied up outside most of them. Emaciated dogs roamed free and barked at their passage. He guessed that when the river ran high the dwellings would be flooded.

He looked down into the slow muddy water of the Mississippi. A yellow foaming scum gathered around the floating logs and branches which were drifting downstream, and he shuddered at the thought of the disease which awaited anyone unlucky enough to fall in.

'Jo! Jo! Get your lazy butt up here.'

Edward looked up as the captain shouted below deck. So there is some other crew! When he'd first come on board he'd glanced around for an implement that he could use if he was set upon, and had spied a rusty spanner. It was just out of reach, but he could dash for it should he need to. But I wouldn't stand a chance against two men, he pondered, not if the other is as muscular as Cap'n Mac.

But Jo wasn't muscular. Jo was nicely rounded with a small waist, long dark hair and a pretty, though sullen, grubby face.

'Don't get any ideas, mister,' Cap'n Mac shouted to Edward. 'You so much as look dirty at her and you're overboard!'

'Wouldn't think of it,' Edward said, nodding towards her. Even if I was so inclined, which I am not, it would be difficult to pay one's respects in the state I am in. What I desire more than anything is a soak in a hot tub and a change of clothes. I will not become embroiled with a woman again, he resolved.

'Get to the fore,' Cap'n Mac ordered the girl. 'Look out for the lumber. And you,' he bellowed to Edward, 'when she rings the bell, take that stave and push the timber away from the hull.'

Edward looked around. A long wooden pole was lying on the deck. He'd noticed it before and wondered what its use was. Now he knew. It was to keep any logs, branches or floating weed away from the paddles.

Jo positioned herself at the head of the boat with her back to Edward. At her side was a large brass bell which she rang regularly. They were coming now into a wide stretch of the river littered with fallen trees whose branches lay above the water and drifted with its movement, their roots submerged beneath the surface. Other craft, mainly flatboats and freight-carrying steam packets, were moving slowly to avoid the obstacles.

'Watch out fer that sawyer,' Jo called to Edward. 'He's a big fella.' She pointed to a huge tree still with green leaves on its branches, which swayed menacingly towards them. 'Git that fella sucked under the paddles and we're done fer.'

Edward heaved with the pole, pushing with all his strength to keep the trunk of the tree away from the boat. 'Stop engines,' the girl cried. 'You'll have to come up, Pa,' she called to the captain. 'This fella's not used to hard work. Bin a gen'leman, have you?' she scoffed.

Edward was about to reply that, yes, as a matter of fact that was what he was, when he remembered who he was supposed to be, or rather not to be. *I must remember that I am not Edward Newmarch.*

'No,' he replied. 'I was a servant, but I didn't do heavy work.'

The girl pealed with laughter. 'Oh, *la-di-da!* A *sarvant!* Is that right? Well in that case you can git below, mister, and make some coffee.'

Cap'n Mac took the pole from him. 'Yip, get below whilst we're stationary. Coffee's on the shelf.'

Whilst Edward felt some degree of relief that the captain had his daughter on board and was therefore unlikely to use violence on him, he was still uneasy as to how he would get back to New Orleans. Though their passage was slow he reckoned that they had travelled several miles. The land beyond the banks seemed swampy and inhospitable. Narrow creeks and rivulets ran off the main artery and dozens of small islands, thick moss and strangling weed had to be negotiated. Frogs croaked incessantly and several times he had seen slithering movements on the banks and rippling eddies in the water. It was also blisteringly hot in spite of the rain, and there was a stench of rotting vegetation.

'I've found the coffee,' he called up from below. 'But where's the water?'

He heard the girl's peal of laughter again and Cap'n Mac's muttered oath. 'Come up here, mister,' the captain called. 'Bring the pan. Look down there.' He pointed into the river. 'What d'you see?' He spoke in a slow derisory tone as if Edward was dim-witted.

Edward gazed down into the water. It was green and slimy and covered with river weed. Mosquitoes hovered over it. 'You're not suggesting we drink that!'

'Ain't nuthin' else,' he replied. 'If you're particular there's a filter somewhere below, but this water is good and wholesome, mister. Ain't done me or my daughter any harm. Why, she was weaned on it, ain't that right, Jo?'

Edward stared at them both in disgust, then lowered the long-handled vessel into the river and brought up a panful of green water. Well, *nothing* will induce me to drink this, he vowed. I'd have to be dying first!

Nevertheless, he was very hot and thirsty, and looked around in the cramped galley for something in which to catch rainwater. He found another pan and also a rusty sieve. He put it to

309

his nose and sniffed. It had an unmistakable reek of engine oil.

An evil-smelling stove was in the galley and after scooping off the weed from the pan of water, he heated it and made the coffee. He felt quite virtuous, as this was the first time in his life that he had done such a thing. He took the other pan on deck to catch rainwater, placing it away from the chimney, which was spurting black soot and smoke.

He handed the chipped coffee beakers to Jo and her father. She took a drink and immediately spat it out. 'Cold! Didn't you boil the water?'

'Well, it's fairly hot,' he began.

'Some *sarvant* you are,' she said scathingly. 'You've got to boil the water to kill off the mozzies! Here.' She handed it back to him and her father did likewise. 'Try agin.'

He glanced in the pan that was catching the rainwater. It was half full already, but had soot and mosquitoes floating in it. He kicked it viciously, knocking it over. I'll do without, he decided.

There were two small cabins and, when darkness fell, Cap'n Mac ordered him below to one of them. It was not much bigger than a cupboard with a narrow shelf, which turned out to be his sleeping bunk. A thin mattress lay upon it and he found that he couldn't stretch out, only lie with his knees tucked up.

There was little chance of sleep, for all night there were bumpings and jarrings as the timber in the river hit the boat and on one occasion he was almost thrown out of his bunk. To add insult to hopelessness he was dripped on by rain

310

coming through the cracks in the timbers.

As day dawned he sat with his head in his hands and pondered on his situation. How was he to get off the boat and back to New Orleans? There hadn't been any opportunity the previous day, and as evening had drawn on they moved into a wider, rolling, rushing stretch of river. Right now, he thought, the prospect of Rodriguez searching me out seems preferable to being stuck here in the middle of a swamp with a boat-steering rogue and his bad-tempered daughter.

He put on his shirt, trousers and jacket, which he had draped over a rickety chair and which were still very damp. He shivered, though the air was muggy. 'I'll probably die of pneumonia,' he muttered. 'And no-one will know.' Or care, he reflected. No-one knows where I am. Not Allen, he'll be expecting me back. Two weeks, I told him. And if I die out here on the boat, this blackguard will throw me overboard. He felt very sorry for himself. He didn't deserve this misery, he thought, quite forgetting that he had brought on his misfortune entirely unaided.

'Hey, mister.' The girl, Jo, shouted down to him. 'You gonna stay in bed all morning?'

'I'm coming.' He roused himself and shuffled up the few steps to the deck. There was a smell of coffee and he licked his dry mouth. Should he risk trying it? If he was going to die it wouldn't matter if he died of pneumonia, malaria or dysentery, though the latter might be the worst, he decided.

'Coffee?' Jo asked, holding up a jug. She looked more presentable this morning. Her face was clean and her hands relatively so, though she was

311

wearing the same mud-spattered dress.

'Yes. Please.' He took the beaker from her and sipped, closing his eyes so that he was spared further sight of the thick soupy liquid which was the colour of the river itself. It tasted surprisingly good if rather gritty. He took another gulp and felt better for it.

'Sorry I was so shrewish yesterday,' Jo said. 'I was feeling outa sorts. You know how it is sometimes with wimmin?'

'Ah, yes,' he said vaguely.

'You married?'

He was caught unawares by her question. Last time he had falsely claimed to be a widower he had almost become a bigamist by promising to marry Elena. 'Yes,' he said. 'I am.'

'So who you running from? Your wife?'

'Erm – no. I owe money,' he lied. 'To a money-lender.'

'You son of a bitch! You left your wife holdin' the baby?'

'No. No. We don't have any children,' he said hastily.

She grimaced at him. 'I didn't mean that, you dolt! I meant holding the can, going to jail 'stead of you?'

'Oh, no. No fear of that.' He was quick to deny it. 'She's not there – she's away, visiting her sister.'

'Yeah, yeah!'

She was unconvinced, he could see that. 'So I mustn't be away too long,' he said. 'She'll start worrying. When shall we be arriving at wherever it is we're going?'

She hunched her shoulders. 'Depends,' she

said. 'On what Pa has planned. Two or three days anyway afore we turn around.'

'I thought your father said he couldn't turn this boat around?'

She rolled her eyes at his stupidity. 'Nor he can when the river's narrow. But once we git to a wider stretch, then he can.'

He heaved a deep breath. Things were looking up. 'So, we can expect to be back in New Orleans in a week or so?'

'What makes you think we'll take you, mister?' Cap'n Mac appeared at the top of the galley steps. 'You said you'd lost your money!'

'Stolen!' Edward said vehemently. 'That fellow who said he was a friend of yours. But I'll pay you for the return trip,' he added quickly. 'I have money back at the hotel.'

'Which belongs to the moneylender?' Jo queried, a cynical smile on her lips.

Edward closed his eyes for a second. How was it that whenever he lied, he seemed to dig a deeper hole for himself?

'I promise you–' he began, but the captain was turning away. 'I need some help,' he barked. 'Get up on deck.'

It was very hot on deck and the mosquitoes constantly buzzed and bit until Edward's face was covered in itchy red weals. There was no need to bail as the rain had stopped, but he was told to 'stay up front and keep lookout'.

The current was strong and faster here. The river rushed and whirled and great globs of crusty yellow foam attached themselves to the floating timber like a frilly hem on a young girl's skirts. They stopped once and took on wood for the fire. The bank was low and the wood was thrown down onto the deck by someone who was obviously waiting for the boat, and who caught the packet that Cap'n Mac threw to him.

Edward looked keenly at the landscape with a view to getting off, but the river was wide and the land was marshy. As he gazed into the distance the swamp seemed to extend as far as he could see, with a few stumpy decaying cottonwood trees and no sign of habitation.

They chugged and wheezed along for two more days and tempers grew short. On the third morning Edward rose and realized they were going much more slowly. When he came up on deck he saw that they were no longer on the river, but had run off it at some point during the night and were moving along a winding sluggish creek with overhanging branches and swampy banks. There were no other boats.

'What place is this?' he exclaimed. 'Dante's Inferno?' It was hot and sticky and foul-smelling. The mosquitoes were alive and hungry, the frogs croaked in deafening cacophony, yet there was no other sound. Everything else was silent in that humid, desolate atmosphere, save for the creak and groan of their paddles.

Cap'n Mac didn't answer him, but only indicated that he should watch out for weed and timber.

Edward ducked his head as a low branch threatened to decapitate him. He felt queasy. There hadn't been much food and what there was he carefully looked over before venturing to eat.

Jo had cooked soup, the base of which he couldn't begin to guess at, which lay heavy and greasily on his stomach along with the stale bread which they had consumed. This is a disease-ridden hellhole! I can't think that I'll get out alive.

On the following morning Edward awoke as the boat shuddered and the engine died. He could hear Cap'n Mac cursing. He went up on deck and found him leaning over the side, trying to prise a tree branch from under one of the paddles.

'Pesky river,' he grunted. 'Jo!' he yelled. 'You should have been up here watching out, gal. I just didn't see this coming.'

Jo appeared from below. She was dressed in only her shift but she didn't seem at all concerned about it. 'Will you have to go over?' she asked, peering down.

'Reckon so. Can't shift it from up here.'

Edward looked about him. They had come into fairly clear water and it was running fast. In the distance beyond the levee he could see a shack and behind it a sparse wood. 'I'll go over if you like,' he offered. 'If you force it from the top, I'll try to move it from below.'

'Can you swim? It's pretty deep.'

'Yes.' As a boy he had occasionally swum in the Humber, though he had been in trouble from his parents when they found out. The Humber estuary was fast and treacherous but, unlike the Mississippi, it didn't have the hazard of trees floating down it. The only debris there was what people threw into it.

He took off his jacket and lowered himself into the water. If I can pull this out, he thought, and whilst Cap'n Mac is starting the engine, I could swim to shore. He's not going to take me back with him, that I know, so I might as well chance my luck here.

It was cool in the water. Slimy strands of weed attached themselves to him as he heaved and tugged at the branch that had become entwined in the paddles.

'That's it,' he shouted as it eventually came free. 'Start the engine.' He trod water away from the paddles. I'll let it start moving and then head for the shore.

'Look out!' Jo, who had been leaning over the side, watching, suddenly screamed out. 'Croc! There's a croc coming up behind!'

Edward glanced over his shoulder. Slithering down the muddy bank and into the water was the grey scaly body of a crocodile, and it was coming straight towards him.

CHAPTER TWENTY-SEVEN

Getting out of the boat had been easy enough, he'd simply lowered himself over the side. But getting back in was a different matter altogether. There was nothing to hold onto, no ledge where he could heave himself up. He swam to the fore of the boat away from the ripples in the water, where he could see the scaly body of the oncoming reptile just below the surface. He shouted, 'The stave! Get the stave!'

316

Jo rushed to fetch the pole they had been using to ward off the floating timber, but her father appeared with a rope, one end of which he threw over, hitting Edward on the head. He grabbed it and heaved and it slipped out of Cap'n Mac's hands. 'For God's sake!' Edward shouted. 'Hurry up and get another rope!'

Cap'n Mac disappeared and Jo called to Edward, 'Watch out, I'm going to throw this over,' and she pushed the stave into the water.

'Stupid girl,' he yelled. 'I wanted you to pull me in by it!'

'Can't,' she yelled back. 'You'd be too heavy. Hit him with it when he comes at you.'

Edward seized the stave and held it in front of him. When the crocodile was near enough for him to see its long body and powerful propelling tail, he lifted the stave and whammed it on its long snout.

'C'mon,' Cap'n Mac shouted from the deck. 'I've got another rope. It's fast. Climb up.'

Edward took another swipe at the reptile and then jumped towards the rope. Clinging tightly and praying it would hold, he pushed upwards with his feet against the hull of the boat, only glancing for a second at the snapping jaws of the crocodile. He fell onto the deck on his knees, gasping and shaking his head.

'You all right?' Jo asked, bending down to look at him.

'Yes,' he breathed. 'I'm just wondering what I did to deserve all this trouble.'

'Trouble!' Cap'n Mac said scornfully. 'You ain't seen no trouble yet, mister.'

'Look,' Jo pointed down at the water. 'It's biting at the stave.' Edward staggered to his feet and followed her gaze. The crocodile was attacking the stave with its huge sharp teeth, its wide jaws spanning the width of the wood.

'It's only a baby,' she remarked as she watched it. 'It ain't full size. These fellas grow to fifteen feet easy. He's only six feet or so.' She shrugged. 'Course, he could've taken your leg off, which would've been a real problem for you as there's no doctor hereabouts.'

Edward stared at Jo. She's mad! Cap'n Mac was bemoaning the loss of his rope, which was floating downriver, and muttering about the price he'd have to pay for another. They're both mad! The sooner I'm off this boat the better I shall like it.

The next day they came into narrow water where a tangle of weed, branches and slimy sludge matted the surface. Willow trees lined the banks, their slender branches bending low over the creek. Here and there through the under-growth, Edward spied an occasional broken-down cabin and sometimes a figure or dog beside it. By midday they reached a gap in the trees and Cap'n Mac steered towards it. The land was low-lying, with stagnant weed and thin saplings growing on it, and there was no sign of habitation.

'Are we getting off?' Edward asked.

The captain nodded. 'For supplies. I'll need a hand.'

For supplies? he thought. But there's nothing here. Is he meeting someone? 'Then are we heading back?' he asked.

Cap'n Mac lifted his chin and viewed Edward

318

through narrowed eyes. 'Mebbe! Mebbe not. Depends.'

I could be on this damned boat for ever, Edward thought, and retorted sharply, 'Depends! You keep saying that! Depends on what? I need to get back. I have to be in New Orleans. This is kidnapping.' He angrily jabbed a finger. 'In England you would be put in jail for this!'

'In England? You English then?' Cap'n Mac pushed back his cap and scratched his head. 'I guessed there was sump'n odd about you.'

'Something odd about me!' Edward screeched. 'I've been robbed. Forced onto a leaky old tub that I wouldn't sail on a garden pond. Poisoned by noxious coffee, been nearly eaten alive by crocodiles and mosquitoes, and you say there's something odd about me.'

Jo had come on deck and was listening to the discourse. 'You could always walk back if you don't want to stay.' She waved a hand in the direction of the bank. 'There ain't nobody stopping you.'

'You're absolutely right,' he said. 'I can!' He swung his leg over the side and then the other and slid into the green water. 'Goodbye!'

'So long,' Jo cried. 'Been nice meetin' you. Watch out fer the crocs.' She had a laugh in her voice, and as Edward struck out the short distance to the land he glanced back and saw them watching him from the deck. He hauled himself out and shook like a dog to be rid of the excess water and weed, then splashed across the quaggy land. He turned back only once to look towards the creek which lay murmuring below the low banks. There was nothing there. No smoking chimney to show where the boat had been. They'd gone.

They didn't even wait to see if I changed my mind! He was swathed in weed and mud, his boots were squelching and tendrils of green hung from his hair. Ahead of him was waterlogged land with gnarled and twisted trees and garlands of moss hanging from them.

He straightened his shoulders and heaved out a breath. No point in hanging around here. I might as well start walking.

He was exhausted by the time he reached a shelter belt of trees. The miry swamp sucked and pulled at his boots and he wondered what venomous creatures might be waiting beneath the surface. The air was humid and sticky and at times he found himself almost up to his waist in stagnant water. The shelter belt which he had pushed towards was little more than a few stringy cottonwood trees, but the land was slightly higher and drier and he plunged into the middle of it and dropped down thankfully beneath the shade.

He licked his dry lips. How have I come to this? His body shook with fatigue and he lay down, pushing some dry leaves beneath his head for a pillow. Have I been so very wicked? His head ached and images swirled around his mind. Images of England and leaving home and the past and present became confused.

I left May and that seems like a thousand years ago, and yes it was wrong of me. Not a gentlemanly thing to do. Martin would never have done that, he mused, his thoughts drifting and his brother coming into his consciousness. But then he was always a good fellow, not like me. I wonder if he married Georgiana Gregory? They seemed to have an understanding.

And what about my poor patient mother? What did she think when I left England? He remembered that he hadn't said goodbye but had only left her a letter. His thoughts flickered to Ruby, his young mistress. Ah, Ruby, darling girl! I shall never forget you, not ever. I should've married you and not May, but, poor girl, it wouldn't have worked. He was dizzy and though his eyes were closed he had the sensation of spinning round and round.

'Wouldn't have worked,' he murmured. 'You said that I would be ashamed of you and of course, then, I would. I was so full of pride. But not now, I wouldn't. Not now. Not now that I have been through so much. My pride has gone.' He was vaguely aware that he was babbling, but couldn't stop. 'Sofia!' he called out. 'You tricked me. It's your fault that I'm in this predicament. Predicament. Predicament. What a predicament!'

He dropped off into an uneasy, dream-filled sleep. He sweated with the heat and then as it grew dark he shivered and hunched into himself. 'Mosquitoes!' he muttered. 'Malaria! Allen! Allen! Where are you? Fetch me some water. Damn your eyes.' He sat up and stared into the darkness at the wizened ghostly shapes of the trees. 'My money!' He patted his damp jacket as if searching. 'My pocketbook! Allen's got it.'

He lay down again and closed his eyes. He was

321

cold and shivery. 'Malaria,' he mumbled. 'I've got malaria, just like Allen had. Or swamp fever. That's it! How long have I been gone? A week? More? I've lost track of time. I told him – what? Two weeks, I think.' His mind was disordered and he sought for dates. 'Allen won't be expecting me back just yet. He won't be concerned. Not yet.'

As the day dawned, he tried to rise from his hard earth bed but his joints had stiffened and he couldn't move. I'll wait for the sun to warm me, to loosen up my joints, he thought, and fell asleep again.

He awoke when the sun filtered through the tree branches and flickered on his face. He slapped at a mosquito and turned over. 'Fetch me that water,' he muttered. 'Be quick about it.' He sat up a little later and roared 'Rodriguez!' at the top of his voice and then fell back and slept.

It was dark when he awoke again and he wondered what it was that had woken him. He was drenched in sweat and had a raging thirst. Then he raised his head and realized that he wasn't sweating, but that it was raining. Raining a great deluge of wonderful clean water. He scrambled to his knees and grasping the nearest tree trunk hauled himself to his feet and staggered to the edge of the grove.

He stood with his arms held wide and his face upturned to the blue-black sky and let the rain pour over him, opening his mouth to let the moisture trickle down his throat. 'There is a God after all,' he gasped. 'I was beginning to think that there wasn't.'

After a thorough drenching he crept back into

the shelter of trees and waited for morning. At the first sign of light streaking the sky he moved off. He didn't pause to look at the shafts of vibrant colour which were heralding a new day, but simply moved one foot in front of the other and knew that if he stopped he would find it difficult to get going again.

He had stumbled on for about a mile when he realized that his direction might be wrong. The creek had been at his back when he set off, but he didn't know from which direction it had run off the Mississippi. Was it east or west? If I turn around and go back then I'll have to cross it. He put his hand to his head. He was dizzy from lack of food and his throat was parched again. His clothes had dried on him and were stiff with mud. I'll go on, there will surely be a settlement or habitation. But as he looked ahead all he could see was a vast stretch of land.

He was still stumbling forward by dusk and now he hadn't any idea of the direction he was following. There was no road, no wheel marks, no animal tracks, but he thought he could see a faint light in the distance, shining through the twilight.

A dog barked and he stopped, startled by the sound, then urged himself on. 'If there's a dog – if there's a dog–' he mumbled, but hadn't even the strength to put into words what he was thinking.

A shack loomed up ahead. The light he had seen was coming from a window. A dog barked again and a woman's voice called to it. But it persisted, its bark angry and urgent. 'Hello!' Edward attempted to hail whoever was inside, but his voice was weak and hoarse. 'Anybody there?'

The planked door opened a crack and he saw a glimpse of someone behind it. 'Hello,' he called again, mustering a cracked plea. 'Can you help me?'

'Stay right where you are, mister.' A woman's voice, low and menacing, answered. 'One move and I'll blow your danged head off.'

Edward dropped to his knees and splayed his hands in front of him. 'I'm not carrying a weapon,' he croaked. 'I need water. I'm lost.'

The door opened and a large woman came out. She had a rifle crooked into her arm and she looked as if she knew how to use it. 'Git outa here if you know what's good fer you, mister,' she said threateningly. 'Otherwise I'll set my dawg on you.'

'Please,' he begged. 'Some water! I've walked for miles. I need to get back to New Orleans.'

'New Orleans?' She came closer. 'You goin' in the wrong direction, mister, if you want New Orleans.' She edged towards him and nudged him with her foot. 'Where you walked from?'

He shook his head. 'I was – on a – boat,' he mumbled. 'On the Mississippi. Then – we came into a creek. I don't know where.'

'Jack!' The woman called back to the house. 'Jack! Come on out here.'

From where he was on the ground he squinted towards the door, wondering vaguely why Jack hadn't come out first instead of the woman, and if he was going to be sent on his way. Then, from out of the lighted doorway, he saw the shape of a large black dog. Its feet were firmly on the ground and its great head looking towards the woman.

'Come on here,' she commanded. 'Seize!'

Edward held his breath for a second as he wondered if he had the strength to run, or if he should simply lie down and be torn to pieces by the brute. But the dog ambled towards him, sat down in front of him and bared his teeth into a grin.

'Don't think he can't bite, mister, cos he can,' the woman told him. 'If he sets about you you'll sure be sorry.'

Edward nodded. 'I can tell,' he muttered. 'I can see he's a vicious brute.'

'He sure is.' She kept her eyes firmly fixed on him and pointed the rifle at his chest. 'Now git up slowly. Don't make a sudden move or he'll have you.'

Edward staggered to his feet, trying to keep his hands in the air. This is a nightmare, he thought. It has to be. A long, long nightmare, and I'll wake up in my own bed back home in England.

'Keep on walking,' she said. 'Go inside and I'll take a look at you.'

The shack was barely furnished with a table, two chairs, a roughly hewn dresser and a mattress in the corner. In the middle of the room was an iron stove with a pan on it and a smell of food cooking. Edward stumbled towards it. 'Could I have some water? Please.'

'Water's in the butt outside,' she said, then pointed to a jug on the table. 'There's some ale in the jug.'

He seized the jug and drank straight from it, not waiting for a cup or glass. 'Thank you,' he gasped. 'Thank you. I'm so grateful. I think I would have died if I hadn't found you.'

His legs suddenly felt weak. 'Can I sit down?' he said and as he asked, a dizzying blackness came over him. 'I think I'm–'

He knew no more until the morning, when he awoke in a bed on the floor. His jacket and boots had been taken off and a coarse grey blanket covered him.

The woman was by the stove with her back to him. She was tall and heavily built, with strong muscular arms below the rolled-up sleeves of her dress. She turned around and saw him watching her. Her hair was fair and hung greasily around her plump cheeks, and he guessed that she was in her thirties.

She nodded at him. 'You back in the land of the living then?'

He tried to raise himself up but found he was curiously weak. 'Yes.' He dropped back on the mattress. There was no pillow. 'How long have I been here?'

'Dunno.' She shrugged laconically. 'Couple o' days, I guess. You hungry?'

'Yes. Very,' he said, making an extra effort to sit up. 'Have I really been here so long?'

She nodded. 'You got up once and went outside to pee, then fell right back to sleep agin.'

He was embarrassed. He couldn't remember anything since coming into the shack with the dog following. 'Where's your dog?' he asked.

She poured something from a pan into a bowl. 'He's on guard outside. Here, have some broth.'

'Thank you.' He took it from her. 'Do you live alone here?'

'Right now I do, but my man'll be back from

326

market any time.'

He drank the soup from the bowl, as she hadn't offered him a spoon. It was thick and hot but he had no idea what the flavour was.

'What does he do? Is he a boatman?'

'You sure ask a lot o' questions, mister.' She sat down on a chair, folded her arms across her ample chest and surveyed him. 'He's a farmer.'

'Really? Can you farm the land around here? It seems like swamp to me.'

'It is swamp. We keep pigs. Where you from? You a city boy? You talk kinda funny.'

His head still ached. *I wonder if I've got malaria like Allen had? Those mosquitoes certainly had a good feed off me.* 'I'm from England,' he said. 'I was robbed in New Orleans, then put on a boat and finished up here. I've no money or papers.'

'Papers? What kinda papers?'

'To say who I am! My identity.'

She laughed, showing gaps in her teeth. 'We don't bother with that kinda thing out here, mister. We know who we are. Don't ya know who you are?'

He pondered for a second and wondered how far Rodriguez' domination stretched. 'Yes, I know who I am,' he said. 'My name is Robert Allen.'

CHAPTER TWENTY-EIGHT

'May I have a wash?' he asked later after he'd got up from the bed and stretched his aching limbs. He felt much better – the soup had given him some energy though his legs still felt weak.

'Sure.' She looked him over. 'The water butt's outside. If you take your pants off I'll wash them for you.'

'Erm–' He cleared his throat. He wasn't sure how he would feel about being in his under-garments in front of a strange woman.

'No need to feel bashful.' She winked at him. 'You ain't got nuthin' Ah ain't seen before. Ah grew up with six brothers and they didn't own a pair of underpants between 'em. Besides,' she gave him a sly look, 'you've bin sharing my bed for the last couple o' nights so it won't matter too much.' She grinned. 'You kept calling me Ruby.'

He stared at her and his mouth opened and closed. He flushed. He hadn't thought to wonder where she had slept! There was only one bed in the room. 'I'm sorry–' he began. 'I didn't think to ask–'

'You were dead to the world,' she remarked. 'So you didn't even notice.'

I wish I could remember, he thought uneasily. How could I have lost a couple of days?

She washed his trousers and jacket and hung them on a clothes line which stretched between the shanty and a dilapidated pig pen. It was empty of pigs but the guard dog lay sleeping inside and only opened one eye when he looked in. A few scrawny chickens clucked around and a nanny goat tied on a long rope bleated at him.

There didn't seem to be a bowl to use for washing, so he dipped his head into the water butt and rubbed his hands through his hair to be rid of the tangle of weed. The woman called to him from the doorway. 'Guess you're a good-lookin' fella when you're cleaned up?'

'Well,' he began modestly. 'This isn't how I usually look or dress.' Then he remembered his role as Robert Allen. 'How can I get back to New Orleans?' he asked. 'My er, my employer will be wondering where I am.'

'Can't say.' She finished pegging out the rest of her laundry. He thought that his trousers and jacket didn't look any cleaner for washing, they were still stained with green, though maybe they smelt a little sweeter. 'I ain't never bin.'

She came towards him and looked him up and down, which he found disconcerting, standing only in his underclothes. 'Why do you want to go back there? You can stay along a' us.'

He gave a tense laugh. 'I must get back. I, er, I have work to do. I need money.'

'You can help us with the pigs. You wouldn't need money out here.' She gave him what he interpreted as a very warm smile, which, with her raised suggestive eyebrows, made him extremely apprehensive.

'There surely isn't enough work for two men to do? You said your man would be back soon.'

'He might be. He might not.' Again she smiled. 'Ah ain't too bothered if he ain't.'

'How long has he been gone?' he asked uneasily.

''Bout five, six, weeks, I guess.'

'That's a long time just to take pigs to market. Did you have many pigs?'

'Just the two,' she said, nodding.

I think I'm going mad! This is as bad as being on the boat. How do I get out of this situation? And, he deliberated fearfully, where do I sleep tonight?

He slept on one of the chairs though she urged him to 'Come alongside o' me,' but he told her that he couldn't possibly sleep in the same bed as another man's wife, not now that he was fully conscious of what he was doing.

'It wouldn't be right,' he insisted. 'And whatever would he think?' he added. 'Your man, if he should come home unexpectedly?'

'Oh, Ah guess Guthrie wouldn't mind too much,' she said. 'Ah was in bed with him when Eli came home.'

'Eli?' he asked.

'My first fella. He was a mite annoyed, but he went quietly enough after Guthrie peppered him with shot.'

I *am* going mad, he decided. Or I will be if I don't get out of here.

He was up early the next morning and dressed in his clean trousers, which appeared to have shrunk, for his ankles showed below them. He was determined to depart, even if it meant walking for miles again. There was no habitation in the landscape around him, only a vast area of swamp and open fields in the distance. I'll have to make a dash when she's doing something, he decided, and I'll have to run, otherwise I'm quite sure I'll be peppered with shot just as Eli was.

She called him in for breakfast and he sat down with her to a bowl of gruel and a slice of bread. 'Here's my neighbour coming,' she said suddenly. 'Ah guessed he'd be along sometime soon.'

He glanced across at her. She hadn't stirred from the chair so how did she know someone was coming? Even the dog hadn't barked. 'Your neighbour? Where does he live?'

'Five, six, miles along the track. He's bringing me my groceries.' She looked at him questioningly. 'Can't you hear him?'

He concentrated hard, then shook his head. She must be so used to living in isolation that she could hear every little rumble or crack of sound that was out of the ordinary.

'Heard you, way back, on the night you came,' she said, keeping her eyes on him. 'That's why Ah had my gun ready. We git some strange folks coming up from that ole river. Folks that have bin tipped off the boats same as you were.'

'Do you mean that fellow back there, Cap'n Mac, knew that I would get off the boat rather than risk travelling any further?'

'Yip. Guess so. Saves him the bother of dumping you.'

The dog barked and Edward got up from the table and looked out. He couldn't see anyone, but there was a dark shape on the horizon which he guessed could be a waggon or cart coming towards them. He felt a tingle of excitement.

331

Perhaps I could get a lift. I don't care where he's going as long as it's out of here.

'Howdy, Rube!' The woman greeted the man driving a waggon as he drew up at the door ten minutes later. 'Heard you comin'.'

'Howdy, Martha. Got yourself a visitor, Ah see.'

'This is Bob,' Martha said. 'He got tipped off a boat.'

Bob? Edward thought. I told her I was Robert Allen. But he nodded at the stranger. 'How do you do.'

'Ah'm doin' all right, thank you kindly, sir.' He looked at Edward from beneath his battered hat. 'Ah've just brought Martha some vittles. Sack o' cornmeal.' He sucked on his teeth, making a whistling sound. 'Cooking oil. Coffee.'

I don't need an inventory, Edward brooded. What I need is to hide in the back of that waggon and drive out of here. A vague notion of stealing the horse and waggon once Rube had unloaded the supplies entered his mind, but he decided against the idea as he wouldn't have known in which direction to travel. If Rube will drive me to the nearest settlement, surely I can then find my way back to New Orleans?

The delivery of supplies also meant Rube sitting down to a pot of coffee and a gossip about neighbours, then partaking of a bowl of gruel and discussing the price of pigs at market, and all the while he kept glancing across at Edward. Then another pot of coffee and Rube told of his son who was set on going to California and who had bought a new wheelbarrow, before he finally rose up from his chair, stating that he would have to rush along.

Edward went outside before him and looked in the back of the uncovered waggon. There were several empty sacks and a coil of rope which had been thrown in haphazardly, but not enough to cover a man.

Rube came out and made a show of attending to the horse, and beckoned with his head for Edward to come closer. 'If you want a ride outa here, mister, just give me ten minutes with Martha. See that tree?' He pointed down the track where a stumpy dead tree was standing alone. 'Wait fer me there.'

Edward stared in astonishment. Rube must have been all of sixty. His face was brown and wrinkled and he was wearing the oldest clothes that Edward had ever seen: baggy trousers, a worn waistcoat with the buttons missing, a striped cotton shirt. On his feet were cracked leather boots without laces.

'Yes,' Edward muttered, thinking that although Rube was not the most handsome man he had ever met, perhaps Martha wasn't too particular. 'Thank you.'

He waited beside the tree as the sun beat down on his head and presently saw the waggon move off from the shack and come in his direction. Rube pulled his hat further over his eyes as he reined in, whilst Edward climbed aboard.

'Pretty good arrangement, Ah reckon,' Rube muttered. 'Sack o' cornmeal. Cooking oil. Coffee.'

'Yes. Yes, indeed,' Edward agreed and wondered who had had the best of the bargain, Rube or Martha. He looked back over his shoulder and wondered if she knew that he had gone, but Rube reassured him.

'Don't you worry 'bout Martha,' he said. 'There'll be some other fella along in no time at all.'

They trundled down the track in silence for a while, then Rube started to tell him about his son Jed. 'Dead set on going to Californy, he is. Going to look fer gold. He's got his pick and shovel. Bought a wheelbarrow, cos Ah said he couldn't have mine. Meetin' his friends at the saloon tonight, then they're off first thing in the morning. Told him, Ah did, that there's no use fer gold around here. Nothing to buy. Not a darned thing. 'Cept fer cornmeal, cooking oil and coffee. But he's dead set on going anyway.' He nodded his head, looked into the distance and sucked on his teeth. 'Got his pick and shovel. Bought a wheelbarrow, cos Ah said he couldn't have mine.'

Edward put his head in his hands. This is a nightmare! When am I going to wake up?

After about half an hour they passed a tumble-down shack and Rube raised a hand though Edward didn't see anyone around, then ten minutes later they passed another, with a man sitting on a bench outside. Again Rube raised a hand and the man responded though neither of them spoke.

'Jest coming into town now,' Rube proclaimed after another fifteen minutes or so, as they approached half a dozen wooden cabins. 'Traffic'll be mighty busy.' A waggon pulled by two horses was travelling in the opposite direction and a horse and rider followed it. 'Yip,' Rube commented.

334

'Traffic's always busy on a Monday.'

'Is it Monday?' Edward had completely lost count of the days.

Rube shrugged. 'Guess it's Monday. Or it might be Wednesday. Traffic's mighty busy on a Wednesday.' He pointed with his whip to a building where the word Saloon had been painted on a board across the front. The S and the l had worn off, but there was no mistaking what it was. Two oak casks were positioned by the door and there were shouts of laughter coming from within.

A covered waggon and two horses were tied to a hitching post. 'Looks like my boy's there already.' Rube drew up and invited Edward to come in and meet his son before he left for California.

'Would there be anyone who could show me the road to New Orleans, do you think?' Edward asked as they went through the door. 'It's most important that I get back.'

'I'll ask around town, Bob,' Rube said. 'There jest might be.'

The saloon seemed to be full of young men, but the room was small and there were only about six or seven of them, all gathered together prior to departure for California.

Edward was introduced as Bob to Jed and the assembly, and a tankard of ale was put in front of him. 'I haven't any money,' he started to explain. 'I was robbed in New Orleans.'

'Drink up,' Jed said. 'Nobody has any money. But we're on our way to find some. We're off to Californy–'

'Yes, yes,' Edward interrupted hastily. 'I heard. You've got a pick and shovel.'

335

'Yip.' Jed put his hands into his pockets. 'And a wheelbarrow.'

Edward took a long gulp of ale. 'Couldn't you have bought a wheelbarrow when you got there?'

'Shucks, no,' Jed said. 'The price will be way out of reach. I've bought mine on credit. I'll pay for it when I find gold.'

'So you'll come back?' Edward asked, thinking that nothing on earth would get him to set foot here again.

'Shucks, no,' he answered. Jed was a young man of about twenty. 'Pa thinks I will. But I know that I won't. When I find gold I'll set up in business, build me a nice little cabin, find a girl to marry and I'm set up for life.'

'Good luck, then.' Edward drained his tankard and found another one had been put in front of him by another man.

'Say, where you from, mister?' the man said. 'Not from these parts?'

'No.' Edward told them part of the story, of how he was walking in New Orleans, was accosted and robbed and put on a boat.

'It's a wicked place, so Ah've heard,' said another man. 'Not that Ah've bin.' And he too put a tankard in front of Edward.

'I shouldn't really,' he protested. 'I don't usually drink ale.'

'You want something stronger?' Jed said. 'Here, Moss,' he called to the man who was serving behind a low counter. 'One of your specials for our visitor here.'

Moss came over with a small glass of clear liquor. 'Where you from, stranger?'

By the time Edward had regaled them several times with variations of his story, he couldn't stand upright without assistance. 'What a lovely town,' he slurred. 'Sluch – flendly – pleople.' He hiccuped and put his arms around Jed and one of the other men. 'Can't think why you should want to leave it.' He heaved a deep breath. 'I've never had friends like you before. I'll miss you when you're gone.'

Jed leaned into him and, putting his head next to Edward's, squinted at him. 'Come with us, Bob. You don't need to go to New Orleans.' He patted Edward affectionately on his cheek. 'Come along with us.'

'Yes.' The others agreed and cheered the suggestion. All but Rube, who was slumped on the floor in a corner of the room.

'Righty-ho.' Edward swayed towards the open door. 'Come on, then. If we're going, let's go.' He raised his arm in the air and waved it. 'Ho, California!'

He stumbled outside to where the waggon and horses were waiting. The men crowded and stumbled after him. Some couldn't quite make it to the waggon and fell in a heap on the ground, but four or five pushed their way in and argued as to who should drive.

'*I'll* drive!' Edward climbed unsteadily into the driver's seat and Jed clambered up at the side of him. The others fell into the back of the waggon. One fell out again and lay on the ground. Edward shook the reins and the horses moved forward, but they didn't go far before they heard a splintering crash as the hitching rail fell over.

Moss came running after them. 'You need to unhitch it from the rail first!'

'Sorry.' Edward grinned. 'Sh'll know better 'nother time.' He cracked the whip and the horses moved off at his command. 'Ho, California!' he yelled.

'Ho, Californy.' A drunken cheer went up from the inside of the waggon. 'Ho, Californy!'

CHAPTER TWENTY-NINE

Edward came to his senses three or four days later. None of the men could remember setting out on the journey, only that some of them who had been coming didn't, and some who had come hadn't intended to.

'My ma's going to be real mad at me,' a seventeen-year-old, whose name was Tod, said dismally. 'Shucks, I only went into town to get a sack o' flour.'

'You could start walking back.' Jed held his hand over his eyes to keep out the daylight. 'Maybe you'd get a lift part-way.'

Tod considered. 'Why, I guess I might as well come along. Ma can get another sack o' flour.'

Edward stared at them. Who were these men? They were not the kind he would normally associate with. Where did he meet them? And where were they going? He vaguely remembered driving a waggon, then someone else taking over the reins when he fell asleep. Days and nights had

338

merged, the ale from the barrels had flowed freely, then they had moved on again and whoever was the most capable had taken the reins.

They had drawn to a halt during one evening, drunk the final barrel dry and slept until morning, then sobered up as they realized that they were on a journey and not quite prepared for it.

'Say! Who exactly are you?' Jed was speaking to him. 'Did my pa bring you in?'

'Somebody called Rube?' Edward squinted at him. His brain felt loose and his tongue thick. 'I was at a place where – Martha – lived.'

'Ah!' Jed nodded at him. 'Martha! Did you get tipped off a flatboat?'

'Yes, I was robbed.' Edward again started to explain.

'I remember now,' Jed said. 'Didn't you want to go to New Orleans?'

'I did,' Edward muttered. 'There'll be no chance of that now. Do you know where we are? Or where we're going?' He felt desperate and wanted to cry like a child. What was happening to him? He didn't want adventure. He wanted a respectable life, plenty of money and someone to look after him, to press his clothes and clean his shoes. 'Allen,' he mumbled. 'He's got my money and my papers.'

'Allen?' Jed asked. 'Is he the fella who robbed you?'

'No. No. It's a long story,' he said quickly. 'Does anybody here know Sancho Rodriguez?'

They all shook their heads. Of course they wouldn't know him, Edward thought. They're all back-country men. They are not of Rodriguez' world.

'So – you coming along with us?' Jed asked. 'To Californy?'

Edward wavered. 'Is that where you're going?' Something clicked in his mind about California. I must have been so very drunk. 'It's a very long way, isn't it? Are we still near the Mississippi?'

'Still in the Mississippi valley.' Another man, Larkin, spoke up. He was older than the others by several years, nearer to Edward's age. 'We've only bin travelling 'bout three days, not counting the stops for sleeping and watering the horses.'

'Three days!' Edward was astounded. This country was so immense. 'How long would it take me to get back to New Orleans?'

'Walking, d'you mean?' Larkin asked. 'Couple o' weeks, I guess. You were well upriver if you came off at Martha's place. And, say – didn't I hear tell you'd no money?'

When Edward nodded miserably that he hadn't, Larkin went on, 'So what'll you do fer food, mister? You can sleep rough if you've no money to pay for a bed, but what'll you do fer eating?'

Edward was silenced. He would not even consider sleeping rough. He had done that already after coming off the flatboat and hadn't liked the experience. He had no desire to walk back to New Orleans, and if he should manage to hitch a lift, and no doubt he could, for waggons had passed them going in the opposite direction, any driver would expect a contribution from him. Besides, he thought, I have to be honest, I don't like being alone. I've always had someone around, my

340

parents, brother, servants. And it seems that whenever I do anything for myself, I make a hash of it.

'What shall I do?' He murmured the words almost to himself, but Jed heard him.

'You can come along with us, Bob – it is Bob, isn't it? We're safer travelling if there's a few of us. We've all got weapons, 'cept for young Tod, but he knows how to handle a gun. What about it? When we git to Californy and strike gold, why, then you can pay us back fer your vittles out of your share, and if you're rich enough you can take a ship back to New Orleans.'

The others nodded in agreement. It seemed odd, Edward thought. These men were taking him at face value. They knew nothing of him except what he had told them, yet they were agreeing, not suggesting, that he should accompany them in their search for gold. It means hard work, he mused. They'll not want anyone who doesn't pull their weight, and I've never done a proper day's work in my life.

But what other options do I have? I can try walking to New Orleans and if I don't die on the way there, I might die at Rodriguez' hands when I arrive! And what if Allen isn't at the hotel? He may have decided to go off on his own rather than wait for me, I'm well overdue. So I would still be penniless. God, what a dilemma!

They were waiting for his answer. Tod was whittling a stick with a knife. Jed was still holding his head as if he thought it might fall off and Larkin was watching him steadily. The other two, Matt and James, were lighting a fire so they could boil water for coffee.

'Do you know the way?' he asked, before deciding.

'Follow up the Mississippi until we reach Red River, then across the plains and follow the cattle trails,' Larkin said. 'Cross the Rocky Mountains and join the Santa Fe Trail. Then head west towards the Pacific. We can team up with others, there's countless folks on the move. We'll follow their tracks.'

It sounded so easy, though they knew it was not. They would have to travel thousands of miles. It meant fording rivers, crossing mountains and arid desert. Even in the swamps of the Mississippi they had heard tales of enthusiastic people joining the migrating hordes, full of hopes for the future, and finishing in despair and often death on the trail.

But I'm setting out without hope and without money, with only the clothes that I'm wearing. Surely nothing worse can happen? Edward considered. What have I to lose? Only my life. And what is that worth? No-one will mourn me, for no-one knows where I am. May will be better off without me. Ruby has someone she cares for.

It came to him that since the onset of his misfortunes he had frequently contemplated his past life, not something he had ever done before. I've been a selfish bounder all my born days, he reflected. I've only ever thought of my own pleasures and even then I've never been completely satisfied. Perhaps, just perhaps, this is a chance for me to make something of myself. To set myself challenges. I might find that I'm a different man from the one I thought I was.

'Yes. All right. I'd like to join you.' He got up to

shake hands with them and they all looked at him in astonishment. They were obviously not used to formality, but each man gave him a firm hand clasp.

'I should tell you something about myself,' he said, as he stood before them. 'Because I'd like to set the story straight. You'll gather that I'm an Englishman and I came to America looking for a new life. Well, it seems as if I've found one, though it isn't quite what I had in mind.'

He wondered just how much he should tell them; perhaps only as much as they needed to know. 'I've made a lot of mistakes in my life and more than a few since I came to this country. But I want to tell you,' he looked at Jed, 'that my real name isn't Bob, or Robert Allen, whose name I was going to take, but Edward Newmarch, and if anyone should come looking for such a person, then you don't know him!'

They all grinned except Larkin, who asked sharply, 'Is it the law that's lookin' fer you?'

'No,' he said firmly. 'It is not. It's a man called Rodriguez who wanted me to marry his daughter.'

'Wa-hoo!' Jed hooted. 'Is she in the family way?'

'She is, but not by me. That's why I fled and then I was robbed and the rest you know.'

'So what name shall we call you?' Matt asked. 'We can't call you Edward if this fella's looking fer you. Rob, Bob, or Ted?'

Edward considered. When he was young his brother Martin used to call him Eddie. He had rather liked it then, it seemed affectionate somehow. But as they'd grown to adulthood he had asked him not to use it. In his arrogance he

343

had thought it wasn't an appropriate name for a man of importance in the town.

'Eddie,' he said. 'I'd like to be called Eddie.'

If he had thought himself superior in intellect to these men he would have been right, but he knew within several days of travelling that they were more than his equal in endurance and endeavour. The terrain was swampy and often the trail was thick with mud and slime which made it heavy going for the horses, so they walked alongside the waggon with just one man driving the team. Without them, as a raw inexperienced Englishman, he would not have survived. When he questioned them on whether the reason for the firearms was to keep off hostile Indians or bandits, they gazed at him as if he had taken leave of his senses.

'Sure,' Jed said patiently. 'We might come across scoundrels and cut-throats, and not all of the Indians are friendly, but have you thought, Eddie, what we'll do fer food? We've brought jerked meat, beans and biscuits, but that won't last long, not with six of us!'

They shot whatever meat they could find in the bush and swamp, they fished in the streams and caught sturgeon and bass, and because Edward couldn't do any of these things he was put in charge of the stores which were packed in the waggon. They also showed him how to jerk the meat that they couldn't eat immediately, to cut it into thin strips and dry it in the sun.

'Pretty soon we'll hit bad weather,' Larkin said, 'and maybe won't be able to find much fresh meat. Then we'll have to rely on our stores.' He was a sober man, not given to jokes or laughter like the younger ones, but he grinned wryly as he said, 'And if you've never had a liking fer bean soup, Eddie, then you're going to hate it by the time we reach Californy.'

Whilst sorting out the stores in the waggon, Edward found a sack with heavy clothing inside: a padded jacket, twill trousers, socks and boots.

'Say, these must be Webster's,' James said, when Edward asked who they belonged to. 'What happened to him? He was coming along a' us!'

Larkin scratched his head. 'Somebody fell off the waggon. Guess it must have been him.'

'Then he won't mind if I borrow them!' Edward said and changed out of his stained shrunken cotton suit into these other more suitable clothes, which fitted him better than Robert Allen's did.

On their route towards Red River they came across an occasional settlement, a collection of cabins, with a general store, and they stocked up with more supplies, filled their casks with water and let the horses graze.

Their funds were meagre, Edward discovered, and they told him they had never earned much money. What little they had, had gone on the waggon, horses and provisions. Matt had bought the horses from his father and he was the one who looked after them, tended their feet and fed and watered them.

The track grew less swampy as they trekked alongside cottonwood trees and maple. The going was easier, though Larkin kept casting his eyes heavenwards and muttering that soon there would be a big one.

'What kind of big one?' Edward asked. 'A storm, do you mean?'

'Yip,' he replied laconically. 'A big one, and that ole Mississippi will flood the banks and come rolling right on up here.' He lifted his head and sniffed. 'I can smell it.'

Edward wiped his brow with his sleeve. The air was heavy, though it was not as hot as when he had been in New Orleans. It's winter, he thought: at home there'll be snow on the ground or fog. They'll soon be preparing for Christmas.

'Surely the river won't flood here?' he said. 'We're several miles from the bank. Isn't that why the settlements are so far back?'

'It'll come,' Larkin said. 'It's a mean ole river! Them folks back there just git themselves settled in their homesteads and in she comes, that muddy ole river, over the levee across the swamp and washes them clean away.'

The storm came at night. They had pitched their canvas tents in a grove and tied the horses nearby. Edward, who hadn't a tent, slept in the waggon. The frogs were especially loud that evening, giving out a high-pitched chorus of croaking. They heard a honking of geese and Jed put his hand out for his rifle and looked up, but the sky was dark and they were gone before he could load, a formation of hundreds heading for safety before the storm broke.

They cooked bean stew, ate rye bread, put more wood on the fire to keep it going during the night, and unanimously decided to turn in and have an early start the next morning.

The first thing they heard was the sizzling of

the fire as the rain came down. The wind began to rise and whoosh through the trees, causing the branches to sway and bend and scatter the dead wood so that it thwacked against the canvas tents and waggon.

'Batten down!' Jed shouted. 'Make sure the provisions are covered, Eddie. We've got to keep the stores dry.'

Edward pulled the sacks and canvas over the boxes of provisions. Matt went to the horses to make sure they were secure and soothed them, for they were stamping nervously. The fire went out as the rain became torrential, and the sky was lit by a flash of lightning followed by a crash of thunder.

They all huddled into the waggon, for the tents were useless against the deluge. 'We'll have to move on to higher ground,' Larkin said presently. 'Another hour and the water'll be up to the axles. We'll never get the waggon out.'

Edward glanced outside. The rain was sheeting down and already the ground was becoming a quagmire. The others agreed with Larkin, knowing the territory and what to expect.

'Let's get moving then,' Jed said. 'Matt, you and James go one on each side of the team. The rest of us will walk behind and push if necessary.'

'Walk?' Edward said. 'Can't we take it in turns to travel in the waggon?'

'Nope,' Jed said. 'We need as little weight as possible else we'll not get rolling.'

They put canvas sacks over their shoulders and Edward, who hadn't a hat, tied his over his head and shoulders with a length of twine. Before they had even put the horses into the traces, they were

347

all soaked. The others didn't seem to notice, but Edward, standing behind the waggon ready to push off, was as dejected as he had ever been in his life. He swallowed hard but tears, which he hadn't shed since he was a child, ran down his cheeks, mingling with the rain.

I must go on, he vowed. I must keep up or I'm finished. I'll die out here in this godforsaken swamp. He stood next to Jed and put his hands on the waggon as he was doing and leaned into it, his back and shoulders tense, waiting for the signal.

'Ready everybody?' Larkin's voice was almost obliterated by a crack of thunder. A flash of lightning lit up the scene, the dark trees bending dangerously and the men and horses illuminated for a second, then darkness, then again light. 'Get set!' Larkin cracked the whip over the horses' heads and gave a great shout. 'Push!'

CHAPTER THIRTY

All the men were weary, their energy sapped, but Edward most of all. They had travelled out of the swampy Mississippi basin, through dust and rocks and desert, and there came a day when he collapsed and had to ride in the back of the waggon. He felt so guilty as the men and horses hauled across the cattle-droving plains and towards the Santa Fe Trail that he staggered out of his jolting bed, insisting that he should do his share.

'You're a city gent,' Larkin told him. 'We didn't

expect that you'd be able to match us swamp-suckers. We're used to heavy work – what did you do?'

'Nothing much,' he admitted. 'Sat at a desk in a cotton mill.'

'What?' Jed exclaimed. 'You were a desk clerk? I had you down for a gentleman of leisure.'

'I would have been,' he said. 'But my father insisted that my brother and I worked at the mill. We had shares in it, and he said we should see how it operated. But I hated it,' he confessed. 'I never wanted to work and I didn't after he died.'

'So you did nothing to earn a living? Wow!' Jed was impressed. 'You must have been mighty rich!'

Edward considered. Compared to these men his means were vast, and he'd left all that behind. 'Fairly rich, I suppose, or at least my wife was.'

'Your wife?' Larkin said. 'So where's she?'

'Back home in England.' He felt a sudden sense of shame. 'We – we had a disagreement, so I came to America to try my luck here. A new life, you know,' he said lamely.

They were sitting around a campfire and the men gazed at him as he finished speaking. Larkin was the first to break the silence. 'So what'll you do if you find gold? Go home to your wife?'

Edward took a deep breath. 'She wouldn't want me. She has her pride. Though if I should decide to, then she'd have to accept me back. That's the way the law works in England.' But I have no intention of doing that, he thought. None at all. If I get to California in one piece, then I shall stay.

'But if we find gold,' he gave a sudden grin, 'I'll stay around you fellows, if you don't mind. I like

349

your company. But tell me. If you knew I couldn't work as hard as you, why did you ask me to come along? Was it just the drink?'

'Larkin and me have been talking about that, and we remembered why we asked you,' Jed said. 'When my pa brought you into the saloon that day, we saw that you were an educated fella and guessed that we could use you if you'd come along.'

'How?' Edward was puzzled.

'Well, we'll need to write letters home, and we don't read or write too well.'

Tod interrupted. 'I can read well enough!'

'Sure,' Larkin said. 'But you only came along by chance. But more than writing letters home, we want somebody who can understand legal things. There's plenty of free land, but we wouldn't want somebody to come along and jump a claim if we should make a lucky strike. We'd want it written down to say that it was ours.'

James chipped in. 'Do you think there'll be any gold left by the time we get there? We'll be weeks yet on the trail.'

'The fever's probably passed,' Larkin agreed. 'But don't forget that some men, if they don't find gold straight away, will move off elsewhere. It's a big country.' He chewed on a piece of twig. 'We'll be patient. We'll find gold.'

There were thousands of other gold-rushers with the same destination in mind. Men with a vision, men with a dream. City men, farm boys, factory workers, shopkeepers and sailors, speculators and law-breakers, all set out on the long trek, by sea or overland, to seek their fortune. Some brought their wives and families to share in the adventure and many of them, worn down by hardship and disappointment, turned around and went home again.

Edward and his party passed broken-down waggons and dead horses, and men walking with packs strapped to their backs and grim determination written on their faces.

They were stopped by the snow at the eastern edge of a high ridge of mountains and it was here that one of the horses had to be shot. Matt had been concerned for some days after finding the horse sweating and a swelling under its jaw.

'Guess it's strangles,' he said eventually when the horse couldn't swallow. 'Can't do anything for him out here.' He stroked the horse's neck. 'Don't know what Pa would say.' His voice was choked.

'Your pa would say shoot him,' Larkin said. 'Come on, boy, put him out of his misery.'

Matt shook his head. 'I can't. It would be like shooting my best friend.'

'If your best friend was suffering,' Larkin said quietly, 'wouldn't you help him out?'

Matt looked up. His eyes were wet and he pressed his lips together. 'Guess so.'

'Go on,' Larkin said. 'I'll do it.'

The boy put his head against the horse's neck. 'So long, old fella,' he croaked. 'You've done us real proud.'

He walked away, leading the other horse with him, so that he didn't see Larkin lift his rifle, though the shot echoed around the mountains.

'So now what do we do?' Edward asked. 'Can

one horse pull the waggon?'

'Sure he can, if we walk to lighten the load,' Jed said. 'But we can't go anywhere until the thaw.' He looked up the pine-covered mountainside, decked out with thick snow. 'We'll just have to dig in until then.'

They found a suitable clearing and began the task of making a shelter for themselves, and another beneath the lee of the trees for the other horse. They felled trees, cut them into logs and built themselves a rough cabin. Edward had taken a breath as he was sawing and looked across the landscape. Below them lay a large lake which glistened in the sparkling cold air. Tall pines and jagged rocks led down to it and over the land lay a covering of crisp snow.

Matt went off on his own several times. He'd been morose after the loss of the horse, but he came back one day bursting with excitement and dragging something behind him. He shouted at them from a distance. 'Look,' he yelled. 'I've shot an elk.'

Edward, James and Matt quickly put together a wooden frame and placed it over the fire, whilst Jed and Larkin skinned and prepared the dead animal for roasting. 'This will keep the store cupboard going very nicely,' Edward said. 'Well done, Matt.' The others laughed at what they considered his quaint way of speaking.

He sorted out the dried food, the beans, the biscuits and horse food, and brought it all into the shanty, for the men had told him that the canvas on the waggon wouldn't hold under a blanket of snow, neither could they keep marauding animals out of it. Then he dug a pit for the remaining meat, wrapped it in a canvas sack, and covered it with logs and brushwood.

They collected kindling for the fire, sawed logs and stacked them by the side of the cabin, and settled down to wait for the spring.

The snow came steadily, drifting down silently in the night and then continuing every day. They made two teams of three and took it in turns to keep the front door of the cabin clear, but each morning the snow had crept up around the cabin until soon only the door was visible. It grew colder and they used every item of clothing to keep themselves warm. Edward dressed in the cotton suit belonging to Robert Allen, and put Webster's clothes on top of it.

'We're going to have to make a hole in the roof,' Larkin said, 'and make a fire inside the cabin. If we don't, we shall freeze to death.'

They stacked one wall with logs, pushed a hole through the middle of the roof and made a small fire beneath it. They coughed with the smoke, but they were warmer, and several times a day they pushed a branch through the chimney hole to keep it clear of snow. Matt dug his way out each morning to feed the horse and make sure he was covered over with his blanket. The snow was too deep for him to take the animal out for exercise but he rubbed him down briskly to keep his circulation going.

Then one morning they couldn't get out. The snow had fallen all night and was above the door, trapping them inside. 'It maybe won't be for long,' Edward said hopefully.

353

'But what about the horse?' Matt said. 'He'll starve!'

'Or freeze,' Jed replied. 'He's got the same chance as us.'

I keep thinking that nothing can get any worse, Edward pondered. I feel as if I am living someone else's life. What happened to the other me, the self-assured gallant with an eye for the ladies? Where did he go?

They had minor skirmishes about someone snoring or the stink of somebody's feet, but on the whole they remained friendly. The younger men bantered with each other about girls they knew. Larkin was of a quiet nature and kept the peace, and Edward became introspective as he thought on his past life, so different from the other men's.

Then Jed found a pack of cards tucked inside a box of biscuits. 'I'd forgotten about these. Anybody for a hand?'

They played for pieces of twig and Edward found his pile of twigs growing much bigger than the others'. 'Well,' he said, as he drew in yet more winnings from the men. 'If I don't find gold, I can make my living as a card sharp.'

Matt suggested they try to get out, so they took down the log door. A thick wall of snow was beyond it. 'Use the fire branch,' Jed said. 'Let's see how deep it is.'

The branch went almost to its full length before it reached the height of the snow. 'I guess about two feet above the cabin roof,' Larkin hazarded.

'Could we tunnel upwards?' Matt said. 'I'm worried about the horse.'

'Sure,' Jed said sarcastically. 'And where do we

put the snow?' The door was replaced and they again settled down to wait, but now they were becoming irritable. The food stocks were running low and they were all heartily sick of beans and biscuits. Then one day they heard shouting, a faint *halloa*, and they jumped to their feet and halloed back.

Edward immediately threw wood onto the fire. They'd managed to keep the exit hole clear, though the air in the hut was extremely acrid. He pushed hard with the stick to let the smoke through, so that whoever was there would know they were still alive.

'You folks all right in there?' A man's voice called dimly through the wall of snow.

'We're all right,' Jed shouted back. 'Any chance of getting us out?'

'Can you check the horse?' Matt yelled. 'See if he's alive.'

'He is.' The voice came faintly back. 'Just.'

A grin of relief suffused Matt's face. 'Thank the Lord for that! *Alleluia!*'

They heard the sound of shovelling and scraping above their heads and felt impotent at not being able to help. As the day wore on the sound came nearer and lower, until at last they took down the door. A shaft had appeared in front of it, just above their heads.

A man with a thick beard and a hooded fur coat leaned down through the hole. 'Howdy,' he said. Then another man's head appeared above him. He too was bearded, and wore a similar coat. 'Howdy.' He grinned. 'Guess you'll be glad to be outa there!'

With their own shovels the men in the cabin shaped some steps up to the shaft and one by one they emerged, blinking at the brightness of the snow. There were three rescuers, all of them trappers, they said, and Edward shook them by the hand. 'Thank you very much,' he enthused. 'So very grateful!'

The trappers nodded and gazed at him. 'Any time,' said one. 'You a long way from home?' asked another, whilst the third said nothing but continued to stare.

Edward ran his hand over his beard – it had grown thick and long since he'd set out on the journey. He hadn't had a shave since leaving Martha's cabin. He glanced at his companions who were stretching their arms and taking in deep breaths of cold air. We all look wild, he thought, with our long hair and beards. Wild men of the wilderness, just like these trappers.

'We saw your smoke,' one of the trappers said. 'Thought it was Indians at first. Then we saw it was coming from beneath the snow. We heard the horse as we came nearer.'

Matt was giving the animal a handful of oats, little by little. It was thin, its ribs showing. It had kept alive by eating the snow which had piled up around the shelter but hadn't covered it because of the protection of the trees.

'Another time I'll stay with the horse,' Edward bantered. 'Though I don't suppose he'll be very good at cards!'

The trappers came inside the cabin and Edward built up the fire and boiled a pan of snow to make coffee.

'You did pretty well,' said one of the trappers, looking around at the rough building. 'Where you fellas from?'

'Mississippi country,' Jed said. 'Swampsuckers all of us, 'cept fer Eddie here. He's a city gent, down on his luck.'

'And heading fer Californy?' one of the others asked.

They nodded. 'Yip. Jest waiting fer the thaw.'

'Another couple of weeks,' the first trapper said. 'Then you can go. But leave your waggon. You'll travel better without it.'

'Go on foot?' Edward quaked at the thought.

'Take the horse and join up with a pack train if you can. There'll be plenty on the trail.' The man nodded from beneath his hood. 'Jest keep on walking right over them mountains, across the prairie and on to Santa Fe. There's a mission there where you can rest and get provisions in the town. It's a civilized place,' he said, glancing at Edward. 'But watch out fer Navajo Indians on the trail. Don't give them trouble. If they see you've nothing worth having they'll leave you alone.'

'How long?' Edward asked, daunted by the prospect.

'To Santa Fe? As long as it takes,' he grunted.

'And to Californy?' Jed asked. 'How long do ya reckon?'

The trapper shrugged. 'Ain't never bin, but I heard tell all kinda stories. But I guess there'll be plenty of folks to put you right in Santa Fe.'

'Head fer the Colorado river,' said one of the other trappers, 'cross over the old Spanish Trail and make fer the Sierra Nevada mountains. Aim

357

to git there before next winter,' he added, 'or you'll have to wait fer the thaw. Jest like now.'

'We'll be there before then,' Larkin said. 'Should the devil bar the way, we'll be there by summer!'

'Sure we will,' Jed agreed.

To Edward the prospect seemed overwhelming. They had already suffered so much privation. They were all leaner than they had been before setting out. He flexed his fingers and looked down at his hands. They were rough and dirty, but strong. He'd sawn and chopped wood, heaved the waggon out of the swamps, tramped over dusty plains where there seemed to be no end in sight, organized the food ration so that whilst they were holed up in the cabin, everyone ate something every day. He wasn't tired, though his limbs ached. And it came to him that he was exhilarated. The other men no longer treated him like a raw recruit, he was part of the team.

He clenched his fist and raised it in the air. 'Sure we'll make it!' he exclaimed. *'Ho, Californy!'*

CHAPTER THIRTY-ONE

'I think we're lost, Kitty!' Georgiana looked over the vista in front of them.

'I think we are, miss.' Kitty followed her gaze. 'I don't remember this at all.'

They had made their way to No-Name without any difficulty, but on arrival there found that there were only women and children at the settlement,

358

and one or two very elderly men. The men, Little Bear explained, had gone to a meeting with other tribes and wouldn't be back for several days.

'We'll chance it on our own, shall we, Kitty?' Georgiana had said. 'Stay here tonight and go first thing in the morning.'

Little Bear didn't want them to go. 'Stay,' she had implored in her husky voice. 'Dekan will set you on the right trail when he comes home.'

But they had decided not to wait and at first the track was as they remembered it. They climbed up stony hillsides and down into the valleys and found the stream where they had previously stopped for water, which they also did this time. They climbed again and then began a descent down the other side into the forested valley, where Lake had taken them to the cabin for shelter.

Only there was no cabin and they had emerged unexpectedly on a plateau which looked out over the tops of miles of dark green pine forest.

'We've taken the wrong path. We're too high,' Georgiana said. 'We should be lower down. We'll have to turn back.'

'But it's getting dark,' Kitty cautioned. 'I don't fancy travelling in darkness. Should we camp here and go on in the morning?'

Georgiana agreed. She was tired and anxious and trembled as she dismounted. 'Yes, I think so. We'll make a small fire, then move off at first light.' What worries me, she thought, is that we might not be able to find the way back to the right track. There were hundreds of miles of forest below them and they could be wandering for days with no hope of finding their way out. We could die here and never be found. Or wolves could attack us. I could never use the knife as Lake did.

Darkness came quickly, but not before they had lit a fire and made up the canvas tent. They fed the horses and mule and tethered them securely.

'If I wasn't so scared, I could enjoy this,' Kitty said, as they sat by the fire. 'I've never seen such a wonderful sunset. It's as if the whole forest is on fire.'

Georgiana nodded and thought about the sunrise she had shared with Lake. Will I ever see him again? she wondered. Has he gone for ever? Was he my one and only chance of love?

'I wish Lake was here.' Kitty echoed her thoughts. 'Or Dekan, or Horse. Somebody, anyway! Were we very stupid setting out on our own, miss? Just two women?'

I wanted independence, Georgiana pondered. I wanted the same rights as men have. I didn't want to be told what I could or couldn't do. I never wanted to feel inferior. 'No,' she answered emphatically. 'Not stupid. And definitely not because we are women! We are just as capable as any man would be in finding our way. Can you imagine Mr Charlesworth coming out here on his own? Would he have done any better? He wouldn't have attempted it! But we did and we made a mistake, but in the morning we shall find the right track and go on our way.'

'I knew it really, miss.' Kitty gave Georgiana a warm smile. 'But I just wanted to hear you say it!'

They both slept fitfully but fairly well, and as daylight filtered through the canvas, Georgiana opened the flap of the tent and put her head out.

She gave an instant gasp, waking Kitty from her dreamy state. Standing by their merrily blazing fire was a man. A man with matted hair and a thick beard, with a wolf pelt thrown over his skin coat.

She put her hand to the knife, which she was about to strap to her ankle, and jumped to her feet to face him. He stared at her, astonishment on his face. He was extremely tall and broad in his chest, and she knew without a shadow of doubt that they would not stand a chance against him should he be aggressive.

'Who are you?' she demanded, trying to keep her voice steady.

His eyes narrowed and she saw him glance at her knife, still in its leather sheath. 'Might ask you the same, lady. Who's that with you?' He had obviously seen movement from within the tent.

Kitty put her head out of the opening and then quickly withdrew it. Georgiana knew she would be scrabbling for her knife.

He took a step nearer. He had a rifle strapped across his back and knives on his belt. 'Have you no man with you?'

'No,' she said tensely. 'But we are armed.' She hoped that she sounded braver than she felt.

'What ya doing out here alone?'

'We're on a journey,' she said. 'We took a wrong path last night.'

He gave a crooked grin which she thought looked very menacing. 'Lost, ain't you?'

'No. Not lost,' she said sharply. 'We need to retrace our steps, that's all.'

'Dangerous out here.' He eyed Kitty, who was now standing outside the tent with her unsheathed knife held in both hands. 'Indians. Wolves. Bears. Men who ain't seen a woman in a long time!'

I'll fight for my virtue, Georgiana thought. But I don't want to die for it. She slipped the knife from the sheath. 'We are prepared for that,' she said. 'Do you mean us harm?'

He made a swift movement and grabbed her wrist so that the knife dropped to the ground. Kitty dashed towards them but he grabbed her too with his other hand. 'How did you come by the knife?' he asked Georgiana. 'It ain't yours.'

She drew in her breath. His hand spanned her wrist and held it tight. She clasped her other hand into a fist and lashed out, but he saw it coming and simply moved his head away from the blow.

'I said – where'd you git the knife, lady?' His grip tightened and she winced.

'It was given to me,' she managed to say.

'Who by?' His grip lessened slightly.

'Lake!' she said vehemently. 'And if he should hear of this–'

'Lake?' He dropped her hand and Kitty's, who rubbed hers furiously. 'You his woman?'

She lifted her chin and stared at him. 'Yes,' she said. 'I am.'

'Well, well! Never thought I'd see the day when Lake had a woman.' He sat down cross-legged by the fire and they both eyed him warily. 'Recognized that knife,' he said. 'It's an Indian knife. Wondered how you came by it.'

'I would hardly have wrestled it from him,' Georgiana said icily.

He leered at her. 'You might have done, lady. Wimmin gets up to all kinds o' things when a man ain't prepared.'

He threw the wolf skin on the ground next to him and unbuttoned his coat. 'Got any coffee?'

'Yes! Yes, we have.' Kitty bustled up in an attempt to placate him. 'I'll make some.' She filled a small pan from the water bottle and placed it on the fire. 'Where've you come from? Where's your horse?'

He pointed a thumb over his shoulder. 'Back there. Followed your tracks. Wondered who it was coming up to this place. There's no way down from here.'

'Are you a trapper?' Georgiana asked. 'Like Lake?'

He pursed his lips and hesitated slightly, then nodded. 'Yip, of a sort. Do whatever I can to eat and drink. Mainly, though, I'm a guide. Take folks like you across the prairie or mountains. Where you from?' he asked suddenly. 'You from England? I met somebody some time back who talked just like you do, all *la-di-da*. He was from England. Going to try his luck in Californy.'

He gave a guttural laugh, and took the metal cup into which Kitty had poured coffee. 'Doubt he'd make it. He was stuck in the snow with some swampsuckers. Not even halfway there!'

'We have to be going,' Georgiana interrupted briskly. 'So when you've finished your coffee...'

He took his time drinking, then drained his cup and got to his feet. 'Want me to escort you back?'

'No, thank you,' she said with as much dignity as she could muster. 'We can manage.'

'Suit yourself.' He shrugged. Then he grinned. 'I'll tell Lake I saw you.' He moved nearer to

363

Georgiana. 'Want me to give him a message?'

She stepped back and at the same time bent to pick up the pan of coffee from the fire. 'You can tell him where you saw us,' she said calmly. 'And say that he was right about New York.'

'What's that supposed to mean?' he growled.

'He'll understand,' she said. 'Now, if you will excuse us. We need to break camp.'

'Miss Georgiana,' Kitty breathed after he'd gone, 'shouldn't we have let him show us the way?'

'To where, Kitty?' Georgiana hoisted one pack onto the mule. 'Not to Dreumel's Creek, because he won't know of it, and I wouldn't have wanted to tell him.' And besides, she thought, he would have wanted some kind of payment, he didn't look the sort who would be prepared to help anyone out of the kindness of his heart.

Aloud she said, 'We'll find our way back to the track. I'm convinced of it.' She secured the other pack. 'And anyway,' she gritted her teeth, 'I'm going to give Hetty her head and see if she remembers the way.'

It took them most of the morning to retrace their route down and Kitty kept looking back to see if they were being followed by the wild man, as they had named him. Eventually she declared that he hadn't followed them after all and had gone on somewhere else.

'I thought that was very clever of you to say you were Lake's woman, Miss Georgiana,' she said after a while. 'He didn't want to get 'wrong side of Lake, you could tell.'

'Yes,' Georgiana agreed after a second, and gave a laugh. 'It was inspirational, wasn't it! I guessed that Lake might be held in some kind of esteem. Look,' she said, as they came to a small clearing. 'Here are the diverging paths. We took the wrong one. This one goes downhill.' She clicked her tongue at Hetty. 'Come on, girl, is this it?'

Hetty snickered and blew, then, as Georgiana shook the reins, she set off on the downward track, picking her way over fallen branches.

They came at last into the forested valley and made their way to where the creek and cabin were situated. As night was falling they decided to stay there until morning. 'I think we'll be all right now, Kitty.' Georgiana felt exhilarated by their success. 'Though I remember wondering how Lake found his way when he brought us.'

'He was looking for signs, miss,' Kitty said. 'I noticed because I was riding up behind him. He was watching out for breaks in the forest floor and where some of the trees divided off the tracks.'

'I should have looked more closely,' Georgiana admitted. 'I just put myself in his hands and trusted that what he did was right. But now we are quite alone and must make our own decisions.'

Once more they lit fires, both outside and inside the cabin. Georgiana recalled the rabid wolf which Lake had shot, and firmly shut and bolted the cabin door from the inside. They had brought their own candle and lit it from the lucifer. 'If we are attacked, Kitty, by man or beast, we must act together and use our knives.' And if we ever get safely to Dreumel's Creek, she decided, I shall ask someone to teach me how to use a gun.

'An hour, Kitty,' she said the next morning as they set off. 'That's how long it took us last time before we began to climb.' But now it took longer because they kept stopping before deciding if they were going the right way. Eventually they recognized some of the landmarks, the streams and rock slides, and they started to climb. They looked at each other triumphantly and in another hour they came out into the clearing where below, miles below, they could see the waggon trail. They both shouted exultantly at the tops of their voices.

'Nearly there, miss,' Kitty said breathlessly. 'But it's so hot, should we wait awhile?'

'Yes, I think so,' Georgiana agreed. 'We must think of the horses too and give them a rest.' She looked up at the rocky outcrop. 'I remember it was difficult climbing in the heat. We'll wait and rest for a couple of hours before we move on.'

They put the animals in the shade and gave them water, then settled themselves down to rest out of the sun. They poured a little water into their tin cups and sipped slowly, for there would be no more until they reached the creek. Kitty fell asleep and Georgiana was closing her eyes when she heard a movement from above. The wild man, she thought, he has followed us after all! Slowly she turned and lifted her head, at the same time reaching for the knife.

Bear! Her breath caught in her throat. Black bear! It hadn't seen them but was standing on a shelf-like rocky promontory not twelve feet above them, sniffing at the ground. Though remembering that they were shy creatures unless disturbed, this gave her no comfort, for she also recalled that they could turn into ferocious killers if alarmed. Slowly she reached for the metal cup and drew the knife from its sheath.

Clink. Clink. Clink. Gently she tapped the knife on the cup and watched as the bear raised its head and looked around, but not down. Then she tapped louder. *Clank. Clank. Clank.* The bear lifted a paw and she saw the unsheathed claws and its powerful limbs. Again she tapped on the cup. *Clank. Clank. Clank.* The bear, with a great heave of its body, crashed away and she saw the black lumbering shadow of it, scaling the rocky boulders before disappearing into the trees.

'What was that?' Kitty suddenly awoke. 'Did I hear something?'

Georgiana put her head on her knees and tried to breathe deeply. Her heart was hammering loudly and her face was flushed.

'What is it, miss?' Kitty asked in concern. 'Are you not well?'

Georgiana put her head back and exhaled. 'Perfectly well, Kitty.' She looked up the mountain which shortly they would ascend. 'Another hour, then we'll move on.'

They mounted once more and prepared for the final part of their journey. 'Kitty!' Georgiana said. 'You said you could sing!'

'I can sing, miss.' Kitty laughed. 'Why?'

Georgiana looked up the mountain again. The trail was steep, the trees thinning towards the top, and there was no sign of bear. But still, she'd like to be sure. 'I think we should sing our way up the mountain. As loud as we can!'

'All right,' Kitty smilingly agreed. 'They'll maybe hear us down in the valley,' she said. 'At Dreumel's Creek.'

CHAPTER THIRTY-TWO

'I cannot believe that you have travelled alone!' Dreumel and the other men gazed at them in astonishment. 'I don't know whether to be delighted or dismayed.'

'I hope you're delighted, Mr Dreumel,' Georgiana beseeched, whilst Kitty grinned triumphantly at Ted.

'Well, I'm danged glad you're back, Miss Gianna,' Isaac declared. 'You too, Miss Kitty, specially your cooking!'

'You could've been lost!' Ted butted in. He seemed to be trying to contain his anger. 'We'd never have found you!'

'You wouldn't have been looking,' Georgiana said quietly. 'As you didn't know we had set out.'

'Did no-one know?' Dreumel asked. He too sounded concerned.

'Dekan's wife, Little Bear,' Georgiana said, adding, 'she knew, though she did ask us to wait.'

As she spoke of Dekan's wife, a notion occurred to her. She drew in a sudden breath as she thought of the black bear she had encountered. Had Little Bear called on her spirit world to protect them? Georgiana could almost believe that she had. Or was it mere coincidence that the bear happened to be there? The Iroquois were children of the wilderness and worshipped all things of nature. In the misty mountains and dark untamed forests it would be quite easy to believe that ancient spirits lived there.

'I'm sorry if we have alarmed you,' she said. 'But we both wanted to come back and we thought that we knew the way. We only made one mistake,' she added in mitigation.

'Now that you are here, dear lady,' Dreumel said softly, 'do not think that your presence is not welcome, for indeed it is, but we may not be staying much longer. I am on the point of going to Philadelphia to try to raise more money. Then we shall make one last attempt to drill another shaft.' He shrugged his shoulders. 'And if there is nothing, then the men will move on.'

'And you,' Georgiana asked. 'What will you do?'

'I shall stay awhile with my few cattle. The grass is lush and green.' He smiled. 'They will thrive even if I don't.'

'Would you take another partner, Mr Dreumel, if there was one willing to take a risk?'

'Like Charlesworth?' He raised his eyebrows. 'No, I don't think so.'

'N-no,' she said slowly. 'I didn't mean like Charlesworth. I meant someone who believed in this valley and was willing to work with you, and not only for profit.'

'If there was such a man, yes, indeed I would.' He glanced around at the men, who all seemed very weary and despondent. He shook his head. 'We have looked into all possibilities, but there is not such a person. Most men only want the certainty of gold.'

She smiled then and glanced at Kitty who was standing next to Ted, their fingers touching. 'I am not a man, Mr Dreumel,' she said. 'But I am willing. I have been to the bank in New York and arranged a transfer of my funds to their branch in Philadelphia. If you are prepared to work with a woman, then I will gladly be your partner. Kitty and I have travelled here only for this purpose. At least – I have.'

Wilhelm Dreumel's gaze flickered for a second between her and Kitty and Ted, who was now gripping Kitty's hand. Then he took a breath. 'You may lose your money, Georgiana.' It was the first time he had called her by her Christian name. 'I cannot promise you good fortune.'

'Can you promise me a challenge?' she asked.

'Oh, yes.' He laughed. 'That I can promise!'

'Then will you accept my offer?' She waited in anticipation, willing him to agree.

His eyes held hers. Such an honest blue, she thought. I would always trust him to do what was right. Then he smiled and his round cheeks dimpled in the way she remembered. He gave a small formal bow, which only he would do, she mused, out here in the mountains.

'Thank you,' he said simply. 'I will be glad to accept.'

They talked into the night, Georgiana, Dreumel and Ted, whilst Kitty went with Isaac to see what was in the stores. They decided on a plan of action. Dreumel wouldn't after all mortgage his newspaper business, which had been his reluctant intention, but they would use Georgiana's capital. He was, though, uneasy about it and suggested that in case the project should fail, he should take

370

her on as a joint partner in the *Star* newspaper.

They would travel to Philadelphia after she was rested and have everything drawn up legally. Then they would buy more equipment for the shaft and explosives for opening up the creek.

The journey took three days of hard riding across the hot rocky plain and then continued by canal boat. Wilhelm had insisted that Kitty should come too. 'You can buy the stores you need,' he had said, but they both knew that she was there as a chaperone.

It was whilst Dreumel was showing Georgiana around his newspaper office and introducing her to his staff that she had an idea, which she put to him when they adjourned for coffee in a nearby hotel.

'I suggested to you once before that you – *we*,' she corrected humorously, 'need people to come to the valley. Not only miners,' for he had said that they would need more men for working on the shaft, 'but people to make the valley into a proper community. Why don't I put together a news article about this rich land? This–' She contemplated. 'This *golden valley*, and invite people – families – to apply.'

'Yes,' he agreed. 'I do remember what you said, and I have given the idea consideration, even though I did not think that it would be possible to carry it out.'

He reached out and touched her arm, letting his hand lie gently and patting her with his fingers. 'But now, because of you, all things are possible.' His eyes for a second seemed sad and moist, but as he withdrew his hand he added cheerfully, 'Together, Miss Gregory, I feel that we can succeed.'

'Mr Dreumel,' she began, 'do you not think that we could be less formal? As you know, my name is Georgiana. I wish you would use it.'

'I would like to,' he admitted. 'I have old-world values. I have only been waiting for permission! It was a slip of the tongue when I used it previously. The men call me Bill,' he added.

'But I would like to call you Wilhelm,' she said softly. 'It suits you so well.'

Their first priority was to open up the creek at the eastern end to let the waters flow out more easily, and to blast an opening through the rock to allow waggons in. Georgiana had been astounded when she and Wilhelm had set out on their journey to Philadelphia when, at the end of the valley, they appeared to be confronted by a mountain wall. As they drew closer she realized that the rocky out-crop in front of them stood apart from the moun-tain and that there was a track leading out behind it. It was a canyon with high rocky walls, which, from the outside of the valley, couldn't be seen.

'At some time in history,' Wilhelm had said as they rode through onto the open plain, 'there has been a rock fall which hid the valley from view.'

She'd looked back. The opening through which they had come could no longer be seen. Even the waters of the creek seemed to have disappeared, emerging as a gushing waterspout through a break in the rocks. 'Except from the Indians, the buzzards and the eagles who could see it,' she had replied, remembering what Lake had said.

'Yes,' he said. 'Only them.'

Georgiana wondered what Lake would think as she sat and wrote the article for the newspaper, extolling the beauty of the valley and creek and its potential for family life. Would he be angry that this once secret valley, which he had shown to Wilhelm Dreumel, was about to be opened up to others and irrevocably changed?

Letters started to pour in and people arrived on the doorstep of the newspaper office after reading the article. Georgiana interviewed the applicants herself, spending several days in the office. The days ran into a week and then another, as more and more people applied.

She chose practical people, men who had a trade but not much money, families with young children, storekeepers and farmers and a young couple who were both teachers and newly married. Wilhelm took on three more men for the mine, older men who had been to California but had grown disillusioned and disappointed with the mediocre returns.

Then, one day, Georgiana had a visit from a woman. She was well built with dyed hair piled beneath a feathered and chiffon concoction, held in place by a glittering hat pin, and wearing a low-cut gown which displayed her rounded curves. She was not young but had been attractive in her day. She wore carmine on her cheeks and lips and said her name was Nellie O'Neil.

'So, why would you want to come to this valley, Mrs O'Neil?' Georgiana asked cautiously. She didn't seem the type to want a quiet life.

'Well, ma'am,' she said in a dry, husky voice.

'I've been around and about quite a lot for most of my life. Had a few ups and downs, some good times, some bad. But now I've come into a little bit of money – don't ask me how, cos I wouldn't want to shock you.' She gazed at Georgiana from bright blue eyes, which had pale threads of red in the whites. 'But I've had a dream, you see. Had this dream for a good many years, that when I was older – and I ain't admitting to being old!' she added hastily. 'That if I made any money I would set up in some nice place and run a saloon.'

'Oh!' Georgiana said. 'A saloon!' She remembered that she had once suggested the same to Wilhelm.

'Nothing rough, you understand,' Nellie O'Neil emphasized. 'Jest a nice place where men could come and unwind after an honest day's work. They don't always want to go straight home, you know!'

'N-no, I don't suppose they do,' Georgiana admitted and, in spite of her first misgivings, found she was warming to Mrs O'Neil.

'I know about liquor,' Mrs O'Neil said. 'And I understand men, and you needn't worry that there would be any hanky-panky, though you'll find that when the word gets around about this place, the dancing girls will start to arrive. I know, cos I've done it myself in my time. But I'd send 'em on their way if you don't want them there.'

'Well–' began Georgiana, her breath quite taken away, but she saw something like pleading on Nellie O'Neil's face. 'I suppose that men would like to have somewhere to meet, and have a game of cards, a drink or a chat.'

Nellie O'Neil raised her eyebrows. 'A chat! Well, I guess you could call it that. I was thinking more of a jaw about what's happening out in the world, gold prices, what price cattle is fetching and so on.'

'Yes,' Georgiana said weakly. 'Of course! That is what I meant.' She smiled at her. 'Can I let you know, Mrs O'Neil?' she asked. 'I shall need to speak to my partner.'

'Sure you can. Call me Nellie,' she said, getting up from the chair and primping her curls. 'I'm staying in Philly for a few weeks.' She bent towards Georgiana. 'Don't worry about funds,' she whispered, though there was no-one else in the room. 'I've got plenty to buy what I need. But I'd need help to build a saloon.'

'There is a longhouse already which could be rented,' Georgiana told her. 'It would only need to be adapted.' And we could build Kitty a new bakery store, she mused, with a proper oven. She put out her hand. 'I'm sure we can do business, Nellie. I'll contact you soon.'

When they arrived back at the creek she put the idea to the men, who were all in favour, though Wilhelm had reservations. But he was soon persuaded. 'You can rent the longhouse to her,' Georgiana said. 'Build another storey onto it and she can take occasional visitors as well as live there herself.'

'Like a small hotel?' he said.

'Why not?' she replied.

The rock was blasted and the waters poured through, leaving the creek shallow. 'It'll find its own path,' Ted said, as he watched the waters run down into the plain.

A committee was formed at Georgiana's suggestion and a plan of action drawn up. Three carpenters and a wheelwright came back with Wilhelm after one of his trips to Philadelphia and they, with Pike and Jason, began to build the bridge across the creek whilst the water was low. At first they had decided on a footbridge, but then it was realized that if the community should grow, as inevitably it would, a wider bridge to take a horse and waggon would be necessary. The sound of sawing and hammering, whistling and sometimes cursing, could be heard all through the days, ceasing only when the sun went down.

Wilhelm, Ellis, Ted and Isaac began the conversion of the longhouse to make it ready for Nellie O'Neil. The upper storey was to be put up later when the carpenters were finished at the bridge. Then an opening for the road was blasted through, the explosion echoing around the valley and reverberating through the mountains. 'Folks will wonder what that was.' Ted shook his head and pressed his eardrums. 'Bet that could be heard down in Philadelphia.'

The men cleared the rubble and ruminated that it needed a second blast to make it wide enough for two waggons driving in side by side. 'Folks will be coming and going along this road,' Pike said. 'We're planning for the future.'

'When we find gold,' Ted said positively, 'I want a piece of land in the next valley. I'll plant corn.'

'Me too,' Pike agreed. 'If we have corn planted for twelve months then no government department can take it from us.'

The summer was almost over and the men were

eager to finish the blasting so that the first of the new settlers could come before winter. As Wilhelm had bought and owned the whole valley, he would sell off plots of land and timber, and the newcomers would build their own cabins.

'We'd like to buy a piece of land from you.' One of the carpenters came to Wilhelm on behalf of himself and the other tradesmen. 'We'd build a community workshop,' he said. 'Not all the folks coming will have the know-how to build for themselves, so we'd buy the timber from you and charge them a daily rate.'

'Things are happening so fast,' Wilhelm said to Georgiana one evening as they sat on the bench outside the freshly painted saloon. 'Before we know what's happened we shall have a new town here!'

'It's so exciting, isn't it?' she said enthusiastically. 'I'm so pleased, Wilhelm, that you allowed me to be a part of it.'

'Allowed you to be part of it?' He was astonished. 'Without you, Georgiana, it would not have happened!'

Have I then accomplished what I set out to do? she mused. Have I achieved equality? Certainly the men here treat me as their equal. They even swear and curse in front of me, she thought wryly. Except for Isaac and Wilhelm, of course. Isaac still calls me Miz Gianna, and Wilhelm is never anything but courteous.

'Why are you smiling?' Wilhelm interrupted her musings.

'I was thinking of how I have changed.' She laughed. 'I am no longer an English lady. I have

377

broken fingernails, rough hands and a sun-browned skin. And I draw water from the creek. I am a different person from the one I once was!'

He smiled back at her. 'I think not, Georgiana,' he murmured. 'You are what you always were. But you were shackled by convention, as you would have been if you had stayed in New York, where propriety rules just as in England. But out here...' His glance took in the valley, the cattle across the creek and up the mountains where the last rays of the sun were glinting red and gold. 'Out here you have cast off those shackles and found the freedom you always wanted.'

She followed his gaze. They scanned the radius of the mountains and both, simultaneously, caught the movement on the eastern edge. Wilhelm put his hand to his eyes to narrow the view, but Georgiana knew, almost without seeing. She could tell, by the throbbing of her temples and the pulsating in her body, just who it was.

'Lake!' Wilhelm murmured. 'I thought he would come.'

'Yes,' she whispered, and Wilhelm turned an enquiring gaze upon her. 'Yes, indeed.'

CHAPTER THIRTY-THREE

Lake showed no surprise at what had happened in the valley since his last visit, but when he had greeted Dreumel, he looked closely at Georgiana. 'I heard that you were travelling in the forest,' he said bluntly.

'The guide told you?' she queried. 'Is he a friend of yours?'

'No. Not a friend,' he stated flatly. 'He's evil. A desperado. A killer.'

She was shaken. 'I hope he didn't follow our trail?'

'He did for some time,' Lake said, still keeping his eyes on her face. 'You wouldn't have heard him. But then his way was barred.'

'Barred!' she said. 'By what? Surely he wouldn't have been stopped by a fallen tree or a rock?'

'Not by either of those. By a bear!' He stared unblinkingly at her. 'It blocked his path and he had to retreat.'

'He didn't kill it?' she asked anxiously.

He shook his head. 'He said he'd no time to load, or he would have done.' His mouth twitched disdainfully. 'He's a braggart. He wouldn't have been able to strike. She would have killed him first.'

Georgiana's heart thudded. 'She?' she asked, in a small voice.

'It was a she-bear. More dangerous than the male.'

'We saw one too,' she murmured. 'At least, I did. I let her know of our presence and she went away.'

'You didn't mention the bear, Georgiana,' Dreumel said quietly. 'Were you not afraid?'

'Yes. I think I was, but I didn't want to alarm Kitty.' Then she gave a sudden smile. 'We sang for the rest of the journey. We frightened all the wild animals and wild men away!'

Both men shook their heads at her in admonishment but said nothing more.

Lake stayed for three weeks. He told Wilhelm and Georgiana that he had known the valley would one day be occupied again. 'The Iroquois moved on to fresh hunting grounds,' he said, 'but their spirits remain here to watch over it.'

He assisted the men by working on the road by day, then he rode into the mountains in the evenings, returning after dark and making his bed on the floor of one of the men's cabins.

'Where do you go?' Georgiana plucked up courage to ask him one evening. She had watched for his return until quite late. 'Are you hunting?'

'No,' he said, in his usual abrupt way. 'Not here.' He looked down at her. 'I go to be quiet. Away from people.'

'I see,' she said, feeling disappointed but not knowing why. 'Of course. You are used to being alone.'

'Yes. Tomorrow you can come.' His tone was decisive. 'You can ride behind me.'

She bit on her lip and pondered. Would that be the right thing to do? Her emotions were in a turmoil whenever he was around, and when he wasn't she was constantly watching for him.

'Are you afraid?' His eyes held hers.

'Yes,' she answered swiftly. 'I am.'

'There is no need,' he said. 'You will be safe with me.'

He doesn't know it is of myself that I'm afraid, she thought, not wolves or bears or wild men! I know I would be safe from all those things when he is there. It is the thought of being alone with him that makes me tremble.

380

The next day the men brought about the first explosion at the western end of the creek, but the rock was harder than they had expected and the gunpowder they were using produced only a small hole which allowed a mere trickle of water through.

Wilhelm and Ted conferred. 'We'll use nitro-glycerine,' Ted said. 'That'll shift it.'

'*No!*' Wilhelm objected harshly. 'It's not stable. Someone could be killed. And in any case we couldn't get it.'

'Yes we can,' Ted said. 'I've got some.'

'Good God!' Anger showed on Wilhelm's usually calm face. 'Where is it? Where is it stored? We could all be blown to pieces!'

'Safe.' Ted's expression was stubborn. 'It's buried and away from the valley.'

'You were going to use it for the shaft!' Wilhelm accused him.

'In the beginning I was,' Ted admitted, looking away from him. 'But then I thought better of it. The site was too confined, it was too dangerous.'

'I've trusted you—' Wilhelm began.

'And you still can,' Ted said quickly. 'It would save us so much time and effort. I'll do it,' he said. 'I won't ask anyone else to use it.'

'No!' Wilhelm was adamant. 'We cannot take the risk. But how can we get rid of it?'

Ted seemed disappointed, but he just shrugged and said that he knew how.

They blew another small hole, which widened the gap but not enough, and the men decided to leave any further blasting until the following day. They were dirty and tired and only wanted to eat and then go to their beds.

'Tomorrow I'll ride to Philadelphia and fetch Miss O'Neil and some of the others,' Wilhelm decided. 'We must make a start.' He seemed very low after the altercation with Ted, Georgiana thought, and she sat with him for a while, talking of this and that to try and make him more cheerful.

'It's all right, Georgiana,' he murmured after a while. 'You do not need to humour me. It is only that I have had a disappointment. Life does sometimes have a way of making us look again at ourselves.'

She agreed that was true, but added that she didn't like to see him cast down.

He gave her a pensive smile and gently patted her hand. 'I have been much lower than this. It will pass, I expect.'

Georgiana, riding off behind Lake as the men were sitting down to their supper, wondered if anyone would notice that they were both missing. She had told Kitty that she was going into the mountains in case she should worry about her. She glanced back as they crossed over the new bridge and saw Wilhelm standing at the longhouse door looking down the valley towards them.

The sun was such a vivid red as they reached a high bluff that they shielded their eyes from it. They dismounted and watched the shadows on the mountains grow longer and darker as the sun went down, leaving flaming scarlet streaks in the sky.

'It is so beautiful,' Georgiana murmured. 'I don't wonder that you escape to be alone here.'

He reached out and drew her towards him. 'There are times when I don't wish to be alone.' He stroked her hair. 'There are times when I am lonely.' He kissed her lips. 'Since I met you, Gianna, I have often been lonely.' He cupped her face in his hands. 'But it is the course I have chosen.'

She put her arms around his waist. 'Is it the only life for you?' she asked softly, knowing that in his world there wasn't a place for her.

'It is the only life,' he replied. 'It is what I know. Out here in the mountains I know who I am.'

'Who are you?' she murmured.

'Not Indian, nor white man. I am at one with the elements of nature, the solitude and silence. The spirits of the forest and the mountains know that I am just one of the many creatures who live here.'

'A mountain man?' she said, understanding by his words that he was more Indian than white man.

'Yes.' He took her into his arms. Gently he lowered her and himself to the ground and she didn't resist. 'You are beautiful, Gianna. If I was a different kind of man I would want you as my woman – my squaw.' He kissed her again. 'But this is a hard life and I would not wish it on you, or any woman.'

'But some women follow the mountain men,' she said, resting her head on his chest.

'Those women have no other choice.' Slowly he unbuttoned her bodice and she drew her head back, exposing her throat and conscious of the pulse throbbing there. 'They are poor Indian

383

women, cast out from their tribe and reliant on the drunken trappers to look after them. They are not women such as you.'

'What kind of woman am I?' She ran her hands over his shoulders and down his arms, feeling the muscular strength beneath her fingers. 'You don't know me.'

'I know you,' he said softly, and slipped her shirt over her shoulders, where she shrugged it free. He buried his mouth in the tender hollow beneath her neck and shoulder and sucked gently on her skin. 'I know that you are my woman. That whilst I am on this earth you are mine.'

He lifted his head and looked into her eyes. 'Isn't that so?'

'Yes,' she breathed, her lips moist and her body yielding. 'It is so.'

He pulled her down to lie in his arms and she smelt the sharp scent of pine needles, the sweet musky odour of animals, and felt his warm breath on her cheek. She heard the rustle and sigh of the wind in the tree tops as he whispered to her. 'You know that you and I have no tomorrow? We only have today.'

She brushed her cheek against his. 'I only know – that I love you and always will.'

The stars were bright in the dark sky as they reached the bridge and a full moon was shining, its luminescence lighting up the creek and the valley and touching the roofs of the cabins with silver. Lake drew in before riding onto the bridge and put his head to one side, listening. He raised his hand to his ear as if to capture whatever it was that he heard.

'What is it?' Georgiana whispered.

He shook his head. 'Something. I don't know.' He sniffed the air like a dog and listened again. His horse too pricked his ears and snorted restlessly.

Then from the western end of the valley came a crack of light and a mighty explosion which echoed and reverberated around the valley.

Georgiana screamed, 'What's happened?' and clung to Lake's waist as the horse reared and he fought to control it.

'The rock face has been blown up! The water's coming! Hold on! We must get across it before it reaches the bridge.'

In the split second before Lake dug his heels into the horse's flanks, Georgiana shot a glance along the valley and saw a force of turbulent foaming water heading down the creek towards them.

Ted, she thought, as they galloped across the wooden structure. He's done it, even though Wilhelm told him not to. Oh, no! Suppose he's been killed! Stupid, stupid man!

They reached the other side as the torrent rushed at the bridge, churning and frothing around the uprights and swirling over the base and sides before continuing its path towards the newly blasted exit at the bottom of the valley.

Shouts were echoing down the valley and in the moonlight they saw people running towards the scene of the explosion. Two men on horseback were already galloping down. Lake urged his horse on and as they reached the longhouse, he drew to a halt. 'Go inside,' he said to her. 'Prepare bandaging in case someone is hurt.'

'But–' she began but he was already urging her off the horse. Then she saw Kitty running down the valley, her skirts and hair flying. 'No,' she refused, clinging onto him. 'If Ted is dead, Kitty will need me with her.'

He nodded and dug his heels in so sharply that she almost slid off, and galloped towards the western end of the vale. He reined in as he reached Kitty, and leaning down he scooped her up in front of him.

'That eejit!' she shrieked. 'Mr Dreumel said he shouldn't use that stuff. He said it was dangerous! But would he listen?' Her voice was high-pitched and tremulous. 'Miss Georgiana! Suppose he's dead!'

Georgiana made no answer. She was looking to the front where a breach had appeared in the rock face and where the waters of the creek from the other valley were pouring through, rushing and tumbling as if escaping at last from a long confinement.

It will never be the same again, she thought as they cantered towards the boundary. Another bridge will be built over the creek and a road through to the next valley, linking the two. In her imagination she could see a community of log houses, a grocery store, a saloon, children playing in the meadows, cattle grazing on the lower slopes, and knew that now it would come.

It has to be shared, she mused. This vast country which has room for everyone to fulfil their dreams. And if Robert Allen – Ted – has taken a risk or even has to die in his attempt to achieve his dream, then so be it. We all take a risk

386

at some time in our lives. I have taken one tonight in declaring my love for a wild mountain man, when I know there is no future with him.

She slipped down from the horse as Lake reined in and grasped Kitty fast to stop her running ahead to where Ted was staggering with his hand to his head and Wilhelm was trying to support him.

'I'm all right! I'm all right!' Ted could hardly stand yet he wouldn't sit down. His face was spattered with blood and he clutched his elbow as if it was painful. 'I got blown by the blast!' He was shouting. 'I'm sorry, Bill. I know you said – said – God, my head hurts!' He collapsed in a heap on the ground just as Kitty, released from Georgiana's arms, raced up.

'You eejit! Are you all right? I could kill you. In God's name, what do you think you were doing?'

Ted looked up. 'What?' he bellowed. 'What do you say?'

'I said you're an eejit,' she screeched at him. 'What about this bairn I'm carrying? I could be a widow woman afore I'm married, so I could!' In her terror and relief, her Irish and Yorkshire phrasing commingled.

'I can't hear you.' He shook his head and pressed his fingers to his ears. 'I'm deaf.'

'Daft, you are, never mind deaf!' Kitty started to cry and Georgiana put her arm around her waist.

'He'll be all right,' she soothed. 'The men will take him back to the longhouse. He probably has concussion.'

The other men were arriving now and some of

them had come on horseback. They put Ted onto one of the horses and slowly walked him back, whilst Georgiana and Kitty cantered ahead with Lake to prepare a bed and bandaging.

'I was going to tell you about 'bairn, miss,' Kitty sniffled. 'But I wanted to be sure and I wanted to tell Ted first. Now everybody knows but him, cos he couldn't hear me. Do you think he'll get his hearing back?' she asked anxiously.

'I don't know,' Georgiana admitted. 'I suppose it will depend on how near he was to the blast. Perhaps it will come back after a day or two.'

Ted was carried in and put to bed and Kitty bathed his head and face, which were covered with cuts from the flying rock. 'You were never much of an oil painting,' Kitty moaned at him as she tenderly applied warm water and washed the blood away. 'Now you're going to be scarred for ever!' Tears ran down her face.

'Can't hear you,' he mumbled. 'Don't know what you're saying.' He reached for her free hand. 'Sorry, Kitty. I didn't want to scare you. My old da was injured in a mining accident, never thought it would happen to me. But it was my choice.' His words were slurred. 'He never had one.' He brought her hand to his mouth and kissed it. Then, putting his head back, he closed his eyes.

Kitty stared at him. 'He's not–?' Her voice was thin and frightened and her mouth trembled.

'No.' Lake stood there. 'Don't worry. Nature has taken over and put him to sleep.' He lifted up a lock of black hair from his forehead to show a scar. 'I fell from a rock when I was a boy and knocked myself out. I slept for two days.' He nodded towards Ted. 'He'll wake up with a bad headache and he might not remember what happened.'

Wilhelm came to stand by the bed. He looked down at Ted. 'The flood is slowing,' he said. 'The water is finding its own channel.'

'Where will it go?' Georgiana asked. 'Will it flood the plain?'

'It will find its own course down the outcrop,' Lake answered. 'It might join up with other waters or make a lake. One day men will change its direction again, but for the moment the water will make its own way.'

Wilhelm looked round the room. Only Georgiana, Kitty, Lake and he were there. The other men had gone outside to watch the progress of the water as it rushed through the valley.

'It's a pity he's asleep.' He nodded towards the bed where Ted lay. 'I shall have to wait until he's recovered before I can tell him the good news.' He jiggled a lump of rock in his hand.

'What news, Mr Dreumel?' Kitty asked.

'I went back to look at the site where he'd placed the explosives.' He held out the rock to show them. He gave a grin. 'There's gold!'

CHAPTER THIRTY-FOUR

Lake left the next day, but before he did he took Georgiana to one side. 'I have something for you,' he said gruffly, and unfastened one of his packs. He handed her a fur cape. 'Beaver. The best.' And she could see that it was. Quite unlike the pelts he had sold to Charlesworth, though it was roughly sewn this was the most beautiful, soft and desirable fur she had ever seen.

'It will keep you warm when winter comes.'

'It's lovely.' She held the fur to her face. 'Will I not see you again before winter?' she asked.

'Perhaps. Perhaps not. I shall go north again.'

And that is how it will always be, she thought as she watched him ride away over the bridge.

Ted awoke two days later and, as Lake had predicted, he had a bad headache. He was also deaf in one ear. But he was jubilant about the finding of gold and keen to be out of bed to start work on the new shaft.

'I want to speak seriously to you,' Wilhelm said to him. He, Georgiana and Kitty were sitting by the stove in the longhouse, now converted to a saloon with a counter, tables and chairs, but with Ted's makeshift bed in the middle of the room. 'There will be no more acting alone. We will consult with the committee and decide what is to be done. Our lives are about to change and our decisions now, at the beginning of this new era, will influence our future.'

Ted nodded. He had been shocked when he realized that he might have been killed. Kitty had told him that she was carrying his child. 'I never thought–' he said. 'I didn't expect to become a family man.'

'Don't tell me that no-one told you how babies are made!' Kitty stood with one hand on her apron-clad hip. 'Didn't you have any learning?'

'Not that kind.' He grinned. 'So I suppose we'd

390

better get married?'

'You suppose right,' she said firmly. 'Just as soon as Miss Georgiana finds us a parson.'

Georgiana and Wilhelm went back to Philadelphia, returning a few weeks later with a parson riding on a small pony. Nellie O'Neil followed behind in a waggon which was laden with barrels and casks. She was dressed flamboyantly in a flounced purple satin gown, with a green feathered hat and travelling cape. Bright beads and glittering jewels bedecked her neck and fingers.

'Well, I'll be danged!' Isaac stood at the saloon door. 'If it ain't Nellie Murphy.'

'Nellie O'Neil,' she answered primly. 'Howdy, Isaac, you old dawg! Fancy seeing you here.'

The parson, a handsome young man, looked around the valley. 'I'd like to stay here,' he said. 'Can I build a church?'

Isaac, after unloading Nellie's waggon and stacking the barrels and casks in the saloon, disappeared for a while. When he reappeared he had trimmed his beard, had a bath, washed his hair and was wearing a bright blue waistcoat.

'Goodness,' Georgiana said to Kitty. 'What a transformation. Isaac looks ten years younger. He must have a sweet spot for Mrs O'Neil.'

'Call me Nellie.' The subject of their conversation appeared from under the bar counter. 'Isaac and me go way back. He was a handsome buck in his time. Gone to seed a bit since then.' She patted her curls. 'But I guess we'll all do that sooner or later.'

One of the carpenters asked Wilhelm for leave of absence. 'Don't sell my plot to anyone else,' he

391

pleaded. 'I just want to go home to fetch my wife and daughter, my boy, my cow and my dawg. I'll be back in five, maybe six, weeks. Then I'll start building us a log house ready for winter.'

'But where will your family live whilst you're building it?' Wilhelm asked. The three carpenters and the wheelwright had been sharing a cabin.

'In the waggon,' he said. ''Cept fer the cow.'

The other carpenters started to build the church for the wedding. Wilhelm, Ted, Ellis, Jason and Pike, the original party who had now formed a committee to run Dreumel's Creek, pondered future developments. Would it be feasible to cross the creek and blow another opening in the rock, so making a road through to the other valley?

'You'll all have a stake in this,' Wilhelm told them at a meeting in the saloon. 'You've shared the hard times. Now it looks as if our fortune is about to change. There is a great deal of work in front of us, but one day we will have a thriving community here.'

'I want to tell you all something.' Ted stood up and faced everyone. 'Kitty and me are going to be married as soon as the church is ready. Now, I've never been one for church-going, but I'm a bit scared of standing in front of God and the preacher and saying words that might not be true.'

He glanced at Kitty, Georgiana and Wilhelm. 'Some of you know my history already, but I'd like to tell the rest of you that my name isn't Ted Newmarch. Edward Newmarch was my employer and he disappeared in New Orleans, so I took his

392

name. It doesn't matter now why I did, but if you're interested then I'll tell you sometime. My real name is Robert Allen and that is the name I'll be married by. Kitty will be Mrs Allen, but if you still want to call me Ted, then that's all right. I've sort of got used to it.' He looked down at his boots. 'I just wanted you to know, that's all.'

Later Georgiana and Wilhelm sat on the bench outside the saloon. There was a drift of conversation and laughter – even the parson Francis Birchfield was in there. He had been helping to build the church and as he swung an axe, sawed logs and hammered nails in preparation for his own place of worship he sang joyful hymns.

'Everything is going well,' Wilhelm was saying. 'Tomorrow we start blasting through the mountain to make a road into the next valley.'

'I'm very worried about that,' Georgiana said. 'None of you are engineers. Suppose the mountain comes crashing down?'

He reassured her. 'It won't. It didn't when Ted made the opening for the creek. Though we won't use that same explosive.' There had been a vast amount of rock fall which had spread around the valley, but the mountain stood as impenetrable as ever.

Georgiana's thoughts turned to Lake. He had said to her that the mountains were immovable, that no matter how man treated them, only the spirits of the mountain could destroy them. She breathed a small sigh. She was missing him, yet she was content. So very happy. Her face creased into a smile.

Wilhelm saw it. 'You're happy, Georgiana?'

She turned to him. 'Yes. I am.'

'I'm glad.' He took her hand and held it. He had a catch in his voice. 'So very glad for you.'

'Do you know what I'm thinking of, Wilhelm?' She put her head back and laughed. 'I'm thinking of my cousin May. I haven't considered her for such a long time, but she came into my thoughts only a few days ago when I was speaking to Nellie O'Neil. Do you remember, when she said she would like a piano in the saloon?'

He nodded. 'I said I would bring one back on our next journey from Philadelphia.'

'Yes,' she said. 'And I said I would play it. And at the time I reflected on how I used to play the piano in my uncle's house. I told you that he was my guardian during my childhood? And I pondered on what he would think of me playing a piano in a saloon! And just now I speculated on May's reaction if she could only see me, sitting under the stars outside a saloon, beneath the mountains in the wilderness, watching the waters of the creek running by, and holding hands with my very dear friend!'

He gave a sudden intake of breath. 'What would she think?' he said softly.

'She would be quite amazed.' She smiled. 'And totally confused. She would probably think that I had taken leave of my senses.' And perhaps I have, she mused, for I know for sure that all reasoning and wisdom left me when I was with Lake.

She squeezed Wilhelm's hand, which was still clasping hers. 'And I regret nothing. Nothing at all!'

Lake came back once more before the winter

and in time for Kitty and Ted's wedding. Wilhelm was Ted's best man and Isaac gave Kitty away, and said with tears in his eyes that she was just the kind of daughter that he would have wanted. 'One that can cook,' he'd added.

It was such a joyful occasion. Georgiana and Kitty had sewn a wedding dress, and on the wedding day all the men washed, shaved and brushed down their clothes. They took off their battered hats as they entered the newly built wooden church. After the ceremony, somebody played the fiddle, Isaac put his mouth organ to his lips and everyone danced, the men with each other when Kitty, Georgiana and Nellie were already taken.

Later that evening, Georgiana rode with Lake into the mountains and he told her that he would leave the following morning and come back in the spring. 'Where do you go?' she asked. 'Why don't you stay with us at Dreumel's Creek until winter is over?' But she knew as she said it that she was asking the impossible. The life he led was the one he had chosen. She must be content that he would come back when he was ready.

'Let me tell you of my life,' he murmured. 'Then you will understand why I cannot ask you to share it. You have seen my possessions. I have two, sometimes three, horses. A rifle, a knife, hatchet, axe, two blankets and a kettle for the fire.' He ran his fingers through her thick hair and kissed her cheek. 'When I find a good place to hunt or trap I build a log shelter where I can sleep. If there is beaver about, then I set my traps by the rivers and streams. Sometimes I must build a canoe and travel along the banks in search of them.

'You would not like to see what I do next. You are a woman who has not been brought up to know this way of life.'

'Tell me,' she urged. 'So that I know.'

He nodded. 'When I have caught and killed beaver I take it back to my lair. I skin it, stretch the skin out to dry, roast and eat the flesh. That keeps me alive throughout the winter.'

She shuddered. It was true, she could not live that kind of life. 'Some trappers are hunted and killed by the Indians,' he continued. 'They are taking the Indians' source of food and trade, and they also steal their women.'

'But they don't attack you, because you are part Iroquois?'

He smiled. 'That's so. I trade with the Iroquois and I don't take their women, though Dekan and Horse try to persuade me to marry one of their maidens and come back to their settlement. I will never do that.' He drew her close to him. 'Especially not now.'

Pike urged the men not to decimate the tree line when they were felling timber for the cabins. 'Thin the trees out. Leave enough to break the snow when it comes, or I'm telling you we'll have an avalanche, for sure,' he warned, but some of the men, and there were many who were arriving now from Philadelphia, were in a hurry to have shelter before the winter and ignored what he said.

First came the rain which swelled the hillside streams. Without the trees to break their progress, they came rushing down into the valley.

The track outside the cabins was awash and boards were put down to walk on. The women's skirts were constantly mud-splashed, and their boots had to be dried every evening.

Ted built a temporary cabin for him and Kitty, for he was still intent on moving to the next valley when the road was finally pushed through. It was taking longer than they had imagined: first they had to build another bridge, which they named the Western Bridge, to take them and their equipment across the waters of the creek.

'Do you realize, Georgiana,' Wilhelm said as they were sitting, as was now their custom, outside the saloon, 'that we two are the only people without a home of our own! Everyone else has their own cabin.'

Georgiana was wrapped in her beaver cape, a shawl around her head and a blanket over her knees, for there was a crisp frost on the ground. 'Yes,' she said. 'If we each had a cabin we could invite the other to sit in comfort by a warm fire, instead of out here in the cold.'

Georgiana was occupying the cabin she and Kitty had shared when they first came to Dreumel's Creek, but it was draughty and not homely, and Wilhelm still shared with some of the other men.

'In the spring,' he declared, 'we will build you a log house of your own.'

She felt suddenly sad. And no-one to share it with, she reflected. Now that Kitty has married and Lake has gone, I'm a woman quite alone.

The snow started to fall one night, and they awoke to a thin white covering over the boardwalks, the bridge, the meadows and the mountain tops. Wilhelm called an emergency meeting of the committee. 'Can we make one last attempt to blast through the rock?' he asked. 'We shall soon be closed in for the winter and won't be able to cross the mountain to the mine. I'd like to think that we can blast out part of the road so that we are ready for the spring thaw.'

It was agreed and everything was set. They crossed the Western Bridge with their equipment and cleared a trail for the explosive. Pike and Jason were to lay the gunpowder and Jason said he would light it. Pike overruled him as he hadn't enough experience, and said he would do it. Everyone in the valley was warned to keep away, for this was to be a big charge. The men watched from a distance and saw Pike kneel and then run back behind a rock. But there was no sizzle, no flame leaping down the black trail. He got up and went towards it again.

'No!' Dreumel and Ted shouted simultaneously. 'Get back. Wait!'

But he didn't hear them and went on further down the trail, towards the rock face, bending to light the powder again. They watched in horror as it suddenly ignited, gathering speed behind him, then overtaking him. He looked up and started to run back, but the flame ran faster and reached the rock face. The detonation ripped the rock apart, exploding a mass of earth, boulders and debris into the air and hurling Pike with it. As the men rushed towards him they saw the gaping hole and through it the snow-covered valley at the other side.

Sprinting across the boulder-strewn valley, Ted reached Pike first, then Jason, followed by Wilhelm. 'He's dead,' Ted choked. 'Stone dead!'

Jason stared down at Pike. 'It could have been me,' he whispered.

'Fetch the parson,' Wilhelm said to Ellis, who had come up behind them.

'He's coming,' Ellis said quietly. 'Everybody's coming.'

The whole community were hurrying down the valley towards the bridge, some running, some riding, just as they had when Ted was injured.

The cleric cantered on his pony up the valley and across the bridge, pushed his way forward and knelt beside Pike. Jason turned away and crossed the bridge, unable to stay or watch or listen as Francis Birchfield closed Pike's eyes and said a quiet prayer. Then the parson stood up and returned down the valley to prepare his church for Dreumel's Creek's first funeral.

CHAPTER THIRTY-FIVE

The winter was long and hard and although the building of cabins went ahead, the men couldn't work outside for long because of the intense biting cold. Georgiana huddled against her smoky stove, wrapped in blankets, shawls and her fur, and wished for a smaller cabin with fewer draughts, for these walls were roughly hewn and daylight showed between the logs. At night she slept on one of the topmost bunks and piled every piece of clothing or blanket over her in an attempt to keep warm, and frequently climbed out of bed to feed the stove with wood.

Jason knocked on her door one day. He had been silent and morose since Pike's death, and was often to be seen staring up the valley at the place where Pike had been killed.

'Can I talk to you, Miz Gianna?' he asked. 'I want to get something off my chest.'

'Of course you can,' she said. 'Come on in. Will you have some hot soup?'

He nodded his thanks and sat down by the stove. 'I've bin thinking,' he began, ''bout going home.'

She looked at him in astonishment. 'Really? But you're going to strike another shaft as soon as winter is over!'

'I know.'

He looked as if he was about to cry and she sat down beside him. 'You're still upset about Pike, aren't you?' she said softly.

He nodded and rubbed his nose. 'He was like a father to me,' he croaked. 'We travelled together, you see, and he was always on at me that I should let my folks know that I was all right.'

'Did Pike have any family?' It hadn't occurred to her that anyone should be informed of Pike's death. Most of the men here had been rovers, travelling on when the mood suited them.

'He said he hadn't, said he'd been a loner since he was a boy.' He heaved a deep sigh. 'It's since he's been gone that I started thinking about Ma and Pa and whether they were worrying 'bout me.'

400

'Couldn't you write to them?'

'No, ma'am. I can't write and they can't read. Besides which there ain't no mail delivered up where I come from.'

'What? Nowhere? Because I could write for you if you thought a letter would get there, and,' she added hastily, 'if there was someone who could read it to them.'

He thought seriously about this suggestion. 'There's a trading store 'bout twenty miles from home. Fella who runs it can read. Yeh!' He gazed at her with a brighter light in his eyes than she had seen for some weeks. 'Pa calls in there for supplies every couple o' months. Guess a letter might get to him.'

'Well, why don't we do that, Jason,' she proposed. 'As soon as the thaw comes we'll ask Wilhelm to take your letter to Philadelphia to catch the mail coach.'

'Thanks, Miz Gianna. I'm really grateful.' He beamed at her. 'I feel better just fer talking 'bout it. Tell the truth,' he gave a little shrug, 'I didn't really want to go. I guess they'd want me to stay on the farm if I went back.'

'And you want to stay to work the shaft?' she asked.

'Yeh! But not only that,' he said. 'You know the carpenter who fetched his family here?'

'Ah!' she said knowingly. 'Yes!' The carpenter had brought his wife, his son and daughter, and the daughter, Rose, was a pretty seventeen-year-old.

Jason blushed. 'Rose and me kinda get on well. And besides, I've got a stake in the mine. Bill

401

Dreumel promised me.'

A few days later Ellis called in and asked her if she would write a letter to his wife. Jason had told him of his own letter to his parents.

'Your wife!' she said in surprise. 'Does she not know where you are?'

'Nope. I set off from New England fer Californy in search of gold. That was in '49. I had trouble all along. Lost my mare, my money, every darn thing. I was on my way home when I met up with Dreumel.'

It was the longest speech she had heard Ellis make. I trust his wife's still waiting, Georgiana mused as she prepared the letters, and thought how strange it was that everyone seemed to have met up with Wilhelm when they were at their lowest ebb. He's given everybody some hope, something to grasp onto. Even me.

When the thaw came there was an avalanche as Pike had predicted, though he wasn't there to see it. Thick blocks of snow fell from the mountainside and left great drifts piled up at the sides and sometimes over the tops of the cabins. When the snowdrifts melted they ran down the meadowland and into the creek, swelling it so high that the bridges were impassable.

Kitty gave birth to a red-haired daughter, whom she named Caitlin after her own mother. 'So now we have a little piece of old Ireland here,' she said. 'Even though I've never been there.'

Lake returned in the spring. Georgiana had watched for him constantly and saw him early one morning etched against the backdrop of the mountain. She felt a lifting of her spirits and wanted to run to greet him, yet old propriety and convention held her back.

Wilhelm saw him too as he came out of his door, and he also saw Georgiana watching. He called to her. 'Georgiana! Go!'

She turned towards him. 'Should I?' she asked.

'Yes, of course.' He smiled at her, though he had a wistful expression. 'You must do what your heart tells you.'

Quickly she fetched Hetty. She had learned to ride without a saddle, and astride the mare she cantered to meet Lake as he came over the bridge.

He was leaner than when she had last seen him, his cheekbones stood out prominently, and his hands grasping the reins were bony. He gave her his peculiar lopsided grin as she greeted him, but he didn't ask how she was as a cultured man might have done, simply saying, 'You look good, Gianna.' They didn't kiss. He held out his hand and she took it. They cantered side by side along the creek towards the settlement, and she felt her heart swelling with contentment.

On one of his visits he asked her to go with him on an expedition. 'Three days we will be away,' he said. 'Tell Kitty and Wilhelm. I will show you what kind of life I lead.'

This time she didn't hesitate, but packed a few things into a saddlebag and rode up behind him. She turned around and saw Kitty with Caitlin in her arms watching them. Wilhelm wasn't there, although she had told him she was going.

They took a different trail from the one she was familiar with, coming down that evening on the other side of the mountain range into an elevated valley with a stream running through it. Here they made camp within the shelter of pine trees. Lake lit a fire, then went in the direction of the stream whilst Georgiana cooked beans in a pot. She watched him as he strode lithely towards the water and lay down on his stomach beside it. When she looked up again he was beside her with a struggling silver fish in his hand.

'Supper,' he murmured, and bashed the fish against a tree. She watched silently as he gutted it, wrapped it in a large leaf and placed it over the fire. It was, she thought later, the best food she had ever eaten.

Georgiana awoke sometime during the night and saw Lake standing by a tree staring up at the dark sky. She lifted her eyes too and saw a myriad stars glinting and flickering, and held her breath as she saw one shooting earthwards.

'Did you see it?' he asked, without turning around.

'Yes,' she murmured. 'How did you know I was awake?'

He came towards her and she heard the smile in his voice as he answered. 'I knew, that's all. And I heard you move.'

How sharp his senses are, she thought, and leant her head on his shoulder when he came to sit beside her. 'You haven't been to sleep,' she said. 'Is it because of me?'

'Yes.' He looked down at her. 'There are many dangers prowling at night.'

Though the fire was flickering she could barely see him. She touched his face with her fingers and felt his cheeks crease as he murmured, 'I

404

mustn't be distracted again.'

They moved off early the next morning and Georgiana's body ached from lying on the rough ground, even though Lake had given her his blanket and a fur pelt to lie on. They travelled until noon, following a tributary stream through narrow gorges, and halted in another lower valley where a swift river rushed alongside a forested area.

'There's beaver here.' Lake looked around him. 'We'll build a shelter.'

They moved back into a clearing with the protection of trees around it. Whilst Georgiana unfastened the packs, Lake built a crude shelter of brushwood and branches and lit a small fire. He then disappeared for a while, and returned dragging a cottonwood tree.

She didn't ask what the purpose was, for this was his world and she didn't want to intrude with meaningless questions, but she watched as with his hatchet, knife and awl he dug out a hollow in the centre of the tree. It's a canoe, she realized, and shifting her eyes to the river below them, wondered if she would have the courage to go in it, if he should ask her.

'You must stay here,' he said, as he finished it, and she felt a sense of uneasy relief. 'There is only room for one and the beaver. I will be away for several hours.' He gave her a sudden intense glance. 'You will be all right. You have a knife and I'll leave you my rifle. If you are in trouble fire it and I will come.'

It was lonely without him and she kept to the shelter, venturing out only to feed the fire with twigs and branches, and twice to look downriver, hoping to see him returning. There were unfamiliar rustlings from the forest floor and screechings from the tree tops, and from time to time she clanked a tin spoon against the bean pot to warn off any wandering bear.

He returned as the light began to fade, carrying the bodies of two beaver. Georgiana averted her eyes as he threw them down and proceeded to skin them. 'Build up the fire,' he said, 'and look for some long branches to make a frame.'

She did as she was bid without query. When he had skinned the animals he built up the branches over the fire and tied the bodies over it, where they swung and roasted.

'I'm not sure I can eat it,' she said, putting her hand over her mouth as he sliced off a piece of the roasted meat.

'Eat!' He held the meat towards her on his knife. 'There is nothing else. Would you rather starve?'

Later, after darkness had fallen and she was sated with the rich meat, she asked him, as they sat by the fire, about his father and mother. 'What happened to them?' she asked. 'Did your mother travel with him?'

He poked the fire with a stick before answering. 'I only know what I was told,' he said softly. 'My mother was very young and she had gone into the forest alone, which was forbidden for the young Iroquois maidens. She was collecting berries and didn't hear him come behind her. She tried to run but he caught her, put her on his horse and took her away with him.'

His forehead creased into a deep frown. 'He took her from the territory she knew and made her his squaw. Two years she was gone, then she became with child and he didn't want her any more. He took her back to the settlement early one morning and left her there. She sat outside in the forest for two days, not daring to go in. Then she thought of the child she was carrying and plucked up the courage to ask the Iroquois to take her in.'

'And they did?' she asked softly.

He nodded. 'The women held a council, and then the men did the same. They decided that it hadn't been her fault. That she hadn't encouraged him and so they let her back into the tribe.'

'Did you ever meet him?'

'No. He was killed by another tribe when he tried to take one of their women.' His eyes narrowed and his voice was bitter. 'It was a pity for I had wanted to kill him myself.'

They set off back to Dreumel's Creek the next morning, arriving as darkness fell. He watched her go into her cabin, then wheeled around and cantered back down the valley and up the wooded mountainside.

Her life took on a regular pattern. Lake rode in over the mountains and they spent a short precious time together, then he gathered his belongings, lifted his packs onto the second horse, fastened the blankets over the top of them and put on his leather hat, which each time he came had a different feather in it. He saddled his horse, hitched up onto it and looked down at her. He didn't speak, but simply nodded his head,

407

raised his hand and cantered away. She never asked him when he would be returning – she knew he would come when he could.

Now that Kitty had her child Georgiana was without any help or maid, but she didn't mind. She felt quite self-sufficient, except on washdays when carrying heavy buckets of water from the rain butts or creek did not appeal, so Kitty arranged for young Rose to help Miss Gianna with the washing. Rose also assisted Kitty in her bakery store. 'What about that, Miss Georgiana?' Kitty exclaimed. 'Who'd ever have thought that I would have a help of my own!'

Georgiana's own cabin was taking shape as Wilhelm had promised, as was the new road into the next valley which they decided would be called Pike's Road. Mining equipment was coming in only gradually, for the men were anxious not to whisper the word that there was gold in the next valley. The ground was staked and a company, made up of the committee, was formed.

In the summer a second shaft was sunk, but there was disappointment when there was no gold. Some of the newer men, employed to work for the company, packed up their picks, shovels and tents and drifted away to look for their fortune elsewhere.

'We're too high,' Ted proclaimed, looking down from the site of the second shaft. 'We should be lower down, nearer the creek.' So another site was chosen for the third shaft. Waterwheels were installed, flumes to divert the mountain streams were dug, a shaft house and rough shanty housing were built so that the men didn't have to journey back to Dreumel's Creek each evening.

Georgiana was sitting on a bench outside the bakery with Caitlin on her knee, whilst Kitty was inside kneading dough. She was building up a good business, supplying the residents of Dreumel's Creek with fresh bread and cakes. Georgiana lifted her head and listened. A shout! Faint, yet definitely a shout. There it was again. It was coming from the direction of the other valley.

'Kitty!' she called. 'Come here a minute.'

Kitty emerged, wiping her floury hands on a cloth. 'What?' she said.

'Something's happening – listen, can't you hear? The men are shouting.'

'Glory to God!' Kitty crossed herself. 'I hope there's not been an accident!' She took Caitlin from Georgiana and hugged her.

'No.' Georgiana stood up and strained to hear. 'I can hear – *yippee!* That's what they're shouting! They're shouting yippee! Oh, Kitty!' She turned to face her, her face flushed and animated. 'Do you think they've struck gold?'

They had. A figure appeared across the creek at the entrance to the new road. A figure waving his arms and jumping up and down. They couldn't hear what he was yelling but he was indicating good news.

'It's Ted!' Kitty shrieked, startling Caitlin and making her cry. 'Look, he's wearing his lucky red shirt!'

Georgiana laughed. 'His lucky red shirt?'

'Yes!' Kitty cried excitedly. 'I'd washed his old one and told him to wear that one. He didn't want to because he said it was his best winter flannel. I said it would bring him luck and then we'd be able to make him another!'

When the men arrived back that evening they brought the news of a strike. 'We struck the lead!' Ted threw his hat in the air and swung Kitty round and round until she shrieked at him to stop. Then he gave Georgiana a smacking kiss.

'Forty feet down,' he bellowed. 'Jason went wandering along the creek and saw the gravel glistening under the water. We went down another ten feet and brought up the richest gravel you ever did see!'

Wilhelm had a huge beam on his face. 'I can't believe it,' he kept saying. 'I can't believe it! After all this time! I almost gave up,' he confessed to Georgiana. 'The men were so tired, yet they wanted to continue, especially Ted. And,' he looked at Georgiana, 'I couldn't bear to think of you losing your inheritance.'

'But I didn't,' she said gently. 'I had faith in you, Wilhelm.'

'Thank you.' He took her hand and pressed it to his lips. 'Thank you.'

Once the news reached Philadelphia, miners started to appear across the plain, carrying their picks and shovels and some wheelbarrows, all heading for Dreumel's Creek. But not all could find their way and some missed the opening into the mountains and lost themselves. Other more determined characters found their way but discovered that the best claims had been staked on the hillside, so they moved further down into the second valley.

Yeller Valley, Jason had named it, and within

weeks a shanty town had been set up alongside the creek. Claims were staked, and men panned and sieved the waters of the river bed. Others struck the rock with their picks but few found gold for it was buried deep, and many moved on.

Nearly four years had passed since Georgiana and Kitty had set sail for America, and they often discussed how different their lives now were. Kitty was a wife and mother and running her own bakery store, whilst Georgiana had swapped her genteel lady's existence for a much simpler one. They were richer than they had ever dreamed they would be, but found that the acquisition of gold had made little difference to their lives here in Dreumel's Creek.

It was whilst Georgiana and Wilhelm were in Philadelphia attending to newspaper business, for Georgiana, at Wilhelm's insistence, had kept her shares in the *Star*, that a letter came for her. She had given the newspaper address to May and May's parents and although she wrote fairly regularly, their replies came only infrequently. In one of them May had told her of the sudden death of Aunt Clarissa.

She sat at Wilhelm's desk now and hoped that it wasn't more bad news. She was dismayed, however, to read in the first line that May's father had died during the year.

'I did not tell you sooner, my dear Georgiana, for I know how you would have depended on poor Papa should you return to England, and I did not wish to crush your spirits too much. However, after much discussion, Mama and I decided that it was best that you know the

411

situation here and that after such a long period away, you must expect now to fend for yourself.

'I had hoped that you would have found a suitable husband to care for you, but I must presume that you haven't as I know you would have written to tell me. I can only hope that your spinsterhood is tranquil and untroubled, and in order to maintain a prudent decorum I suggest that you refrain from reading any romantic novels as you used to, which might induce any craving of unrequited passion.'

Georgiana smiled to herself as she turned the page, and thought of riding up into the mountains with Lake. She thought of his lithe strong body, his tender, yet passionate loving, and knew that she couldn't speak of any of this happiness to her cousin.

'However,' she read on, and her eyebrows rose at the content. 'The main reason for my writing to you now is to ask a favour of you, which I know you will consider it your duty to fulfil, in view of your obligation to us, your adoptive family, who have sustained you as a daughter and sister since the early death of your unfortunate parents.

'Dearest Papa was always of the opinion that one day Edward would return to me and that our marriage would be resumed. I was therefore never allowed to entertain any gentlemen, not even in a most discreet manner, and have lived a virtuous and moral life since my husband left. But now that Papa is gone, I have a suitor, a Mr Melville, a very worthy gentleman, who would marry me if I was free. I am asking you therefore, dear Georgiana, if you will do all in your power to ascertain whether my husband, Edward Newmarch, is alive or dead.'

Georgiana put down the letter. But how? Surely May does not want me to search for him? Does she not realize how big this country is? She glanced again at the letter and read it to the end. She does! She is obligating me to seek him out! There was no doubt that her cousin was calling on Georgiana's integrity and gratitude for the benevolence shown to her in the past.

She showed the letter to Wilhelm and he read it with a grave expression on his face. 'Did they bestow compassion on you when you lost your parents?' he asked.

'My uncle supported me and never grumbled,' she admitted. 'But I lived with his elderly sister, my aunt. I did not live with them as a daughter or a sister, as May implies. May was very young when I came into their care and I don't think they wanted another child in the house.

'Nevertheless,' she conceded, 'I have every reason to be grateful to my uncle and aunt. And I did accompany May as a companion as we grew into womanhood.' She sighed and thought of how very often she had become weary of May and her constant demands.

'Then we must endeavour to find him.' Wilhelm teased his beard thoughtfully. 'If he is alive she must file for a divorce, which would perhaps be distasteful for her, or if he is dead be declared a widow. She cannot marry otherwise.' He gazed at Georgiana. 'An advertisement in the newspaper for a start?'

She considered. 'Yes. And perhaps in a New

413

Orleans paper also, if you have contacts. That is where he was last seen.'

But weeks went by and there was no response to their advertisements. Autumn was coming up fast, the foliage on the oaks was turning to red-gold and the willows by the creek were shedding their leaves. Lake would be coming for the last time before winter and Georgiana felt that if she was to be positive regarding the search for Edward Newmarch, then she should act soon.

'Wilhelm! I think I must travel to New Orleans to enquire about Edward.'

He looked startled. 'But someone must accompany you. You cannot possibly travel alone.' Then he blinked his blue eyes and smiled. 'Even though you are an intrepid traveller!'

'Wilhelm,' she warned jocularly. 'You know better than to say that I cannot do something!' She considered. 'I'll speak to Ted again. Perhaps he might remember more about what might have happened to Edward Newmarch.'

Ted couldn't shed more light on the mystery. 'I was ill with malaria at the time he disappeared,' he said. 'I won't ever forget that because it keeps recurring.' He shook his head. 'I reckon the Spaniard, Rodriguez, found him. Newmarch told me he had become involved with a woman. Women were always his downfall,' he added cynically.

'Well, you cannot go alone, Georgiana,' Wilhelm insisted. 'It is too dangerous. Ask Lake,' he said quietly. 'He'll tell you.'

'Lake is not my keeper,' she answered defiantly, for although she realized that Wilhelm knew of her relationship with Lake, she did not care for it to be acknowledged. She regretted her words instantly when she saw the hurt on his face. 'I'm sorry, Wilhelm,' she whispered. 'But I must do what *I* think is best.'

'I only meant,' he said, turning away from her, 'that Lake would know of the dangers of crossing the country alone. As indeed I do, and Ted and the other men do.' He looked back at her. 'But you are a stubborn, independent woman, Georgiana, and nothing I will say will make the slightest difference!'

She caught hold of his sleeve. 'You are wrong, Wilhelm. I value your opinion very highly. I will go to Philadelphia and travel by ship to New Orleans.' She gave him a warm smile. 'I shall be perfectly safe on a ship, so you need not worry.'

'But I will,' he answered.

Lake had his misgivings when she told him of her plans. 'Are you in this woman's debt? Is she so important to you that you will risk your life for her?'

She suddenly felt frightened, just as she had when she first set out on the voyage to America. 'I owe my life to her father, who is dead. I would have been destined for an orphanage otherwise.'

He didn't understand the term and so she explained. He simply nodded his head and gave a small grunting noise. 'You must pay that debt,' he agreed. 'And then you are free for ever. You can do whatever you wish with your life.'

'I only wish to be with you,' she whispered. 'I don't want to go away. I'm happy with my life here, but when I come back I will be ready to

415

follow you if you will let me.'

They were up on the plateau overlooking the valley, and he put his arms around her and drew her towards him. 'My freedom is not the same as yours, Gianna. I am beyond civilization, which is where you belong. My freedom is on the plains and in the mountains. It is on the riverbanks and beside lakes. It is being able to make my shelter where and when I choose.'

He kissed her gently on the lips. 'I can travel in the heat of the sun or in the depths of winter snow. If I am tired I rest, and if I am not I keep on travelling. You and I know it is not a life that I can share.'

'Do you love me?' she asked.

'I will love you always.' He looked down at her, then closing his eyes he touched her face, tracing her features with his fingers as if he wanted to imprint them into his own quintessence. 'Look for me when you return and I will be here.'

CHAPTER THIRTY-SIX

When Edward and the other men looked on San Francisco for the first time, they were looking through weary, yet eager eyes. 'We've been through hell,' Edward had muttered, 'and we've reached El Dorado.'

They were triumphant at having arrived as there had often been times on their long journey when they were on the verge of giving up, and

416

would have done so but for the hazards of going back. They were also astounded by the size of the city. The previous year a conflagration, lashed by the wind blowing in across San Francisco Bay, had caught hold of the crude wooden shacks, canvas tents and waggons, and within minutes had reduced the town to smouldering timber.

Now a new city had arisen. Cheap hotels, bars, brothels, gambling dens, quarters where Chinese, Mexican, Negro, and countless nationalities had settled in their own domain to speak their own language and continue their customs. The city was a conglomerate mass of cultures. Educated men with pen and paper, parsons with bibles, seamen jumped from their ships, cooks with recipes, farmhands with hayseed in their hair, scoundrels and card sharps, all eagerly converged on this once small settlement of Yerba Buena to seek a quick fortune.

Following on behind the gold prospectors were merchants selling their goods at inflated prices. The whores set up brothels, theatre groups put up their stages and vigilante bands held trials and hangings, sometimes on the same day. Justice was swift, rough and conclusive.

'Why did we come here?' Jed had muttered as they pitched their tents on a hillside outside the town. 'Just look at those ships, all filled with prospectors! We should have gone straight upriver, the strikes will be all worked out!'

Down in San Francisco Bay the ships crowded together on the wharf, having disgorged hundreds more men to swell the city to bursting point.

'No, they won't,' Larkin asserted. 'There's gold

all over Californy. We've just got to look for it, that's all, but we need to be here in San Francisco to hear of the best sites.'

I might have made my fortune with a ship if I had stayed with Rodriguez, Edward had thought as he'd gazed down at the seething city. I suppose fate has brought me here. He hardly ever looked back to his life in England, and rarely thought of his wife May, though often of his mistress Ruby.

She had come into his mind many times as he had tramped over mountains and along rutted trails, forded rushing creeks, crossed dusty plains and rocky valleys, and he had longed for her to be by his side.

The gold rush had started in 1849 when thousands of men and some women left their homes in search of gold, but it had been the year before that James Marshall had discovered gold in the tailrace of John Sutter's sawmill at Coloma on the American river. Once the secret was out, towns and cities emptied and the long trek to California began.

Edward and the other men had disregarded the trappers' advice about leaving the waggon behind and trekking on foot after the snow had dispersed, and had travelled many more miles with it, following a pack train. Eventually an axle had cracked and the canvas tore in a storm, so they packed as much as they could onto the horse and on their backs, abandoned the waggon and set off to walk.

The trail was well used and they passed many burnt-out waggons, much discarded equipment and the bodies of horses and mules which had been left to rot. They had encouraged each other whenever any one of them was weary, but once they had arrived in San Francisco, dissent began to set in.

James and Matt called a meeting one day to say that they had decided to move off together. They were going up a tributary of the Sacramento river. 'It makes sense,' Matt pronounced. 'If we split we can cover more ground. We can meet up here – say, in a couple of months – and compare findings, and,' he added, 'if any of us finds a good vein then we can join forces and set up as a team again.'

Jed, Larkin and young Tod had glanced at each other and Edward realized that they probably wanted to do the same, but he knew that he would hold them back. He was not as physically strong as they were, he had developed a cough and his chest often ached. He also realized that his skills at reading documents were probably not now needed as they had picked up plenty of information on what to do and how, from other experienced travellers.

'Well, look here,' he'd said. 'I think I'll hang about San Francisco for a while. Rest up a bit and have a look around. See what's happening, you know.'

'You've no money,' Larkin reminded him. 'And nuthin' to sell.'

'Ah! No. So I haven't. But then none of us have!'

'I'll give you my cards.' Jed fished in his bag and handed Edward the dog-eared pack. 'You play a good hand. You might make some money.'

Edward looked down at the pack in his hand and felt strangely touched. It was the only thing Jed had managed to hang onto. He had pushed his precious wheelbarrow when the waggon had gone, then borne it on his back for miles, before finally discarding it on a mountain top when he couldn't carry it any further. He had looked back as he'd walked away and wept.

'I'd leave you my horse,' Matt said. 'But we'll need him. Besides, he's not going to last much longer and I want to be with him when the time comes.' He gave an embarrassed grin. 'I guess I'm just a sentimental ol' farm boy!'

Edward was aware that he looked rough and dirty, so on his first foray alone into the city he had found the cheapest, lowest bar possible and joined a table of men at cards. They'd guffawed on hearing his English accent, but curiosity had inclined them to let him play. Whilst they'd questioned him on where he was from, he had taken stock of them, seen they were drunk and ignorant, and managed to win enough to pay for a trip to the barber.

With his hair cut and beard trimmed and his clothes brushed down, he ventured into another slightly less rough saloon, where he made sufficient money for a bath and something to eat. The other men had left him one of the canvas tents, which he carefully rolled up every morning and carried with him, for the last thing he wanted was for someone to steal it, leaving him without shelter. He pitched it every evening as near to a baker's shop as possible, in the hope that the following morning he could steal a loaf of bread or pastry from the tray which the baker left cooling near his open door.

He lived by his wits, which had been considerably sharpened since escaping from the Mississippi river boat. He obtained work as a porter down on the wharf, which bought him food, a second-hand coat and boots and a blanket, for the nights were cold. Then he applied for work as a barman in a saloon. He called himself Eddie Newsom. Word got around about the Englishman, for he couldn't disguise his accent, and he would be offered drinks just so that they could hear him say *Thank you so much. So very kind*, phrases which became more and more cultured and refined as he perceived their effect. The miners would hold their sides as they bellowed with laughter, and mimic him, whilst he would smile and pocket the money and make one drink last all evening.

The saloon owner increased his wages when Edward told him he was thinking of moving on, for there was no doubt that he was a big draw. The saloon girls trusted him because he treated them with respect and not as whores, which was what they were. One of them, Dolly, invited him to her bed. 'For you, honey, there'll be no charge,' she whispered, and when he asked why, she winked and said she was curious.

He accepted her offer. She was nicely rounded and attractive and it was a pleasure to make love to her. Afterwards she cried. 'Honey,' she said. 'I've been with many men, but none like you. It's the first time I've been treated like a lady.' She raised her eyebrows and gave a little wriggle of her hips. 'And I'd been told that Englishmen were cold!'

Larkin, Tod and Jed turned up from time to time and if Edward had any money he bought them supper and a bed for the night, for he was very conscious of his debt to them. They had panned river beds and sluiced the streams and came away with a small handful of gold dust. They used this to buy food and more tools, but they could only afford the simplest troughs and sluice boxes. Of James and Matt nothing was heard.

Edward took to wandering around the city, looking for some opportunity or the chance to gamble, for he didn't attempt this in the saloon where he worked. There were numerous bar rooms which seemed to spring up overnight; stores where anything could be bought, from picks and spades to sacks of flour, providing the customers could pay cash. Boards were placed outside the doors proclaiming *Cash only. No credit. Don't ask.*

The city was awash with humanity, a congestion of shacks, shanties and hovels. Desperate men stood on street corners begging for bread or trying to sell a washed-out claim which, they assured anyone prepared to listen, hadn't yet petered out. Indians roamed the streets, their faces vacant as they succumbed to the white man's liquor. Chinese sat outside their dark cabins smoking pipes of opium, and Edward would stop for a moment and wish that he could buy an ounce to raise his spirits.

He was careful not to venture into the city at night, for that was when drunken fights broke out. He worked from six in the evening until four in the morning, when he fell into the bed above the saloon, which came as part of his wages. He then slept until eleven, when he began his prowl around the city.

He watched the gold prices as they fluctuated, and saw them rising higher. He pondered on whether, the next time Larkin and Jed came by, as they'd promised they would, he should travel out to the diggings with them.

A fight erupted one evening. A group of miners, already well inebriated, came into the saloon. They had struck it rich and were buying drinks for everyone. Edward and the owner, Benton, accepted theirs as usual and Edward put his money in his pocket. Then someone said something disparaging about Edward's accent. A regular at the saloon took exception on his behalf and in the next minute tables were being overturned, guns were drawn and fists pulled back.

Edward and Benton swiftly cleared the counter of glasses and bottles and crouched behind it to avoid the flying glasses, chairs and knives. Edward huddled contemplating his beer-stained apron. How have I come to this? Hiding behind a counter of a seedy saloon, thousands of miles from civilization! Not a chance of making any real money or improving my situation.

When the fighting stopped he worked his way around the saloon, picking up chairs and broken glass and wiping down tables with a cloth, whilst Benton carried on serving at the counter. Some of the girls had gone upstairs with their customers, someone was playing a mouth organ and for a few moments there was calm. Edward bent down beneath a table to clear up some glass and picked up a leather hat that had been knocked off during the fight. He put it on his head whilst he swept up the slivers of glass into a shovel.

As he swept, he caught sight of a small stone or rock and within it a glint of yellow. He put his cloth over it, scooped it up and stuffed it into his apron pocket.

'Hey! Hey, you English son of a bitch.' A drunken miner, one of those who had previously been fighting, staggered back into the saloon. 'You're wearing my hat!'

Edward took it off his head and threw it to him. 'You left it behind,' he said.

'*Left it behind*,' the man mimicked. 'You damn well stole it.' He swayed towards Edward and poked him in the chest. 'What you doin' here anyway in this country? It ain't yours no more. Damned English!'

Edward turned away but the man hauled him back. He was big and rough and Edward had no desire to get into an altercation with him, yet he couldn't help saying, 'Well, it hasn't always been yours either.'

The man glared at him, his eyes bloodshot. 'You a redskin lover?'

'Not especially,' Edward replied calmly. 'But they were here before you, as were the Spaniards.'

The drunk hit out, catching Edward on the chin and making him stagger. Some of the men sitting at the tables got up, always ready to join in a fight. Edward found himself surrounded, and the faces were not friendly. He was not a fighter and looking for a way out saw Dolly beckoning him from a side door. Beside her was the Chinese girl who washed the dishes and cleaned the floors.

He ducked as a blow was hurled his way and it found its mark on someone else's nose. He dropped to the floor as a mêlée erupted and crawled on his hands and knees towards the door. Not the most dignified way of making an exit, he considered, keeping his head down. But I have no wish for a cut lip or a broken nose.

He rose up as he reached the door, where he could see Dolly's skirts and the Chinese girl's bare feet, and then sank into oblivion as a chair crashed over his head.

CHAPTER THIRTY-SEVEN

'It seems quite amusing now,' Edward related later to Jed and Larkin when they finally found him, living in a wooden cabin with the Chinese girl Tsui.

Whilst the fight was continuing, Dolly and Tsui had managed to drag Edward to his room above the saloon. Dolly asked Tsui to look after him. He had a nasty wound on the back of his head and Dolly had no stomach for blood. She gave Tsui money for ointment and bandages which she bought from a medicine man in Chinatown. Edward moved out of the saloon as soon as he was fit and the girl went with him.

He wanted to give Jed and Larkin money. The

rock which he had found beneath the table, when it was split open, was worth more than he would ever need in the simple life he was leading. But they grinned and refused it, and handed him a leather purse filled with gold dust and pieces of quartz with gold embedded in it.

'We worked out your share, Eddie,' Larkin told him. 'Taking into account the fact that you came with nuthin'.'

Edward shook his head. It was true they had an agreement that they would share if ever they struck gold. 'But I haven't worked for it,' he said, thrusting it back to them. 'I haven't been to the diggings. I've done nothing to deserve it. You fellows rescued me when I was really down. Keep it,' he said. 'Jed, you wanted to build a cabin.'

'Sure I do, and I will.' His face dropped and he glanced at Larkin.

'When we set out,' Larkin said, 'we were all greedy fer gold. That yeller stuff was a magnet drawing us to it. Well, since we got here we've seen men go crazy fer it. We've seen them hang a man fer jumpin' somebody's claim. We finally caught up with James,' he added. 'He and Matt worked a claim and had a lucky strike, or so they reckoned, but it ran out and they only made a few dollars.'

He rubbed his fingers over his stubbled chin. 'Matt decided to go home. His horse died and he missed his ma and pa. He set off on his own and we'll never know whether or not he made it back.'

'And James?' Edward asked quietly. 'Where's he?'

426

'When we found him he was drunk and lying outside a bar. We took him back to his camp and saw the shack he shared with some other miners.' Larkin shook his head despondently. 'It was a hovel and I wouldn't have kept pigs in it. We've stayed in some pretty rough places but none so bad as that one. We asked him to come along o' us, but he said he was on the verge of a big strike.'

'And was he?' Edward contemplated them as he asked the question. They were sombre men now and the brightness in their eyes had dimmed.

'Nope.' Jed continued the story. 'We caught up with him again couple o' weeks later. In one of his sober moments he told us he'd panned a stream, then somebody jumped his claim. He came away with a sprinkling of gold dust which he spent on liquor. We asked him again to come with us but he refused. He was convinced he was going to make it big.' He stared down at the floor, rubbing his rough hands together. 'He's sure got gold fever,' he said softly. 'And he'll not be cured.'

'Jed and me found gold,' Larkin said. 'As much as we need. And the agreement was that we'd share, but Matt's gone along home and if we give James his due, then he'll sure enough kill himself with drink.'

Edward was silent and thought of the handsome quiet young man who hadn't had much conversation but got on with whatever was expected of him and never complained.

'Tod,' he said, suddenly remembering the seventeen-year-old. 'Where's he?'

'Used his share on a ticket home.' Larkin grinned. 'Said his ol' ma would be wondering where he was!'

The visitors looked up as Tsui came in, but she hastily backed out again when she saw them. 'So who's the Chink?' Jed said admiringly.

'Tsui,' Edward said. 'I can't pronounce her full name. And she's not a Chink,' he admonished. 'She's Chinese and she lives with me.'

Jed pursed his lips. 'Didn't think they lived with Europeans!'

'Usually they don't. She was sold out of her family. She escaped from the man who bought her and made her way to San Francisco where she thought she would find work.'

'As a whore?'

Edward shook his head. He was very protective of her. 'No. She scrubbed bar-room floors, washed dishes. Anything but that.'

'So–?' Jed lifted his eyebrows questioningly. 'Is she–?' He let the question hang in the air, but Edward ignored it. He liked to have Tsui around. She kept the cabin clean, shopped and cooked for him and did his washing. She asked for no payment, but she ate with him and they had conversation, she was tender and considerate and sometimes she shared his bed.

'Will you stay in California?' he asked Larkin and Jed as they took their leave of him.

'Sure we will.' Larkin answered for both of them.

'So we'll see you around, Eddie.'

With some of the money from the rock of gold, as he liked to call it, Edward made a down

428

payment on a run-down saloon and put Dolly in charge of it. She had a stage built and brought in dancing girls and entertainers, and within a few months it was called a theatre saloon. He bought new clothes, cigars and a gold watch and chain, and spent his evenings talking to his customers, giving the big spenders an occasional drink on the house, knowing that they would come back again after such a show of hospitality. But each early morning as the customers drifted away he went home to his cabin and Tsui.

Then one morning when he arrived home, she wasn't there. He went to bed and rose at his usual time and she still wasn't there. He ate a solitary breakfast and then went looking for her.

He tried in Chinatown but he only met with impassive faces and a silent shake of heads. She hadn't been to the saloon and the shops which she frequented hadn't seen her either.

He sat on his bed and contemplated that he didn't have any luck with women and if Tsui didn't come back, then that was the last time he would ever have a relationship. His marriage to May was a sham, Ruby hadn't wanted him and the affair with Sofia had been disastrous.

Dolly commiserated, but remarked, 'The Orientals have a code of their own. Somebody in Chinatown will know where she is, but they won't tell you.'

He spent restless nights worrying about whether she had been snatched and sold again. She was small and pretty and, though he didn't love her, he was fond of her and missed her calming presence, her delicate hands and sweet smile. After six months, he reluctantly decided that she had gone for good, and went to bed with a compromising Dolly.

CHAPTER THIRTY-EIGHT

Wilhelm travelled with Georgiana in a waggon over the plain, and then by canal boat to Philadelphia. Here she would join a steamship for New Orleans. He was plainly anxious about her and had given her names of contacts in the newspaper world who would, he assured her, provide help if it was needed.

'You worry too much, Wilhelm! It cannot be any more dangerous than travelling from England to America,' she said, placatingly. 'People are doing it all the time. I shall be all right.'

'You had Kitty with you then,' he said gruffly. 'You were not alone.'

'Yes,' she agreed. 'But as Kitty was then in my employ, I had to make any decisions.'

'Just as you do now,' he grumbled. 'You are a difficult woman, Georgiana.' But he smiled as he said it, and bent to kiss her hand.

Georgiana had misgivings which she kept to herself. It was true that she would miss Kitty, for she was so very practical, but she couldn't come with her, not now she had a husband and child and a business to run. The colony at Dreumel's Creek was steadily becoming established. Ted had set up a trading store which Isaac was running.

Kitty had her bakery, and the carpenters had started a co-operative venture where the community could buy or borrow the tools they needed. Wilhelm had bought his cattle which grazed on the fertile meadowland, and other families had moved in with their cattle and livestock.

Georgiana left Hetty in Kitty's care and advised her to teach Caitlin to ride. 'She's steady,' she said. 'She won't throw her.' She picked up the tiny girl and hugged her. 'I'll miss you, Caitlin,' she whispered. 'Just as I'll miss your mama.'

When she boarded the steamship for New Orleans, Georgiana was reminded of her journey from Hull to London, and was struck, she knew not why, by a sudden and unexpected pang of homesickness. She recalled sailing out of the Humber dock and seeing the spires and turrets of the churches, the mills and factory chimneys on the skyline. She looked back now and saw Wilhelm watching from the wharfside and felt a warm glow for him, for his dependable character and his strong friendship.

Lake had gone back to the mountains before she departed. He had looked down at her from his horse, his eyes searching her face before silently turning away, and she had watched from the valley as he rode up the mountainside until at last she could no longer see him.

She had chosen to travel to New Orleans before the winter snow closed in on Dreumel's Creek, and also because Ted had advised that New Orleans was much more pleasant for English people in the winter or spring than in the summer. 'The mozzies really bite, Miz Gianna. I was almost eaten alive.'

She smiled to herself. Miz Gianna. That was the name which everyone in the community now gave to her. Everyone, that is, but Wilhelm, who called her Georgiana.

The boat was crowded with farmers and businessmen and some ladies and their maids, who kept to their own little cabins. Georgiana, however, walked the deck several times a day to escape the stifling atmosphere of the saloon and cabins. She had to endure an acrid smell from the black smoke which issued from the furnace, chimneys and boilers.

The passage was long and tedious and the sultry journey up the Mississippi slow, but on their arrival in New Orleans she thanked the captain for a safe and uneventful journey. Although on several days they had hit bad weather, the boat was stable and there was no sickness on board.

He asked her if she was staying long in the city. 'I have an introduction to the editor of the *New Orleans Gazette*,' she said. 'I am here to search for a relative and am hoping that they will advertise for him.'

'An Englishman?' he asked.

She answered that he was and asked if he got many English passengers.

'From time to time, ma'am,' he said. 'Our sister ship brings the Mormons here; some of them are English, but mostly Welsh. She anchored only yesterday.' He pointed up the levee, where there were ships and boats of every size and shape packed along the length of the embankment.

Georgiana shook her head. 'He isn't a Mormon,

432

unless he's changed his religion, which I very much doubt. His name is Edward Newmarch,' she said. 'And he came here, oh – about six years ago.'

'Don't recall the name, but then I've only been sailing this stretch of water for the last two years. Now, ma'am, I must warn you, seeing as you're a lady on your own. Watch out for the wharf thieves. These fellows seem real friendly and obliging, but they know every trick there is and they'll steal your luggage and smile at you whilst they're doing it. Don't be afraid of the blacks, and if you have any trouble at all, then ask for Rodriguez. He owns most of the town, including this ship.'

Rodriguez? she wondered as she disembarked. I know that name.

It had been raining hard and the streets were ankle-deep in muddy water. Boards had been put down so that people could walk across to the wide and high footpath at the other side of the road without getting their feet wet. The captain had asked a porter to obtain a carriage for her, and whilst she was waiting she was approached several times by men offering to help her with her luggage. The porter, a big black Negro who was loading crates into a cart, shouted at them to leave the lady alone. Drays and waggons trundled along the levee, which was crowded with cargo and merchandise, and she was beginning to feel oppressed by the noise and commotion.

'Here you is, missy,' the porter said as a carriage rolled up. 'This fella'll take care of you real good.'

She considered, as they bowled along, that she

would be fortunate if she arrived at her hotel in one piece and with her luggage intact. Although the streets were wide, they were thronged with carriages and carts and a mass of people who appeared to have nothing to do but merely stroll in the sunshine and were disinclined to move out of the way of the carriages, in spite of the drivers shouting at them or cracking their whips.

How lovely the women are, she thought, looking out of the carriage window. And the colours of their gowns, like those of a peacock! Even the young slave girls – for I must assume that is what they are, as they are following behind their mistresses with baskets and shopping – even they are dressed so beautifully in their crisp cotton skirts. She turned her head to watch a barefoot mulatto girl in a colourful shawl and red skirt who was singing as she walked. If Ted is to be believed, there is no wonder that Edward became entranced by the women here, she reflected.

The next day, after settling in at the hotel, she decided to walk to the newspaper office. The streets were laid out in squares and on enquiring the way she was told she should walk for two blocks to get there. She asked the desk clerk for Carlos de Lassus, telling him that she was expected. Wilhelm had written to de Lassus previously, asking if he would place an advertisement in his paper regarding Edward Newmarch, and had written again when Georgiana had determined to travel to New Orleans.

Carlos de Lassus greeted her with a courteous bow and bade her be seated, and then sent out for a jug of orange juice when she declined wine or coffee.

'I am delighted to meet you, Miss Gregory.' He smiled. 'I trust you had a good journey?'

She replied that the steamboat, *Sancho*, had been comfortable, though extremely full of passengers, which had worried her a little.

'Ah, yes, the *Sancho*,' he said. 'It belongs to my cousin Rodriguez. It is well maintained, you need not have worried. Though it is true,' he admitted, 'that some steamboats do have fatalities; the boilers overheat or if the paddles are not properly protected ladies' skirts can get caught. But not Rodriguez' vessels, and he owns several. The *Sancho* is named for him and he has another beautiful ship which sails between your country and New York which he has named for his wife, *Sofia*.' He added, 'The *Sofia* carries the Mormons from Liverpool.'

'I see,' she said. 'Señor de Lassus, I was given your name by Wilhelm Dreumel, who runs the *Philadelphia Star* and who thought perhaps you could help me to find a relative.'

'Ah, yes indeed.' He took a letter from a drawer in his desk and perused it. 'You wish to find Edward Newmarch. Is that so?' He looked up at her and his eyes scrutinized her intensely. 'May I ask what relation he is to you? Your husband?' His eyebrows rose quizzically. 'Your fiancé?' His voice softened on the words.

Her lips parted in surprise. 'Neither of those, señor, and I wonder why you should ask if he is my husband. I gave my name as Miss Gregory, which must surely imply that I am unmarried!'

He shrugged and smiled. 'What is in a name,

435

Miss Gregory? In this country people often change their names. Some of the foreigners who come here have to, for their own are unpronounceable. I am even thinking of changing mine!'

She laughed. 'Yours is quite easy to pronounce.'

'Ah, but–' He leaned towards her. 'You called me *señor*, which is Spanish, whereas I am an American – but no matter,' he said. 'It is not important. What is important, and you may well be surprised to know, is that your relative Edward Newmarch and I met some time ago.'

'Really? Goodness! Do you know where he is?'

He didn't immediately answer her question, but commented, 'He left New Orleans in rather a hurry.'

'So I heard,' she said. 'His former valet, Robert Allen, told me that he had become involved with a woman.'

Carlos de Lassus put his finger to his lips in a swift movement and looked towards the door. He dropped his voice. 'We are in New Orleans, Miss Gregory. It is a city of intrigue. I would advise you to be circumspect and guarded in conversation.'

She stared at him. 'But why? Did Mr Newmarch do something he shouldn't?'

'Perhaps!' He smiled in a charming way. 'Miss Gregory. Would you give me the honour of dining with me? I will then tell you the story of Edward Newmarch, or as much as I know of it.'

'You have just warned me that I must be careful of conversation,' she said wryly. 'Does that advice not apply to discourse with you?'

'Indeed not.' His eyes perused her again. 'And

may I ask, if Newmarch is not your husband or fiancé, what concern is he of yours?'

She pondered for a moment and scrutinized de Lassus. He reminded her by his stature and demeanour of Wilhelm, except that she considered he might be inclined to be more light-hearted and possibly flirtatious, but he had an open honest face, like Wilhelm.

'He is of no real concern to me,' she said truthfully. 'But I come at the request of my cousin who is married to him. She wishes to marry again, therefore needs to know if he is alive or dead.'

She agreed to meet de Lassus for lunch the next day at her hotel. She dressed in a cream silk gown, one she had purchased in Philadelphia, and wore a dainty hat with white feathers and lace which perched on her forehead, emphasizing her eyes. She had come down early, so she walked through the lobby of the hotel and stood at the door looking out at the hustle and bustle of the street. The day was pleasantly warm and the air not so heavy as it had rained during the night.

A carriage drew up outside the hotel. De Lassus got out, then turned to assist a woman and a child. Georgiana drew in a breath. The woman was beautiful. Small and dainty with a creamy complexion. A lace cap covered her thick dark hair, which hung in curls about her neck. Her rustling silk gown was in a shade of rose, her ears and arms shimmered with gold jewellery. She held the hand of a small boy.

'Miss Gregory,' de Lassus greeted her. 'I do hope we haven't kept you waiting?'

'Of course not. I am enjoying watching the

activity of this colourful city.'

They followed her into the hotel and de Lassus made the introductions. 'I took the liberty of bringing Señora Rodriguez,' he explained. 'My cousin's wife and their youngest child, Antonio.'

The two women gave a slight dip of their knees in greeting. 'Delighted to meet you, Señora Rodriguez,' Georgiana said, though she was at a loss to know why de Lassus had brought her. Perhaps it is an old Spanish tradition, she thought. Designed to protect my reputation!

'I wished to meet you, Mees Gregory.' Sofia Rodriguez spoke English with an attractive soft accent. 'Carlos told me why you were in New Orleans.' She fluttered her eyelashes and Georgiana marvelled at their length. 'I 'ave met your relative, Ed-ward Newmarch,' she trilled.

'He seems to have become well known whilst he was here,' Georgiana commented. 'So perhaps he will be easy enough to find?'

'I don't sink so,' Sofia replied. 'I 'ave thought all of this time that per'aps 'e is dead.' She looked wistful for a moment and absent-mindedly stroked her son's head.

Is this the woman Edward was involved with? Georgiana was curious. He would be playing with fire if she was.

They sat down for lunch and de Lassus continued the conversation. 'I advertised in our newspaper when Dreumel first contacted me some months ago, but heard nothing. Then about four weeks ago, I received this note. I cannot say that it is a letter, for it is written by someone who has not a good hand.' He took a scrap of paper

438

from his pocket and handed it to her.

'The man you speak of mite be Bob. Englishman gone to Californy with sum of our boyz. Matt came back and said he was in San Fran. If there's a reward send it to me, Moss at the saloon.'

There was an address which she could not decipher.

'It's somewhere in the Mississippi swamps,' de Lassus told her. 'And it ties in with what we know of Newmarch.'

'Which is?' Georgiana asked.

'My 'usband sent someone to look for 'im,' Sofia said huskily. ''E was angry wiz 'im. Edward was going to marry my daughter, Elena.' She lowered her lashes. 'But 'e ran away when we found out 'e was already married to a wife in England.'

'Indeed he is,' Georgiana said, and pondered that there was something that this lovely woman wasn't revealing.

'Rodriguez sent someone after Newmarch,' de Lassus said. 'He was followed from his hotel then put onto a Mississippi flatboat, and the captain was ordered to dispose of him.'

Georgiana was aghast. 'What – not to kill him?'

'Tst,' Sofia censured. 'No! That I would not allow. I sent a message to Sancho that 'e must not kill Edward. Just for 'im to disappear for a while. But 'e escaped from the boat.' She smiled and her eyes sparkled. 'But as you see by the letter, it seems that Ed-ward survives!'

'California,' Georgiana murmured. 'That's a long way from here. However would he get there?'

'Cross-country. Waggon or pack train, there are

regular trails to follow, though they are very difficult.' De Lassus shrugged. 'Who knows?'

'Is there no railway yet?' she asked.

'No. The railroad has not reached here, but it is coming. Soon we will have a railroad from the east into New Orleans, but not yet. As for further west...' Again he shrugged. 'Even the mail has difficulty in getting through. There is much debate in Congress, but ship and stagecoach, freight waggons and the Pony Express is our only option for the time being.'

'So, how then will I travel to California?' Georgiana murmured.

They both stared at her. 'I beg your pardon, Miss Gregory,' de Lassus said. 'Did I hear you correctly?' His expression was one of amused astonishment. 'You cannot possibly travel to California! Not alone. It is too dangerous to contemplate.'

'I travelled alone to New Orleans,' she said briskly. 'I have to go. If Edward Newmarch is there, then I must seek him out.'

She saw what she thought to be admiration in de Lassus's eyes and a wariness in Sofia's.

'Are you so very fond of Ed-ward that you travel thousands of miles to look for 'im?' Sofia asked softly.

'Fond? No! I had considered him to be dishonourable and irresponsible even before he married my cousin! But,' Georgiana gave a slight sigh as she thought of what was in front of her, 'I owe it to her. If Edward is dead she can marry again, and if he isn't, she can't.'

'She is very 'ard, this woman,' Sofia said with a sudden spurt of fire. 'This May! She wishes Edward dead, yes? And yet she is a cold wife, she did not welcome him to her bed!'

There was a sudden silence. How does she know this? Georgiana wondered. Edward must have told her. And why would he do that?

Sofia seemed to realize her blunder, and said petulantly, 'I know this is what some English-women are like. And that is why their 'usbands take a mistress. I 'ave been told of this!'

Their lunch over and de Lassus having promised he would enquire into the best route if Georgiana was adamant about travelling, he left them and went to order a carriage for himself and Sofia.

Georgiana smiled down at the little boy who had been very well behaved during lunch, though she wondered why Sofia had brought him with her. They must have servants in abundance to look after him, she thought. Wealth seemed to ooze from Sofia's pores.

'My little Antonio is 'andsome, yes?' Sofia said indulgently.

'He is,' Georgiana concurred. Though without your striking good looks, she considered. He must take after his father.

'We waited a long time for a son,' Sofia continued. 'I 'ave two daughters. One from my first 'usband and one from Sancho. But Sancho always wanted a son.' She smiled down at Antonio. 'And now 'e has one.'

'I believe that most men desire a son,' Georgiana said politely. 'Señor Rodriguez must be very proud?'

'Yes, indeed he is,' Sofia agreed, then added

swiftly as de Lassus appeared across the lobby, 'Mees Gregory, if you find Ed-ward in San Francisco, you will tell 'im, please, that we 'ave a fine boy?'

CHAPTER THIRTY-NINE

'It is madness,' de Lassus told her when they met again. 'You cannot possibly travel alone. There are several routes but they are all fraught with danger!'

'Tell me about them,' Georgiana said. 'I do not wish to put my life in danger. But I do know that women go to California. I have been told that they do.'

'But not women such as you, Miss Gregory!'

'Perhaps not,' she said, privately disagreeing and wondering why it was that men always said that of her. *He thinks that I have lived a sheltered life, which I did until coming to this country.* Isaac had told her about the women he had met in California. Saloon girls, dancers, whores. But even so, she had thought, *these are women trying to survive in a man's world and they must be applauded for that. And there are other women too, women who travel with their menfolk and who endure hardship in the search for a better life.*

'I will describe the worst aspects to you,' de Lassus continued solemnly, 'and then perhaps you will see sense and change your mind.'

442

'You do not know me, Mr de Lassus. If you did, you would realize that I won't change my mind.' She gazed squarely back at him. 'But, please, do tell me.'

'There is a route by Santa Fe and the Colorado River. Or up the Mississippi to St Louis in the State of Missouri. It is a distance of over a thousand miles.' He gazed at her in concern. 'Then along the Missouri, across rapids and falls, where you must change boats, then trek westwards across the plains to Salt Lake City.'

She took in a breath. She had seen a map showing Salt Lake City, the home of the Mormons. It was a long way, thousands of miles, and she knew in her heart that she couldn't travel that route, not alone.

'Most of these trails are the old fur-trading routes,' de Lassus told her. 'They are meant for travellers with packhorses or waggons. I have heard many stories of men setting out on this journey and never arriving. Some stage- and mailcoaches ply the route from Sacramento to San Francisco, but the journey there is hazardous and uncomfortable. There are hostile Indians and dangerous men to contend with. I beg of you, Miss Gregory,' he said earnestly. 'Please do not attempt it!'

She hesitated for only a second. 'I won't,' she said. 'I have much to live for. What is the alternative?'

He closed his eyes for a moment, then opening them said in exasperation, 'Has anyone ever told you that you are a very stubborn woman?'

'Yes.' She laughed. 'Many times.'

'Then – if you are determined to go, I advise that you should travel from here by ship across the Gulf of Mexico to the Isthmus of Panama. Cross that stretch of land by whatever means you can – since Columbia's treaty with America, a railroad is being built, but it is not yet finished – then from there you go again by steamship north along the coast to California.'

When she was alone in her hotel room she lay on her bed and wept with pent-up emotion. 'I am a madwoman! Why am I doing this?' Not for the first time was she asking herself this question. 'Do I owe my cousin so much? Can I not just live my own life? Cousin May doesn't know what she is asking of me!'

Georgiana knew that if she wished, she could just return to Dreumel's Creek and live a simple life amongst her friends. With Kitty and Wilhelm, and most of all with Lake. 'I don't have to do this,' she declared aloud and passionately. 'I am a relatively rich woman. I have a share in a newspaper, a share in a gold mine! I have a log house of my own!'

She paced the floor of the room talking to herself. 'I don't care about Edward Newmarch! Why doesn't May just divorce him? There's no shame in that!'

But of course there was, as her conscience reminded her. In England, her cousin May would not be able to hold up her head if she went through the divorce courts. Georgiana pursued this line of thought. Perhaps the man she wants to marry won't marry a divorced woman. Poor May!

She suddenly felt sorry for her cousin, trapped

in a loveless marriage with a missing husband. I am so lucky, she thought. I came to this country to gain my independence. And I have! I have! I can make my own decisions! Even if I should ever return to England, I know that I would not be hidebound by convention. I am a different person.

All right, May! She made her decision. I will do this for you. I will search for your wayward husband and if I find him alive and well, I will ask him if he will declare himself dead and give you, his wife, her freedom.

Time and time again on the long journey she regretted the undertaking. Hurricane winds and mountainous seas blew across the Gulf of Mexico. She was tossed in her cot, holding on desperately for what seemed to be the last hours of her life, listening to the moaning and retching of her fellow passengers, and then succumbing herself to an attack of seasickness. She sweltered with perspiration, her empty body on fire, then shivered with chattering teeth and gooseflesh as her skin dampened and she was chilled to the marrow.

'Damn you, Edward Newmarch! If you're not dead when I find you, then I swear I'll kill you myself!' She moaned and bent over the bucket as the nausea and the stink of vomit overtook her once more.

She arrived in Panama, weak and thin, and checked in at an hotel before continuing her journey. She stayed only three days before she heard, quite by chance, that there was an outbreak of yellow fever in that steamy city peopled by Spanish, Indian, American and European mixed race. Immediately she booked another passage out. Being in a weakened state already, she was fearful of becoming a victim of the dreadful disease. If I died here, how would anyone know where I was? she thought wretchedly, and immediately penned a letter to Wilhelm to keep on her person, should such an event occur.

A thick bank of mist obscured the long coast of California and San Francisco Bay as the steamship drew steadily onwards towards the Golden Gate strait. Then the mist slowly lifted and the passengers rushed to the rails to watch as the ship entered the waterway of San Francisco. El Dorado, golden city of so many dreams and hopes.

Georgiana was feeling much better now at the end of her journey. The final sea voyage had been pleasant and she had sat in a corner of the deck, enjoying the sunshine and the breezes, though she had kept well wrapped in her beaver cape and a blanket around her knees.

Now she watched with the other passengers as the ship docked. The city was not as she had imagined. She had thought it would still be a jumble of tents and shanties, rough buildings to house the miners. She saw from the deck that it had become a city of wide streets and pavements, fine buildings and houses, theatres and hotels.

It was also thronging with thousands of people, many of whom appeared to be waiting for the ship. 'They're waiting for mail.' A man, a stranger, standing by her side, spoke to her. 'They're hungry for news from the outside world. All they know about here is news of gold.' He gave a scornful laugh. 'Humbug, most of it! Nobody ever tells of when gold runs out, only of when it is found.'

'I beg your pardon,' Georgiana said. 'Do you know the city?'

'Some.' He nodded. 'This is my second trip.'

'Could you then advise me?' she asked. 'If I wanted to find someone, how would I set about it?'

He thought for a moment. 'There's a local newspaper printed here. The *Gazette*. You could ask if they'd print a message. Best I can suggest, ma'am.' He looked her up and down. 'You looking for your husband? There's hundreds of 'em who just disappear.'

'Erm – yes,' she said, unwilling to confide. 'That's right.'

'He'll be up at one of the mines or along a river bed if he's gone looking for gold,' he said. 'You might never find him, there's thousands of men here. Some of them, though, have left to find their luck elsewhere. I heard there's been a strike in Utah and one in Carson City, but it might just be rumour.'

She thanked him and turned away to assemble her belongings. The ship was being unloaded and the wharfside was strewn with drays, waggons, coaches, packhorses and mules, all waiting to collect passengers and their baggage.

She booked in at a small hotel and then went to look around the city. There were stores of every description and not only catering for the miners.

It was evident from the goods which were displayed that here was a settled community which, over a few short years since the gold boom had begun, had built up their homes and businesses and were going to stay.

There were separate areas where different nationalities had made their homes. Mexicans, Cubans and Chileans, Irish and Spanish, Russians, Americans and thousands of Chinese. A colourful noisy babble of people with a conglomeration of language and cultures. Georgiana wandered around in a daze. How on earth can I possibly find Edward Newmarch within this seething multitude?

She did as the man on the ship had advised and contacted the newspaper, citing both Wilhelm and de Lassus as references. The editor agreed to put in a message and said he would ask for replies to be sent to him. 'There'll be all kinds of odd folks coming in,' he warned. 'Some will claim that they know him and expect a reward. Then there'll be others who'll claim to *be* him in the hope that there's something in it for them. You know, like a long-lost relative leaving something in a will. They won't have any proof of course: anybody can be anybody they want to be out here and no questions asked.'

A week later and a queue of people were claiming that they knew Edward Newmarch, but wouldn't say where he was last seen until they were told why he was wanted, and what was the advantage to them.

The editor, Seth Hanson, made a list of possibilities. 'Don't think much of any of them,' he said. ''Cept maybe one.' He pondered, his eyebrows bristling as he frowned. 'Don't quite know what to make of her.'

'Her!' Georgiana laughed. 'She might be the one to know. He was always a ladies' man. Perhaps he's crossed this one.'

Hanson shook his head. 'Don't think so. She's a hard case. I know her slightly. She runs a theatre saloon. It's not hers, belongs to some big shot. Anyway, she wanted to know who was asking and did they have an axe to grind. She said she wasn't sure if the man she knew was the one we wanted.'

'Should I see her?' Georgiana asked. 'It doesn't sound as if she wants anything for herself.'

'That's what I thought,' he said. 'When she left she said she might come back with someone else.'

The next day a messenger boy arrived at her hotel, asking her to come to the newspaper office. She walked to the building. It wasn't far and she wanted to give herself time to prepare what she would say to Edward Newmarch, if he was there.

But he wasn't. She walked into the lobby and there was no-one who looked remotely like him, though various men who were sitting waiting stood up as she entered and doffed their headgear, some of them giving her a feeble grin of familiarity. She was shown into Hanson's office and said, 'None of those men out there are the type who Edward Newmarch would even condescend to speak to! I'm beginning to think it's a hopeless task.'

'The woman came back,' Hanson told her.

'She's sending a fellow round. He'll be here any time now. If this is the man you're looking for, I'd like to run an article about him and you. *Woman travels thousands of miles in search of long-lost relative.*' He grinned and winked. 'That kind of thing. It's only fair,' he added. 'That's what newspapers are for.'

'You wouldn't make it into a romance?' she said in sudden concern. 'Because it's not. I can't stand the man!'

'Come on, lady!' he interposed scathingly. 'All right, then. What about *Love turns to revenge?* Was he your lover?'

'Certainly not!' She was furious. 'I told you! He's my cousin's husband.'

'Lady,' he said sardonically, 'I've heard all kinds of stories in this business, and I know that nobody, just nobody, least of all a woman, travels thousands of miles unless there's something in it for them.'

She was about to draw breath and tell him to forget the whole thing, when there was a knock on the door. A man of medium height, spruced up in a respectable if unfashionable coat and waistcoat and buckskin breeches, was shown in. He clutched a leather hat in his hand. 'Howdy.' He seemed ill at ease and shuffled his feet and didn't look directly at her. 'Larkin's the name. Dolly asked if I'd come along – find out what it was all about.'

'My name is Georgiana Gregory.' Georgiana stood up to greet him and thought by his country drawl that it was unlikely that Edward would have kept company with him. 'I'm looking for

450

Edward Newmarch. Do you know of him?'

Larkin switched his gaze to her. 'Mebbe. Depends. Who wants to know?'

'I'm a relative of his wife's. The wife he left in England.' Her voice was haughtier than she intended, but she was still smarting and riled by Hanson's insinuations. 'Of course,' she continued, in the same manner, 'he may not have told anyone he was married. He might even have married again, for all we know. It's the kind of thing he would do!'

She saw, barely perceptibly, a slight negative shake of Larkin's head, before he redressed the movement. He does know him, she thought, and drew in her breath. 'I only want to know if he is alive or dead,' she explained in a softer voice. 'His wife wishes to marry again.'

'Ah!' Larkin's face opened up. 'So you ain't nuthin' to do with any folk from New Orleans?'

She frowned. 'New Orleans? No!' Oh, she thought. I see. The Rodriguez family! 'Mr Larkin,' she said. 'We're taking up Mr Hanson's valuable time. Do you know somewhere we can talk without bothering him?' She smiled sweetly at Hanson. 'I'll come back to tell you if my mission has been successful,' she said, and was gratified to see him looking annoyed.

Larkin took her to an eating house nearby. It was a wooden building, probably one of the original ones, Georgiana surmised. It had a planked floor and wooden chairs and tables. Men were leaning on a polished bar counter; others were playing cards and one a mouth organ. A few of the men nodded to Larkin and he seemed

451

more at home here than in the newspaper office.

'Like a cup o' coffee, ma'am?' he drawled.

'Please.' She looked around her. There were no other women there and some of the men had turned around from the bar, leaning with their elbows on it to gaze at her.

'Are they not used to seeing women in here?' she asked Larkin, who collected the coffee from the counter and brought it to her, with a small glass of what looked like whisky for himself.

'Not during the day. Night-times the fellas bring along their gals.'

He seems to be a laconic kind of man, she thought. Not used to a great deal of conversation.

'Sorry, I ain't bin too forthcoming,' he said, taking a drink from his glass. 'But that fella you bin lookin' fer.' He nodded his head and rocked precariously backwards in his seat. 'Well!' He rocked forward again, putting his elbows on the table and dropping his voice. 'He jest might be a friend o' mine.'

She eyed him as she drank her coffee. It was strong and bitter. 'I don't mean him any harm,' she said, and wondered how Edward, if it was he, would come to know such a man as this. 'And there isn't a reward.' Though I could offer one, I suppose, she mused.

He pursed his mouth, then gave a slight grin. 'Don't need no money, ma'am. Made a lucky strike some time back, me and Jed.'

'Where did you meet Edward?' she asked suddenly.

'Eddie? Mississippi country.' Then he stopped and looked warily at her. 'Might not be him!' She

452

had caught him out – he obviously hadn't meant to say too much.

'Eddie?' she queried. 'I've never heard him called that name!'

'Eddie Newsom,' he told her. 'He was called Bob when we first met him.'

'Oh! Then it's not the same man,' she began, then had a sudden thought. Bob – Robert? 'Did he call himself Robert Allen?'

He slowly nodded. 'Guess he did, but how d'ya know 'bout that?'

'I met the real Robert Allen in New York. Oh dear,' she said. 'It's getting very confusing.'

'Sure is,' Larkin agreed. 'But when we met Eddie in the swamps he'd bin running away from some woman in New Orleans. He changed his name so they wouldn't find him.'

'So, is he still alive? Is he here in San Francisco?'

Larkin rubbed his beard. It was neatly trimmed, though there was a nick of blood on his cheek. His checked shirt was clean and his heavy boots freshly polished.

'Dolly said jest to find out first.'

'Who is Dolly?' she asked.

'She runs Eddie's saloon and kinda looks after him.' He chewed on his lip. 'She was the one who saw it in the *Gazette*. I can't read. Eddie tried to larn me some time back, but it weren't no good.'

I can't believe that this is the same Edward Newmarch that I know, she pondered. There has to be a mistake. Owns a saloon? Teaching someone to read? Impossible! 'So can I meet this man?' she asked.

'Don't know if he'd be pleased to see you,' he said slowly. 'But Dolly said it was worth a try.'

He scraped back his chair and stood up. 'He might be mad at us. We sort o' made a promise long time ago not to tell anybody 'bout him.' He gave what seemed like a sigh. 'But I guess it'll be all right now.' He put his hat on. 'So if you've finished your coffee, ma'am, we'll go. We ain't got a great deal o' time.'

CHAPTER FORTY

What does he mean, not much time? Georgiana pondered as she sat in the creaking waggonette which Larkin had whistled for and which the sweating horse was pulling up a steep hill away from the waterfront. Is Edward going away? If indeed it is him, and I feel now that it might be. The woman in New Orleans that Larkin mentioned must surely be Sofia Rodriguez. Though she said that Edward was going to marry her daughter! I can't believe that even he would stoop so low as to consider going through a bigamous marriage ceremony! Is that why he ran away? Did he get too deep into something?

Larkin called to the driver to stop outside a cluster of wooden buildings. There was a saloon bar, with the sound of music and laughter coming from within, and two stores, one selling fruit and vegetables which were piled high in a colourful pyramid outside the windows, another which sold groceries and had a rich smell of coffee and ripe cheese emanating from its doorway. Through the shop window Georgiana saw layers of pasta hanging from a ceiling rack and bread heaped up on the counter. Set slightly to the side and behind these buildings was a wooden house with a small yard in front of it, where two children were playing.

They looked up as Georgiana and Larkin approached. ''Ello, Larkin.' A dark-haired chubby boy greeted him, but didn't move from his game with pebbles which were piled precariously into a wobbly tower. The younger child, obviously a girl in spite of being dressed in wide trousers and a cotton shift, was tiny and pretty with high cheekbones and dark oriental eyes. She jumped up and wrapped her arms around Larkin's legs, trapping him so that he couldn't walk without falling over her.

Larkin bent and picked her up and swung her into the air, holding her there. 'Hello, Jewel. Give me a kiss.'

The child reached down and kissed his bearded face, then, rubbing her cheek, struggled out of his arms to resume her game in the dust.

Larkin was about to tap on the half-open door when it opened up fully and a younger man came out. He glanced first at Georgiana, then at Larkin, then back again at Georgiana. He nodded at her in greeting and mumbled, 'Pleased to meet you, ma'am. I'm Jed. See you tonight, Larkin.' After patting the children on their heads, he walked swiftly down the hill.

Georgiana hesitated. There was something

amiss here. 'Is this where Edward Newmarch lives?' she asked Larkin, who was holding the door open for her.

'Yes, ma'am.' He spoke in a low voice. 'He don't know you're here in the city. We didn't tell him.'

'We?' Still she hesitated and tried to look through the doorway into the room. She saw the red glow of a stove and a rocking chair beside it, but couldn't see more because of Larkin blocking her view. 'Who are *we*?'

'Me and Jed and Dolly. We wasn't too sure if he'd want to see anybody from home.'

From home! Is that how Edward still thinks of England? Is that how I think of it?

'Please come in, ma'am. Now that you're here.' He beckoned to her and with a slight reluctance she followed him inside.

The room was larger than she would have thought from outside. It held a sofa which was draped with a colourful woollen shawl, a rocking chair, two easy chairs with rich brocaded coverings, a circular polished table and four chairs. An open staircase led upstairs and at the far end of the room was an archway with a beaded curtain over it, leading, she supposed, to another room.

'Would you like to sit fer a minute?' Larkin said. 'I'll jest make sure it's convenient.'

Bemused, Georgiana sat on the sofa and looked around. There were pictures and mirrors on the wall, shelves with books, but no ornaments or knick-knacks. Comfortable, but a man's room, she decided, without a feminine touch. She glanced up at the mirrors. Just like Edward to

456

have mirrors, she thought cynically. He was always vain.

Larkin signalled to her from behind the beads. 'You've got a visitor, Eddie.' He spoke to someone over his shoulder. 'A lady. She's bin asking 'bout you.'

'I don't know any ladies,' a low gruff voice answered. 'Not any more.'

Georgiana pushed aside the curtain. Though the room was dim, lit only by an oil lamp and a fire in the grate, she saw that it had been made into a bedroom. Facing her, a thin man was sitting in a chair with a blanket over his knees. It's not him! she thought. Not in the least like him, and she was strangely relieved.

'Who is it?' The man's voice was hoarse. 'Do I know you?' He lifted his head and peered at her.

'I fear there has been a mistake, Mr Newsom,' Georgiana apologized. 'I'm so sorry to have bothered you. I'm looking for someone by the name of Edward Newmarch, who left England six or seven years ago.'

There was a hesitation, then he said, 'Come closer.' It was a polite bidding and Georgiana wavered. Was there something in that slightly imperious accent that could have belonged to the Edward she once knew?

She stepped forward and faced him. The man in front of her was gaunt and most decidedly ill. His eyes were large in his pale face, and his fingers, as he teased his dark beard, were white and bony.

'I know you,' he said huskily. 'How do I know you?'

457

She took a shallow breath, then, 'Is it – is it you, Edward?'

'Georgiana?' There was a puzzled frown on his forehead. 'Georgiana Gregory? How in heaven's name–?'

There was a slight sound behind them, a rattle of the beads as Larkin went out.

There was another chair in the room and Georgiana, unbidden, sat down. She suddenly felt quite weak, unexpectedly emotional and perilously close to tears.

'Georgiana! I don't believe it. Can't believe it!' Edward's voice was croaky as if with shock. 'How are you here? When did *you* come to America?'

She gave a short nervous laugh, glad to release the tension welling up inside her. 'I arrived in New York in the spring of '52. I wanted a new life. I thought that in America women would be equal to men.'

'Ah! You were always a campaigner, I remember.' His mouth lifted into a lazy smile and she was reminded that he could be charming. 'And are they?'

'Some,' she said. 'Though in the cities women still drag behind men and they don't have a vote either. But there have been improvements,' she admitted. 'Women have qualified as doctors, and two sisters founded the New York Infirmary for women and children in '54.'

'Did they? You're very well informed,' he said. 'Though I suppose it would be expected of you.'

'I part-own a Philadelphia newspaper,' she said. 'I keep abreast of the news.'

He shook his head in astonishment. 'You are an

amazing woman, Georgiana! So, what does your husband do? Is he an American? You decided against marrying my brother Martin, did you?'

'Edward!' she exclaimed. 'Have you never written or had any news at all since you came out here?'

'Eddie,' he corrected her. 'My name's Eddie now. The old Edward has been gone a long, long time. But no, in answer to your question, I have not.' He looked away from her and rubbed his chest. 'I didn't think they would want to hear from such a man as I was.' He examined his long thin fingers. 'Though I have been tempted recently to write and make my peace, with my mother and May at least. And maybe even Martin. You didn't want to marry him, then?' he asked again.

'No. I did not. He has married someone else.'

The beaded curtain rattled again and Larkin came in, awkwardly carrying a tray with a teapot and cups and saucers on it.

'Ah! The cup that cheers. See how well trained my minions are,' Edward joked. 'Larkin knows that when times are difficult a cup of tea always soothes.' He peered at the tray. 'You forgot the lemon, dear fellow, and my guest may prefer milk with her tea. She's English, you know!'

Larkin muttered something incomprehensible and returned in a moment with half a lemon on a saucer and a jug of milk.

'Does Larkin work for you?' Georgiana asked after he had gone out again.

'No,' he replied promptly. 'He's a good friend. As is Jed. I wouldn't be alive but for them.'

'And Dolly?' she queried.

'You've heard about Dolly? Yes, she does work for me. She runs my theatre saloon down by the waterfront and runs it very successfully. But she's a friend too. Warm-hearted. Generous.' He became pensive. 'The three of them are the best friends any man could wish for.'

'And who is Matt?' she asked.

'Matt!' He stared at her. 'How do you know about Matt?'

She told him about the advertisement and the letter received by the *New Orleans Gazette*.

'So he made it home after all!' His voice was choked. 'Oh, I'm so glad. So very glad. I must tell Larkin and Jed. They'll be relieved. They all came from the Mississippi Basin, you know.' He gave a laugh which turned into a cough and he put a handkerchief to his mouth. 'Swampsuckers, every one of them!'

He said it in such a light-hearted manner that though the term might have sounded derisory, she could tell he held them in great affection.

'But back to you,' he said gruffly and glanced at her left hand. 'So you didn't marry anyone? Still independent. No man good enough, eh?'

'There is a man that I love,' she said softly. 'And who loves me. But marriage is out of the question.'

'Married already, eh? Don't go down that road, Georgiana. Take my advice. Forget him, find someone else.'

'Like you did?' she said grimly. 'You left a trail of havoc behind you, Edward; even here in America, from what I've heard!'

He blinked, startled. 'What? What have you heard?'

460

'I came looking for you. I went to New Orleans! I met Sofia Rodriguez. Her husband's cousin, Carlos de Lassus, runs the newspaper.'

He gave a soft groan and shook his head. 'I knew they'd find me eventually.' He pressed his fingers to his eyes. 'Oh, God! What a mess I've made of everything.'

'They're not looking for you now,' she said gently. 'You don't have to worry about that.'

'Really?' Relief showed on his face. 'Are you sure?' When she nodded, he said, 'So, go on. Why were you, of all people, looking for me?'

She poured more tea for them both, and took a sip from her cup before continuing. 'May wrote to me. You remember May? Your wife?' She couldn't help but be acerbic. 'She wants to marry again and she can't because she doesn't know whether you're dead or alive!'

He gave a sudden exclamation and covered his mouth with his hand. 'Couldn't she just have divorced me?' he muttered. 'Proclaimed me dead? I might have been. Almost was, several times!' Then he looked into space and appeared to deliberate. 'Of course not.' His voice was muted. 'It wouldn't do, would it? Her father wouldn't allow it. They would worry over what people would think. As if it mattered!' he added bitterly.

'It matters to May,' she said quietly. 'And her father is dead. I think that is why she wants to make another life.'

'I'm sorry,' he apologized. 'I was always thoughtless where other people were concerned. And – so you travelled across this vast country to find out whether I was still alive? I am amazed,

461

Georgiana. You are a remarkable woman. But why? Are you still tied to May's petticoat strings?'

She was piqued, annoyed with him. He hadn't really changed. He was still blunt, arrogant and outspoken. 'I owe it to the family.' She was defensive. 'They brought me up – at least, they were responsible for me when my parents died. After this, I owe them nothing. Except gratitude. My debt will be paid!'

He was silent. It was as if he was caught up in another train of thought. 'Of course,' he said at length. 'You lived with your aunt, Clarissa Gregory. I'd forgotten about that.'

He seemed suddenly tired and he took a deep breath and closed his eyes for a second.

'You're not well, Edward. I'm sorry, I can't think of you as Eddie! Would you like me to come back another day?'

'Yes.' He gave a wan smile. 'I would. I'm tired now. Tomorrow? I'll send a cab for you if you'll tell Larkin where you're staying.' His eyes were eager, worried almost, that she might not agree. 'Please come back.'

'I will,' she began, when the beads rattled and the little girl who had been playing out in the yard suddenly burst in and flung herself onto Edward's knees.

'Papa! Papa! Please may I go and eat at Renzo's house?'

'Lorenzo's? Sure, but mind your manners. Don't forget please and thank you. Wait! Wait! First, come and say how de do to this nice English lady.' He turned the child to face Georgiana. 'She's travelled a long way to come and see us.

462

This is Miss Gregory. Miss Gregory, this is my daughter, Jewel.'

Georgiana gazed at the little girl and smiled as the child gave her a dainty curtsy, which seemed very odd, dressed as she was in her strange clothes.

'Papa showed me how to curtsy, just like the ladies in England do,' she lisped. 'Is that how to do it?' She looked at Georgiana with dark appealing eyes.

Georgiana stood up and bent her knee and her head in response. 'That is exactly how to do it, Jewel. I must admit, I have almost forgotten myself.'

'May I go now, Papa?' the child said breathlessly, turning to Edward. 'The pasta will be ready.'

He nodded and she shot out again, the curtain streaming behind her. He faced Georgiana, saw the question which was plainly written on her face, and stated mildly, 'It's quite a long story. Shall we leave it until tomorrow?'

'I think perhaps we should!' She gathered up her cape and reticule. 'I'm glad to find you alive at least, Edward. But we should discuss May and what she could do under the circumstances. No matter that it will be distasteful to her, it seems that she must divorce you.'

A thin smile touched his lips. 'Perhaps,' he said softly.

'By the way.' Georgiana paused as she lifted the curtain to leave. 'I have a message for you.' She turned to look at him hunched in his chair. 'From Sofia Rodriguez.'

'Ah!' he sighed and smiled. 'The beautiful passionate Sofia. Is she still beautiful, Georgiana?'

'She is indeed, very beautiful. She asked that if
I found you, would I tell you – that she has a son.'
She raised her eyebrows in a quizzical manner.
'Her husband always wanted a son apparently,'
she added. 'She insisted that I must be sure to tell
you!'

Georgiana was haunted all night by the image of
Edward as he was now, gaunt and thin with
ashen face and pale trembling hands, and the
man he once was, handsome, arrogant, a ladies'
man, with a young mistress from the poorest
streets of Hull. Even after he had married Cousin
May he had refused to give her up, causing May
much distress. He had then left them both and
sailed for America.

He is different now, she admitted, as she lay
awake in her bed. He's chastened, perhaps. More
modest and mellow than he once was. And much
nicer, though he is still opinionated! The child!
Chinese? But where was her mother? Jewel! An
unusual name. Such a sweet child.

When she arrived mid-morning at Edward's
house, Jed opened the door and invited her in,
telling her that Eddie was still in bed. 'I'll wait,'
she said. 'I'm not in a hurry.'

'No, ma'am. He said fer you to go right on in.
Would you like some coffee?'

She thanked him and accepted and, after
knocking on the door jamb of the room, parted
the beaded curtain and went inside. Edward was
propped up on several pillows. A jug of water and

a glass were on a table by the side of the bed.

'I'm so glad that you came back, Georgiana,' he said. 'I was worried that you might not.'

'I said that I would,' she replied. 'Why would I not?'

'Well, I've made promises throughout my life and not kept them,' he said wearily. 'Though not lately.' He gave a wry grin. 'I've changed. You wouldn't believe how I've changed or what I've been through.'

He started to tell her about New Orleans and Robert Allen, and being kidnapped, but she interrupted him in mid-flow. 'I know about Robert Allen,' she said, 'though I didn't know about you being kidnapped until I met Sofia and she told me.'

He sighed. 'I guessed that it was Rodriguez' men who put me on that creaky old tub, though how they got to me so quickly, I'll never know.'

They talked for an hour, piecing together both their stories. Jed brought in more coffee and said that Eddie shouldn't talk so much. Georgiana sat in the living room so that he could rest for half an hour. Jed joined her and told her of how he and Larkin and the others had met Edward in the Mississippi swamps, and of their journey to California.

At one o'clock Lorenzo's mother from the store next door brought in a dish of pasta and a plate of thinly sliced meat, and urged Georgiana in a strong Italian accent to make Meester Eddie eat.

'Everyone is so good to me,' he said, forking the pasta into his mouth. 'And I don't deserve it.'

'Where is Jewel's mother?' Georgiana was

465

unable to contain her curiosity any longer.

'Dead.' He wiped his mouth on a large white serviette. 'She left one day and didn't come back. I didn't know that she was expecting a child. I would have looked after her,' he said pensively. 'I was very fond of Tsui. But for whatever reason she chose to leave. A Chinese woman brought the child to me twelve months later. She told me that it had been a difficult birth and Tsui had died two weeks after Jewel was born. This woman, I never knew her name, had looked after the baby until she was weaned, but now her husband had said that they must sell her.'

He saw her shocked expression and nodded. 'It does still happen sometimes with a girl child. They become slaves or prostitutes when they're old enough. Tsui had told the woman that I was the father, and she wouldn't have lied. The woman said that I must take the child if I wanted her to live.' He shrugged. 'What could I do? I got a woman in to help me, and Dolly, though she's not what you'd call the motherly type, did what she could.'

He smiled contentedly. 'She's a happy child and I've never once wished that she wasn't here. I love her more than anyone else in the world, and she's changed my life.'

'Her name?' Georgiana asked. 'It is most unusual. Why Jewel?'

He put his head back against the pillows and closed his eyes for a moment, then he opened them and looked at her. 'I loved someone else once. Still do, I suppose. But she didn't love me. Not enough anyway.'

'Your mistress. The young mill girl?'

'Yes.' He nodded. 'Ruby. I was completely and utterly obsessed by her and maybe I stifled her, I don't know. But there was never another woman, not May, not Sofia, not Tsui, who could ever make me forget her.' He sighed. 'I called Jewel after her. Ruby was like a precious gem, vibrant, sparkling – but Jewel loves me,' he said, almost fiercely and possessively. 'She belongs to me as no-one else ever did or can. I am her father and – and I hope that she remembers how much I loved her.'

'What is it that's wrong with you, Edward?' Georgiana asked quietly. 'What ails you?'

'Nothing now.' He reached for the glass with a trembling hand. 'Nothing at all.' He drank and swallowed as if it hurt. 'I am over my illness; now I am only waiting. I've had all the medicines that the doctors can give me, English, Indian, Chinese. I've had herbs from the forests, opium, everything.'

She sat silently, knowing that there was something more he had to say.

'Another month, Georgiana, and you would have been too late.' He gazed at her from sunken eyes. 'As it is, you have come in time. Someone has answered my prayers by sending you here just when you were needed. I feel – reprieved, as if I have been forgiven for my wrongdoings after all.'

'I don't understand,' she said. 'What do you mean?'

'I'm dying, Georgiana, you can surely see that?' There was a plea hidden behind his husky voice. 'I'm not afraid, though I feel it's unfair. But I badly need your help.'

467

CHAPTER FORTY-ONE

'I'm so very sorry.' Her voice broke. He was right, it didn't seem fair. 'But how can I help you? You said you had seen doctors?'

'I don't mean help me with my malady,' he said patiently. 'There's no cure for that. No, I'm on my way to eternity for sure. But I've been fighting it, Georgiana. Fighting so hard because I wasn't ready to go, not until I had resolved my dilemma.'

'Which is?' she asked softly.

'It's as if–' He didn't answer her directly, but seemed to be searching and deliberating in the furthest reaches of his mind. 'As if,' he continued, 'I've been waiting for something to happen. Or waiting for someone.' He lifted his eyes to hers and gave a weak grin. 'And then you walked through the door! Thousands of miles have divided us and I haven't thought about you in years, yet you came just when I needed you most.'

'I don't understand you, Edward,' she said. 'What is it you want of me?'

He sat forward in bed. His face was flushed, his eyes bright. 'Jewel!' he said. 'I want you to take Jewel!'

'Take Jewel? Take her where?' She was astonished and not a little alarmed, for she feared he was feverish.

'Back with you,' he whispered. 'Don't you see? It's as if it was ordained! She can't go to Larkin, he's a single man and doesn't know about children – I know, I was too, but she is my child. Jed is married with a wife who is expecting a baby, and Dolly, darling Dolly, she'd teach her all the wrong things.'

She stared at him, her lips apart. 'But – I can't,' she breathed. 'She doesn't know me. I don't know her. Besides,' her voice became stilted and she stammered in her confusion, 'wh-what about my life? I came to this country to be independent, to do what *I* wanted. And then – then there's Lake.'

She told him about Lake, who he was and what he did.

'All the more reason,' he softly persuaded. 'When your mountain man is away, she would be a great comfort to you.'

'You don't know what you are asking of me, Edward.' An uncalled-for tear trickled down her cheek. My dreams are vanishing, she reflected miserably, as they seem to do. I don't want to be responsible for anyone else.

'I do know,' he answered. 'I really do. But you know, better than most, what it is like to lose your parents. Can you imagine how Jewel will feel when I am dead? She has never known her mother – and with her father gone–' He swallowed hard and blinked away his own tears. 'My friends would do their best for her, but she would be alone.' He wiped his eyes with pale thin fingers. 'And God alone knows what will happen to her when she's older. She'll be so vulnerable.'

He covered his face with his hands. 'And I won't be here to protect her,' he wept.

'Please, Edward. Don't upset yourself.' She

469

could no longer control her own tears and she reached out to him.

He squeezed her hand, took a great breath and leaned forward. 'I've been a terrible person, Georgiana,' he snuffled, and rubbed his nose with the back of his hand. She silently handed him her own wet handkerchief. 'But I can't bear to think that Jewel will suffer because of what I have done. The sins of the father and all that.

'I'm sorry.' He blew his nose on the dainty scrap of linen. 'Of course I shouldn't have asked you. You're quite right. You have your own life to lead. You were fettered for so long by your relatives. You must have been pleased to have your freedom.'

'It wasn't all bad,' she murmured. 'I was treated well enough.' She thought of May's parents who had provided for her, and of her Aunt Clarissa with whom she had lived. A single woman who had been kind to the orphaned child and did her best for her. But Aunt Clarissa had lived a quiet sheltered life and didn't know anything about the outside world. Not as I do, she pondered. I could teach a child so much more, especially a girl. A small girl like Jewel would grow up with different expectations. She could have hopes and dreams that could be realized.

She took a shuddering breath. 'I'll think about it, Edward,' she said at length. 'I promise. I will think about it.'

She visited every day for nearly a month, talking to Edward about the past, for he could no longer talk about the future. When he wasn't too tired, he told her of the journey from the Mississippi swamps, of being buried in the snow, and of the long journey across the plains, fording rivers and creeks and crossing mountains.

'I came across a trapper in the mountains once,' she said to him. 'He told me he had met an Englishman travelling to California. He said this la-di-da Englishman was with some swampsuckers who were stuck in the snow!' She laughed. 'I could never have dreamed that it might have been you!'

She told him of her journey to Dreumel's Creek with Kitty, and of Wilhelm, whom she described as a very dear friend. He nodded thoughtfully when she said that Wilhelm still grieved for his dead wife, and told him of the mining shaft which had produced gold.

'So you're a rich woman, Georgiana,' he said one day. He was in bed, too weak to get up.

'Yes, I suppose so. A woman of independent means, at any rate!'

'Jewel will be well provided for,' he said. 'I'm giving Dolly the saloon. She's worked hard on my account. The least I can do is give it to her. But I've made plenty of money and I too have some gold.' He reached into the drawer at the side of the bed and brought out a small leather bag. He threw it across the bed towards her.

'Gold dust,' he said. 'It's for May, in return for her dowry.'

'For May? How do you propose to get it to her?'

He gave her a droll glance and shook his head.

'You're not expecting me to take it?' She asked the question in a teasing voice.

471

He raised his eyebrows. 'Only if you decide to take Jewel to meet her English relations. Her grandmother – her uncle.'

She gave an exasperated exclamation. 'I haven't yet said I will take Jewel into my care!' She had played with her, read to her, taken her shopping. Walked hand in hand with her around the streets of San Francisco and eaten pasta with her and Lorenzo.

'But you will, Georgiana, won't you?' His voice was pleading. 'There isn't much time left,' he whispered.

She pressed her lips together. She had grown fond of the child. She was sweet-natured and merry, ready to do anyone's bidding, eager and intelligent. She could, she knew, grow to love her as her own.

She put her hands into his. His were cold, his fingertips blue. 'Will you do this for me, Georgiana?' His voice was so low that she had to bend her head to hear him. 'In the name of our new friendship and the bond, tenuous though it was, that we once had. Will you take my child and love her? Will you do this for me?'

'Yes,' she vowed, her mouth trembling. 'I will.'

The following week flew past as arrangements were made. Georgiana booked a passage on a clipper ship sailing to New York around Cape Horn. During that long three-month voyage she knew that there would be plenty of time for her and Jewel to get properly acquainted. But they hadn't yet told the child that she was leaving.

'*You* must tell her, Edward,' Georgiana said.

'You must tell her yourself, for she will always remember, young as she is, your final words of farewell.'

He wept. 'I can't. How can I look at her and know that I will never see her again? It's breaking my heart, Georgiana!'

'You must be strong for her sake,' she said gently. 'Be brave. That is how she will remember you.' And then she wept with him.

'Jewel, my darling,' he said to her. 'Papa has to go on a long journey.'

'Can I take my new coat and bonnet?' she asked, for she and Georgiana had been shopping for clothes.

'I'm afraid you can't come with me.' He shook his head. 'This is a journey only for grown-up people. But Aunt Georgiana has said that you could go on a journey with her! On a ship! To see where she lives and stay with her for a while.'

'Will you bring me back, Aunt Gianna?' Jewel piped up at her. 'Or will you come for me, Papa?'

'I will be away a very long time, Jewel,' he said huskily. 'Aunt Gianna has said she will look after you until you are old enough to travel alone.'

'I'm nearly big enough now,' said the tiny girl, and Edward blinked away his tears at the realization that he would never see her grow into a young woman. He leant towards her and Georgiana bent to pick her up and place her on the bed beside him.

'I will always love you, my darling,' he whispered. 'Even when I'm far away. Will you remember that?'

She nodded and as if she realized that there was something momentous happening that she didn't understand, she put her arms around his neck and hugged him.

On the day of departure, Edward managed to get out of bed and go to the door. Larkin and Jed stood at each side of him propping him up. Dolly, sniffling and crying, came to say goodbye to the little girl.

'We'll write,' Georgiana promised them. 'We will, won't we, Jewel? You can learn your letters and write a letter to everyone.'

'And one to Papa,' she said. 'A special one for Papa.'

Edward kissed her on her cheek and hugged her, then kissed Georgiana on both hands, pressing them to his lips. 'I can't tell you what this means to me,' he whispered. 'You will reap your reward one day, Georgiana.'

As they crossed the yard and turned for one final wave before they climbed into the waggonette, he called weakly. 'When you write to May, tell her – tell her I'm sorry, and wish her well in her new life. I trust that she gets a better second husband than her first!'

Georgiana gave a trembling smile. 'I will tell her that she didn't really know him, that none of us did.'

'And my brother – and my mother,' he called breathlessly and urgently, as if he had to pack a lifetime of words and sentiments into the last few precious minutes. 'Tell them–'

'I will tell them, Edward.' She came halfway back across the yard. 'I will tell them everything they need to know and nothing that they don't. I'll tell them that you made a good life and found happiness here with your friends and your daughter.'

He nodded, hardly able to speak. 'Yes,' he whispered. 'You will know what to say.'

By the time the ship anchored in New York, Georgiana had been away almost a year and had travelled twelve thousand miles. The whole of America from east to west was opening up with the advent of new railroads and canal systems, but the territory was so vast and funds so limited that debates and discussions delayed the start of projects, and companies and private investors fell into bankruptcy before new rail tracks could be laid or water routes diverted. Coaches, waggon or mule trains plied across the old dusty and rutted trails, and overland routes were still the favoured form of travel, difficult though it was.

She had written to Wilhelm explaining the situation and saying that they were returning on the clipper ship *Hope*. She was not sure, though, whether the overland mail would have arrived in time for him to meet her. He wasn't at the wharfside, so she took a horse cab to the Marius, where she and Jewel would rest for a few days and she would show her the city of New York.

Jewel had cried for her father many times and sometimes couldn't be pacified. Georgiana kept having to remind herself that Jewel was still little more than a baby. Edward had said that he thought she was four years old, though he didn't know her exact birthday.

'We will buy you a present whilst we are in New

York, Jewel, and one for Caitlin,' she said as they booked in at the hotel. 'Caitlin isn't a big girl like you, but she will soon be able to play with you.'

Jewel jumped up and down in excitement at the prospect of having a new friend, for she had also cried for the little boy Lorenzo.

'So glad to see you again, Miss Gregory,' the desk clerk greeted her. 'Mr Dreumel will be along soon, I reckon. He's been expecting you.'

She had been given accommodation with a sitting room next to the bedroom. They had lunch, then Georgiana put Jewel to bed for a sleep. She was repacking their travelling clothes when there came a soft knock on the door.

'Who is it?' she called.

'Wilhelm,' the familiar voice replied.

She rushed to open the door. 'Wilhelm! Oh how lovely to see you after so long–' Her voice trailed away, her enthusiasm diminished. He was thinner and although his face was weather-browned and he smiled, he had an aura of tension and a deep worried furrow on his forehead.

'Come in. Come in. Wilhelm!' She put out both her hands to his, and he bowed low, then kissed them.

'It is good to see you, my dear Georgiana,' he murmured. 'So very good. It has been such a long time.'

She ushered him towards a chair, but he declined, shaking his head. 'No. No. I will stand. Thank you.'

'What is it, Wilhelm? Something is wrong?' She searched his face for the reason for his reticent manner. 'Are you ill? Please say you are not!'

'No.' Quickly he reassured her. 'I am not. I – I would have met you at the wharf, but–'

'Did you not receive my letter?'

'Yes. I have been here for some time, checking the arrivals, waiting for the ship.'

'So why did you not come to the wharf? Not that it matters,' she added quickly. 'We managed perfectly well.'

'I did come,' he said. 'But I saw the little girl – I had forgotten that she would be with you and – I – so I went away again and waited for you here.' He took a deep breath, then put out his hands to hers. 'I have something to tell you, Georgiana, and I didn't want to tell you in front of the child.'

'What?' she whispered. 'What's wrong? Is it Kitty? Caitlin?'

'No. They are both well.' He drew her towards him. 'There is not an easy way to tell you this. It's Lake! I'm so very sorry, my dear. Lake is dead.'

CHAPTER FORTY-TWO

He held her close as she trembled with shock, though she didn't immediately cry. Then he gently placed her onto a sofa and left her, returning a few minutes later with a glass of brandy and hot water.

Her hand shook as she lifted the glass to her lips, and he steadied it as she sipped. 'How?' she whispered. 'How did he die?'

'He was killed,' he said softly. 'He died in the mountains.'

477

'Killed?' She stared at him, her face blank. 'A wolf? A bear?'

'No. By another trapper. They were old enemies.'

Georgiana thought of the trapper who had appeared when she and Kitty were travelling in the mountains, and wondered if it had been him.

'How do you know this?' she asked, her voice thick as tears began to well in her eyes and clog in her throat.

'Horse and Dekan found him and came to tell me. Lake had been expected back at No-Name, but when he didn't arrive they set out to look for him. When they found his body they sent out a search party for his killer. Lake's gun and knife were missing. When they found the trapper he had them both. He was also injured with knife wounds to his arms and chest.'

'What will happen to him?' she whispered. 'This killer?'

Wilhelm was silent for a moment, then, with a catch in his voice, said, 'Justice has been done. Lake was half Iroquois, and although the tribe is normally peaceable, vengeance for the death of a brother was exacted.'

Georgiana shuddered. 'What did they do?'

'They killed him with Lake's own knife.'

There is more to it than that, Georgiana thought. But it is all I need to know, and it was then that she started to cry.

He sat with his arm around her as she sobbed, and silently handed her his handkerchief. She leaned against his shoulder and wet his jacket with her tears and never once did he implore her not to upset herself or cease her crying.

478

'It is a bad time, I know, Georgiana,' he whispered into her hair, which had strayed from her chignon. 'And nothing can ease the terrible pain. I remember that so very well. You think your world has come to an end, your dreams and hopes shattered when a loved one dies.'

She nodded and blew her nose. Wilhelm above all people would understand that, having lost his young wife. 'We had no plans,' she sobbed. 'How could we have? But we had our love and that was enough.'

But was it? She searched her soul, even as she wept. Was it enough or did I want more? She knew that there had been no real future together for her and Lake, not in the conventional sense. He couldn't leave his forests and mountains and she couldn't live there. Was this what he meant when he said she couldn't be with him? That they only had today and no tomorrow? He knew that death lurked behind every tree and every rock. And what would have become of her if she had been with him?

'Dekan and Horse want you to go to No-Name,' Wilhelm said. 'For a special ceremony. I said I would take you if you agreed.'

'Yes.' She wiped her eyes and tried to compose herself. 'I would like to see them and hear of what they think happened, and why – perhaps they would show me where he died?'

Wilhelm entertained Jewel during the journey, telling her stories, playing tricks with a coin, telling her of the Indian people she was going to meet, whilst Georgiana fell into a silent reverie, wondering what life had in store for her now.

'The mine, Wilhelm? Is it still producing gold? And the settlement? Are there any new people?'

He seemed relieved that she was showing an interest in other things and smiled, first shaking his head and then nodding.

'Your head will fall off, Mr Dreumel.' Jewel laughed and shook her own vigorously.

'No, it is tied on very firmly. Look!' He bent his head to show her the back of his neck. 'I have a very long string.'

To Georgiana he said, 'The mine has dried up. We dug three more shafts but there was a mere trickle of gold, barely enough to pay the men. Then word got out that we had found gold in the creek, and we were inundated with hundreds of miners swarming all over Yeller Creek. The upper valley was like a shanty town with shacks, tents, waterwheels and all the usual equipment.' He smiled at her. 'But most of them have now gone off to search elsewhere, some up north, some to Montana and Idaho.'

'And the rest? Those who have stayed?' she asked.

'Farmers mostly, blacksmiths, wheelwrights, a haberdasher. They liked it there, and they'd heard about the railroad coming, so they decided it would be a good place to settle.'

They were now approaching No-Name. For this last part of the journey they were riding on horseback, with Jewel up behind Wilhelm. Georgiana was painfully reminded of when she and Kitty had ridden out of the settlement with Lake. *I can't believe that I will never see him again. Never see his crooked smile or his dark*

480

eyes gazing on me.

'Georgiana!' Wilhelm interrupted her thoughts. 'It may be difficult for you at the settlement. The tribe wish you to be their guest of honour at the ceremony.' He looked across at her and said softly, 'Where love has been, it never completely disappears. There will always be a place in your heart where Lake will live. Think of him with joy, not with sadness.'

'Is that what you do with Liesel?' she asked.

He nodded and gave her a wistful smile. 'Now I do.'

In the longhouse where the ceremony was to take place, the Indian women were wearing shawls over their heads, partly covering their faces. The men were dressed in cotton fringed trousers and tunics, though some were bare-chested. Silver bracelets adorned their arms and bright beads were strung around their necks. The older men draped coloured shawls over their shoulders and wore braids and feather headdresses in their sleek hair and carried long canes.

Dekan and Horse greeted them and Little Bear took Georgiana and Jewel to her cabin for refreshment before the ceremony began. 'We miss Lake very much,' she said huskily. 'But we must be happy for him that he has returned to his spiritual home.'

Jewel was taken to play with the children and Georgiana was led back into the longhouse, where she was seated on a bench draped with a red blanket. Wilhelm sat next to her and she felt the comfort of his hand in hers.

Dekan rose to his feet and the others in the

tribe followed suit. Slowly, in single file they shuffled around the room in a death march, chanting in low sepulchral voices. Then they stopped and Dekan addressed them.

'We have come today to honour our brother who has gone to join the spirit of his fathers. Though he had white man's blood he had the true soul of an Iroquois. He was felled as a tall tree full of leaf is cut down, by his enemy who dared to call us savages.

'Our brother was descended from our prophet Handsome Lake, who taught us that we must love one another and make peace not enemies, and that beyond the grave we will find happiness or punishment for the life we have lived on this earth.'

He paused, and glancing at the senior tribesmen, went on. 'In ancient times, in our old way of life, we believed that our spirit families would protect us from harm.' Some of the elderly men nodded their heads sagely and grunted or thumped the floor with their sticks. 'Our brother's death has been avenged and he is now resting with his ancestors. But times are changing,' Dekan went on firmly. 'And we must ready ourselves against those forces who wish to remove us from our rightful land, or else face death and destruction of our race. Our brother warned us of this and told us that we must be prepared.'

They all rose to their feet once more and marched, chanting, around the room and then filed outside to where a feast was awaiting them.

Dekan came to speak to Georgiana. He had a piece of paper in his hand which he handed to

482

her. 'The man who killed our brother had this in his possession when we found him. It is yours, I think.'

Georgiana looked at it. It was the receipt for the mining claim which Charlesworth had given to Lake in exchange for the pelts. She gave a deep sigh. 'Not mine,' she said softly. 'Lake intended it for Wilhelm.'

Georgiana had felt quietly comforted by the ceremony and when discussing this with Wilhelm later, he said that he had also. 'I felt a great loss when I heard of his death,' he said. 'For I admired Lake and the way he conducted himself. Though he was brought up by the Iroquois, he was caught between two worlds, that of the Indians and the whites. He was a brave man.'

'What did Dekan mean about the warning that Lake had given them?'

'The Indians are resisting the loss of land which is being taken from them for the settlers and the railroads. The treaties are being broken. The trappers had heard of unrest in various tribes. Lake was warning the Iroquois that war will come.'

She became thoughtful and sad that the peaceable people she knew, Dekan, Horse and Little Bear, should be involved in conflict. 'You saved Lake's life once, didn't you?' she asked. 'What did you do?'

His eyes clouded. 'The trapper who killed Lake was his half-brother, Odie. Son of the Frenchman and a saloon woman. They met when they were boys and were sworn enemies from the start. Odie always referred to Lake as a half-breed. I came across them quite by chance as I was travelling towards Philadelphia. Odie had followed Lake and jumped him, intent on stealing his horse and his pelts. He had his knife to Lake's throat when I happened to come along. I drew my gun and told him I would shoot him if he didn't drop it.

'Lake repaid me by showing me the valley and the creek.' He gave a worried sigh. 'I hope I have not betrayed his trust in me.'

'In what way could you have done that?' she asked.

'The land belonged long ago to the Indians. When they moved out the valley was silent and peaceful, given back to nature. We have changed it by opening it up and by turning the earth inside out looking for gold.' He seemed downcast, she thought.

'But you have had control over it,' she encouraged him. 'You are making it into a good settlement where people want to be, just as the Indians once did. But it is time for change and I think that Lake knew that.' Georgiana touched his arm and gently reassured him. 'That is why he showed it to you. That is why he left you Charlesworth's claim. He knew it would be in safe hands.'

Kitty was delighted to see her, though sorry she had had a sad homecoming. She was pregnant again and had taken on help in her bakery shop. Ted was engaged in salvaging the equipment that had been left behind by the miners, and had now given up searching for gold. 'We've enough,' he said. 'More than I ever dreamed of. We're going

484

into business, Kitty and me. We're going to build an hotel up on Yeller Creek. When the railroad comes, folks will want somewhere to stay.'

Georgiana told him about Edward Newmarch and his trek, from the swamps of Mississippi to California. Ted was astonished. 'I didn't think he had it in him,' he said. 'I thought he was just a priggish English sop.'

'He might once have been,' she agreed. 'But how we all have changed.' She gave a little smile. 'Before I left, he said to tell you that you could keep his suit of clothes!'

He nodded at the joke, but didn't smile. 'I'm sorry I misjudged him,' he said. 'Really sorry.'

'You didn't,' she replied. 'He became a different man from the one you knew.'

Winter was almost upon them, but Georgiana wanted to make her own lone journey into the mountains to say a final goodbye to Lake. She left Jewel with Kitty and took Hetty out of the stable, mounted her and rode out of the settlement, which had, as Wilhelm had told her, grown considerably since she had left. It had an air of cheerful activity as people went about their business, and there was a buzz of children's voices coming from the schoolroom.

She crossed the bridge and cantered towards the foothills and up the mountain track. The air felt crisp and sharp as if there would soon be snow. The sky was blue, with soft white clouds floating above the mountain tops. Hetty snickered and put up her ears. 'Yes, Hetty,' Georgiana murmured. 'It's a long time since you and I had such a ride.' She stroked the horse's neck. 'And

485

there have been many changes since we were last here.'

When she reached the ridge she turned to look back as she always did. Smoke was curling from the chimneys of the cabins, sawing and hammering reverberated along the valley as more buildings were being put up. The valley had a permanent, established look to it, she thought. As if the cabins and buildings were putting down roots and settling themselves comfortably into the ground.

She turned again and rode into the forest. She had asked Dekan if he would show her where Lake had died, but he had shaken his head and told her it was a faraway place. 'But you will find his spirit in the forests and the mountains, or by the rivers and streams,' he had said. 'He will always be there if you look for him.'

'I know that to be true,' she murmured now. 'For that is what Lake himself said. *I am at one with the elements of nature, the solitude and the silence.*' She drew into a space between a group of trees and listened. She could almost hear his low voice, his breathing and his presence. Something scuttled nearby and she turned her head. The tops of the trees rustled as a cool breeze blew and she thought she could hear the distant howl of a wolf.

'I know you are here,' she said softly. 'And you told me that whilst you were on this earth, you would always love me.' Her breath caught in her throat. 'But you have left me alone and I miss you so much.' She started to sob and, covering her face with her hand, she allowed the mare to find her own way back down to Dreumel's Creek.

CHAPTER FORTY-THREE

Wilhelm went on a final journey to Philadelphia before winter. He brought Georgiana a letter from Larkin, though written by Dolly, to tell her that Edward had died a peaceful death. 'He sent his last words of love to his little girl,' they wrote. 'And asked that we tell you he trusts her life to you.'

Georgiana folded up the letter, swallowed a lump in her throat, heaved a sigh and considered that she was now totally and morally responsible for Jewel's upbringing. She called the child to her and, holding her in her arms, told her quietly and gently of her father's death and that she would be looking after her from now on.

As time passed, Jewel often cried and pensively asked about her papa and questioned why he had to die. Sometimes at bedtime as Georgiana tucked her up, she would cling to her and ask when she would be going home. Georgiana decided one night that in order to distract her she would tell her of her father's life before he went to live in California.

'Before me, do you mean, Aunt Gianna?' she asked, and her mouth trembled. She sat up in bed. 'And before Larkin and Jed and Dolly!'

'Yes,' Georgiana replied, and realized how Edward had sheltered his daughter, and that apart from her little friend Lorenzo and his mother, these were the only people that Jewel knew. So she told her of her father's brother Martin, and of her grandmother, then reluctantly told her of May, Edward's wife.

'So, she's my mama!' Jewel said eagerly. 'May we go and see her?'

'She isn't your mama,' Georgiana explained. 'Your mama was a lovely Chinese lady, called Tsui. May is an English lady who lives in another country.'

Jewel seemed confused. 'Does my grandmother live in another country?'

'She does. She lives in England.' Gently she pulled the covers over her and tucked her in again. 'I'll tell you more another day. Now, time for sleep.'

Over the winter, Jewel asked many questions about her uncle and if he had any children, and about May, and demanded why she lived in a different place from her papa, and Georgiana answered as best she could. The child often followed Wilhelm about, tugging on his sleeve or holding his hand as if she needed the reassurance of a male presence, used as she had been to her father, Jed and Larkin. Wilhelm responded warmly to the little girl, building her a toboggan and playing with her in the snow. Then Jewel asked Kitty if she was Caitlin's mama and looked curiously at Ted when he said that he was Caitlin's da.

'Poor little mite,' Kitty said. 'She's all mixed up. Perhaps you should take her to England to see her gran and her uncle! I know I would take Caitlin home to see my ma if she was alive.'

Georgiana was thoughtful. The idea had crossed

her mind more than once, not only for Jewel's sake, but her own. She was restless, couldn't concentrate on any project and whenever she looked up into the mountains, she imagined she could see the image of Lake riding down the track towards her.

Wilhelm came into her log house for supper one night as he often did. It was cosy and warm, unlike her old cabin, and they sat together after Jewel was put to bed, watching the flames dancing in the stove.

'There's a shadow enveloping me, Wilhelm,' she confided, knowing that he would understand, having been through this sorrow himself. 'Wherever I go, wherever I look, Lake is there, and–' She swallowed hard as emotion threatened to overwhelm her. 'I don't ever want to forget him.'

She wiped away a tear which had escaped onto her cheek. 'But – I am in limbo. He's holding me fast. Whilst I am here within the sight of his mountains and forests, I cannot proceed with my life.' She lifted a melancholy face to him. 'Am I being disloyal? Am I forgetting our love so quickly?'

'No,' he said softly. 'You are not being disloyal, but you are still young.' He smiled as she shook her head and denied that she was. 'Yes, you are. You still have youth and vigour running through your veins.'

'Dearest Wilhelm.' She put her hand into his. 'Whatever would I do without you? You are so wise.'

'No.' His voice cracked as he spoke. 'I am not wise at all. I am the most foolish man in the world.'

She gave a tearful laugh. 'Why do you say that?'

489

He wiped his eye as if he had something in it. 'Because I know that I am.'

'I think I might go to England in the spring,' she said suddenly, and didn't notice his sharp intake of breath. 'Jewel should meet her father's family and they should meet her. Her grandmother might want to bring her up.'

'But you will come back to Dreumel's Creek?' he asked quietly. 'Your home is here, isn't it?'

'I don't know.' Her voice was sad. 'If it is my home, I mean. I have travelled so many thousands of miles since I came to America that I'm unsettled and can't tell if I'm ready to put down roots. Since Lake died I have no conception of where I belong.' She thought for a moment, then added, 'And I'm not sure if I knew before.'

'I would miss you,' he murmured. 'Dreumel's Creek isn't the same without you. I discovered that when you went to California.'

She nodded absent-mindedly. 'I know.' She looked up at him and was surprised at how downcast he was. 'I would miss you too, Wilhelm. Everyone. But it needn't be for ever.' She bit on her lip as she considered. 'I feel that I owe it to Jewel. Her father entrusted her to my care and I must do what I think is best for her.'

He gave an exasperated exclamation. 'And what is best for you, Georgiana? You escaped to America to find freedom! To prove that you are an independent woman. Yet you cannot let go of what you consider your obligations – your – allegiances!'

She stared at him. She had never seen him so roused. He was the calmest, steadiest man she

490

had ever known, yet now he was flushed with what seemed to be outrage.

'So – is that wrong? Should I disregard my inner feelings of loyalty? My conscience? Please advise me, Wilhelm, for I value your opinion.' She gazed at him beseechingly. 'Because I no longer know what is right or wrong or indeed what I want.'

He put his hand wearily to his forehead and rubbed it. 'I'm sorry, Georgiana. So very sorry. I spoke hastily. Of course you must do what you think is best. You have the right to choose. That has always been your aim. Jewel is a dear sweet child and, yes, she must visit her family. It is only just and fair.'

He got up to leave and patted her shoulder as she sat on the sofa looking up at him. 'I'm being selfish.' He gave a whimsical laugh which didn't quite convince her. 'I am thinking only of our evenings together – our conversations. I will miss those. Who will I talk to when you go away?' She saw him take a deep breath as he continued. 'As of course you must.'

Am I making the right decision? she wondered as the ship left New York the following spring. I asked myself this same question when I departed from England over five years ago. Am I now merely retracing my steps? Why am I leaving my friends whom I love so dearly?

Kitty had given birth to a boy during that long harsh winter, and had called him Robert, his father's real name. Wilhelm had been subdued all winter, concerned, she thought, about his cattle surviving the cold. But he had come to see her and Jewel off at New York, waving both arms in the air as the packet ship pulled away up the river Hudson on course for Liverpool, from where they would travel by railway across to Hull.

For the first fortnight the weather was fair and the sea calm, but then a hurricane blew in, the ship tossed and rocked on the high seas, their belongings fell from shelves and the lantern swayed precariously from its hook in the ceiling. Both Georgiana and Jewel were so sick they couldn't eat anything but thin soup and biscuits. The sea was rough for several days, with wind and hail to add to their discomfort, and they kept to their cabin, which was hot and stuffy. When they finally emerged as the storm abated and there was a fresh breeze carrying them, they saw that there had been considerable damage on deck, with a ripped and tattered jib sail and a broken mast. The rest of the journey was long and tedious and they spent weary days walking around the deck for exercise.

A train was leaving Liverpool early the following morning after they disembarked. It was cold, dark and wet in Liverpool and as the train chugged and hissed its way towards Hull, Jewel leaned exhaustedly against Georgiana. She had lost weight during the journey and her face was drawn and pallid, making her dark oriental eyes look enormous.

'Are we nearly there, Aunt Gianna?' she whispered. 'I am so very, very tired.'

'Poor darling.' Georgiana put her arm around her. 'Rest if you can; it is a long journey but we'll be there before nightfall.'

492

An elderly woman sitting across from them in the carriage had been eyeing them surreptitiously since the start of the journey. Now she leaned towards Georgiana and asked curiously, 'Is your husband a Chinaman, my dear?'

How very impertinent, Georgiana thought. 'No,' she answered plainly.

'Oh? Then the child is not yours?'

Georgiana didn't see fit to answer her, but the woman stared at Jewel and continued. 'My son has gone to America. I was to have gone too but I changed my mind at the last minute, which is why I am travelling back on this train. He told me just before we were due to board that there were all kinds of people in America. Black and yellow, Red Indians even!'

'So there are,' Georgiana replied coldly. 'And pink and white just like you and me.'

Surely Jewel won't be turned away because of her Chinese blood? she pondered. I hadn't thought of that. Perhaps her grandmother will not accept her as part of her own family? Will Martin? And whatever is May going to say when she sees her?

Georgiana was quite disorientated when they stepped from the train in Hull. She felt cramped and hemmed in, used as she was to the wide open landscape of America. The smells of the blubber and seed oil which drifted over the town made her feel nauseous. She was disturbed too at the sight of beggars, men, women and barefoot children, sitting in the station waiting for the arrival of visitors with their hands outstretched and a desperate appeal in their eyes.

493

I'd forgotten about them, she thought, as she dropped a copper into a woman's eager hand. How could I? Why did I not remember when I was desperate for my own independence that there were so many others in need? Her thoughts turned to the young girl Grace, who had so actively campaigned for women in poverty. She had then married Edward's brother Martin, who had fallen in love with her. I wonder if she has given up that cause now that she is married to a rich man. It would be so easy to forget, she thought guiltily. Just as I have done.

They walked from the railway concourse into the Royal Station Hotel, where they were to rest for a few days before proceeding to make their visits. Georgiana had written to Edward's mother telling her of his death, and also to May so that she could make preparations for her marriage. She had also told them that she was journeying back, but she hadn't mentioned Jewel, preferring to tell them in person.

The hotel, though newly built the year that Georgiana and Kitty left for America, had been refurbished and decorated for the visit of Queen Victoria two years earlier. The manager proudly showed Georgiana and other special visitors the apartments which the Queen had occupied, and which had been furnished in a rich and sumptuous manner.

'Nowhere in the world can you find an hotel finer than this,' he exclaimed, pointing out the elegant pillars and arches and handsome glass roof above the entrance court. Georgiana, having seen the Astor and many other New York and

Philadelphia hotels, agreed that the Royal Station Hotel compared very favourably in every degree.

The next day she showed Jewel the old shipping town of Hull and found that she had, after all, a warm feeling inside her when she saw the familiar landmarks of the town and the choppy brown waters of the Humber. They walked down the shopping street of Whitefriargate, where the rich bought their fripperies and the poor queued at the workhouse door. She showed the child the ships in the old dock which had been renamed the Queen's Dock since Her Majesty's visit, and the golden statue of King William, and then she posted a short letter to Wilhelm telling him that they had arrived safely.

'I like it here, Aunt Gianna!' Jewel, more cheerful now that she was rested, skipped alongside Georgiana as they walked along the bustling Market Place which was crammed with canvas-covered stalls, and listened to the call of market traders as they competed with one another. 'I could find my way in this town without getting lost. Not like in San Francisco. Papa wouldn't let me go out on my own in case – in case – I got lost – Papa!' she suddenly cried and, clinging to Georgiana's hand, started to weep with great racking sobs and copious tears. 'Papa! Where are you? Papa!'

'Oh, Jewel! Don't cry.' Georgiana bent down to comfort the little girl. How quickly her laughter had turned to tears as she was reminded of her father. But she wouldn't be comforted and she stood shaking and crying and rubbing her small fists into her eyes.

They were jostled from behind by people who looked curiously at them. Georgiana moved Jewel against a shop window and, taking out a handkerchief, bent down again. 'Come, darling. Blow. Be a brave girl.'

'No.' Jewel stamped her foot, shook her head and howled. 'I don't want to be brave. I want my papa!'

'I beg your pardon!' A man walking behind almost fell over them, and lifted his top hat in apology. 'I'm so—' His words faded away. 'Georgiana? Georgiana! Can it be you?'

She looked up and gave a sudden smile. 'It can, Martin! It is!' She put out her hand and eagerly he grasped it and bowed.

'How extraordinary!' he gasped. 'Just amazing! Mother said, of course, that you were coming – but didn't know when, so – to meet here—!'

He laughed in his enthusiasm and she thought that he seemed more handsome, more lively and vigorous than she remembered him. Marriage obviously suits him, she thought. I was mistaken in thinking him sombre.

Jewel tugged impatiently on her skirt as if to remind her of her presence and Georgiana looked down at her, as did Martin.

'Your daughter?' he asked. 'I – didn't know.' There was a slight hesitation in his voice, though he smiled down at Jewel, whose face was wet with tears.

'No,' she said huskily. 'Not my daughter.' She put her arm protectively around Jewel. Suppose he rejects her, his brother's child? Suppose he doesn't acknowledge her because she was born

496

out of wedlock? And she is half-Chinese. She was suddenly tense, concerned that Jewel shouldn't be hurt again. 'This is Jewel. Edward's daughter.' She stroked the little girl's cheek. 'Jewel,' she said. 'This is your uncle. Martin. Your papa's brother.'

'Edward's daughter?' he breathed. 'But why didn't he tell us? We heard nothing from him.' A veil of anguish flitted across his face. 'Mother said you'd written that – about–' He hesitated, his concerned glance skimming from Georgiana to Jewel.

'Jewel knows of her father's death,' she said quietly. 'That's why she is crying: she was just now reminded of him.' Then she felt a joyous relief as Martin crouched down beside the child and took hold of her hand.

'I'm very pleased to meet you, Jewel.' His voice was low but Georgiana felt that he was battling with a strong emotion. 'So very pleased. What a charming name. Is it an American name?'

Jewel pressed her lips together, then shook her head. She blinked, teardrops clinging to her dark lashes, and stared back at Martin, who was gazing gravely at her. 'Are you Papa's brother?'

'Yes.' His voice was tight. 'I am. We were great friends when we were young, but we haven't seen each other in a long time.'

'He's dead now,' she told him solemnly. Her mouth trembled and her tears overflowed. 'And I wanted to see him!'

'I know, darling.' Martin's words were choked. 'So did I.'

He held both hands out to her and she lifted

her arms and put them around his neck. He stood and swung her up into his arms, then held her close while she sobbed onto his shoulder.

CHAPTER FORTY-FOUR

'You must come home with me,' Martin insisted. 'We live in the High Street. It's not far. Grace will be so pleased to see you.' He patted Jewel's wet cheek. 'And so will our two little girls.'

Jewel heaved a sobbing breath. 'W-will I be able to p-play with them?'

'Of course!' He hitched her higher into his arms and looked anxiously at Georgiana. 'You will come? Please.'

'Now? Well, yes! Thank you. If it won't be inconvenient.' She wondered how his wife would react to having visitors calling without notice.

His eyes sparkled as if he knew what she was thinking. 'We have open house at all times. Grace doesn't believe in calling cards.'

'How is Grace? Is she coping well with her new life?' She felt she had known him well enough in the past to ask an honest question.

'She's wonderful, Georgiana.' He beamed. 'I can't tell you how lucky I am. She wanted to live in Hull, so we chose the High Street, which is near enough for her parents and old friends to call.' He glanced significantly at her. 'She doesn't want to forget her beginnings, and,' he added, 'it is very convenient for my day-to-day activities.'

He led her down the narrow Bishop Lane and into the High Street, where presently they stopped at the door of a tall substantial house. Martin put Jewel down, rang the bell and withdrew a key from his pocket. Before he could put it in the lock, the door opened and Grace stood there with a joyous look on her face. 'Martin,' she said excitedly. 'What do you think–'

How lovely she is, Georgiana thought as they gazed at each other. More than ever she was when I last saw her. She has matured into a beautiful woman, and she felt a small pang of envy for these two happy people.

'Miss Gregory!' Grace greeted her warmly. 'How lovely to see you. Come in. Come in, please!' She opened the door wide. 'Martin? Did you expect–?' She beamed with delight at Georgiana. 'We heard you were coming back.' Then she looked down at Jewel. 'Hello! How do you do! Have you come to play with our little girls?'

Jewel nodded and started to unbutton her coat. 'Yes, please. I'm called Jewel Newsom. What are they called?'

'Elizabeth and Clara Newmarch,' Grace answered. 'They're twins and they're nearly five years old.'

Georgiana bent down to Jewel. 'Do you remember what your papa said to you before we left San Francisco? About your name?'

Jewel stared up at her. 'I shall cry again about Papa!' she said petulantly.

'Dear. Do try to remember,' Georgiana urged.

'He said I was called after a lovely lady in England.'

'Yes, I know that.' Georgiana was embarrassed. 'But your other name? Your proper surname.'

Jewel screwed up her face in an effort to remember. Then she looked up at Grace. 'It was Newmarch, like your little girls.'

Grace blinked and, glancing from Georgiana to Martin, murmured, 'So whose child is she?'

'My papa's called Eddie,' Jewel interrupted, and Georgiana considered that one thing Edward hadn't taught his daughter was that she shouldn't break into adult conversation. 'And my mama is dead. Can we go and play now?'

Grace put out her hand to her. 'Yes, of course.' She raised her eyebrows at Martin and he nodded at her implied query. 'Come along then.' She smiled. 'Come and meet your cousins.'

Martin and Grace insisted that Georgiana and Jewel should stay with them. Martin ordered the carriage and went to fetch her belongings from the hotel himself. Georgiana was introduced to the twins, who were slender and fair as Grace was, but with Martin's dark eyes.

She and Grace drank tea by the sitting-room fire and Georgiana told her of her life since leaving England.

'Such an exciting life you have had, Miss Gregory.' There was a hint of deference in Grace's manner to Georgiana, as if she still considered her to be her superior.

'Please call me Georgiana,' she said. 'In America I haven't been called Miss Gregory for many years, except by people in New York, and one elderly Englishwoman whom I met on the voyage out.' She recollected the eccentric Mrs

Burrows with affection, and wished that she had had the chance to see her before she had sailed for England.

'Most people at Dreumel's Creek call me Miz Gianna.' She laughed. 'Old Isaac started it and it seems to have stuck.' She paused and suddenly felt melancholy. 'Except for Wilhelm,' she murmured. 'He always gives me my full name.'

'And who is he?' Grace asked. 'A friend?'

'Yes.' Georgiana felt a lump in her throat. 'My very dear friend. I miss him terribly. He's so steady and sensible and – and caring.'

Grace nodded and gazed at her. 'Martin was my friend for a long time before he declared himself,' she said quietly. 'I was very young, but I could say or ask him anything. I trusted him completely but I never knew that he loved me.'

'Oh, Wilhelm doesn't care for me in that way,' Georgiana said wistfully. 'He loved his wife. She died in childbirth when they were newly married.' She lifted her eyes to Grace. 'He has never recovered from that loss, and I understand that. I too have loved and lost.'

Grace rose from her chair and came to kneel by her side. 'I am very sorry,' she whispered. 'That must be so hard for you. Is that why you have undertaken Jewel's welfare? To fill a part of your heart?'

'No.' Georgiana struggled to compose herself. 'I didn't know that Lake had been killed when I agreed to look after Jewel. I promised Edward because – because there was no-one else,' she explained in a rush.

'But now there is,' Grace said softly. 'If you

501

would desire it. We will take care of her and bring her up as our own daughter. We would be happy to. Martin would say the same, I know.'

'But!' Georgiana gazed at her. 'She will be considered an illegitimate child! It will get out. There will be such scandal. I haven't seen May yet, but I can guess what she will have to say about Edward and his daughter.'

May had many things to say about Edward and even more about Jewel when Georgiana and the little girl visited her. 'I wonder how many more children he has fathered?' she said blisteringly. 'Chinese! Indian? Who knows? There could be any amount! He was a loose fish, a Lothario, and I was unfortunate enough to marry him!'

Almost certainly there was one more, Georgiana considered, as she remembered the lovely Sofia and her handsome son. But she said nothing about that and simply explained how Edward had changed, and that he had asked her to say he was sorry he had been found wanting as a husband, and sought her forgiveness. She fished in her reticule for the small leather bag which Edward had given her.

She handed it to May and pondered that her cousin hadn't improved in temperament since she had been away. She had become more peevish and querulous than ever.

'What's this?' She snatched the bag from Georgiana. 'Atonement? He took my dowry, you know!'

'Of course I know,' Georgiana answered sharply. 'I was here at the time. This is to make amends! It's gold.'

May's eyes widened. 'Gold!' She pulled the bag

502

open. 'How much is it worth?'

'I don't know the gold prices at the moment.' Georgiana tried not to be caustic. 'But it will be worth more than your dowry ever was.'

Her cousin looked at her suspiciously. 'Is there a proviso?' she asked. 'Because legally he didn't have to return it. Women have no rights. You know that better than most after all your campaigning.' Her pretty mouth curled into a sneer. 'Didn't make any difference, did it? Any more than that woman Grace, who married Martin, did any good with that silly book she wrote. *The Emancipation of Women* or some such thing. It was quite unreadable!'

'We women have to try, May.' Georgiana felt her patience ebbing away. 'And people have read Grace's book. She has told me that every copy has been sold.'

'You've been to see them already?' May flushed. 'And what did Martin think of Edward and his philandering?'

'They were sorry that he had died,' she said softly, and reflected that May had not once shown any sorrow or asked about her husband's life. 'And they offered to have Jewel live with them.'

'Good heavens,' May exclaimed. 'But the child is a bastard! How can they think of it?' She shot a withering glance at Georgiana. 'You were not thinking of asking me to have her, were you?'

'Certainly not! She needs love and understanding.' Georgiana was very conscious of Jewel's presence. Surprisingly, the little girl was sitting quietly on a chair next to her without making any interruptions. 'She has just lost her father, who was very dear to her.'

'Hmph,' May said grudgingly. 'Well, I suppose the child can't be blamed. But I can't possibly have her. I'm about to be married. You can come to the wedding if you wish, Georgiana.' She tossed the invitation casually into the conversation. 'Only, don't bring the child. People might think she's yours, which would be very embarrassing for you as you are not a married woman.'

'I would not be in the least embarrassed.' Georgiana rose determinedly to her feet. 'But I will not be coming. I wish you every happiness in your future life. I have travelled thousands of miles on your behalf in order to repay a debt of gratitude which I considered I owed your parents. Those obligations are now discharged. Goodbye, May. I doubt that our paths will cross again.'

May opened her mouth to say something but Georgiana was already walking to the door, calling Jewel to follow her. Jewel slipped down from her chair and stood in front of May. 'I'm glad you're not my mama.' Her almond-shaped eyes were dark and unfathomable and May shrank back. 'I don't like you.'

Martin drove Georgiana and Jewel to meet his mother. 'I'm concerned that she will be upset. Though she has always been stoical, I feel she has been holding back her emotions since you wrote to tell her of Edward's death.' He gave a little smile. 'He was always our mother's favourite; she used to spoil him when we were children.'

Mrs Newmarch greeted her cordially. Georgiana had known her socially and considered that

504

she had aged in the last five years. 'So good of you to visit, Miss Gregory. So very kind of you to write to tell us of Edward.' She seemed not to take notice of Jewel, even though the little girl gave her a polite wobbly curtsy. She sighed and clutched her throat nervously. 'I wish he had written from America. I worried so.'

'He thought that no-one would want to hear from him in view of his behaviour.' Georgiana sat down as she was bid and drew Jewel towards her.

'We were angry, of course, when he went away. Were we not, Martin?' She glanced at her son. 'But a mother's love is always there, my dear, no matter what, and he has been constantly in my thoughts.'

'I haven't got a mother,' Jewel suddenly piped up. 'She died when I was a baby.'

Mrs Newmarch turned to her as if seeing her for the first time. 'I'm so sorry to hear that, my dear. And your father? Do you have a father?'

Jewel shook her head. 'My papa is dead too, but before he died he sent me on a journey with Aunt Gianna to see Wilhelm and Kitty and baby Caitlin. And,' she took a breath and gazed steadily at the old lady, 'he said that one day I might go and meet my grandmama.'

'Oh!' Mrs Newmarch seemed perplexed. 'And have you met her?'

Jewel's lips moved wordlessly.

'Mother!' Martin went to sit on the sofa by her side. 'Mother. This is Jewel, Edward's daughter. Miss Gregory has brought her home to us.'

Georgiana shuddered uneasily. No! No! It isn't like that, she thought.

Mrs Newmarch looked intensely at Jewel. 'But how can that be? Edward was married to May. She doesn't have any children!'

'No, Mama.' Martin spoke patiently. 'Not May. Jewel's mother was called Tsui, but Edward was her father.'

Mrs Newmarch beckoned to Jewel to come closer. She stroked the little girl's long tresses which hung below her bonnet. 'So dark and silky,' she murmured. 'Who was your mother, did you say?'

'Tsui.' Jewel blinked her long lashes. 'She was a beautiful Chinese lady and lived with Papa.' She looked wistful. 'I don't remember her, but that is what Papa said. I only remember Jed and Larkin and Dolly.'

'And who were they?' Mrs Newmarch asked.

Georgiana cleared her throat and interrupted. 'Jed and Larkin travelled with Edward to California, Mrs Newmarch,' she said. 'And Dolly managed Edward's business. They were good friends,' she added. 'Edward was proud to know them. He valued their friendship – and they were with him at the end.'

Mrs Newmarch put her head down and rubbed her fingers over her eyes. 'My poor Eddie,' she murmured. 'My poor darling Eddie.'

Jewel, on hearing the familiar name of her father, stepped closer to her grandmother and touched her arm. 'Don't cry, Grandmama,' she whispered. 'Try to be brave,' and Mrs Newmarch put her arms around the little girl and wept.

CHAPTER FORTY-FIVE

One more person to visit, Georgiana pondered, and then I must decide what to do with my life. And Jewel's. Mrs Newmarch wanted Jewel to live with Martin and his wife, even though she was concerned about her illegitimacy.

'If she has the name of Newmarch, she will be known in this district and possibly have a finger pointed at her,' she told Georgiana. 'But Martin and Grace are known for their philanthropy. Grace has helped many a wretched woman who has a child out of wedlock. I must say,' she added, 'that my views have changed considerably since knowing Grace and although, of course, I don't condone impropriety or infidelity, I do declare that some poor women have many difficulties and some men have much to answer for!'

Georgiana had raised an eyebrow and a slight smile at Mrs Newmarch's words. Perhaps women's expectations were changing, after all, if a matron of Mrs Newmarch's class and upbringing could alter her opinion.

She had asked Grace for the address of her friend Ruby, and Grace, without a moment's hesitation, had given it to her. 'Visit during a morning,' she had discreetly advised. 'Her husband is a toy-maker and chooses his timber mid-morning and visits the bank and so forth, whilst Ruby minds the shop.'

The toyshop was situated in Manor Street, just off the Land of Green Ginger. Jewel danced and clapped her hands when told the name of the street. 'It sounds like magic, Aunt Gianna. Will it disappear before we get there?'

'I'm sure it is a magical street, Jewel, for no-one knows how or why it came to be named,' Georgiana explained. 'But I'm certain it will still be there.'

The shop, which was tucked into a corner, was small and had a bow window full of brightly coloured wares. A painted wooden tree was decorated with small toys, a clown hung from the ceiling and twirled his soft body in the breeze drifting in from the open door. A wooden duck bobbed its head up and down into a bowl of water and on a shelf sat wooden dolls with painted faces, dressed in silk and satin gowns and bonnets.

From the open doorway came the sweet smell of burnt sugar and cinnamon. Jewel, whose eyes had opened wide at the splendour of the window display, licked her lips and asked if they could please go inside to have a further look.

A bell jangled as they pushed the door wider and stepped in. Arranged around the shop were pieces of wooden furniture, stools and chairs and small tables, just the right size for children. A pretty dark-haired woman came out from an inner door. 'Good morning, ma'am.' She smiled pleasantly and bobbed her knee, and said hello to Jewel.

'Have you come to look at our lovely toys?' she asked Jewel, then, taking another look at her, said, 'Why – you're prettier by far than any of our dollies. I haven't seen you before. Are you a visitor?'

She had an accent which Georgiana recognized as belonging to the Hull area. So this is Ruby, she thought, and I can see why Edward was so attracted to her. She had a natural vivaciousness which seemed to bubble from within her.

'Yes, we're visiting relatives,' Georgiana began, when Jewel broke in. 'What's that nice smell?'

'It's toffee.' Ruby smiled. 'Perhaps you would like a piece?' She offered a tray of sticky golden honeycomb toffee. 'I make it to draw in my young customers,' she admitted to Georgiana.

Jewel took a piece, then, pushing the toffee to the side of her cheek with her tongue, remarked chattily, 'I've got a new grandmama.'

'Then you are very lucky,' Ruby acknowledged gravely. 'My little boys don't have a grandmother of their own, but their friends let them share theirs.'

'I'm about five,' Jewel told her and idly picked up a wooden box. 'How old are your little boys?'

'Dan is six and Thomas is nearly five. They're both at school this morning, otherwise you could have met them.'

'At school?' Georgiana was delighted to hear of it, for she knew of Ruby's deprived background.

Ruby nodded proudly. 'Dame school just around 'corner. We – that is, Daniel, my husband, and me – want them to get on in life. We want them to have an education.'

'Ruby,' Georgiana said softly. 'You won't know me, but my name is Georgiana Gregory and–'

'Oh!' Ruby exclaimed. 'Miss Gregory! I know

509

about you through my friend Grace.'

'Ah!' Jewel had pressed the box lid and it popped open, revealing a bobbing black-faced toy. 'Look!'

'Put it down please, Jewel,' Georgiana said firmly. 'Don't touch!'

'It's all right, Miss Gregory,' Ruby assured her. 'The toys here are almost unbreakable.' She laughed. 'My husband tests them out on our boys. You went to America, didn't you?' she went on. 'I thought you were so brave to travel alone.'

'I met Edward Newmarch whilst I was in America,' Georgiana said, and Jewel looked up at his name. 'He asked me if I would call to see you if ever I came back to England.'

'Grace told me that he'd died,' Ruby murmured. 'I'm so very sorry. I've often thought of him. He–' She looked pensive. 'He saved my life. I admit I was ashamed of what I did, but without him I would have finished up in 'workhouse.'

She took a handkerchief from her apron pocket and blew her nose. 'I'm sorry if I upset his wife. I didn't mean to do that. But in the end I did care for him. Onny, not enough to go with him. I loved Daniel, you see.'

Georgiana nodded. 'I think he understood.' Ruby would never have survived, she thought. Not in the rough and tumble of California or the genteel life of New York. She would have been too vulnerable. I would think that she needs someone to look after her, and now she has a husband and two sons who will do that. 'Edward sent a last message for you, Ruby,' she said quietly. 'He wanted me to tell you that he loved you always.' She glanced down at Jewel, who was once again amusing herself with the jack-in-the-box. 'He named his daughter after you. Jewel.'

'Yes?' The little girl looked up again at the mention of her name. 'I wish I lived here with all these toys!'

A tear trickled down Ruby's face. 'Where is her mother? Is she – is she an orphan, Miss Gregory? Cos if so, I'd ask Daniel if we could take her. I would, gladly!'

'Yes, she is an orphan, and it seems that everyone wants you, Jewel.' Georgiana felt a warmth stealing over her at Ruby's generosity towards her former lover's child, but also a sensation of melancholy and loneliness.

Jewel came and took hold of Georgiana's hand. 'I'm going to live with Aunt Gianna.' She leaned against her and looked up at Ruby and spoke in her determined childish treble. 'Aunt Grace has two little girls and you have two little boys, so you don't need any more children. Aunt Gianna does, because she doesn't have anyone else of her own, except for Uncle Wilhelm, and he's far away in America.'

Georgiana considered Jewel's comments as they walked back towards the High Street. Jewel was clutching the jack-in-the-box which Ruby had presented to her, and Georgiana carried gifts for Elizabeth and Clara. She had offered, as Edward had requested she should, to give monetary help to Ruby if she should need it. But she had refused the offer.

'Don't think I'm ungrateful, Miss Gregory,' she had said. 'But we manage quite nicely and Daniel wouldn't take kindly to me taking money from Edward.'

I've fulfilled my duty to everyone, Georgiana thought. To May on behalf of her parents' benevolence towards me, and Edward to whom I made a promise. But what shall I do now? There was an empty place in her heart now that Lake was gone, though since coming to England his presence was no longer so dominant. He is alive in the mountains and forests, dwelling where his ancestors are, she mused sadly, looking vaguely around her at the bustling town. There is no place for him in city streets or busy towns.

During the afternoon, Jewel went to the nursery to play with Elizabeth and Clara under the watchful eye of a maid. Martin and Grace were both out and Georgiana sat in a chair by the window of her room and contemplated the life in front of her. She looked down at the narrow street below, which was filled with drays and waggons. The river Hull ran behind these houses and this was a street where shipping merchants lived and worked.

I can't stay here, she deliberated. I'm hemmed in by the closeness of the buildings. Grace has lived her life in the confines of the town and feels comfortable within these familiar narrow walls. She got up and paced the room. I have become used to the open spaces of America, but can I take Jewel back there when her family is here? You could leave her, a voice inside her head told her. She is not your child. She will be loved and cared for with her family. You could have your freedom once again.

'No!' She spoke out loud. 'I cannot.' She groaned. What should I do? Wilhelm, if only you were here, you would advise me. She lay down on her bed, but then, still disturbed, got up again. Why am I so distracted? I have always made decisions before. She put her hands to her head as she paced. I miss them all so much. Kitty and the babies. But most of all I miss Wilhelm. He has been my rock, my advisor, my friend.

The image of Wilhelm with his round dimpled cheeks came swiftly to mind as she recollected their shared conversations, either in her log house or sitting on a bench of an evening, watching the sun go down on the mountains, turning the rippling water of the creek to flame. She thought of their rides together on the long journeys to Philadelphia, and of their animated discussions over the articles which were to be printed in the *Star* newspaper. But most of all she thought of his warm and caring presence when he comforted her after Lake's death. I was so comfortable in his company, she remembered. So sheltered and at ease. She swallowed hard. And now I am so alone.

'Georgiana! Come in, do.' Martin beckoned to her from within the open door of his library a few days later as she came down the stairs. He was working at his desk in his shirtsleeves, which he rolled up his arms. 'You are unhappy. Grace and I have both noticed it. Is there anything we can do?'

Grace had taken the three children out into the town with the vague promise that they just might pass by the shop in the Land of Green Ginger.

Georgiana shook her head. 'Just a trace of

melancholia, Martin. It will pass.'

'Do you want to go back to America?' His eyes were kind, not unlike Wilhelm's, she thought. In fact, she pondered, they are very similar in nature. I used to think that Martin was very conventional and sober, without any fire, but I was so wrong.

'I don't know what I want,' she admitted. 'I think I am lost.'

'Would you like to talk about it?'

Her eyes brimmed. 'Perhaps I would. I need a friend to talk to because I have lost my one and only true one.'

She told him of the impossible love she had had for Lake and of his trapper's life in the forests. She told him of the tall and handsome Iroquois Indians who had once been forest warriors and hunters. Of their wives, who had equality and their own council of women who made decisions. She spoke of Dekan and Horse who had conducted the ceremony for Lake's last spiritual journey to join his ancestors. She described Dreumel's Creek, where a settlement was now growing, and told him of Kitty and Ted, Jason and Ellis, of Pike's death, and Isaac and Nellie O'Neil. And finally of Wilhelm.

Martin had not interrupted her with questions and as she finished speaking he shook his head in wonder. 'Such rich memories you have gathered, Georgiana,' he said softly. 'How favoured you have been to see so much of another country, to gather such knowledge and to make so many friends.'

He leaned towards her and hesitated as if

choosing his words carefully before speaking. 'I'm so sorry that you have lost the man you loved. But I can only say, in the words of Tennyson, when you sorrow most, *"'Tis better to have loved and lost than never to have loved at all."'*

Georgiana bowed her head and nodded. 'Yes, that I know, and I will forever hold Lake dear in my memory.' She lifted her head and gazed at him. 'But when I said I had lost my one and only true friend,' her voice dropped to a whisper, 'I meant Wilhelm.'

CHAPTER FORTY-SIX

Two weeks later Georgiana had almost made up her mind to return to America with Jewel, but then she would hear Jewel's excited shrieks as she played with her cousins, and wonder if it was fair to take her away from them.

'You must not let us hold you here, Georgiana.' Grace, in her gentle way, was concerned about them both. 'Jewel will have a good life with you if you return to America, and she will make other friends.'

'It is so difficult to know what to do for the best,' Georgiana confessed. 'I enjoy your company, Grace. It is such a pleasure for me to know you and Martin again. I'm sorry that I'm so downcast.'

'We've all changed, haven't we?' Grace said. 'You were always so sure and confident and I was such a poor hapless creature. But your good spirits will return,' she added kindly.

And now you are the one who is positive and I am so wretched, Georgiana brooded. Only not for the same reasons. Grace has come up through the misery of poverty to become what she now is. I should be grateful for what I have. And indeed I am, but I'm still miserable and feel so alone!

The following evening the doorbell rang and the clock struck six as the three of them were finishing supper. They heard the maid's footsteps in the hall as she went to the front door. 'Are you expecting anyone this evening, Grace?' Martin asked.

She said that she was not unless her father or mother had chosen to call. The maid tapped and announced, 'A gentleman to speak to you, Mr Newmarch.'

'Will you excuse me?' Martin pushed back his chair. 'Please do start coffee without me.'

They heard the murmur of voices in the hall and Grace poured the coffee and remarked, 'We quite often get callers. Martin's business associates visit and people know that they can come here if they are in trouble or need.'

'I do admire you, Grace,' Georgiana said. 'I must seem very selfish to you. I do nothing for other people, only for myself.'

'Look at what you have done for Jewel,' Grace argued. 'And what's more, you've made great strides for women. You've shown that women can be independent. That they can travel alone, even across another continent, and make decisions for themselves too! You should be proud of that,

516

coming as you did from a sheltered background.'

She paused and considered. 'Can you imagine your cousin May travelling thousands of miles as you have done? She's been sitting at home all these years bemoaning the fact that her husband had gone off and left her, instead of making a fresh life for herself!'

'Grace!' The door opened and Martin stood there. 'I'm sorry to interrupt.' His eyes looked merry. 'Could you come for a moment?'

Grace rose to her feet. 'Is there someone in trouble?' she enquired.

'Possibly,' he conceded. 'But it can be resolved.'

Georgiana sipped her coffee as she waited for them to return. I will stay, she determined. I'll find something to do here as I did once before. There will be some worthwhile campaign. And Jewel will grow up with her family. It isn't fair to take her away from them.

The door opened. 'I've come to a decision,' she stated without turning around. 'At least – I think I have made up my mind.'

'Without consulting me?' a man's voice asked and she whirled around, almost spilling her coffee.

'Wilhelm! Wilhelm!' She put down her cup and jumped up from her chair. 'Oh, my dear, dear Wilhelm.' She put out her hands to receive him. 'Whatever are you doing here? How did you find me? You can't have received my letter?'

'No.' His face was wreathed in smiles as he bent to kiss her hand and then her cheek. 'I did not. I – I left America in rather a hurry – not long after you, in fact.'

517

'Really?' She drew him towards an easy chair and offered him coffee, finding that her hand was shaking as she poured.

'Yes.' He stretched his hands out to the fire and then rubbed them briskly together. Though the weather was pleasant, it had been a lovely day, she thought that perhaps he was cold, being unused to the cooler air of northern England.

'I, erm, I had some business to attend to,' he said, 'and – and, and I was advised by someone whom I trust implicitly to sail for England immediately.' He spoke quickly and rather nervously, which wasn't like him. He was usually so measured and controlled.

'It is good to see you, Wilhelm,' she said softly. 'I have been thinking of you so often.'

His face brightened. 'Oh?'

'Yes.' She gave a little sigh. 'I need your advice. I can trust your judgement and your impartiality. But tell me first how you found me here.'

He gazed at her for a second, then gave a small shrug. 'I simply got on a train in Liverpool, and when I got off in Hull I enquired where I could find the Newmarch family. I asked a gentleman at the station. He seemed to be the kind of person who might know who was who. But he said he was a stranger to the town and had just arrived on the train, as I had.'

She watched him as he continued speaking and saw the familiar dimples appear in his round cheeks as he smiled. 'But there was a young girl sitting on the pavement who heard my enquiry, and she immediately jumped up and said she knew Mrs Newmarch and would bring me to her!'

'One of Grace's waifs,' she murmured. 'The poor know them better than most.'

'I didn't realize that you would be here, of course. But I thought at least they would know where I could find you. Jewel?' he asked. 'How is she? Is she here? I've missed her!'

'She is well. Much happier and brighter than she was. She's a dear child, and it is of her I wish to hear your advice, Wilhelm. She's out at present. She is already socializing! Though her manners are not quite what they might be! She has gone to spend the day with the children of a friend of Grace's.'

'Is your business here concluded?' she asked, curious about the connections he had in England. Nothing that he had ever discussed with her. Perhaps, then, I don't know him as well as I thought.

'No,' he said solemnly. 'There is still much to be discussed. Georgiana!' he said abruptly. 'Could we – could we perhaps take a walk? I don't wish to intrude on the Newmarches' hospitality.'

Grace came into the room as he was speaking. 'Mr Dreumel, will you have supper? We have finished ours but Cook will prepare something for you.'

He stood up. 'Thank you, Mrs Newmarch, but no. I am not at all hungry and Georgiana has kindly given me coffee.'

Which is still in the cup, Georgiana thought. He has barely touched it.

'I was just suggesting that perhaps we–' He looked down at Georgiana. 'That is, Georgiana and I could take a short walk. I'm in need of some fresh air, having been cooped up on the train since early this morning. I came in a horse cab from the railway station. I was prepared to walk but my young guide insisted that it would be too far for me.' He grinned. 'She was most animated on the journey and waved and whistled to several of her friends!'

Grace and Martin, who had also come into the room, burst out laughing. 'It will be the highlight of her day, Mr Dreumel,' Grace said. 'Her week, even. I remember very well my first ride in a carriage with a very fine lady.' She smiled at Georgiana. 'Do you remember, Georgiana? Though I didn't know it then, it was the start of a new life for me.'

Georgiana nodded. She remembered very well the cold wet day when she had offered a carriage ride to the poorly clad young girl.

Martin came towards Grace and put his hand tenderly on her shoulder. 'It's a pleasant evening. Perhaps we might suggest a walk towards the estuary?' he suggested. 'People seem to gravitate towards the Humber when they have things to discuss or think about.' He spun one of Grace's curls around his finger as he spoke. 'We do still, even though we are staid married people!'

He smiled down at Grace as he spoke and Georgiana felt a surge of emotion at their obvious love and contentment. 'Yes,' she said quickly to hide her feelings. 'Let's do that. I'll get my coat and hat.'

Wilhelm took her arm as they walked. She led him, first of all, to the river Hull, which ran behind the houses and warehouses in the High

Street and then flowed into the Humber. 'This was once the main harbour,' she told him. 'The whaling fleet came in here and discharged their cargo. Now there are other docks in the town, but this is still in use and flows into the Queen's Dock.'

They looked across the narrow waterway where barges and small ships were moored. Porters and seamen jumped on and off the vessels, and clerks scurried along the staith side with consignment sheets in their hands. 'Perhaps one day, Dreumel's Creek will be as busy as this,' Wilhelm remarked, then, glancing up at the old buildings, added, 'though our log houses will never last so long!'

'This is an ancient town,' Georgiana agreed. 'So much antiquity.' She smiled up at him. 'But Dreumel's Creek is making history and we were part of it.'

A stiff breeze was blowing by the estuary and Georgiana had to hold onto her hat. Eventually she unpinned it and let the breeze ruffle her hair.

'That's better,' Wilhelm remarked. 'That's the Georgiana I know. I hardly recognize this elegant lady with ribbons in her hat!'

'Oh, come!' she replied gaily. 'I was wearing my most fetching outfit when we first met in New York!'

'You were playing the piano when I first set eyes on you,' he said softly. 'You were lost in another world and you were wearing a silver-grey gown. When we met later for supper you wore blue with a bustle.'

'Goodness, Wilhelm. Imagine you remembering!' She was both flattered and unnerved at him recalling such things.

'If you had asked me in Dreumel's Creek what you were wearing on that day, I would not have remembered.' He turned away from her and gazed down at the choppy brown water lashing against the wooden structure of the pier. 'It is since we have been apart that my memory has improved. So many things that I remember and few that I ever want to forget.'

'Wilhelm!' She touched his arm and for a second held her breath. 'Wilhelm. I have missed you so much. And not only because you have given me support and guidance since I have known you.'

He turned back and took hold of her hand. 'I trust you above anyone and there is something I must tell you,' she said weakly, not able to look into his face, and wondering how far she dare go in her confession. Would he be embarrassed? Would she be humiliated? No, she considered. She knew him well enough to be sure that he would always treat her kindly. He was, after all, her very dear friend.

'Georgiana!' He lifted her chin with a finger so that she had to look at him. 'Georgiana. Why do you think that I came to England?'

'Business, you said,' she replied in a whisper. 'Though I didn't know you had any business in England.'

'I don't!' He pressed her hand. 'After you sailed, I went back to the Marius. On the way I met Mrs Burrows. You remember Mrs Burrows?' he asked gently.

'Of course! I regret that I didn't say goodbye to her before we sailed. She is a very special lady.'

He nodded. 'And very wise. She asked me why I was so glum and downcast, and when I told her, she said I must stop being so foolish and book a ticket at once on the very next ship to England.'

She gazed at him. What was he saying? 'What did you tell her?' Her voice was uncertain. 'For her to give you that advice?'

'Aunt Gianna! Aunt Gianna!' A childish voice hailed her which was followed by a chorus of others. 'Aunt Gianna!'

They both turned. Jewel, with her coat undone and bareheaded, her black hair streaming behind her, was waving to her. With her were Elizabeth, Clara, Ruby and two young boys. 'Aunt Gianna!' She came rushing towards her, then stopped as she saw Wilhelm smiling at her. 'Oh!' she cried. 'Oh! Wilhelm!' Wilhelm put out his arms and she jumped into them, then smothered him with kisses. 'Oh, Wilhelm, I'm so glad that you have come. I've missed you. Have you brought Kitty and Caitlin?'

He squeezed her tight. 'No. Only myself. I wanted to see you and Georgiana, so I got on the next ship to England.'

She pressed her cheek close to his. 'I'm so glad,' she whispered. 'I wanted to see you, Wilhelm, and so did Aunt Gianna. I love you and I cried cos I thought you had gone away, just like Papa did.'

Georgiana saw Wilhelm swallow hard and his eyes were bright as he kissed the little girl upon her cheek.

'I haven't gone away, and I love you too,' he said softly. 'Both of you.' He looked at Georgiana. 'Very much. That is what I came to tell you.'

Georgiana couldn't speak. For all her bravado as an independent woman, she hadn't found the courage to say what she felt, what she really wanted. It didn't matter, she thought, where they lived, she and Jewel, as long as they were with those whom they loved. When love beckons you must follow. That was what was important.

From the corner of her vision she saw Ruby gather up her other charges and melt away.

'Wilhelm,' Georgiana said shakily. 'What was it that you told Mrs Burrows, for her to say what she did?'

He eased himself from Jewel's embrace. 'I said that I had let the woman I love go away, without telling her first that I love her.' His voice was soft and low and his eyes held hers. 'That I had loved her for a long time, but feared that she was tied eternally to someone else, as I once had been to Liesel.'

'And you are no longer?' Her voice trembled as she asked the question.

'No.' With one free hand, he took hers. 'I won't ever forget her, as you won't forget Lake. They have been part of our lives. But you and I are still here, Georgiana. We must go on with our lives and I want – I want more than anything in the world, for us to do that together.'

'I want that too,' she whispered. 'I hadn't realized it before, but I love you, Wilhelm, and I want to be with you, wherever that might be.'

'Me too!' Jewel reached out and patted

Georgiana's cheek. 'I want to come too!'

They both smiled and put their arms around each other, holding Jewel in their midst and oblivious of the glances of passers-by. 'How could we possibly go anywhere without you, Jewel?' Georgiana laughed and cried at the same time.

'Look.' Wilhelm pointed down the river. A steamboat was heading towards the tip of Spurn with a pilot boat guiding it. 'Down there is the mouth of the Humber. I looked at a map when I was on my way here, and I saw that at the end of this estuary is the sea. And on the other side of the sea is the country where my father and grandfather were born. The Netherlands.'

His eyes were bright and eager and he gazed at Georgiana. 'I would like to visit that country where my family came from, but I don't want to go alone.'

She shook her head. 'You don't have to,' she said softly and breathed a kiss on his cheek. 'We will come with you. The world is ours, Wilhelm. We just have to reach out together and grasp it.'

AFTERWORD

The air was sharp, the night sky full of stars and the snowflakes softly falling as the man on horseback rode across the bridge at Dreumel's Creek towards the mountain track. There were no prints on the white ground, no creak of leather or thud of hoof beat.

A small red-haired girl, hearing the bark of a wolf, lifted the heavy curtain at her bedroom window and looked out. She saw the rider and waved her hand to him as she always did, though her mother, whenever she had told her of his presence, would hush her and shake her head, even though she smiled wistfully as she followed her gaze up the mountain.

He reached the high ridge and looked back. Moonlight glinted on the rushing creek so that it sparkled like crystal. Smoke spiralled from the chimneys of the log houses, which seemed to sigh and settle their roots down into the ground. Chinks of lamplight were showing beneath doors and most of the windows, except for one cabin which was in darkness.

He nodded and, giving his rare crooked smile, lifted his hand and raised his battered leather hat in farewell before turning into the forest. He felt the remembrance of the woman's arms tighten around his waist and her warm breath against his neck. He smiled again. He was home. He was happy.

The publishers hope that this book has given you enjoyable reading. Large Print Books are especially designed to be as easy to see and hold as possible. If you wish a complete list of our books please ask at your local library or write directly to:

Magna Large Print Books
Magna House, Long Preston,
Skipton, North Yorkshire.
BD23 4ND

This Large Print Book for the partially sighted, who cannot read normal print, is published under the auspices of

THE ULVERSCROFT FOUNDATION